For my parents

MATTHEW PEARL

The Poe Shadow

VINTAGE BOOKS
London

Published by Vintage 2007

2 4 6 8 10 9 7 5 3 1

Copyright © Matthew Pearl 2006

First published in Great Britain in 2006 by
Harvill Secker

Vintage
Random House, 20 Vauxhall Bridge Road,
London SW1V 2SA

www.randomhouse.co.uk/vintage

Addresses for companies within The Random House Group Limited
can be found at: www.randomhouse.co.uk/offices.htm

The Random House Group Limited Reg. No. 954009

A CIP catalogue record for this book
is available from the British Library

ISBN 9780099478225

The Random House Group Limited makes every effort
to ensure that the papers used in its books are made from
trees that have been legally sourced from well-managed and
credibly certified forests. Our paper procurement policy
can be found at: www.randomhouse.co.uk/paper.htm

Designed by Simon M. Sullivan
Printed and bound in Great Britain by
Bookmarque Ltd, Croydon, Surrey

PUBLISHER'S NOTE: *The mystery related to the strange death of Edgar Allan Poe in 1849 has been uncovered through the following pages.*

❁   ❁   ❁

I PRESENT TO YOU, *Your Honor and Gentlemen of the Jury, the truth about this man's death and my life. The narrative has not been told before. Whatever has been taken away from me, one last possession remains: this story. There are those of our city today who tried to stop it. There are those sitting here among you who still believe me a criminal, a liar, an outcast, a clever, vile murderer. Me, Your Honor: Quentin Hobson Clark, citizen of Baltimore, member of the bar, a fond reader.*

But this story is not about me. Please think of this, if you think of nothing else! It never was about me; ambition had never been my chosen stimulus. This was not motivated by my own fortunes among my fellow class or reputation in the eyes of higher judges. It was about something greater than I am, greater than all this, about a man by whom time will remember us though you had forgotten him before the earth settled. Somebody had to do it. We could not just keep still. I could not keep still.

All that follows will be the plain truth. And I must tell you it because I am the one nearest the truth. Or, rather, the only one still living.

It is one of life's peculiar facts that it is usually those no longer alive whose stories preserve the truth. . . .

These statements above I scribbled in the pages of my memorandum book (the last sentence is crossed out, I notice, with "philosophical!" written in my hand beside it as critique). Before walking into that courthouse, I scribbled these words in desperate preparation to face my defamers, those who thought ruining me rescued themselves. Because I am an attorney, you may think the prospect of all this—I mean standing before a courtroom of onlookers and former friends, and two women who might love me—you might think the prospect of doing that would be fairly effortless to the experienced Baltimore attorney. Not so. To be an attorney, you must be interested above all else in the interests of others. It does not prepare a man to decide what must be saved. It does not prepare a man to save himself.

—BOOK I—

OCTOBER 8, 1849

I REMEMBER THE day it began because I was impatient for an important letter to arrive. Also, because it was meant to be the day of my engagement to Hattie Blum. And, of course, it was the day I saw him dead.

The Blums were near neighbors of my family. Hattie was the youngest and most affable of four sisters who were considered nearly the prettiest four sisters in Baltimore. Hattie and I had been acquainted from our very infancies, as we were told often enough through the years. And each time we were told how long we'd known each other, I think the words were meant also to say, "and you shall know each other evermore, depend upon it."

And in spite of such pressure as might easily have pushed us apart, even at eleven years old I became like a little husband toward my playfellow. I never made outward professions of love to Hattie, but I devoted myself to her happiness in small ways while she entertained me with her talk. There was something hushed about her voice, which often sounded to me like a lullaby.

My own nature while in society as it developed was markedly quiet and tranquil, to the degree that I was often asked at any given moment if I had only just then been stirred awake. In quieter company, though, I had the habit of turning unaccountably loquacious and even rambling in my speech. Therefore, I savored the stretches of Hattie's animated conversation. I believe I depended upon them. I felt no need to call attention to myself when I was with her; I felt happy and modest and, above all, easy.

Now, I should note that I did not *know* that I was expected to propose marriage on the afternoon with which we begin this narration. I was on my way to the post office from the nearby chambers of our law practice when I crossed paths with a woman of good Baltimore society, Mrs. Blum— Hattie's aunt. She pointed out immediately that the errands of retrieving waiting mail should be assigned to one of my lesser and less occupied legal clerks.

"You are a specimen, aren't you, Quentin Clark!" Mrs. Blum said. "You wander the streets when you are working, and when you're not working, you have a look upon your face as though you were!"

She was your genuine Baltimorean; she suffered no man without proper commercial interests any more than she would tolerate a girl who was not beautiful.

This was Baltimore, and whether in fine weather or in this day's fog it was a very red-brick type of place, where the movements of the people on well-paved streets and marble steps were quick and boisterous but without gaiety. There was not much of that last quality in supply in our go-ahead city, where large houses stood elevated over a crowded trading bay. Coffee and sugar came in from South America and the West India Islands on great clipper ships, and the barrels of oysters and family flour moved out on the multiplying railway tracks toward Philadelphia and Washington. Nobody *looked* poor then in Baltimore, even those who were, and every other awning seemed to be a daguerreotype establishment ready to record that fact for posterity.

Mrs. Blum on this occasion smiled and took my arm as we walked through the thoroughfare. "Well, everything is quite perfectly arranged for this evening."

"This evening," I replied, trying to guess what she could be referring to. Peter Stuart, my law partner, had mentioned a supper party at the home of a mutual acquaintance. I had been thinking so much of the letter I anticipated retrieving, I had until then forgotten completely. "This evening, of course, Mrs. Blum! How I've looked forward to it."

"Do you know," she continued, "do you know, Mr. Clark, that only yesterday I heard dear Miss Hattie spoken of on Market Street"— this generation of Baltimoreans still called Baltimore Street by its former name— "yes, talked about as the loveliest unmarried beauty in all Baltimore!"

"One could argue the loveliest above all, married or not," I said.

"Well, isn't that clever!" she replied. "Oh, it won't do at all, twenty-seven and still living bachelor and— now don't interrupt, dear Quentin! A proper young man doesn't . . ."

I had trouble hearing what she said next because a loud rumble of two carriages grew behind us. "If it is a hackney approaching," I thought to myself, "I shall put her into it, and offer double the fare." But as they passed I could see both were private carriages, and the one in front was a sleek, shiny hearse. Its horses kept their heads low, as if in deference to the honorable cargo.

No one else turned to look.

Leaving behind my walking companion with a parting promise of seeing her at the evening's gathering, I found myself crossing the next avenue. A herd of swine swarmed past with belligerent shrieks, and my detour ran along Greene Street and across to Fayette, where hearse and mourning-carriage were parked together.

In a quiet burial ground there, a ceremony began and ended abruptly. I strained through the fog at the figures in attendance. It was like standing in a dream— everything blurred into silhouettes, and I swallowed down the vague feeling that I should not be there. The minister's oration sounded muffled from where I stood at the gates. The small gathering, I suppose, did not demand much effort from his voice.

It was the saddest funeral ever seen.

It was the weather. No: the mere four or five men in attendance— the minimum needed to lift an adult coffin. Or perhaps the melancholy quality came chiefly from that brisk, callous completion of the ceremony. Not even the most impoverished pauper's funeral that I had observed before this day, nor the funerals of the poor Jewish cemetery nearby, not even those exhibited such *unchristian* indifference. There wasn't one flower, wasn't one tear.

Afterward, I retraced my steps only to find the post office had bolted its doors. I could not know whether there was a letter waiting for me inside or not— but I returned to our office chambers and reassured myself. *Soon, I'd hear more from him soon.*

That evening at the social gathering, I found myself on a private stroll with Hattie Blum along a field of berries, dormant for the season but shadowed with summer remembrances of Champagne and Strawberry Parties. As ever, I could speak comfortably to Hattie.

"Our practice is awfully interesting at times," I said. "Yet I think I should like to choose the cases with more discrimination. A lawyer in ancient Rome, you know, swore never to defend a cause unless he thought it was just. We take cases if their pay is just."

"You can change your office, Quentin. It is your name and your character hanging on the shingle too, after all. Make it more like yourself, rather than make yourself more suited to it."

"Do you believe so, Miss Hattie?"

Twilight was settling and Hattie became uncharacteristically quiet, which I fear meant that I became insufferably talkative. I examined her expression but found no clues to the source of her distant bearing.

"You laughed for me," Hattie said absently, almost as though I would not hear her.

"Miss Hattie?"

She looked up at me. "I was only thinking of when we were children. Do you know at first I thought you were a fool?"

"Appreciated," I chuckled.

"My father would take my mother away during her different sicknesses, and you would come to play when my aunt was minding me. You were the only one to know just how to make me smile until my parents returned, because you were always laughing at the strangest things!" She said this wistfully, while lifting the bottom of her long skirts to avoid the muddy ground.

Later, when we were inside warming ourselves, Hattie talked quietly with her aunt, whose entire countenance had stiffened from earlier in the day. Auntie Blum asked what should be arranged for Hattie's birthday.

"It is coming, I suppose," Hattie said. "I should hardly think of it, typically, Auntie. But this year . . ." She trailed off into a cheerless hum. At supper, she hardly touched the food.

I did not like this at all. I felt myself turn into an eleven-year-old boy again, an anxious protector of the girl across the way. Hattie had been such a reliable presence in my life that any discomfort on her part upset me. Thus it was perhaps from a selfish motivation I tried to cure her mood, but at all events I did wish her to be genuinely happy.

Others of the party, like my law partner, Peter, joined in attempting to raise her spirits, and I studied each of them vigilantly in the event that one of them had been responsible for bringing Hattie Blum into a fit of blues.

Something was hindering my own role in cheering her on this day: that funeral I had seen. I cannot properly explain why, but it had thoroughly exploded my peace. I tried to call to mind a picture of it again. There had been only the four men in attendance to listen to the minister. One, taller than the others, stood toward the rear, his gaze floating off, as though the most anxious of all to be somewhere else. Then, as they came toward the road, there were their grim mouths. The faces were not known to me but also not forgotten. Only one member delayed, staying his steps regretfully, as though overhearing my private thoughts. The event seemed to speak of a terrible loss and yet to do it no honor. It was, in a word, Wrong.

Under this vague cloud of distraction, my efforts exhausted themselves without rescuing Hattie's spirits. I could only bow and express my helpless regrets in unison with the other guests when Hattie and her Auntie Blum were among the first to depart from the supper party. I was pleased when Peter suggested we bring an end to the evening, too.

"Well, Quentin? What has come over you?" Peter asked in an eruption. We were sharing a hired carriage back to our houses.

I thought to tell him of the sad funeral, but Peter would not understand why that had been occupying my mind. Then I realized by the gravity of his posture that he referred to something altogether different. "Peter," I asked, "what do you mean?"

"Did you decide *not* to propose to Hattie Blum this evening, after all?" he demanded with a loud exhalation.

"Propose! I?"

"She'll be twenty-three in a few weeks. For a Baltimore girl today, that is practically an old maid! Do you not love the dear girl even a little?"

"Who could not love Hattie Blum? But stay, Peter! How is it you came to assume we were to be engaged on this night? Had I ever suggested this was my design?"

"How is it I— ? Do you not know as well as I do that the date today is the very same date *your own parents* were engaged? Had this failed to occur to you even once this evening?"

It had indeed failed to occur to me, as a matter of fact, and even being reminded of this coincidence provided little comprehension of Peter's queer assumption. He explained further that Auntie Blum had been sagely certain I would take the opportunity of this party to propose, and had thought I had even hinted such earlier in the day, and had so informed Peter and Hattie of this likelihood so they would not be surprised. *I* had been the unwitting, principal cause of Hattie's mysterious distress. I had been the wretch!

"When would have been a more reasonable time than tonight?" Peter continued. "An anniversary so important to you! When? It was as plain as the sun at noon-day."

"I hadn't realized . . ." I stammered.

"How couldn't you see she was waiting for you, that it is time for your future to begin? Well, here, you're home. I wish you a restful sleep. Poor Hattie is probably weeping into her pillow even now!"

"I should never wish to make her sad," I said. "I wish only that I knew what seemed to be expected from me by everyone else." Peter gruffly muttered agreement, as though I had finally struck upon my general failing.

Of course I would propose, and of course we would marry! Hattie's presence in my life had been my good fortune. I brightened whenever I saw her and, even more, whenever we were apart and I thought about her. There had been so little change all this time knowing her, I suppose it had just seemed odd to call for it now with a proposal.

"What *do* you think about?" Peter seemed to say with his brow as I closed the carriage door to bid him good night. I pulled the door back open.

"There was a funeral earlier," I said, deciding to try to redeem myself with some explanation. "You see, I watched it pass, and I suppose it troubled me for a reason I had not . . ." But no, I still could not find the words to justify its effects on me.

"A funeral! A stranger's funeral!" Peter cried. "Now, what in heaven does that have to do with you?"

Everything, but I did not know that then. The next morning I came down in my dressing gown and opened the newspaper to distract myself. Had I been warned, I still could not have predicted my own alarm at what I saw that made me forget my other concerns. It was a small heading on one of the inside pages that caught me. *Death of Edgar A. Poe.*

I would toss the newspaper aside, then would pick it up again, turning pages to read something else; then I'd read again and again that heading: *Death of Edgar A. Poe. . . . the distinguished American poet, scholar, and critic in the thirty-eighth year of his age.*

No! Thirty-nine, I believed, but possessed of a wisdom worth a hundred times that . . . *Born in this city.* No again! (How questionable it all was, even before I knew more.)

Then I noticed . . . those four words.

Died in this city.

This city? This was not telegraphed news. This had occurred here in Baltimore. The death in our own city, the burial, maybe, too. Could it be that the very funeral on Greene and Fayette . . . No! That little funeral, that unceremonious ceremony, that *entombment* in the narrow burial yard?

At the office that day, Peter sermonized about Hattie, but I could hardly discuss it, intrigued instead by these tidings. I sent for confirmation from the sexton, the caretaker of the burial yard. Poor Poe, he replied. Yes, Poe was gone. As I rushed to the post office to see if any letter had arrived, my thoughts revolved around what I had unknowingly witnessed.

That cold-blooded formality. That had been Baltimore's farewell to our nation's literary savior, my favorite author, my (perhaps) friend? I could barely contain the sense of anger growing within me; anger of a sort that blocked out everything else. I know, looking back on this, that I never wanted to hurt Hattie through the commotion that crept over my mind beginning that afternoon. Yes, this was my favorite author, who had died in my midst, but even then it was far more than that. Perhaps I cannot in one breath fairly describe why it was so devastating to a man with youth, with romantic and professional prospects enviable to anyone in Baltimore.

Perhaps it was this fact. I— without having appreciated the fact— *I* had been the one to see him last; or, rather, as all others rushed past, I had been the last to watch the indifferent earth rattling over his coffin, as over the nameless corpses of the world.

I had a dead man for a client and the Day of Judgment as my hearing date.

That was the sardonic way Peter put it a few weeks later when I began my fateful inquiries. My law partner did not have enough of the wit about him to be sardonic more than three or four times in his life, so you can imagine the agitation behind the words. Peter, a man of height and bulk, was my elder by only a few years, but he sighed with the sigh of an old man, especially at the mention of Edgar A. Poe.

By my teen years, two facts in my life were as fixed as destiny: my admiration for literary works by Edgar Poe and, as you have heard, my attachment to Hattie Blum.

Even as a boy, Peter talked about Hattie and me being married with the focus of a man of business. In his prudent heart, the boy was older than all other boys. When his father had died, my parents, through my father's church, had assisted the widowed Mrs. Stuart, who had been left nearly destitute by debt, and my father treated Peter like another son. Peter was so thankful for this that he dutifully and genuinely adopted all of my father's positions on affairs of the world, far more than I could ever seem to do. Indeed, it might have seemed to a stranger that he was the rightful Clark, and I a second-rate pretender to the name.

Peter even shared my father's distaste toward my literary preferences. *This* Edgar Poe, he and my father were both prone to say, this Poe that you read with such compulsion is *peculiar* beyond taste. Reading for the relief of *ennui* was simply pleasuremongering, no more useful to the world than dozing in the middle of an afternoon. Literature should improve the heart; these fantasies cripple it!

That is how most people saw Poe, and I would not have disagreed at first. I was hardly out of boyhood the first time I came upon Poe's work, a *Gentleman's Magazine* tale called "William Wilson." I confess I could not make much of it. I could find neither beginning nor end and could not distinguish the portions that exhibited reason from those of madness. It was like holding a page up to a mirror and trying to read it. Genius was not looked for in the magazines, and I saw no greater amount of it residing in Mr. Poe.

But I was only a boy. My judgment was transformed by a story of a class peculiar to Poe, a story of criminal detection entitled "The Murders in the Rue Morgue." This story's hero is C. Auguste Dupin, a young Frenchman who ingeniously unravels the truth behind the shocking slayings of two women. One woman's body is found in a house in Paris, thrust up the chimney feetfirst. Her mother, meanwhile, has been sliced at the neck so severely that when the police try to raise her body, her head falls off. There were valuables in plain view in their chambers, yet whatever deranged intruder had been inside had left them unmolested. The singularity of the crime was entirely baffling to the Paris police and the press and the witnesses— well, to everyone. Everyone except C. Auguste Dupin.

Dupin understood.

He understood that it was the strikingly singular nature of the deaths that made them at once *easily solvable,* for it separated the event instantly from the indistinguishable muddle of everyday crimes. It seemed to the police and the press that the murders could not have been done by even an irrational person, because they had been done by no person. Dupin's reasoning followed a method Poe called *ratiocination*— employing one's imagination to achieve analysis, and one's analysis to climb the heights of imagination. Through this method, Dupin showed how a rare orangutan, provoked to a rage by abuse, had committed the horrible atrocities.

From the hand of an ordinary person, the particulars would have seemed stuff and nonsense. But at the very moment the reader expresses disbelief at the course of events, every difficulty is eliminated by an unbreakable chain of reasoning. Poe whetted the curiosity for what is possible to its sharpest edge, and that brought the soul along with it. These tales of ratiocination (with sequels touching Dupin's further cases) became Poe's most popular among a mass of readers, but, in my opinion, for the wrong reasons. Mere spectator readers enjoyed seeing an unbroken puzzle solved, but there was a higher level of importance. *My ultimate object is only the truth,* said Dupin to his assistant. I understood, through Dupin, that truth was Edgar A. Poe's only object, too, and that precisely is what frightened and confused so many about Poe. The genuine mystery was not the particular riddle that the mind aches to know; *the mind of man,* this was the tale's true and lasting mystery.

And I found something new to me as a reader: recognition. I felt suddenly less alone in the world with his words before me. Perhaps this is why the occasion of Poe's death, which might have riveted another reader for a passing day or two, inhabited my thoughts.

My father liked to say that truth resided in honest professional gentlemen of the world, not in the monstrous tales and hoaxing stories of some magazine writer. He had no use for Genius. He said that most men in the armies of the world were required to attend to homely duties of life, where Industry and Enterprise were more in need than Genius, which was too squeamish at men's dullness to succeed in the world. His business was packinghouses, but he took to the notion that a young man should be an attorney, a complete business in itself, he said admiringly.

Peter positively thrilled at the plan as though he were boarding the first ship to California on whispers of gold.

Upon achieving maturity, Peter situated himself as an apprentice to a law office of some distinction and while there achieved notice for compiling a thorough work, *An Index to the Laws of Maryland, from the Year 1834 to 1843*. My father soon financed Peter's own practice, and it was clear that I was to study and work under my friend. It was a plan too reasonable to object to, and I never once thought to do so— not once that I can remember, at least.

You are fortunate, Peter wrote to me when I was still at my university. *You shall have a fine office here with me under your Father's auspices and you shall marry as soon as you wish. Every beautiful young woman of high standing on Baltimore Street smiles on you, by the bye. If I were you, if I had a face half as handsome as yours, Quentin Clark, how well I would know what to do with ease and luxury in society!*

By the fall of 1849, where you joined me some pages earlier, I had my profession in place so securely I hardly took notice of it. Peter Stuart and I made excellent partners. My parents were both gone by then, killed by a carriage accident while they were traveling in Brazil for my father's business. There was an empty spot where there once had been guidance from my father. And yet, the life he'd arranged for me flowed on in his absence— all this, Hattie, Peter, the well-pressed clients appearing daily in our offices, my stately family house shaded by ancient poplars and known as Glen Eliza, after my mother. All this ran on as though operated by some noiseless and ingenious automatic machine. Until Poe's death.

I had the young man's weakness of wishing others to understand everything that concerned me— of needing to *make* others understand. I believed I could. I can call to mind the very first time I told Peter we should work to protect Edgar A. Poe. Believing that, as a result of the compliance I imagined on the part of Peter, I would be able to report back the good tidings to Mr. Poe.

My very first letter to Edgar Poe, on March 16, 1845, was brought about by a question I had when reading "The Raven," then a recently published poem. The final verses leave the raven sitting atop a bust of Pallas "above my chamber door." With these last lines of the poem, the

impish and mysterious bird continues to haunt the young man of the
poem, perhaps for eternity:

> *And his eyes have all the seeming of a demon's that is dreaming,*
> *And the lamp-light o'er him streaming throws his shadow on the floor;*
> *And my soul from out that shadow that lies floating on the floor*
> > *Shall be lifted— nevermore!*

If the raven sits at the top of the chamber door, though, what lamp-
light would be behind him in such a way as to cast his shadow to the
floor? With the impetuousness of youth, I wrote to Poe himself for an answer, for I wanted to be able to envision every crevice and corner of the
poem. Along with the question, I enclosed in the same letter to Mr. Poe
a subscription fee for a new magazine called *The Broadway Journal,*
which Poe was then editing, to make sure I'd see whatever else flowed
from his pen.

After months without receiving any reply, and without a single number of *The Broadway Journal,* I wrote again to Mr. Poe. When the silence
persisted, I addressed a complaint to an associate of the magazine in New
York and insisted that my subscription be refunded in full. I no longer
desired to ever see it. One day, I received my three dollars back, along
with a letter.

Signed Edgar A. Poe.

How startling, how uplifting that was, such a lofty visionary bringing
himself to personally address a mere reader of three and twenty years! He
even explained the minor mystery regarding the raven's shadow: "My
conception was that of the bracket candelabrum affixed against the wall,
high up above the door and bust— as is often seen in the English palaces,
and even in some of the better houses in New-York."

There was the very nature of the raven's shadow explained just for me!
Poe also thanked me for my literary opinions and encouraged me to send
more. He explained that his financial partners in *The Broadway Journal*
had forced its termination in yet another defeat in the struggle between
money and literature. He had never regarded the journal as more than a
temporary adjunct to other designs. One day, he said, we might meet in
person and he would confide in me his plans, and inquire my advice. "I
am entirely ignorant," he stated, "of all law matters."

I wrote nine letters to Poe between 1845 and his death in October 1849. I received in return four courteous and sincere notes in his own hand.

His most energetic comments were about his ambitions for his proposed journal, *The Stylus*. Poe had spent years editing other people's magazines. Poe said the journal would finally allow *men of genius* to triumph over *men of talent*, men who could feel rather than men who could think. It would cheer no author who did not deserve it, and would publish all literature that was unified by clarity and, most importantly, truth. He had waited many years to begin this journal. He wrote to me the last summer before his death that if waiting until the *Day of Judgment* would increase his chances of success, so he would! But, he added, he instead hoped to have the first number of it out the next January.

Poe anticipated with excitement a trip to Richmond to gather finances and support, commenting that if everything went as he intended, his final success was certain. He needed to raise funds and subscriptions. But he continued to be hindered by the rumors in the so-called professional press of irregular and immoral habits, questions about his sanity, unfit romantic dalliances, general excessiveness. Enemies, he said, were always at his throat for publishing honest criticisms of their writings, and for having had the great nerve to point out the complete lack of originality in revered authors like Longfellow and Lowell. He feared that the animosities of small men would attack his efforts by painting him as a sot, an unworthy drunk not deserving any public influence.

That is when I asked. I asked plainly, maybe too plainly. Were these at all true, these accusations I had heard for years? Was he, Edgar A. Poe, a drunkard who had given himself over to excess?

He wrote back without the least air of offense or conscious superiority. He vowed to me— me, a practical and presumptuous stranger— that he was wholly abstemious. Some readers might question my ability to judge his truthfulness from afar, but my instincts spoke with unclouded certainty. In my next letter, I replied that I put full confidence in his word. Then, just before sealing my reply, I decided to do better.

I made a proposal. I would bring suit against any false accuser attempting to damage his efforts to launch *The Stylus*. We had represented the interests of some local periodicals before, providing me with the proper experience. I would do my part to ensure that genius would not be trampled. This would be my duty, just as it was his duty to astonish the world now and then.

"Thank you for your promise about *The Stylus*," answered Poe in a letter replying to mine. "Can you or will you help me? I have room to say no more. I depend upon you implicitly."

That was shortly before Poe began his lecture tour in Richmond. Emboldened by his response to my offer, I wrote again, pouring out a myriad of questions about his *Stylus* and where he planned to raise money. I expected he would respond while he was touring, which is why I visited the post office and, when business consumed my time, checked the lists of waiting mail the postmaster regularly inserted in the newspapers.

I had been reading Poe's work more than ever. Particularly after my parents died. Some considered it distasteful that I would read literature that frequently touched on the topic of death. Yet in Poe, while death is not a pleasant subject, it is not forbidden. Nor is it a fixed end. Death is an experience that can be shaped by the living. Theology tells us that spirits live on beyond the body, but Poe believes it.

Peter, of course, had at the time vocally dismissed the idea of our law practice taking up the cause of *The Stylus*.

"I would sooner cut off my hand than spend my time worrying about magazines of blasted fiction! I would sooner get run down by an omnibus than— " You can see what he was driving at.

You'd probably guess that the real reason Peter objected was because I could not answer his questions about the *fees*. Poe was regularly reported in the papers as penniless. Why take upon ourselves, Peter argued, what others wouldn't? I pointed out that the source for our payments was obvious: the new journal. Success was guaranteed for it!

What I wanted to say to Peter was "Do you not ever feel you are becoming hackneyed by the lawyer's routine? Forget the fees. Wouldn't you wish to protect something you knew to be great that everyone else sought to desecrate? Wouldn't you wish to be a part of changing something, even if it meant changing yourself?" That line of argument would have accomplished nothing with Peter. When Poe died Peter was quietly satisfied that the matter had ended.

But I was not, not in the least. As I read newspaper articles eulogizing Poe with bitter voices, my desire to protect his name only grew. Something had to be done *even more* than before. When he was alive, he could defend himself. What enraged me most deeply was that these carping muckworms not only embellished the negative facts about Poe's life, but that they crowded around the scene of Poe's death like little hungry flies. Here was the ultimate evidence, the crowning symbol— ran their logic— of a lifetime of moral frailty. Poe's dismal and low end served to confirm the darkness of his life and the imperfections of his morbidly inclined literary productions. *Think of Poe's miserable end,* groaned one paper.

Think of his miserable end!

Think not of his unprecedented genius? Not of his *literary mastery?* Not of how he sparked life in his readers at times when they felt none? Think of kicking a lifeless body into the gutter, and striking the cold forehead of a corpse!

Go visit that grave in Baltimore (the same paper advised) and receive from the very air around it the awful warning of this man's life to ours.

I announced one day that something must be done. Peter laughed.

"You cannot bring suit— the man is under the sod now!" said Peter. "You shall have no client! Let him rest; let *us* rest." Peter started whistling a popular tune. Whenever he was unhappy, he whistled, even if it was in the middle of a conversation.

"I tire of being hired for a little money to say or do other than what I believe, Peter. I made a commitment to represent his interests. A promise, dear friend, and do not tell me that promises should end at someone's death."

"He likely agreed to your help only to keep you from badgering him on the matter." Peter saw that this statement bothered me and he pressed the point with a more sympathetic but insightful tone. "Is that just possible, my friend?"

I thought about something Poe had said in one of his letters regarding *The Stylus: This is the grand purpose of my life,* wrote Poe. *Unless I die, I will accomplish it.* Poe insisted in the same letter that I stop paying advance postage in our correspondence. He signed the letter "Your Friend."

And so I had written the same words to him— the same two simple words in plain ink, and signed my name below them as I would a deadserious oath. Who would ever have argued then that I should not keep it?

"No," I answered Peter's question. "He knew I could defend him."

2

THE THREAT CAME on a Monday afternoon. There were no guns, no daggers, no swords, no near hangings involved (nor would I have believed these were coming for me). The utter astonishment on this day proved more forceful.

My visits to the Baltimore athenaeum reading rooms were becoming regular. A certain prominent debtor's lawsuit, commenced around that time, obliged us to gather diverse news clippings. In times of pressing business, Peter would have been happy to construct a bunk in our chambers and never meet with a ray of sunlight, so it fell to me to travel the short distance to the reading room to perform the researches. While I was there, I would also research Edgar Poe and his death.

A typical biographical account on Poe, which had increased as news of his death spread, might name some of his poems ("The Raven," "Ulalume"), where he had been discovered (Ryan's hotel and tavern, which on that day of election was also a polling place, at High and Lombard streets), when he had died (Sunday, October 7, in a hospital bed), and so on. More Poe-related articles began appearing in the larger presses of New York, Richmond, and Philadelphia that preferred events with a bit of sensation to them. I was able to find some of these mentions at our reading room. Mentions! Mentions indeed!

His life was a regrettable failure. He was a gifted mind who squandered all his potential. Whose fantastical and affected poems and weird tales were too frequently tainted by the fatal, miserable fact of his life. He lived as a drunkard. Died a drunkard, a disgrace and a blackguard who injured sound morals through his writings. Not to be missed by many (said one New York journal). Not long to be remembered.

Have a look with your own eyes:

> Edgar Allan Poe is dead. We have not learned the cir-
> cumstances of his death. It was sudden, and from the
> fact that it occurred in Baltimore, it is to be presumed

that he was on his return to New York. This announcement will startle many, but few will be grieved by it.

I could not watch this desecration. I wanted to look away, yet at the
same time I found myself thirsting to know everything that had been
written, however unjust. (Or— think of the peculiarities of the human
mind— the more unjust it was, the more I needed to see it, and the more
unfair, the more essential it seemed to me!)

Then came that cold, drizzling afternoon when the noon-day sky was
the same at six in the morning as it would be at six at night. Fog everywhere. It drifted like fingers in your face and jabbed in your eyes and
down your throat.

I was on my way to the athenaeum reading rooms when a man bumped
into me. He was approximately my height, and probably the age my father
would have been. The stranger's collision would not have normally
seemed deliberate but for the fact that he had to coil his body in rather an
unnatural way in order to extend his elbow against me. It was not a blow
but rather a drifting tap, actually tender. I listened for an apology.

Instead, there came this warning.

"It is unwise to meddle with your lowly lies, Mr. Clark."

He flashed a glare at me that cut right through the dense air, and then,
before I could think, he had vanished in the fog. I turned to look behind
me as though he had been addressing someone else.

No, he had said "Clark." I was Quentin Hobson Clark, twenty-seven
years old, an attorney chiefly in cases of mortgages and debt. I was Mr.
Clark, and I had just been threatened.

I did not know what to do. In my confusion, I had dropped my memorandum book, and it opened promiscuously on the ground. It was at
that moment, retrieving it before it could be trampled by a mud-crusted
heel, that I recognized how much I had been researching Poe. The name
Poe was written on practically every page. I apprehended with sudden
clarity what the stranger had meant. It was about Poe.

I confess that my own response astonished me. I grew calm and collected, so notably calm that Peter would have grasped my hand with
pride; that is, if this were relating to any other affair. I could never be a
lawyer like Peter, a man who had *passion* for the dullest affidavit or suit,
especially the dullest of them all. Though I had a respectably quick
mind, ability could never outdo passion however much one memorized

the pages of Blackstone and Coke. But in this moment, I had a client and I had a cause that I would not see extinguished. I felt like the finest lawyer ever known.

Regaining my senses sufficiently I plunged into the crowd of umbrellas and soon located the back of the man. He had slowed to a stroll, almost a summer saunter! But I was deceived; this was not the same man. Upon gaining ground, I noticed that in the clouds of fog everyone looked approximately like the subject of my search, even the fairest ladies and darkest slaves. That creeping mist concealed and blended us together, disturbing the regulated order of the streets. And I own that each person tried their best to hold their heads and to stride in perfect indifferent imitation of that one man, that phantom.

There on the corner a stream of gaslight broke through the thick air from a window half hidden underground. It came from the outside lamps of a tavern, and thinking this might be a beacon to attract someone of conniving motives, I rushed down and burst inside. I pushed through the clusters of men intent on their drinks, and at the end of a long row I saw one crumpled over a table. His once-fancy coat was just the one I'd noticed worn by my phantom.

I took his arm. He weakly lifted his head and gave a start upon seeing my intent countenance.

"A mistake. Sir. Sir! A grave mistake on my part!" he cried. His words died together drunkenly.

This was not the man either.

"Mr. Watchman," a nearby inebriate explained to me in a sympathetic loud whisper. "That's John Watchman. I drink to him, the poor fellow! And I drink to you, too, if you'd like."

"John Watchman," I agreed, though at that point this name meant nothing to me (if I had seen it in the newspaper columns, it was with only passing attention). I left some copper coins for the continuation of the man's indulgences, and quickly returned above to the street to press ahead with the search.

I saw the true culprit revealed to me where the fog lessened. At one given time it seemed, in my distress, that all the inhabitants of the street were giving chase to him, summoning their courage to hunt him.

Did I say our Phantom was my height? Yes, and that is true. But this is not to suggest that he resembled me in any way. Indeed, I was perhaps the only one on the streets then not bearing a strict similarity to my subject.

I, with dusty hair of a color like the skin of a tree, which I kept well-groomed, and small, reasonable, clean-shaven features too often called boyish. He— this Phantom— had different proportions to his body. His legs seemed nearly double mine in length, so that however briskly I went along, I could not reduce that gap between us.

As I ran through the prickly mist, I was filled with frantic and excitable thoughts with nothing tying them together except that they thrilled me beyond any logic. I collided with a shoulder, another, and once almost the entire body of a large man who could have flattened me out on the red brick of the side pavement. I slipped on a track of dirt, coating my left side with mud. After that I was all at once alone— nobody in sight.

I stood perfectly still.

Now that I'd lost my prey— or he had lost his— my eyes focused, as though I had put on a pair of spectacles. Here I was, not twenty yards away from it: the narrow Presbyterian burial ground, where the thin slabs of stone sloping out from the ground were only barely darker than the air. I tried to think whether the interloper had actually led me here through half of Baltimore as he fled my pursuit. Or had he been gone for the whole length of the chase, before I came near this place? This place where Edgar Poe now rested, but could not.

Many years earlier, when I was but midway through my teen years, there was an incident on a train I should recount. I was riding with my parents. Although the ladies' car permitted family members of women to sit with them, it was quite full, and only my mother was able to stay. I sat with my father a few cars away, and we walked through the train to visit Mother at regular intervals, into that compartment where no spitting and cursing could take place. After one such excursion, I returned to our seats ahead of Father and found two gentlemen in the seats moments ago occupied by us. I politely explained to the men their mistake. One of the men flew into a violent passion, warning me that I would have to "walk over his dead body" to get our seats back.

"I shall do that very thing if you do not step aside," I replied.

"What did you say, lad?"

And I repeated the same absurd statement with equal calm.

Imagine me as rather a thin boy at fifteen— stringy, you can say. Typically, I might have begged the pardon of the occupant and diligently

searched out inferior seats. You wonder meanwhile about the second interloper in this episode, the other thief of our seats. He, it appeared by a
similar look around the eyes, was the brother of the first; from his bob-
bing head and stare, I believed him to be slow-witted.

You may wonder also as to my reaction. I had been enveloped in my
father's presence shortly before. Father was always a *sovereign* to all
around him. You see, in the moment, it was perfectly natural to me to assume that I, too, could adjust the world as fit my sense of things. This had
been the sneaking nature of the delusion.

I may as well finish the story. The villain did not stop landing severe
blows to my face and head until my father's return to the train car. Less
than a minute later, my father and a conductor had banished the men
into another car of the train to be removed at the next depot.

"Now, what did you do, my boy?" my father asked me afterward as I
lay prostrate across our seats in a haze.

"I had to, Father! You were not here!"

"You provoked someone. You might have been killed. What would you
prove then, Quentin Hobson Clark?" I looked back at the blurry image
of this man lecturing me, standing above me with his usual composure,
and knew the difference between us.

Now I thought of the new warning I had received. *It is unwise to
meddle . . .* The Phantom's image locked up my mind beside the demon
of the train from my childhood. How I burned to talk about it! My great-
aunt at this time was residing with me for a few days to help oversee the
housekeeping. Could I tell Great-Auntie Clark about the threat?

"You ought to have been caught young and trained carefully," she
would say— or something along those lines. She was a great-aunt on my
father's side, and applied the sternness of my father's business principles
to promoting sober behavior more generally. Great-Auntie Clark praised
Father for his "strong Saxon thoughts." Her affection for my father
seemed to accrue partially to me, and she watched over me with dutiful
vigilance.

No, I did not tell Great-Auntie Clark and soon she had departed from
Glen Eliza. (Could I have told my father if he were alive?)

I wanted to tell Hattie Blum. She had always been pleased to hear
of my personal enterprises. She alone had been able to speak to me after
my parents' deaths in a tone and confidence that understood that though

my parents had died, they were not corpses to me. Yet, as I had not seen her since the day we were supposed to have been engaged, I could not fathom how she would perceive my interest in this.

In a way, the Phantom's words attracted as much as they startled me. *It is unwise to meddle with your lowly lies.* Though he was warning me away, the cryptic words acknowledged that the perception of Poe could be *meddled* with— in other words, they could still be changed by me. In a way, that warning encouraged me.

I felt an excitement that was only remotely familiar and only half unwanted. It was different from anything I had known in our work.

One long afternoon at the office I sat looking at the street from my desk. Peter was nearby. He was in the middle of reprimanding our copying clerk over the quality of some affidavit when he glanced over at me. He returned to his speech, then glanced abruptly at me again. "All right, Quentin?"

It was a habit of mine that I occasionally fell into a sort of staring spell, glaring in the air at nothing in particular. Peter was especially fascinated and appalled whenever these reveries occurred. He noisily shook the bag of ginger-nuts I'd been eating. "All right, Quentin?"

"All right," I assured him. "Tolerably well, Peter." Upon seeing that I would say no more, he returned to the clerk with the precise word of reprimand where he had left off.

I could no longer keep buttoned up. "All right, certainly! If there is anything all right about being threatened!" I cried out suddenly. "All wrong!" Peter quietly dismissed our clerk, who gratefully scurried from the room. When we were alone, every detail spilled from my tongue. Peter sat at the edge of his chair, listening with interest. At first, he even shared in the thrill of the incident, but soon enough remembered himself. He declared the Phantom nothing but a cracked lunatic.

I somehow felt the need to defend, even *commend* the threatening party. "No, Peter, he was no lunatic in the least! In his eyes was a rational purpose of some kind— a rare intelligence."

"What cloak-and-dagger business! Why— ? Why should he bother to— ? What, one of our mortgage cases?"

I responded with a hoarse laughter that seemed to offend Peter— as though denying a would-be lunatic's potential interest in our mortgage disputes devalued the whole legal profession. But I was sorry for the tone, and I more calmly explained that this affair was something to do with Edgar Poe; I explained that I had been studying clippings about Poe and had noticed important inconsistencies.

"For instance, there is the common innuendo, the suggestion, that Poe died of his 'fatal weakness,' they say, meaning drinking. Yet who was a witness? Hadn't some of the same newspapers reported, only a few weeks earlier, Poe joining the Sons of Temperance in Richmond and successfully keeping their oath?"

"A thorough scamp and a poet, that Edgar Poe! To read him is like being in a charnel-house and breathing the air."

"You say you never read him, Peter!"

"Yes, and that's precisely why! I would not be half surprised if more people never read him each day. Even the titles of his tales are nightmares. Just because you cared about him, Quentin Clark, should that mean anyone else did? None of this is about Poe, it is about you wanting it to be about Poe! Why, this warning you think you heard surely had nothing to do with him at all, except in some disordered current of your mind!" He threw his hands in the air.

Perhaps Peter was right; the Phantom hadn't *specifically* said anything pertaining to Poe. Could I be so certain? Yet I was. Someone wanted me to stop inquiring into Poe's death. I knew someone had to hold the truth of what had happened to Poe here in Baltimore, and that is what others must have feared. I had to find that truth to know why.

One day, I was checking over some of the scrivener's copies of an important contract. A clerk thrust his head into my office.

"Mr. Clark. Mr. Poe. Here."

Startled, I demanded to know what he meant.

"From Mr. Poe," he repeated, waving a piece of paper in front of his face.

"Oh!" I gestured to him for the letter. It was from one Neilson Poe.

The name had been familiar to me from the newspapers as a local attorney representing many defaulters and petty thieves and criminals in court and, for a time, as a director on the Baltimore & Ohio Railroad committee. Addressing a note to Neilson a few days earlier, I had asked whether the man was a relative of the poet Edgar Poe's, and had requested an interview.

In this reply, Neilson thanked me for my interest in his relation but averred that professional duties made any appointment impossible for some weeks. Weeks! Frustrated, I recalled an item about Neilson Poe I had read in the latest court columns of the newspapers and quickly gathered up my coat.

Neilson, according to the paper's advance report of the day's activities at court, was at that very moment defending a man, Cavender, who had been indicted for assault with attempt to commit an outrage against a young woman. The Cavender case had already adjourned for the day when I reached the courthouse, so I looked in the prisoners' cells that were housed in its cellar. Addressing a police officer with my credentials as an attorney, I was directed to the cell of Mr. Cavender. Inside the chamber, which was dark and small, a man garbed as a prisoner sat in deep communion with one wearing a fine suit and a lawyer's fixed expression of calm. There was a stone jug of coffee and a plate of white bread.

"Rough day at court?" I asked collegially from the other side of the prison bars.

The man in the suit rose from the bench inside the cell. "Who are you, sir?" he asked.

I offered my hand to the man I had first seen at the funeral on Greene and Fayette. "Mr. Poe? I am Quentin Clark."

Neilson Poe was a short, clean-shaven man with an intelligent brow almost as wide as the one shown in portraits of Edgar, but with sharper, ferret-like features and quick, dark eyes. I imagined Edgar Poe's eyes having more of a flash, and a positively opaque glow at times of creation and excitement. Still, this was a man who, at a casual glance in these dim surroundings, could almost have doubled for the great poet.

Neilson signaled to his client that he would be stepping outside the cell for a few moments. The prisoner, whose head had been in his hands the moment before, rose to his feet with sudden animation, watching his defender's exit.

"If I'm not mistaken," Neilson said to me as the guard locked the prisoner's door, "I'd written you in my note that I was pressed with business, Mr. Clark."

"It is important, dear Mr. Poe. Regarding your cousin."

Neilson set his hands stiffly on some court documents, as though to remind me there was more pressing business at hand.

"Surely this is a topic of personal interest to you," I ventured.

He squinted at me with impatience.

"The topic of Edgar Poe's death," I said to explain it better.

"My cousin Edgar was wandering about restlessly, looking for a life of true tranquillity, a life as *you or I* are fortunate enough to possess, Mr. Clark," Neilson said. "He had already squandered that possibility long ago."

"What of his plans to establish a first-rate magazine?"

"Yes . . . plans."

"He would have accomplished it, Mr. Poe. He worried only that his enemies would first— "

"Enemies!" he cut me short. Neilson then paused as his eyes widened at me. "Sir," he said with a new air of caution, "tell me, what is your particular interest in this that you would come down into this gloomy cellar to find me?"

"I am— I was his attorney, sir," I said. "I was to defend his new magazine from attacks of libel. If he did have enemies, sir, I should like very much to know who they were."

A dead man for a client . . . I heard Peter in my ear.

"A new trial, Poe!"

Neilson appeared to be weighing my words when his client threw himself against the cell door. "Petition for a new trial, Mr. Poe! A fair shake, at least! I'm innocent of all charges, Poe!" he cried. "That wench is an out-and-out liar!"

After a few moments, Neilson pacified his despondent client and promised him to return later.

"Someone needs to defend Edgar," I said.

"I must attend to other work now, Mr. Clark." He started walking briskly through the dismal cellar. He paused, then turned back to me, remarking grudgingly, "Come along to my office if you wish to speak further. There is something there you might like to see."

We walked together down St. Paul Street. When we entered the modest and crowded chambers of his practice, Neilson commented that when he'd received my letter of introduction he'd been struck by the resemblance between my handwriting and his late cousin's. "For a moment I thought I was reading a letter from our dear Edgar," he said lightheartedly. "An intriguing case for an autographer." It was perhaps the last kind word he had for his cousin. He offered me a chair.

"Edgar was rash, even as a boy, Mr. Clark," he began. "He took as his wife our beautiful cousin, Virginia, when she was thirteen, hardly out from the dew of girlhood. Poor Sissy— that's what we called her— he took her away from Baltimore, where she'd always been safe. Her

mother's house on Amity Street was small, but at least she was surrounded with devoted family. He felt if he waited, he might lose her affections."

"Edgar surely cared for her more dearly than anyone," I replied.

"Here, Mr. Clark, is what I wanted you to see. Perhaps it will help you
understand."

Neilson removed from a drawer a portrait that he said had been sent
by Maria Clemm, Sissy's mother (and Edgar's aunt and mother-in-law).
It showed Sissy, a young woman of around twenty-one or twenty-two with
a pearly complexion and glossy raven-black hair, her eyes closed and her
head tipped to the side in a pose at once peaceful and unspeakably sad.
I commented on the life-like quality in the portrait.

"No, Mr. Clark." He turned pale. "*Death*-like. It is her death portrait.
After she died, Edgar realized they had no portrait of her and had this
done. I do not like to show this, though, for it poorly captures the spirit
she possessed in life— that pale and deathly look about her. But he val-
ued it beyond measure. My cousin, you see, could not relinquish her
even to death."

With the portrait were some verses written by Virginia to Edgar the
year before her death, speaking of living in a blissful cottage where the
"tattling of many tongues" would be far away. "Love alone shall guide us
when we are there," her tender poem read. "Love shall heal my weakened lungs."

Neilson put aside the portrait and poem. He explained that during her
last years Virginia had required the utmost medical attention.

"Perhaps he did love her. But could Edgar have properly provided for
her care? Edgar might have done better all along finding a woman of
wealth." Neilson paused at this thought and seemed to shift topics. "Until
I was about your age, you know, I myself edited newspapers and journals
and wrote columns. I *have* known the literary life," he said with fallen
pride. "I know its appeal to the raw spirit, Mr. Clark. Yet I have always
had dealings with reality, too, and know better than to keep at something
for personal gratification after it proves a losing proposition, as Edgar's
writing did. Edgar should have stopped writing. This alone might have
saved Sissy, might have saved Edgar himself."

Regarding Poe's final months, his final attempt to obtain financial success, Neilson referred to his cousin's aim to raise money and subscriptions for the proposed *Stylus* magazine by delivering lectures and visiting

people of good society in Norfolk and Richmond. It was in the latter city that he renewed an acquaintance with a woman of wealth, as Neilson described her approvingly.

"Her name was Elmira Shelton, a Richmond woman whom Edgar had loved long before." In their youth, Edgar and Elmira had promised themselves to each other before he left to attend the University of Virginia, but Elmira's father disapproved, and confiscated Poe's constant letters so his daughter would not see them. I interrupted Neilson to ask why.

"Perhaps," he replied, "it was that Edgar and Elmira were young . . . and that Edgar was a poet . . . and do not forget, Elmira's father would have known Mr. Allan. He would have spoken with him and he would have known Edgar was likely to receive no inheritance at all from the Allan fortune."

When Edgar Poe was forced to return from college after John Allan would not pay his debts, Edgar attended a party at Elmira's family home only to find, to his heartbreak, that Elmira was engaged to another.

By the summer of 1849, when they met again, her husband had died, as had Virginia Poe. The carefree girl of so many years ago was now a wealthy widow. Edgar read her poems and reminisced with good humor about their past. He joined a local chapter of a temperance society in Richmond and swore to Elmira to keep their oath. He said love that hesitated was not a love for him and he gave her a ring. Theirs would be a new life together.

Only weeks later Edgar Poe would be found at Ryan's, here in Baltimore, and rushed to the hospital, where he'd die.

"I had not seen Edgar for some years toward the end. It was a great shock, you will imagine, Mr. Clark, when I was told he was found at one of the places of election in Old Town in poor condition and carried to the college hospital. My relation, a Mr. Henry Herring, was called to the scene at Ryan's. At what time Edgar arrived in Baltimore, where he spent the time he was here, under what circumstances, all this I have been unable to ascertain."

I showed my surprise. "You mean you sought this information on your cousin's death, and could not find it?"

"I felt it my duty to try, relationships and so on," he said. "We were cousins, yes, but we were also friends. We were the same age, Edgar and I, and he was not old enough to see the end of his life. I hope my own death is peaceful and in plain sight, somewhere surrounded by my family."

"You must have found something more?"

"I'm afraid that whatever happened to Edgar has accompanied Cousin into the grave. Is this not sometimes the course of a life, Mr. Clark, for death to swallow a man up so wholly there are no traces left? To leave not a shadow, not even the shadow of a shadow."

"That is not all that is left, though, Mr. Poe," I said, insistently. "Your cousin will be remembered. His works are immensely powerful."

"There is a kind of power to them. But it is usually the power of disease. Tell me, Mr. Clark, do you know something more about Edgar's death?"

I did not tell him about the man who warned me to stop looking at Poe's death. Something stopped me. Perhaps this hesitation was the true beginning of the investigation. Perhaps I already suspected that there was more to this situation, more to Neilson Poe, than I'd yet been able to see.

He could not even say much about Edgar Poe's condition after he was rushed to the doctors from Ryan's. Once Neilson had arrived at the hospital, the physicians advised that he not enter Edgar's room, saying the patient was too excitable. Neilson only saw Poe through a curtain, and he looked from that vantage point like another man altogether, or a ghost of a body he had known. Neilson did not even have the chance to view the body before it was closed into the coffin.

"I'm afraid there's nothing more I can tell you about the end," he sighed. Then he said it. The eulogy that I could not forget. "Edgar was an orphan in every way. He had seen much of sorrow, Mr. Clark, had so little reason to be satisfied with life that, to him, the change, death, can scarcely be said to be a misfortune."

My frustration at Neilson Poe's complacency inspired me to call on the offices of a few newspapers with a faint hope of persuading them to at least pay better tribute to the genius of Poe. I described Poe's paltry burial and the many erroneous facts in the short biographies so far published in the papers, hoping they would improve. But these visits were useless. At the office of one of the Whig newspapers, the *Patriot,* some reporters overheard me and, calling to mind that Poe wrote for the press, suggested with great solemnity that they take up a subscription to pay for a marker on Poe's grave to honor a fallen fellow. As though Edgar Poe were simply another spinner of newspaper tales! Note, too, that I would not make the error of saying, as the periodical press had taken to doing,

Edgar *Allan* Poe. No. The name was a contradiction, a chimera and an unholy monster. John Allan had taken in the poet as a young child in 1810, but later ungenerously abandoned him to the whims of the world.

Passing the Presbyterian burial yard on my way home late one afternoon, I decided to see the poet's resting place again. The old cemetery was a narrow block of graves on the corner of Fayette and Greene streets. The location of the grave was near the fine marker of General David Poe, a hero of the Revolutionary War and Edgar Poe's grandfather. But there was something disconcerting.

Poe's own spot was still unmarked. It looked as though it had never been prayed over.

Invisible Wo! I could not stop from thinking of the ravages of the "conqueror worm," as Poe had called our bodies' final attacker. *And the angels sob at vermin fangs in human gore imbued.*

With sudden purpose, I marched deeper into the burial ground. Peering around I saw steps leading down into one of the old underground vaults. Following these steps straight down, I found the sexton, Mr. Spence, reading a book in a low-arched granite crypt deep below the surface. There was a table, a bureau, a washstand, a medium-sized looking-glass. Even once a church was built on the burial ground a few years later, it was said that George Spence still preferred these vaults. But it rather astonished me then.

"You don't live down here, do you, Mr. Spence?" I asked.

He was troubled by my tone. "When it is too cold down here, I stay above. But I like it better here. It's more quiet and independent. This vault, in all events, was emptied out some years ago."

Several decades earlier, he explained, the family who owned this particular tomb had wanted to move the bodies of their ancestors to more spacious accommodations. But when the tomb was opened, it was discovered— by the previous sexton, Spence's father— that one of the bodies exhibited that rare occurrence: human petrifaction. The body, top to bottom, was entirely stone. Superstitions spread quickly. No member of the church since would agree to bury their dead in that particular vault.

"Devilish horror, coming upon a stone man when you are no more than a boy," the sexton said. He found a chair for me.

"Thank you, Mr. Spence. There is something wrong. The grave of Edgar Poe, buried last month, is still unmarked! The grave lies level with the ground."

He shrugged philosophically. "It is not my decision, but that of the party that had charge of burying him. Neilson Poe and Henry Herring, Poe's relations."

"I passed here the day of the funeral, and could see it was small. Were there other relatives of Poe's besides them present?" I asked.

"There was one other. William Clemm, of the Caroline Street Methodist Church, performed the service and I believe he was a distant relation of the family. Reverend Clemm had prepared a lengthy discourse, but there were so few present for the funeral, it was decided he would not read it. There were only two mourners in addition to Neilson Poe and Mr. Herring. One was Z. Collins Lee, a classmate of Poe's. Peace be to his ashes!"

"Mr. Spence?"

"That is something I remember the minister said over Poe's grave. Peace be to his ashes. I was surprised to hear about Mr. Poe's death at first. He will always be a young man in my mind, not much older than you."

"You knew him, Mr. Spence?"

"When he lived in Baltimore, in Maria Clemm's little house," the sexton replied musingly. "It was years ago. You would have been hardly older than a boy. Baltimore was a quieter city then; one could keep track of names. I used to see Edgar Poe wander about the burial ground now and again."

He said Poe would stand before the graves of his grandfather and his older brother, William Henry Poe, both of whom he'd been separated from in childhood. Sometimes, said the sexton, Edgar A. Poe would examine names and dates on the tombs and quietly ask how this one was related to that one. When Spence would meet Poe out on the streets, the poet would sometimes say "good morning" or "good evening," and sometimes he would not.

"To think such a fine gentleman should look *as he did* at the end." Spence shook his head as he spoke.

"How do you mean, Mr. Spence?" I asked.

"I recall he always had a fastidiousness about his dress. But that suit he was wearing when he was found!" he said as though I should know perfectly well. I motioned for him to continue, so he did. "It was thin and ragged and did not fit him at all. It could not have been his. It was for a body perhaps two sizes larger! And a cheap palm-leaf hat one would not bother to pick up from the ground. A man from the hospital offered a better black suit to bury him in."

"But how did Poe come to be wearing ill-fitting clothes?"

"I cannot say."

"Do you not think it utterly strange?"

"I suppose I have not thought of it much since then, Mr. Clark."

Those clothes were not meant to be worn by Poe. *Poe's death had not been meant for him,* I thought, an irrational and abrupt notion. I thanked the sexton for his time and began rapidly to ascend the long stairs that rose from the vaults, as though once I'd secured the top there would be some immediate action to take. Suddenly seized by a momentary foreboding, I stopped in the middle of the stairs, tightening my grip on the handrail. The wind had grown worse outside, and as I reached the top I could barely direct myself to cross back into the upper world.

When I emerged, my eyes drifted to the spot of Poe's unmarked grave for one last look. I nearly jumped at what I saw. I blinked to make certain it was real.

It was a flower, a fragrant, blossoming flower lying incongruously atop the grass and dirt of Edgar Poe's plot. A flower that had not been there just a few minutes before.

I gasped for Mr. Spence, as though there was something to be done, or as though he could have seen something I hadn't while we were both sitting together below the earth in that tomb. Down in the vault the sexton could not hear me calling. Dropping to my knees, I inspected the flower, thinking perhaps it had blown from another grave. But no. Not only did the flower sit there, *there,* but also its stem broke firmly through the dirt on top.

Suddenly there was the noise of horses stepping and wheels clicking slowly to life. I peered around and could see a medium-sized carriage cloaked by the mist. I ran toward the gates to try and see who was there, but I was instantly blocked. A dog bounded into view. The dog barked voraciously at my ankles. I tried to steer around her, but the canine pounced to the side, growling and snarling from behind the gravestones.

The dog had clearly been trained to prevent Baltimore's "resurrection men" from attempted thefts of our corpses, and perceiving me run had identified me as one of those miscreants. Finding some ginger-nuts in my coat, I offered them up, and the mongrel soon befriended me. But by the time I could safely reach the street, the carriage had vanished into the distance.

3

I WAS STIRRED awake the next morning only by the muffled sounds from the servants below. I washed and dressed rapidly. But at this hour, no carriages were found for hire near my house. Luckily, I found a public omnibus that happened to be boarding.

Having not traveled by public conveyance as of late, I was struck by how many strangers to Baltimore were aboard. This I thought from their dress and speech, and their watchfulness of the people around them. It led me to wonder. . . . I happened to be carrying among my papers a portrait of Poe from a biographical article published a few years before. At the next stopping-place I turned to the rear of the bus. When the conductor finished collecting tickets from the newcomers, I asked him whether the man pictured in the magazine had been his passenger in the last weeks of September. That was the time— I had estimated from the more reliable newspaper accounts— that Poe would have arrived to Baltimore. The conductor murmured "Don't recall 'm," or something in the same fashion.

A slight comment, I know! Hardly worth any excitement? Yet I felt the flash of accomplishment. In a single moment, though rebuffed, I had acquired knowledge that Poe had not been in this particular omnibus during this conductor's watch! I had solicited a small share of the truth behind Poe's final passage through Baltimore, and that contented me.

Since I had to move about the city anyway, it could not hurt to ride the omnibus more frequently and, when I did, ask such questions.

You have no doubt noted that Poe's time in Baltimore had not seemed to be premeditated. After becoming engaged to Elmira Shelton in Richmond, he had announced his intentions of going to New York to complete his future plans. But what had been the poet's whereabouts and purposes here in Baltimore? Baltimore should not be so indifferent as simply to lose a man, even in its dingiest shipping quarters— it was not Philadelphia. Why had he not traveled straight to New York after sailing here from Richmond? What had happened over the course of five days between leaving Richmond and being discovered in Baltimore and what had brought him into such a state that he would be wearing someone else's clothes?

After my visit to the burial ground, I'd been bent on directing to these questions my own faculties of intelligence, which I would humbly measure against those of any man— at least any man I had yet known (for this was about to change).

There was that one momentous afternoon when the answers seemed to come improbably into view. Peter had been delayed at court, and our desks were empty of new work. I was walking away from the Hanover Market and was stepping to the Camden Street curb with an armful of packages.

"Poe the poet?"

At first I ignored this. Then I stopped and turned around slowly, wondering if my ears had been fooled by the wind. Truly, though, if this voice had not pronounced on its own power "Poe the poet" it had said something *just* like that.

It was the fish dealer, Mr. Wilson, with whom I had just done business at the market. Our law office had recently arranged some mortgages for him. Though a few times he had come to our offices, I preferred finding him here, as I could then also select the finest fish to be prepared for supper at Glen Eliza. And Wilson's crab-and-oyster gumbo was the best this side of New Orleans.

The fishmonger motioned me to follow him back to the large market. I had left my memorandum book at his table. He wiped his hands on his streaked apron and handed it to me. It was now wrapped in the distinct odors of his store, as though it had been lost at sea and then pulled out.

"You don't want to forget your work. I opened it to see who it belonged to. I see you've written the name Edgar Poe." The fishmonger pointed to the open page.

I returned the book to my bag. "Thank you, Mr. Wilson."

"Ah, Squire Clark, here's something." He excitedly unwrapped a package of fish from its paper. Inside was a hideously ugly fish, piled upon its identical brothers. "This was ordered especially from out west for a dinner party. It is called a *dog-fish* by some. But it's also called a 'lake lawyer,' for its ferocious looks and voracious habits!" He chuckled uproariously. He quickly worried he had insulted me. "Not like you, of course, Squire Clark."

"Perhaps that is the problem, my friend."

"Yes." He hesitated and cleared his throat. He was now hacking at fish without looking down at his hands or at the heads shooting off them. "Any event— poor soul, must have been, that Poe. Died over at that creaky ol' Washington College Hospital some weeks back, I heard. My sister's husband knows a nurse there, who says, according to another nurse who spoke to a doctor— *demonish* busybodies, these women— who said Poe wasn't right in his upper story, that as he lay there he called out a name over and over before he . . . well, that is," he shifted to a whisper of great sensitivity, "before he *croaked*. God have mercy on the weak."

"You said he called a name, Mr. Wilson?"

The fishmonger sloshed around his words to remember. He sat at his stool and began picking out unsold oysters from a barrel, carefully prying each one open and checking them for pearls before discarding them with philosophical regret. The oyster was the consummate Baltimore native, not only because it was enterprising and could be traded but because it possessed the always-present possibility of an even more valuable treasure inside. Suddenly the fish dealer clucked exultantly.

"'Reynolds,' it was! Right, that's it, 'Reynolds'! I know because she kept saying it when she told me over supper, and on our plates were the last good soft-shell crabs of the season."

I asked him to think hard *and be certain*.

"'Reynolds, Reynolds, *Reynolds!*'" he said with some offense at my doubt. "That's how he was calling it out, all through the night. She said she couldn't pluck it out of her brain after she heard of it. Creaky ol' hospital— should be burnt down, I say. I knew a Reynolds in my youth who threw stones at infantrymen— he was a demonish character, no mistake, Squire Clark."

"But did Poe ever mention a Reynolds before?" I asked myself out loud. "A family member, or . . ."

The fish dealer's enjoyment of the scene lessened, and he stared at me. "This Mr. Poe was a friend of yours?"

"A friend," I said, "and a friend of all who read him."

I bid my client a hasty good evening with much gratitude for the remarkable service he had provided me. I had been permitted to hear Poe's very last utterance to this earth (or nearly the last, anyhow), and in it some retort, some revelation, some remedy to the slashing and the cutting of the press might be recovered. That single word meant there was something to be found, some life left of Poe's for me to discover.

. . .

Reynolds!

I spent countless hours searching through Poe's letters to me and through all of his tales and verse to detect any sign of Reynolds. Tickets to exhibitions and concerts went unused; if Jenny Lind, the "Swedish Nightingale," were singing in town, I would have been among my books all the same. I could almost hear my father direct me to put all this away and return to my law books. He would say (so I imagined), "Young men like yourself should observe that Industry and Enterprise can slowly do anything Genius does with impatience— and many things Genius cannot. Genius needs Industry as much as Industry needs Genius." I felt suddenly, each time I opened another Poe document, as though I was in an argument with Father, that he was trying to tear the very books out of my hands. It was not a wholly unwelcome feeling to encounter: in fact, I think it actually pushed me forward. Besides, in my capacity as a man of business I had promised Poe, a prospective client, that I would defend him. Perhaps Father would have commended me.

Hattie Blum, meanwhile, called at Glen Eliza with her aunt frequently. Whatever disapproval on their part had developed from my recent transgression had passed, or at least been suspended. Hattie was as thoughtful and generous in our conversations as ever. Her aunt, perhaps, was more watchful than usual, and seemed to have developed the dark eyes of a secret agent. Of course, my intense preoccupations, along with my general tendency to grow quiet when others talked, meant the women in my drawing room addressed each other more than me.

"I do not know how you bear it," said Hattie, looking up at the high domed ceiling. "I could not suffer a house as enormous as Glen Eliza alone, Quentin. It takes bravery to have too much space for yourself. Don't you think, Auntie?"

Auntie Blum snorted out a laugh. "Dear Hattie becomes terribly lonesome when I leave her for an hour with only the help for company. They can be *dreadful.*"

One of my domestics came from the hall and refreshed the ladies' tea.

"Not so, Auntie! But with my sisters gone," Hattie began, then paused, with a slight and uncharacteristic blush.

"Because they've all married," her aunt said quietly.

"Of course," I agreed after a long pause from both Blum ladies suggested a comment on my part.

"With my three sisters out of the house, well, it can seem awfully desolate at times, like I must fend for myself but I do not even know against what. Haven't you ever had a feeling like that?"

"On the other hand," I said, "dear Miss Hattie, there is a certain peace to it, separated from the bustle of the streets and the concerns of other people."

"Oh, Auntie!" She turned jovially to the other woman. "Perhaps I crave the bustle too much. Do you think our family blood runs too warm for Baltimore after all, Auntie?"

A word about the woman being addressed, the one sitting in front of the hearth on an armchair as if it were a throne, the stately dame with a shawl wrapped around her as though it were a monarch's robe, Auntie Blum—yes, a word more about her since her influence will not diminish as our story's complications set in. She was one of that stalwart species of lady who seemed lost in her choicest bonnets and social habits but in fact possessed an ability to jostle her listener to his core, in the same trifling tone with which she critiqued the table of a rival hostess. For instance, during the same visit to my parlor she found occasion to comment offhandedly, "Quentin, isn't it fortunate, Peter Stuart finding you for his partner?"

"Ma'am?"

"Such a mind for business he possesses! He is a man of flat-footed *sense*, depend upon it. You are the younger brother of the pair, *allegorically* I mean, and soon shall be able to boast you are like him in all respects."

I returned her smile.

"Why, it is like our Hattie and her sisters. One day she shall be as successful in society as them— I mean if she becomes a wife in time, of course," Auntie Blum said, taking a long taste of the scalding hot tea.

I saw that Hattie looked away from both of us. Her aunt was the one person in the world who could remove Hattie's wonderful self-assurance. This angered me.

I placed my hand on Hattie's chair, near her hand. "When that time comes, her sisters will learn how to be true wives and mothers from this woman, I assure you, Mrs. Blum. More tea?"

I did not want to mention anything related to Edgar Poe in their hearing on the chance that Auntie Blum would find some excuse to inform Peter, or write a concerned epistle on the state of my life to my great-aunt, with whom she had been very hand and glove over the years. I found myself relieved, indeed, when each interview with that woman closed without my having said a word about my investigations. However, the restriction would make me anxious to resume my recent searches as soon as the Blums had departed.

On this occasion, when I boarded an omnibus I was addressed by the conductor as though I had just spit tobacco juice on the floor. "You!"

I had forgotten to hand over my ticket. An inauspicious start. After correcting this, the bus conductor painstakingly studied the portrait I held up for him before deciding the face was unfamiliar.

This portrait of Poe, published after his death, was not of the highest quality. But I believed it captured the essentials. His dark mustache, straighter and neater than his curling hair. The eyes, clear and almond shaped— eyes with restlessness almost magnetic. Forehead, broad and prominent above the temples, so that from certain angles he must look to have no hair— a man who could be all forehead.

As the doors closed and I was bumped into a seat by the line of on-coming passengers, a short and wide fellow tugged at my arm with the end of his umbrella.

"Pardon me!" I cried.

"Say, the man in that illustration, I think I'd seen him a while ago. Sometime in September, like you said to the conductor."

"Truly, sir?" I asked.

He explained that he rode the same bus almost every day and remembered someone who looked just like the man in the portrait. It happened as they were leaving the omnibus.

"I recollect it because he asked for help— wanted to know where a Dr. Brooks lived, if I remember. I'm an umbrella mender, not a *city directory*."

I readily agreed with the point, although I did not know if the latter comment was meant for me or Poe. N. C. Brooks's name was familiar enough to me— and certainly would have been to Edgar Poe. Dr. Brooks was an editor who had published some of Poe's finest tales and poems, which had helped introduce Poe's work to the Baltimore public. Finally, some real proof that Poe had not entirely disappeared into the air of Baltimore after all!

The horses' rumbling was starting to slow, and I jumped out of my seat as the vehicle began rolling to its next stop.

I hastened to my law chambers to consult with the city directory for Dr. Brooks's address. It was six in the evening, and I had assumed Peter had retired already after finishing his appointments at the courthouse. But I was wrong.

"My dear friend," he bellowed over my shoulder. "You look startled! Nearly jumped out of your skin!"

"Peter." I paused, realizing when I spoke that I was out of breath. "It is only— well, I suppose I was presently on my way out again."

"I have a surprise," he said, grinning and lifting his walking stick like a scepter. He blocked my way to the door, his hand groping for my shoulder.

"There is to be a grand blow-out this evening at my home, with many friends of yours and mine, Quentin. It was very lately planned, for it is the birthday of one who is most— "

"But you see I'm just now . . ." I interrupted impatiently, but stopped myself from explaining when I saw a dark glint in my partner's eyes.

"What, Quentin?" Peter looked around slowly, with mock interest. "There is no more to do here this evening. You have somewhere you must rush to? Where?"

"No," I said, feeling faintly flushed, "it is nothing."

"Good, then let us be right off!"

Peter's table was overrun with familiar faces, in celebration of Hattie Blum's twenty-third birthday. Shouldn't I have remembered? I felt a terrible tinge of remorse at my insensitivity. I had seen her for every one of her birthdays. Had I strayed so far from my ordinary path to forsake even the most *pleasurable* affairs of society and intimate friends? Well, one visit to Brooks, and I believed my preoccupation could be happily concluded.

There were as highly respectable ladies and gentlemen there that night as could be obtained in Baltimore. Yet wouldn't I have preferred to be in Madame Tussaud's chamber of murderers just then, anywhere just then but caught in slow and smooth conversation, when I had such a momentous task tempting me!

"How could you?" This was spoken by a large, pink-faced woman who appeared across from me when we sat down to the elaborate supper.

"What?"

"Oh dear," she said with a playful and humble moan, "looking at me— plain old me!— when there is such a specimen of beauty next to you." She made a gesture at Hattie.

Of course, I hadn't been looking at the pink-faced woman, or not intentionally. I realized I had fallen into one of my staring fits again. "I am surrounded by pure beauty, aren't I?"

Hattie did not blush. I liked that she did not blush at compliments. She whispered to me with a confidential air, "You are fixated on the clock, and have overlooked our most fascinating guest, the duck braised with wild celery, Quentin. Will not that demon Mr. Stuart allow you one evening free without work?"

I smiled. "It is not Peter's fault this time," I said. "I'm just picking, I suppose. I have little appetite these days."

"You can speak to me, Quentin," Hattie said, and seemed at that moment of a gentler cut than any woman I had ever met. "What do you think about now with such trouble on your face?"

"I am thinking, dear Miss Hattie . . ." I hesitated, then said, "Of some lines of poetry." Which was true, for I had just reread them that morning.

"Recite them, won't you, Quentin?"

In my excessive distraction I had taken two glasses of wine without eating properly to balance the effects of the spirits. So with a little persuasion, I found myself agreeing to recite. My voice hardly sounded familiar to me; it was round and bold and even resonant. To convey the style of presentation, the reader should stand wherever he happens to find himself and venture to pronounce in solemn and moody tones some of the following. The reader must also imagine meanwhile a cheery table exhibiting that species of abrupt, grating silences that accompany imposed interruptions.

> And all with pearl and ruby glowing
> Was the fair palace door,
> Through which came flowing, flowing, flowing,
> And sparkling evermore,
> A troop of Echoes, whose sweet duty
> Was but to sing,
> In voices of surpassing beauty,
> The wit and wisdom of their king.

> But evil things, in robes of sorrow,
> Assailed the monarch's high estate.
> (Ah, let us mourn!— for never morrow

> *Shall dawn upon him desolate!)*
> *And round about his home, the glory*
> *That blushed and bloomed*
> *Is but a dim-remembered story*
> *Of the old time entombed.*

When a period was put to this poem, I felt triumphant. There reached my ears thinly scattered applause, drowned out by a few coughs. Peter frowned at me, and simultaneously threw a pitying glance at Hattie. Only a few guests who had not been listening, but were pleased for any distraction, seemed appreciative. Hattie still applauded after all the others had stopped.

"It is the finest recitation ever spoken on a girl's birthday," she said.

Soon, one of Hattie's sisters agreed to sing a song at the piano. Meanwhile, I'd taken more wine. Peter's frown, which had quivered into place during the recitation of the poem, remained fixed when, after the ladies excused themselves to another room and the men began smoking, he brought me to a private corner where the massive hearth sequestered us.

"Do you know, Quentin, that Hattie came quite close to not wanting to celebrate her birthday tonight, and relented at the last moment upon my insistence on a supper?"

"Not because of me, Peter?"

"How could someone who thinks so much of the world depends on him not see what *does* depend on him? You did not even remember it was her birthday. It is time to stop, Quentin. Remember the words of Solomon: 'By slothfulness the building decayeth, by idleness of the hands the house droppeth through.'"

"I don't know what you're driving at," I said irritably.

He looked straight at me. "You know well enough! This queer behavior. First, your strange preoccupation with a stranger's funeral. And riding the omnibuses back and forth without destination like a gadabout—"

"But who told you that, Peter?"

And there was more, he said. I had been seen running through the streets a week earlier, my dress out at the elbows, chasing someone like I was a police officer making an arrest. I had continued to spend inordinate amounts of time in the athenaeum.

"Then there is the idea of imagining strangers are threatening you on the streets for the poems you read. Do you think your reading is so im-

portant that people would harm you for it? And you wandering around
the old Presbyterian burial ground like a pretty resurrection man looking
for bodies to steal, or like a man who walks under a spell!"

"Hold on," I said, regaining my composure. "How do you know that,
Peter? That I was at that old burial ground the other day? I am certain I
hadn't mentioned it." I thought of the carriage hurrying away from the
burial yard. "Why, Peter! Was it you? You followed me!"

He nodded and then shrugged. "Yes, I followed you. And found you at
that cemetery. I confess openly I have been most anxious. I wanted to be
certain you were not involved in some trouble or that you hadn't joined
some cracked Millerites, waiting in white robes somewhere for the Savior to descend from heaven two Tuesdays from now! Your father's money
will not last forever. To be rich and useless is to be poor. If you are occupied in strange habits, I fear you will find ways to squander it— or that
some woman, some lesser member of the kinder sex than Miss Blum, by
the bye, finding you in such a lonely state, will squander it for you— even
a man with the strength of Ulysses must fasten himself to his mast when
facing the artful woman!"

"Why would you leave that flower at his grave?" I demanded. "To
mock me?"

"*Flower?* What do you mean? By the time I found where you had
gone, you were kneeling on the grave, as though praying before some
idol. That's all I saw, and it was enough. Flower— do you think I have
time for such things!"

On this point, I could not help but believe him, as he truly sounded as
though he had never heard the word "flower" before or beheld one.
"And did you send that man to me? That warning not to meddle. To try
to dissuade me from my interests outside the office? Tell me at once!"

"Absurd! Quentin, listen to your own flat nonsense before they send
for a straitjacket! Everyone understood you needed time after what happened. Your depression of spirits was . . ." He looked away from me for a
moment. "But it has been six months." Actually, it had been five months
and one week since my parents had been laid to rest. "You must think of
all this, beginning now, or . . ." He never finished this statement, only
nodded with decision to impress the point. "It's that other world you're
fighting against."

"The 'other world,' Peter?"

"You think me at odds with you. But I tried to gain greater sympathy with you, Quentin. I sought out a book of tales by *that Poe.* I read half of one tale— but I could go no further. It seemed . . ." Here he lowered to a confessional whisper. "It seemed as I read that God was dead to me, Quentin. Yes, it's that other world that I worry about for you— that world of books and bookmen who invade the minds that read them. That imaginary world. No, *this* is where you belong. These are your class, serious and sober people. Your society. Your father said that the idler and the melancholy man shall ever wander together in a moral desert."

"I know what my father would say!" I protested. "He was *my* father, Peter! Do you not think I keep a memory of him as strong as yours?"

Peter glanced away. He seemed embarrassed by the question, as though I was challenging his very existence, though in fact I sincerely wished to know his answer. "You have been like a brother to me," he said. "I mean only to see you contented."

A gentleman obliviously interrupted us, ending our discussion. I refused his offer of tobacco, but I did take a glass of warm apple-toddy. Peter was right. Unspeakably right.

My parents had given me a post in society, but it was now my place to earn its luxuries and fine associations. What dangerous restlessness had I been dandling! It was to be able to enjoy the comforts and delights of good circles that I labored at our law practice. To enjoy the company of a lady like Hattie, who never failed as a friend and a steady influence. I closed my eyes and listened to the sounds— friendly sounds of contentment, which cordially surrounded me from every side and drowned out my riotous thoughts. In here people knew themselves, and never doubted for a moment that they understood the others around them and that they themselves were perfectly understood in return.

When Hattie returned to the room, I signaled her to come to me. To her surprise, right away I took her by the hand and kissed it, then kissed her cheek in front of everyone. The guests one by one fell silent.

"*You* know me," I whispered to her.

"Quentin! Are you unwell? Your hands feel warm."

"Hattie, you've known my feelings for you, whatever those who babble about me say, haven't you? Haven't you always known me, though they gape and simper? You know I am honorable, that I love you, that I loved equally yesterday and today."

She took my hand in hers and a thrill ran through me to see her so happy merely by a few honest words from me. "You've loved me yesterday and today. Tomorrow, Quentin?"

At eleven o'clock on this night, her twenty-third birthday, Hattie accepted my marriage proposal with a simple nod. The match was declared suitable by all present. Peter's smile was as wide as anyone's; he forgot entirely about his rough words to me, and more than once he took credit for the arrangement.

By the end of the evening, I had hardly even seen Hattie again, we were so bombarded on every side. My head was clouded by drink and exhaustion together with a feeling of satisfaction that I had done what was perfectly right. Peter had to gingerly put me in a carriage and direct the driver to Glen Eliza. Even in my stupor, though, I took the slender Negro driver aside before he left me at my house.

"Can you return first thing in the morning, sir?" I asked.

I laid down an extra silver eagle to ensure our rendezvous.

The next day, the driver was there at my pathway. I almost sent him away. I was a different man than the morning before. The night had impressed me with what was real in this life. I would be a husband. It seemed, in this light, that I had obviously already gone far beyond any acceptable interest in the final hours of a man whose own cousin did not care a pin. And what of that Phantom, you ask?— why, it seemed obvious now that Peter was completely right about him. The man had been some uneasy lunatic who happened to have heard my name before in a courtroom or some public square, and merely was babbling to me. Nothing to do with Poe! With my private reading! Why had I let it (and Poe) drive away my peace to such a degree? Why had I felt so grand when thinking I could find an answer? I could hardly think about it at all now. I decided to send the carriage away. I think if the honest driver had not looked so anxious to please me, I would have done so; I would not have gone. I wonder sometimes what would now be different.

But I did go. I directed him to the address of Dr. Brooks. Here would be my last errand in that "other world." And as we drove, I thought about Poe's tales, how the hero chose, when there were no longer any good choices, to find a certain impossible boundary— as did the fisherman traveler lost in "A Descent into the Maelström," plummeting down into the whirlpool of eternity— which most would not dare cross. It is not the simplicity of a tale like Robinson Crusoe's, who chiefly must survive, which is what we would all try accomplishing; living, surviving, is only a beginning for a mind like Poe's. Even my favorite character, the great analyst Dupin, voluntarily and cavalierly seeks entrance uninvited into a realm that brings unrest. What is miraculous is not only the display of his reasoning, his ratiocination, but that he is there at all. Poe once wrote in a tale about the conflict between the substance and the shadow inside of us. The substance, what we know we should do, and the shadow, the dangerous and giggling Imp of the Perverse, the dark knowledge of what we must or will do or secretly want. The shadow always prevails.

As we passed through shady avenues among some of the most elegant estates, heading to Dr. Brooks's house, I was suddenly jostled forward out of my seat.

"Why have we stopped?" I demanded.

"Here, sir." He came around to open my door.

"Driver, that cannot be."

"Wha'? Sir . . ."

"No. It must be farther, driver!"

"Two-seven-zero Fayette, as you asked. Right here."

He was right. I leaned far out the window, looking upon the scene, and steadied myself.

4

WHAT I HAD imagined: conversation with Brooks, perhaps a dish of tea. He talking of Poe's visit to Baltimore, recounting the poet's purposes and plans. Revealing Poe's interest in finding one Mr. Reynolds for some urgent purpose. Perhaps Poe even having mentioned me, the attorney who had agreed to protect the new magazine. Brooks offering all the particulars of Poe's demise that I had thought Neilson Poe could have provided. I would convey Brooks's story to the newspapers, whose reporters would grudgingly correct the languid reporting made since his death. . . .

That was the encounter for which I had been prepared when I had first heard Brooks's name.

Instead, outside No. 270 Fayette, the only person in sight was a free black, solitary and determined, dismantling a piece of the charred, broken wooden frame of the house. . . .

I stood before the address of Dr. Brooks and wished again that it were the wrong number. I should have brought the city directory itself to be certain I was at the right place— although I had even written the address on two slips of paper now in separate pockets of my vest. I checked one slip—

Dr. Nathan C. Brooks. 270 Fayette st.

then reached into my pocket for the other—

Dr. N. C. Brooks. 270 Fayette.

This *had* been the house. Of course.

The lingering stench of burnt, damp wood threw me into a fit of coughing. Broken china and charred scraps of ruined tapestries seemed to compose the floor inside. It was as though a chasm had opened up beneath and pulled out all the life that had been there.

"What happened here?" I asked when I had regained my breath.

"Pray God," the joiner, a type of carpenter skilled in woodwork, repeated to himself under his breath. Thank the Lord, he said, the Liberty engine company had prevented more destruction. "If Dr. Brooks hadn't hired himself an unskilled man first," he told me, "and without the blasted rain, the repairs would long be done, and splendidly." In the meantime, the owner of the house was living with relatives, but the joiner did not know where.

The laborer was able to tell me further that the fire had occurred about two months earlier. I rapidly compared the dates in my mind and realized with numbness what it meant. The fire would have been just around the time . . . the very time Edgar Poe arrived in Baltimore looking for the house of Dr. Brooks.

"What is it you wish to report?"

"I have told you, if you could call for the officer, I shall give all the particulars." I was standing in the Middle District police station house.

After several exchanges similar to this, the police clerk brought out an intelligent-looking officer from the next room. All of my urges to see something done had returned forcefully, but with an entirely different bent. As I stood in front of the police officer and narrated the events of the last weeks, I felt a wave of relief. After what I'd seen at the Brooks house, after having breathed the last traces of destruction and looked upon the sleepy, now-vacant windows and the scarred tree trunks, I knew that this had surpassed me.

The officer examined the newspaper cuttings I handed to him as I explained the questions the press had neglected or misunderstood.

"Mr. Clark, I know not what can be done. If there were reason to believe there had been some wrongful act associated with this . . ."

I grasped the officer's shoulder as though I had found a lost friend. "You believe so?"

He looked back faintly.

"Whether there was a wrongful act," I repeated his words. "It is precisely the sort of question for which you must find an answer, my good officer. Just that! Hear me. He was found wearing clothes that did not fit him. He was shouting out for a 'Reynolds.' I know not who that could be. The house he went to upon his arrival burnt down, perhaps near the very same hour he arrived at it. And I believe a man, one I had never seen before, tried to frighten me from inquiring into these matters. Officer, this mystery must not remain untreated a moment longer!"

"This article," he said, returning to the newspaper cutting, "says Poe was a writer."

Progress! "My favorite author. In fact, if you are a magazine reader, I would wager you have come upon his literary work." I listed some of Poe's best-known magazine contributions: "The Murders in the Rue Morgue," "The Mystery of Marie Rogêt," "The Purloined Letter," " 'Thou Art the Man,' " "The Gold-Bug" . . . I thought the subject matter of these tales of mystery, dealing in crime and murder, might hold special interest to a police officer.

"That was his name?" The clerk who had greeted me upon my entrance interrupted as I recited my list. "Poe?"

"Poe." I agreed, probably too sharply. The phenomenon had always vexed me. Many of Poe's stories and poems achieved great fame, yet managed to deprive the writer of personal celebrity by overshadowing him. How many people had I encountered who could proudly recite all of "The Raven" *and* several of the popular verses parodying it ("The Turkey," for instance) but could not name the author? Poe attracted readers who enjoyed but refused to admire; it was as though his works had swallowed him up whole.

The clerk repeated the word "Poe," laughing as though the name itself contained great, illicit wit. "You've read some of that, Officer White. That story"— he turned chummily to his superior— "where the bodies are found bloody and mangled in a locked room, the Paris police can't turn anything up, and don't you know, it ends up all of it was done by a sailor's damned runaway ape! Imagine that!" As though part of the story itself, the clerk now slouched over like a simian.

Officer White frowned.

"There is the funny French fellow," the clerk continued, "that looks at things with all his fancy logicizing, who knows the truth at once about everything."

"Yes, that is Monsieur Dupin!" I added.

"I do remember the story now," said White. "I shall say this, Mr. Clark. You couldn't use that higgledy-piggledy talk from those stories to catch the most ordinary Baltimore thief." Officer White topped this comment with a coarse laugh. The clerk, at a loss at first, then imitated his example in a higher pitch, so that there were two men laughing while there I stood, somber as the undertaker in war.

I had little doubt that there were an infinite number of talents these police officers could have learned, or tried to learn, from Poe's tales—

indeed, the prefect of police whom Dupin embarrassed in the stories had more aptitude than my present companions for understanding that which is classed as mysterious, inexplicable, unavoidable.

"Have the newspapers agreed with you that there is more to find?"

"Not yet. I have pressed the editors, and will continue to use my influence to do so," I promised.

Officer White's eyes wandered skeptically as I gave him further details. But he ruminated on our talk and, to my surprise, agreed it was a matter for the police to examine. He advised in the meantime that I dismiss it from my mind and not speak of it to anyone else.

Nothing particular occurred for several days after that. Peter and I prospered with some important clients who had recently retained our services. I'd see Hattie at a dinner or on Baltimore Street as she strolled on her aunt's arm, and we would exchange tidings. I would be blissfully lost in her restful voice. Then one day I received a message from Officer White to call on him. I rushed over to the station house.

Officer White greeted me at once. From the twitch of his grin he seemed eager to tell me something. I inquired if he had made progress.

"Oh, there has been much of it. Yes, I should say 'progress'!" He searched a drawer and then handed me the newspaper clippings I had left in his possession.

"Officer, but you may wish to refer to these further in your examination."

"There will be no examination, Mr. Clark," he said conclusively as he settled back into his chair. Only then did I notice another man gathering his hat and walking stick from a table. He had his back to me, but then turned around.

"Mr. Clark." Neilson Poe greeted me quietly, after a slow blink as though making an effort to remember my name.

"I called on Mr. Neilson Poe," Officer White said, gesturing with satisfaction at this guest. "He is known to us from the police courts as one of our most highly esteemed citizens and was a cousin to the deceased. You gentlemen are acquainted? Mr. Poe was kind enough to discuss your concerns with me, Mr. Clark," Officer White continued. I already knew what would come next. "Mr. Poe believes there is no need for any examination. He stands quite content with what is known about his cousin's premature death."

"But, Mr. Poe," I argued, "you yourself said you were not able to learn what had happened in Edgar Poe's final days! You see there is some great mystery!"

Neilson Poe was busy covering himself in his cloak. As I looked upon him, I thought of his demeanor during our meeting and his manner toward his cousin. "I'm afraid there's nothing more I can tell you about the end," he had said to me in his office chambers. But, I now considered, did he mean he *knew* nothing else or he *would tell me nothing else*?

I leaned in close to where Officer White sat, trying to confide in him. "Officer, you cannot— Neilson believes Edgar Poe is better dead than alive!" But Officer White cut me short.

"And Mr. Herring here agrees with Mr. Poe," he went on. "Perhaps you know him— the lumber merchant? He is another one of Mr. Poe's relations, and he was the first relative to be present at the Fourth Ward polls, which were at Ryan's hotel, the day Mr. Poe was found delirious there."

Henry Herring stood at the door of the station house, waiting for Neilson Poe. At the mention of his early presence upon Edgar Poe's discovery, Herring dropped his head. He was of a stouter build and shorter stature than Neilson, and wore a dour expression. He took my hand stiffly and without the least interest. I knew him immediately as another one of these four negligent mourners at Poe's lonely burial.

"Let the dead rest," Neilson Poe said to me. "Your interest strikes me as morbid. Perhaps you are like my cousin more than in handwriting alone." Neilson Poe bid us all a quiet good afternoon and walked briskly out the door.

"Peace be to his ashes," said Henry Herring in solemn tones, and then joined Neilson in front of the building.

"We have enough problems to concern ourselves with in all events, Mr. Clark," Officer White began once we were left without Poe's relatives. "There are the vagabonds, the night-strollers, the foreigners, harassing, corrupting, robbing our stores, demoralizing the good children more every day. No time for *small issues*."

The officer's speech went on and, as he spoke, I cast a glance out the window. My eyes followed Neilson Poe and Henry Herring to a carriage. I saw a petite woman waiting inside as the door was opened. Neilson Poe climbed in next to her. It took me a moment to realize how eerily familiar she looked. In another moment, I remembered with a chill through my bones where I had seen her or, rather, a woman just like her. That death portrait in Neilson Poe's office that had so disturbed him. This woman was almost a double, a twin, for Edgar Poe's deceased young love, Virginia. She was Virginia— Poe's darling Sissy!— as far I was concerned.

Remembering the countenance of Sissy Poe, captured only hours after her death, some lines of Edgar Poe's inserted themselves in my mind.

> For her, the fair and debonair, that now so lowly lies,
> The life upon her yellow hair but not within her eyes—
> The life still there, upon her hair— the death upon her eyes.

But stay! I could not believe it. Poe's description of the beautiful girl Lenore at her death— "that now so lowly lies"— were the same two words at the end of the Phantom's warning. *It is unwise to meddle with your lowly lies.* The warning *had* been about Poe after all, just as I had thought! Lowly lies!

I leaned out the window and watched the carriage disappear safely.

Officer White sighed. "Realize it, Mr. Clark," he said. "There is nothing more here, sir. I beg you to give these concerns to the wind! It seems you have an inclination to think of affairs as extraordinary that are quite ordinary. Do you have a wife, Mr. Clark?"

My attention was pulled back to him by the question. I hesitated. "I will soon."

He laughed knowingly. "Good. You should have much to occupy yourself without needing to think of *this* unhappy affair, then. Or your sweetheart might give you the mitten."

Faithful use of the blank page before me would describe the ensuing despondency as I sat at my misted window overlooking the exodus of people from the offices surrounding ours. I stayed until even Peter had gone. I should have felt at ease. I had done all I could. Even speaking with the police. There was nothing remaining for me to attempt to do. A pall of routine seemed to stretch out before me.

Days passed like this. I entered into an advanced state of *ennui* that no comforts of society could diminish. It was then I received a knock at the door, and a letter. It was a messenger sent from the athenaeum; the reading room clerk, not having seen me for some time, had decided to send me some newspaper cuttings he had come upon. Newspaper cuttings

from several years before; noticing some that had occasion to allude to
Edgar Poe, and no doubt remembering my inquiries, he had thought to
enclose them in a letter to me.

One seized me entirely.

Think of it.

He had been out there all along.

September 16, 1844

☞ Our newspaper has been informed by a "Lady Friend" of the brilliant and erratic writer Edgar A. Poe, Esq., that Mr. Poe's ingenious hero, C. Auguste Dupin, is closely modeled from an individual in actual life, similar in name and exploit, known for his great analytical powers. This respected gentleman is recognized widely in the regions of Paris, where that city's police frequently request his involvement in cases even more baffling than those Mr. Poe has chronicled in his truly strange accounts of Mr. Dupin, of which "The Purloined Letter" marks the third installment (though the editors hope more will be produced). We wonder how many thousands of burning questions occurring these last years in our own country, and how many yet to come, this real genius of Paris could have effortlessly unriddled.

I HELD THE newspaper clipping in my hands. I felt an unnameable difference in myself and in my surroundings as I read it. I felt transported.

A few minutes after the messenger from the athenaeum had exited my chambers, Peter burst in with an armful of documents.

"What are you looking at with such intolerable excitement, Quentin?" he asked. I think it was only a rhetorical question. But I was so enthused that I answered him.

"Peter, see for yourself! It was sent over with some other articles by the clerk at the athenaeum."

I do not know why I did not restrain myself. Perhaps consequences no longer mattered to me.

Peter read the newspaper clipping slowly, his face dropping. "What is this?" he asked with clenched teeth. I cannot pretend not to understand his ensuing reaction. After all, we had an appointment at court the next morning. Peter had been running about the office, frantically preparing, until he'd come in just now. Imagine how he found his partner. Studying documents for our client's hearing? Checking them one last time for errors? No.

"There is a real Dupin in Paris— I mean Poe's character of a genius investigator," I explained. " 'Recognized widely in the regions of Paris.' You see? It is a miracle."

He slapped the extract onto my desk. "Poe? Is this what you have been doing here all day?"

"Peter, I must find out who this person spoken of in the article is and bring him here. You were right that I could not do this myself. *He* can do this."

There was an edition of Poe's *Tales* I kept on my shelf. Peter grabbed the book and waved it in front of my face. "I thought you were finished with this Poe madness, Quentin!"

"Peter, if this man exists, if a man with a mind so extraordinary as C. Auguste Dupin's is really out there, then I can complete my promise to Poe. Poe has been telling me all along how to do it, through the pages of his own tales! Poe's name can be restored. Snatched away from an eternity of injustice."

Peter reached for the newspaper extract again, but I grabbed it out of his hand and folded it into my pocket.

He seemed angered by this. Peter's massive hand now shot forward, clutching, as though needing to choke something, even the air. With his other hand, he flung the book of Poe tales straight into our hearth, the flames of which had been stoked up into a cheerful fire by one of the clerks just a half hour before.

"There!" he said.

The hearth fizzled with its sacrifice. I think Peter was instantly sorry for his action, since the fierceness in his face transformed into sourness as soon as the flames reached for the pages of the book. Understand, this was not one of the volumes I prized for its binding or from any particular sentimental attachment. It was not the copy I had found myself reading in the quiet days after receiving the telegram of my parents' deaths.

And yet, unthinkingly, with the swiftest motion I had ever shown, I reached in and pulled out the book. I stood there in the middle of my chambers, the book ablaze in my hand. My sleeve became a burning ring at the cuff. But I stood resolutely in place as Peter blinked, his helpless eyes large and glinting red with the fire as he took in this sight: the sight of his partner gripping a flaming book while the sizzling fire was beginning to engulf his arm. Strangely, the more delirious his expression became, the more tranquil I felt myself become. I could not remember ever having felt so strong, so decided in my purpose as in this single moment. I knew what was necessary for me now.

Hattie had come into the room looking for me. She stared at me, stared at the burning object I held in front of me, not shocked, exactly, but with a rare flash of anger.

She threw a rug from the hall over my arm and patted the flames until the fire was out. Peter recovered himself enough to gasp at the incident and then check the rug's damage before conferring with Hattie. The two clerks hurried over to me to stare, as if at a wild beast.

"Get out! Out of these offices now, Quentin!" Peter shouted, pointing with a trembling hand.

"Peter, no, please!" Hattie cried.

"Very well," I said.

I stepped out of my chamber door. Hattie was calling for me to return. But I did not turn back. I could see only faraway things in my mind as though they were stretched out before me in the wings of these halls: the long promenades, the din of the busy cafés, the unabashed, dreamy musical chords of dancing and fêtes, the redemption waiting to be uncovered in a distant metropolis.

—BOOK II—

PARIS

7

I ARRIVED AT my first appointment in Paris by way of kidnapping.

In our American cities the stranger is left modestly to himself, with great cruelty and politeness; but in Paris a stranger has a constant sense of being shoved and directed by the citizens and officials; if you are lost, the Frenchman will run half a mile at great speed to point at your destination, and will accept no thanks. Perhaps kidnapping is the inevitable culmination of their aggressive kindness.

I made my voyage to Paris approximately a year and a half after I pulled that book out of the fire. My first shock upon arrival came at the railroad terminus, where screams of *commissionnaires* lure visitors to one or another hotel. I tried to avoid their outstretched hands.

I stopped where I met a man barking for the Hôtel Corneille, named after the great French playwright. I had read of the hotel in a novel of Balzac's (for I had brought some books of his and the novelist George Sand's for entertainment and study on my voyage) and it was reputed to be an establishment welcoming to those who indulge in the various branches of the humanities. I considered my own purposes as having a degree of literary character.

"You are for the Corneille, monsieur?"

At my assent he released a hoarse sigh, as if to thank heaven he could rest from shouting. "This way, if you please!" He brought me to his carriage, where he labored to secure my bags above, occasionally pausing to examine me with an air of exuberant happiness at having a New World visitor as a passenger.

"You have come on business, monsieur?"

I contemplated an answer. "I suppose not exactly. I am a lawyer back home, monsieur. But I have left my situation as of late. I am attending to a rather different type of affair— to say sooth, as I feel already I can hold your confidence, I am here to procure the help of someone who will attend to it."

"Ah!" he replied, not listening to a word. "You are friendly with Cooper, then?"

"What?"

"Cooper!"

After we repeated the exchange, it became clear he meant the author James Fenimore Cooper. I'd discover that the French thought America quite too intimate for any two people of the country not to know each other, even were one a backwoodsman and the other a Wall Street speculator. The adventure novels of Cooper were inexplicably popular in even the finest circles of Paris (bring an American copy and you shall be deemed a regular hero!), and we were all presumed to live among those stories' wild and noble Indians. I said I had not met Cooper.

"Well, the Corneille will fulfill every one of your needs, upon my honor! There are no wigwams there! Watch the step up, monsieur, and I'll retrieve the rest of your bags from the porter."

I had not misjudged my first choice of transportation in this city. The carriage was wider than the American kind and the interior fittings indeed very comfortable. It was the most enjoyable luxury I could imagine at that moment, to sink against the cushions of a carriage as we neared a well-appointed private chamber of my own. This ride, remember, had followed two weeks at sea, starting from the Baltimore harbor, stopping in Dover for a night before sailing again, and finally arriving in France, where I then began six hours on the train into Paris. Just the idea of sleeping in a *bed* enthralled me! I could not know I was about to be removed from my newfound comfort, and at the threat of a sword.

My tranquillity was jolted when the coach abruptly tilted at a sharp angle before coming to a jagged and rough stop. The *commissionnaire* cursed and stepped down from his box.

"Just a ditch!" he called to me with relief. "I thought a wheel had come loose! Then we'd be— "

From my window I could see the features of his face suddenly flatten as he fell into an overrespectful silence. This expression mingled with one of fear before he skulked away.

"Now see here, driver!" I shouted. "Monsieur, where are you going?" Leaning out the window, I observed a squat man, buttoned to the collar in a flowing great-coat of bright blue. He had a large mustache and an exquisitely sharpened beard. I thought to step down and ask the stranger if he had seen the path taken by the runaway *commissionnaire*. Instead, this man opened my door and climbed in with great suavity.

He was saying something in French, but I was too flustered to employ my improving knowledge of the language. My first thought was to slide myself out the other side; I shifted my position only to find, upon opening that door, the way blocked by another man in the same kind of single-breasted coat. He was pulling his coat back to reveal a saber falling perpendicularly from his shiny black belt. I felt mesmerized by the sight of the weapon glinting with sunlight. His hand casually found its hilt and tapped at it as he nodded to me. *"Allons donc!"*

"Police!" I exclaimed, feeling half relieved and half frightened. "You men are from the police, monsieur?"

"Yes," the one inside said, his hand reaching out. "Your passport now, if you please, monsieur?"

I complied and waited in confusion as he read it. "But who are you looking for, Officer?"

A brief smile. "You, monsieur."

It was explained to me at a later time that the watchful eye of the Parisian police fell on any American entering their city alone who was a young man— and especially an unmarried young man— as potential "radicals" who had arrived with intent to overthrow the government. Considering that the government had been overthrown quite recently, when King Louis-Philippe was replaced three years earlier by a popular republican government, this imminent fear of radicalism seemed mysterious to one not well versed in the politics of France. Did they worry that the mobs, having gotten their legislature and duly elected president, and now bored of republicanism, would be instigated to riot to have their kings back again?

The police officers who had intercepted my coach merely explained that the prefect of the police proposed for me to call on him before beginning my stay in the city. Mesmerized and strangely captivated by the sabers and elegant uniforms, I followed willingly. A different carriage, with a faster span of horses, brought us directly to the Rue de Jerusalem, where the prefecture was located.

The prefect, a jovial and distracted man named Delacourt, sat beside me in his chamber as had his functionary in the carriage and performed the same ritual of reading my passport. It had been properly made up by the

French emissary in Washington City, Monsieur Montor, who had also provided a letter attesting to my respectable character. But the prefect seemed
to have little interest in any written proof of my harmless intentions.

Was I here on "business," "touring," or "educational"? I responded in
the negative on all counts.

"If not these, then how have you come to be in Paris this summer?"

"You see, Monsieur Prefect, I am to meet a citizen of your city regarding an important affair back in the United States."

"And," he replied, hiding his interest with a casual smile, "who is that?"

When I told him, he became quite still, then exchanged a glance with
the officer sitting across the prefect's chambers. "*Who?*" the prefect then
said, as though entirely moonstruck, after some moments had passed.

"Auguste Duponte," I repeated. "You do know him then, Monsieur
Prefect? I have communicated with him by mail over the last months—
"

"Duponte? Duponte has written *you?*" the other police officer, a small
and fat old man, interrupted gruffly.

"No, of course not, Officer Gunner," said the prefect.

"No," I agreed, though irritated by the queer presumption of the prefect.
"I have written Duponte, but he has not written in return. That is why I have
come. I am here to explain myself in his private ear before it is too late."

"You shall have a hard time of *that*," mumbled Gunner.

"He is not . . . he is alive?" I inquired.

I think the prefect replied, "Almost," but he swallowed his word up
whole and returned abruptly to his more jovial and freewheeling personality. (I had not noticed the reduction in his joviality, you see, until it was
just then restored.) "Never mind this," he said of my passport, handing it
to his colleague to be stamped with an apparently meaningful series of
hieroglyphics. "A tool of the next Inquisition, no?"

He abruptly dropped the subject of Duponte, welcomed me to Paris,
and assured me that I could call upon him if I should ever need assistance during my stay. On my way out, several *sergents de ville* regarded
me with hard glares of suspicion or dislike, which provoked my great
sense of relief upon reaching the anonymity of the busy street.

That same afternoon, I paid Madame Fouché, proprietress of the Hôtel
Corneille, for a full week's stay, though in fact I anticipated a quicker end
to my business.

I suppose there were signs, though, that I should have noted. For instance, the attitude of the concierge at the grand Paris mansion where I had addressed my letters to Duponte. This was my first stop the morning after arriving. When I inquired at the door, the concierge narrowed his eyes at me, shook his head, and spoke: "Duponte? Why would you want to see him?"

It did not seem inconceivable to me that the concierge for a person of this stature would dissuade casual callers. "I require his skills in a matter of moment," I replied, at which a strange hissing sound emanated from the man and revealed itself as laughter as he informed me that Duponte no longer lived here, had left no further information, and that Columbus probably couldn't find him now.

As I took my leave, I thought about the "Dupin" I had known well. I mean from Poe's tales— that liaison who had opened the portal into Poe by convincing me the inexplicable must yet be understood. "My French hero" was Poe's reference to the character in one of the letters he wrote to me. If only I had happened to inquire to Poe about the identity of the real Dupin; if only I had exhibited more curiosity— it would have saved me the last year and more that had been required to trace this singular man to Paris!

In his tales, Poe never physically described the character of Dupin. I realized this only after freshly reviewing this trio of particular tales of detection with that question in mind. Previously, if asked of this, I might have answered, as if talking to a perfect ass, "Of course Poe describes one of his most important characters, the character that *embodies* perfectly his writing, and in great detail, too!" But on the contrary, Dupin's form, you see, is strikingly imparted— but only to the careful and estimable reader who enters the tale with his full heart.

I mention here as illustration a rather frothy short tale by Poe called "The Man That Was Used Up." It features a celebrated army general whose sturdy physical appearance is widely admired. But the general has an unfortunate secret: each night he falls apart physically from his old war wounds and must have his body parts stitched back together by his Negro manservant before breakfast. I believe this was Poe's shove at those lesser writers, mere blots in the deep shadows of his genius, who thought physical description of features the key to enlivening their characters. Likewise, it was from the untellable soul of C. Auguste Dupin's character, not his choice of waistcoat, that he had long ago stepped into my consciousness.

When I had first received the newspaper cutting mentioning the real Dupin from the athenaeum clerk in Baltimore, I'd found fruitless all my attempts to secure the investigator's name from the New York newspaper where the column had appeared. However, a mere few weeks of research into French periodicals and directories produced a fairly impressive list of possible models for Poe's character.

All of their personal histories matched in some manner the two sources: the cutting's description as well as the traits of Poe's character. One possibility I turned up was a Parisian mathematical celebrity who wrote textbooks used to solve various scientific problems; and there was the lawyer, called sometimes the Baron, who acquitted persons accused of the most scandalous crimes, who had since gone to London; another, a former thief who acted as a secret agent of the Parisian police before operating a paper factory in Brussels. Each one of these and other possibilities were considered dispassionately and objectively and with the expectation that one would rise above the others as the clear source for Dupin.

And yet, another year and a half passed from the start of that research. Correspondence across the Atlantic proved slow and inconclusive. Promising candidates accumulated quickly before each one gradually dropped into a well of doubt after further inquires and exchanges.

Until one clear day in the spring of 1851. That's when I discovered in the French journal *L*— — — the name Auguste Duponte. The name naturally caught my attention, but it was not the sound of the name only that struck a distinct harmony with Poe's C. Auguste Dupin. This fellow, Auguste Duponte, had gained prominence in France in the sensational case of Monsieur Lafarge, a gentleman of strong physical constitution and some local importance found mysteriously dead in his home. After some useless maneuvers by the Parisian police, one officer invited in his acquaintance, the young tutor Duponte, to translate the comments of a Spanish visitor who was a witness in the case (though that angle ultimately proved irrelevant).

Within the space of ten or twelve minutes after hearing the facts from the police officer, it was said Duponte conclusively showed the police that the dead man had been poisoned by Madame Lafarge at the end of a meal. Madame L. was convicted for the murder of her husband. She was later spared from death by sympathetic officials.

(Asked by the French newspaper *La Presse* what he thought about the murderess's sentence having been commuted, Duponte reportedly said, "Nothing at all. Punishment has little relation to the fact of a crime, and the least to do with the analysis of the crime.")

The news of Auguste Duponte's feat spread widely through France. The government officials, police, and citizens in Paris sought his analysis of other incidents. This swift introduction to the public eye— I discovered with immense satisfaction— occurred a few years *before* the appearance in an 1841 issue of an American journal of "The Murders in the Rue Morgue." Poe's description of Dupin's rise to fame in the second of the tales could be used with equal effect to describe the real history of Auguste Duponte: *It thus happened that he found himself the cynosure of the policial eyes; and the cases were not few in which attempt was made to engage his services at the Prefecture.*

My confidence that I had identified the right man was bolstered further when I happened to meet a knowledgeable Frenchman who had been living in America for the last few years, since the overthrow of King Louis-Philippe, as part of a diplomatic corps for the new French republic. This was Henri Montor. I was in Washington City researching Auguste Duponte in its libraries when he noticed with interest that I was struggling through some French newspapers. I explained my purpose and asked if he had known Duponte.

"Whenever there was a crime of great impact," Monsieur Montor said animatedly, "the people of Paris had always called for Duponte— and the criminal on the street would curse the year Duponte was born. A treasure of Paris is Duponte, Monsieur Clark."

During my subsequent visits, Henri Montor tutored me in French over supper and engaged me in long hours of conversation, comparing the French and American governments and people. He found Washington City rather desolate compared to Paris, the climate positively stifling and injurious to one's health.

By this time, when I met Monsieur Montor, I had already written to Duponte himself. I had outlined the events of Poe's death and described the urgent need to resolve the matter before Poe's sickly reputation worsened. After another week had passed, I had written Duponte two more letters, both marked "Immediate," with addendums and more details of the unwritten history of Poe.

Though our acquaintance was short, Montor invited me to join him at a dress ball that hosted several hundred guests at a lofty mansion near Washington City where I could meet numerous French ladies and gentlemen. Most had one title or another, and some, to my delight, humored my unpolished French, which I sought to perfect as much as possible. Jérôme Bonaparte was there— he was the nephew of Napoleon Bonaparte, born to an American woman whom Napoleon's younger brother Jérôme the senior met nearly fifty years before while on excursion in the United States. This regal offspring was now standing before me dressed in a garish Turkish costume, with two curved swords hanging from his belt. After we had been introduced, I complimented his costume.

"No need for 'monsieurs,' anyway, Mr. Clark; we are in America," Jérôme Bonaparte said, his dark eyes lit with good humor. Henri Montor fidgeted at this a bit. "As for this monstrosity," Bonaparte continued with a sigh, "it was my wife's pretty idea. She is in the next room somewhere."

"Oh, I believe she and I met. She is dressed as an ostrich?"

Bonaparte laughed. "There are feathers on her. Your guess of what animal is as good as mine!"

"Our American friend," Montor said, putting his arm through mine, "is trying to practice our native language for his private researches. Have you been back to Paris recently, my dear Bonaparte?"

"Father used to try to sway me to live there, you know. I cannot think for a moment of settling myself out of America, though, Montor, for I am too much attached and accustomed to it to find pleasure in Europe." He tapped an intricately detailed gold snuffbox and offered some to us.

A woman paraded toward us from where the host played his violin accompanied by an orchestra. She was calling out to Bonaparte by a nickname, and for a moment I thought it was his ostrich-feathered wife, until I saw that she wore the flowing robes and jewels of a queen. Montor whispered to me: "That is Elizabeth Patterson, Jérôme's mother." His whisper was so discreet it was clear I should pay attention.

"Dear Mother," said Jérôme formally, "this is Quentin Clark, a Baltimorean of some wit."

"How whimsical!" replied this costume-queen who, though not at all tall, seemed to tower over all of us.

"Mrs. Patterson." I bowed.

"Madame Bonaparte," she corrected me on both points and offered her hand. There was an irreducible beauty about her face and her pristine eyes that was almost tragic. One could not help but be in love with her, it seemed to me. She looked at me with sharp disapproval. "You are uncostumed, young man."

Montor, who was dressed fabulously as a Neapolitan fisherman, explained my lack of disguise by way of his last-minute invitation to me. "He is studying French customs, you see."

Madame Bonaparte's eyes flared at me. "Study hard."

I would realize once I arrived in Paris that this dress-ball queen was right about my grasp of French customs. Moreover, as I looked around at the extraordinary room of masked and obstructed faces, I understood that this was what both Peter and Auntie Blum wanted, in some way. There was something here, something beyond the liveried servants and banks of flowers glowing with lamps inside them, something powerful that had very little to do with money and that Baltimore desired to add to its commercial triumphs.

By that point in time after the occasion of the burning book, I had returned to our law office to complete certain unfinished work. Peter hardly acknowledged my presence. He would whistle whole staves of music up and down our stairs in frustrated displeasure. Sometimes I wished he would simply yell at me again; then in reply I could at least detail the progress I had made.

Hattie seemed to follow the example set by Peter, seeking me out less and less, but she did take much trouble to convince her aunt and family to be patient regarding our engagement and to give me time. I tried my best to reassure Hattie. But I had begun to feel wary at saying too much— begun to see even Hattie's pure devotion as part of their arsenal, another instrument to stifle the aims that commanded me. Even her face began to look to my eyes more like her busybody aunt's. She was part of a Baltimore that had failed to even notice that the truth behind a great man's death mattered. Hattie, why didn't I trust that you could see me, as usual, more clearly than a looking-glass could!

Weeks after the dress ball, there were still no letters from Duponte in reply to mine. I could not abide the slow exchange of mailable communications. Mail could be stolen, or destroyed by accident or mischief.

Here I had found the identity of the Dupin of real life, the one person probably in all the known world able to decipher the blank spot of Poe's last days! I was still only serving Poe as I had promised him. I had reached this far, and should not cede my position through lack of action. I would not wait for *this* to be lost. In June 1851, I made my plans and set off for Paris.

Here I was in a different world. Even the houses seemed to be built from entirely different materials and colors, and to position themselves differently on the wide streets. There was a feeling of secretiveness to Paris, yet everything was open, and existence in Paris was entirely out of doors.

The latest city directories I found upon arriving had no listings for Duponte, and I realized that those I'd consulted in Washington City were a few years out of date. Nor did recent newspaper columns that had previously spoken breathlessly about him have a word to say.

In Paris, the post office delivered the mail directly to the houses of residents— a practice newly begun in some American cities by private arrangement; though in Paris, it was said, its convenience for citizens was less important than the surveillance it provided to the government. It was my hope that the postal officers would not have continued to carry Duponte's mail to an incorrect address. In another peculiarity of the Parisian rules, I was refused (rigidly and politely, as with everything French) any admittance to the administrators of the post office, where I wanted to ask about Duponte's present address. I would need to write for permission to the appropriate ministry. Guided in composing this letter by Madame Fouché, my hotel's proprietress, I sent it by post. (This was another rule, even though the ministry was hardly three streets away!) "You will *certainly* receive a letter of permission within a day or two. It could be quite longer, though," she added thoughtfully, "if there is an error by some functionary, which is *awfully* common."

As I waited for any sign of progress in my search for Duponte's address, I wrote to Hattie. Remembering the pain it had caused me whenever I'd seen her sad, I had been experiencing deep regret that the timing of this endeavor had caused her even the slightest grief. In my letters to Baltimore I promised her as little a delay as possible to our plans and entreated her in the meantime to come to Paris, however short a stay and dull a program my present venture might require. Hattie wrote that nothing would please her more than such a voyage, but she was needed to help care for the two new children recently added to her sisters' households.

Peter, for his part, wrote a farewell letter explaining that I had ruined my life, and nearly ruined his, by yielding to the decadence and indecency of Europe.

What he must have been imagining! If only he could see how different the reality here in my chambers!

The nightly gaieties of the Parisian summer drifted recklessly through my window, the open-air orchestras and gala dances, the theaters that seated happy audiences by the hundreds. I, by contrast, opened and closed my two chests of drawers and stared at the clock on my room's mantelpiece— waiting.

One day Madame Fouché came into my room and offered to tie a strip of black crêpe around my arm. Bothered by the interruption to my indolence, I assented.

"My deep condolences," she said.

"Appreciated. How so?" I asked, suddenly alarmed.

"Hasn't someone died?" she gasped importantly, as though her pity was in short supply and I had wasted it. "Why have you entered such a melancholy state, if not?"

I hesitated, frowning at the black cloth now wrapped on my coat.

"Yes, madame, some have died. But that is not the nearest cause of my agitation. It is the address, this blasted address! Pardon my language, Madame Fouché. I must find Monsieur Auguste Duponte's residence soon, or leave Paris empty-handed and my actions shall be declared even more fantastic by my friends. That is why I wish to visit the postal office."

The next day, Madame Fouché brought me breakfast herself in lieu of the regular waiter. She badly hid a smile and handed me a piece of paper with some writing on it.

"What is this, madame?"

"Why, it is the address of Auguste Duponte, of course."

"I thank you infinitely, madame! How marvelous!" I was at once up and out the door. I was too excited to even pause to satisfy my curiosity as to how she had come upon it.

The place, not fifteen minutes away, was a once-bright yellow structure connected to a scarlet-and-blue house around a courtyard, a good example of the fashion of Paris's gingerbread architecture and colors. The neighborhood was more removed from cafés and shops than the first residence I had visited— a tranquillity conducive to the demands of ratiocination, I supposed. The concierge, a thick man with a hideous double mustache, instructed me to go up to Duponte's rooms. I paused at the bottom of the stairs and then returned to the concierge's room.

"Beg your pardon, monsieur. Would it not be preferable to Monsieur Duponte's tastes if I were announced first?"

The concierge took offense— whether because the suggestion questioned his competence or because the notion of announcing a visitor demeaned his role to that of a house servant, I did not know. The concierge's wife shrugged and said, with a touch of sympathy that she directed with an upturned glance to God, or the floor above, "How many visitors does he have?"

The odd exchange no doubt contributed to my nervous rambling when I first met the man himself in the doorway to his lodging. The employment of his skills was even more exclusive and rare than I had imagined. Parisians, to judge from the comment of the concierge's wife, did not think it worthwhile even to *attempt* to secure his help!

When Duponte opened the door to his chambers, I poured out an introduction. "I wrote you some letters— three— sent from the United States, as well as a telegraph directed to your previous address. The letters spoke of the American writer Edgar A. Poe. It is crucial that the matter of his death is investigated. This is why I have come, monsieur."

"I see," said Duponte, screwing his face into a grimace and pointing behind me, "that this hall lamp is out. It has been replaced many times, yet the flame is out."

"What? The lamp?"

That is how it went with our conversation. Once inside, I repeated the chronicle narrated in my letters, urged that we strike at once, and expressed my hope that he would accompany me back to America at his earliest convenience.

The rooms were very ordinary and oddly devoid of all but a few unimportant books; it felt uncommonly cold in there, even though it was summer. Duponte leaned back in his armchair. Suddenly, as though only now realizing I was addressing him rather than the blank wall behind, he said, "Why have you told this to me, monsieur?"

"Monsieur Duponte," I said, thunderstruck, "you are a celebrated genius of ratiocination. You are the only person known to me, perhaps the only person in the known world, capable of resolving this mystery!"

"You are very far mistaken," he said. "You are mad," he suggested.

"I? You *are* Auguste Duponte?" I responded accusingly.

"You are thinking of many years ago. The police asked me to review their papers from time to time. I'm afraid the journals of Paris were excited with their own notions and, in some cases, assigned me certain attributes to meet the appetites of the public imagination. Such tales were told . . ." (Wasn't there a flicker of something like pride in his eyes when he said this?) Without a blink or a breath, he overthrew the topic altogether. "What you should know, might I say, are the many worthwhile outings in Paris in the summer. You will want to see a concert at the Luxembourg Gardens. I might tell you where to see the finest flowers. And have you been to the palace at Versailles? You will be pleased by it— "

"The palace at Versailles? Versailles, you say? Please, Duponte! This is monstrously important! I am no idle caller. Nearly half the world has passed by my eyes to find you!"

He nodded sympathetically and said, "You certainly should sleep, then."

The next morning I awoke after a deep, uncomfortable July sleep. I had returned to the Corneille the night before in a state of dull shock at my reception by Duponte. But in the morning my disappointment faded, eased by the thought that perhaps it was my own weariness that had clouded my first talk with Duponte. It had been unwise and unseemly to burst in on him like that, tired and anxious, disheveled in my appearance, without even a letter of introduction.

This time I took a leisurely breakfast, which in Paris looks just like dinner minus soup— even beginning with oysters (though Cuvier himself could not put these small, blue, watery objects in any class of true oyster for an appetite born of the Chesapeake Bay). Arriving at Duponte's lodgings, I lingered near the concierge's chambers, and was glad to find that the concierge was out on business. His more talkative wife and a plump daughter sat mending a rug.

The older woman offered me a chair. She blushed easily at my smile, and so I tried to smile liberally in the pauses between my words to induce her cooperation. "Yesterday, madame, you mentioned that Duponte does not receive very many callers. Are there not those who visit him professionally?"

"Not in all the years since he has lived here."

"Had you not heard of Auguste Duponte before?"

"Why certainly!" she answered, as if I had questioned her very sanity. "But I did not think it could have been the same one. They say that man was of importance to the police; our boarder is a harmless fellow, but quite in a stupor much of the time, a *dead-alive* sort of a man. I presumed it was a brother or some distant relation of his family. No, I suppose he hasn't many acquaintances to visit him."

"And no lady-friends," mumbled the bored daughter, and that was all you will hear the girl say for the whole two months in Paris.

"I see," I said, thanking both ladies before climbing to Duponte's door. They both blushed again as I bowed.

I had been thinking earlier that morning of Poe's tales about C. Auguste Dupin. In the first one, Dupin abruptly and unexpectedly announces that he will investigate the horrible murders that occurred in a house on the Rue Morgue. *An inquiry will afford us amusement*, he says to his surprised friend. *Let us enter into some examinations for ourselves.* He searched for amusement. Of all the details I had spilled out in almost a single breath the day before, I had not once presented an enticing reason for Duponte to direct his genius to the case of Poe's death! Perhaps, in the last few years, when Duponte seemed to have become inactive, no affair had come about worthy of his interest, and as a result he had settled into what seemed to most to be an aimless torpor.

Duponte did not turn me away when I knocked at his door. He invited me for a stroll. I walked alongside him through the crowded and warm Latin Quarter. I say "alongside" even though his steps were abnormally deliberate and slow, one foot hardly passing the other in each of his strides; this meant that in trying to remain at the same pace, I sometimes felt like I was dancing a half circle. As with the day before, he spoke of commonplace matters. This time I engaged him in idle topics before making my latest attempt at persuasion.

"Do you not find a desire to be occupied in more challenging dealings, though, Monsieur Duponte? While I have compiled all the particulars of Mr. Poe's death available, others have employed the confused public knowledge to spit upon his grave. I should think an inquiry into a difficult, timely matter such as this *would offer you great amusement . . .*" I repeated this once more, as a heavy truck had rumbled by the first time. In response to this there was not a stir in the man. He clearly did not think himself in need of greater amusements, and I again was obliged to retreat.

On a subsequent visit to Duponte's apartment, I found him smoking a cigar in his bed. It seemed he used his bed for smoking and for writing— he detested writing anything, he said, for with obnoxious consistency it stopped him from thinking. For this visit I had been rereading and reflecting on the "liberal proposition" offered to C. Auguste Dupin by the police in Poe's sequel tale, "The Mystery of Marie Rogêt," to penetrate the case of a young shopgirl found dead in the woods. Though agreeable compensation had certainly been implied in my own letters to Duponte, I now assured him expressly, in homage to Poe's own words from the tale, that I would provide him "a *liberal fee* for your undivided attention to Poe's death, beginning immediately." I removed a check. I suggested an amount of considerable value, and then a few numbers even higher.

With no resulting success. It seemed he was not moved at all by money, despite his less than luxurious circumstances. To this, as to other attempts to direct his attention to my own agenda, he would take my elbow as he pointed out an architectural oddity; or praise the Parisian summers extensively for their loveliness; or remove any need for a reply by letting his eyes linger shut in a ruined blink. Sometimes, Duponte seemed almost an imbecile in his placid stare as we passed shops and the blooming flowers and trees of the garden— "the horse-chestnuts!" he would say suddenly— or maybe it was a stare of sadness.

One evening after leaving another interview with Duponte, I passed a group of police officers sitting at tables outside a crowded café eating ices. They were a formidable blur of single-breasted blue coats, mustaches, and small, pointed beards.

"Monsieur! Monsieur Clark, bonjour!"

It was the squat young policeman who had commandeered my carriage upon my arrival in Paris. I attributed his enthusiasm at seeing me to the congenial spirits of their party.

Each of the officers rose to greet me.

"This is a gentleman and a scholar who has come from America to see Auguste Duponte!" After a moment of interesting silence, the policemen all burst into laughter.

I was confused by this reaction to Duponte's name. I sat down as the first one continued: "There are many stories to hear of Duponte. He was a great genius. Duponte, they say, would know a thief was going to take your jewels before the thief did."

"He *was* a great genius, you say?" I asked.

"Oh, yes. Long ago."

"My father was in the police when the prefects would engage Monsieur Duponte," said another policeman, who displayed a scowl that may have been permanent. "He said Duponte was a clever young man who merely created difficulties so he could *seem* to surmount them."

"In what manner?" I asked with alarm.

He scratched his neck viciously with his overgrown fingernails; the side of his neck looked red and inflamed from this habit. "It is what he heard," the Scratcher muttered.

"It is said that Duponte," continued the more amiable officer, "could judge the morals of all men with precision just by their looks. He once offered to walk through the streets on the day of a public fête and point out to the police all the dangerous people who should be removed from society."

"Did he?" asked another.

"No— the police would have had no business to attend to if he had."

"But what happened to him?" I asked. "What of the investigations he performs today?"

One of the officers who looked thoughtful and quieter than the others spoke up. "They say Monsieur Duponte failed— that the woman he loved was hanged for murder, and his powers of analysis could not rescue her. That he could do no more investigations— "

"Investigations!" balked the Scratcher. "Of course there can be no more. Unless he manages to carry them out as a ghost. He was killed by a prisoner who had vowed that he would avenge himself on Duponte for arresting him."

I opened my mouth to correct him, but thought better of it— there was a deep venom in that man's voice that seemed better not to rouse.

"No, no," one of the others disagreed. "Duponte is not dead. Some say he lives in Vienna now. He grew tired of the ingratitude. What stories I could tell you! There is no living soul like that in Paris in this age, in all events."

"Prefect Delacourt would not hear of it," added the squat officer, and the others cackled raucously.

❋   ❋   ❋

Here was one of the officers' anecdotes.

Years earlier, Duponte one evening had found himself in a *cabinet*, or private chamber, of a tavern in Paris, sitting across from a convict who had only three days earlier sliced the throat of a prison guard from one side to the other. Every agent of the Paris police had been on watch for him since he'd escaped, including several who sat with me at the café. Duponte, employing his varied skills, had deduced where in the city the rogue would most likely think it safest to conceal himself. So there they sat together in the *cabinet*.

"I will be safe from capture from the police," the villain confided. "I can outrun any one of them— and could beat any one of them in a pistol fight if I had to. I'm safe, as long as I do not meet with that wretch Duponte. He is the true criminal of Paris."

"I should think you would know him when you see him," Duponte commented.

The scoundrel laughed at Duponte. "Know him . . . ? God bless!" He now emptied his wine bottle at a breath. "You have never dealt with this knave Duponte, have you? He's not to be seen twice in the same dress. In the morning, he appears to be just another person, like yourself. Then, an hour later, so changed that his own mother would never recognize him and, by evening, no man or demon would ever remember having seen him before! He knows where you are, and can auspicate where you go next!"

When this bad fellow had drunk more than he'd intended, Duponte went downstairs for another bottle of wine and then returned to the *cabinet* with perfect calmness. Duponte reported to the convict that the barmaid had said she'd seen Auguste Duponte there, looking in on the private rooms. The villain was thrown into a wild fury at the news, and Duponte suggested that the fellow hide in the closet so he might come out and kill the investigator when he entered. When the villain stepped into the closet, Duponte locked it and fetched the police.

That had once been Duponte. It was *that Duponte* I had to bring to America. Nor had my limited communion with him proved totally void of his talents. One afternoon, during one of Duponte's walks, the heat was strong and I convinced him to share a coach with me. After some time driving through Paris in silence, he pointed out the window of our coach to a cemetery. "That," he said, "upon the other side of the wall, is the small burial place of your people, Monsieur Clark."

I saw a sign in French for the Jewish cemetery. "Yes, it *is* quite small . . ." I paused, leaving my statement in the air. Thinking of what had just been said to me, I turned in astonishment. "Monsieur Duponte!"

"Yes?"

"What did you say a moment ago? Of that burial place?"

"That in it are the people of your faith, or perhaps partially of your faith."

"But, monsieur, whatever leads you to believe I am Jewish? I have never said so to you."

"You are not?" Duponte asked in surprise.

"Well," I answered breathlessly, "my mother was Jewish. My father, Protestant; he has died too. But however did you think of that?"

Duponte, seeing I would press the question, explained. "When we neared a particular lodging house in Montmartre some days ago, you realized from the newspaper accounts that it was the place where a young girl was brutally murdered." Articles about the gruesome case, indeed, had daily pervaded the Paris newspapers I had been reading to improve my French. Duponte continued: "Feeling it was something of a sacred place, a place of recent death, you reached for your hat. However, rather than taking off your hat— as the Christian does automatically upon entering a church— you secured it tighter on your head— like the Jew in his synagogue. Then you fumbled with it for another moment, showing your uncertain instincts in the matter to remove or tighten it. This made me consider that you had worshipped, at times, in church and in synagogue."

He was correct. My mother had not yielded her Jewish heritage upon entering wedlock, despite the collective urgings of my father's family, and once the Lloyd Street Synagogue was completed in Baltimore she had brought me with her.

Duponte returned to his usual silence. I kept my excitement to myself. I had begun to break down Duponte's walls.

❖ ❖ ❖

I tried delicately to solicit Duponte for more facts about his past, but his face would stiffen each time. We developed a friendly routine. Each morning I would knock at his door. If he was stretched on his bed with the newspaper, he would invite me inside for coffee. Usually, Duponte would announce his departure for a walk and I would ask permission to accompany him, to which he would assent by ignoring my question.

He had an impenetrability, a *moral invisibility* that made me want to see how he would be in all the possible variations of life: to see him in love, in a duel, to see what meal he would select at a certain establishment. I burned to know his thoughts and wished him to desire to know more of me.

Sometimes I would bring him an item related to my original purpose that I hoped might strike his interest. For example, I found a guidebook of Baltimore in one of the Paris bookstalls and showed it to him.

"You see, inside there is a folded map— and this part of town is where Edgar Poe lived in Baltimore when he won his first newspaper prize for a tale called 'Ms. Found in a Bottle.' Here is where he was discovered in an insensible state in Baltimore. Look here, monsieur; that is his burial place!"

"Monsieur Clark," he said, "I am afraid such things are of as little interest to me as you can imagine."

You see how it was. I tried every approach to uplift him from his inactive trance. For example, one hot day when Duponte and I were walking across a bridge over the Seine, we decided to pay twelve *sous* each to one of the floating establishments on the river to take a bath under a canvas roofing. We plunged into the cooling water opposite each other. Duponte closed his eyes and leaned back, and I followed his example. Our bodies were rocked up and down by the happy splashing of children and young men.

Quentin: "Monsieur, surely you know the importance of Poe's tales of C. Auguste Dupin. You have heard of them. They were published in the French journals."

Duponte (inattentively, a question or statement?): "They were."

Q: "Your own achievements in analysis provide the character of the main figure with his abilities. That must mean something to you! The exploits involve the most intricate, seemingly impossible, and miraculous triumphs of reason."

D: "I have not read them, I believe."

Q: "Not read the literature of your own life? That which will make you immortal? How could this be?"

D: "It is of as little interest to me as I could imagine, monsieur."

Should that last comment have an exclamation mark? Perhaps a grammarian could answer; it was quite sharply enunciated but without any greater volume than a waiter at a restaurant repeating an order back to his customer.

. . .

It was just a few days later when there came an important turn in my companionship with Duponte. I had walked with Duponte through the Jardin des Plantes, where not only the finest plants and trees were enjoyed in the summer but also one of Paris's best scientific zoological collections. After a tunnel of clouds had darkened above the trees, we had begun walking for the exit when a man rushed up behind us. He spoke with great consternation.

"Kind monsieurs," he said, panting out the words, "have you seen somebody with my cake?"

"Cake?" I repeated. "What do you mean, monsieur?"

He explained that he had walked to the street-vendors and purchased a seedcake, a rare indulgence for him, to enjoy on what had been a beautiful sunny day before the rain began. This fellow had placed his treat lovingly on the bench beside his person until such a time as he would feel his earlier dinner properly digested. He had turned his back only for a brief moment to secure his umbrella from the ground upon noticing the storm gathering overhead. However, when he turned back finally ready to savor his sweet luxury, it had vanished completely, and there was not a man around!

"Perhaps a bird picked it up, monsieur," I suggested. I tugged at Duponte's arm. "Come along. It is beginning to rain, Monsieur Duponte, and we haven't any umbrellas."

We parted from our cakeless friend, but after a few steps Duponte turned around. He called back this despondent man.

"Monsieur," said Duponte, "stand where I am now and likely your cake shall return in two to seven minutes. Approximately speaking." Duponte's voice exhibited neither joy nor particular interest in the matter.

"Indeed?" the man cried.

"Yes. I should think so," said Duponte, and he began walking away again.

"But— how?" the man now thought to ask.

I, too, was held dumbstruck by Duponte's proposition, and Duponte saw this.

"Imbeciles!" said Duponte to himself.

"What?" the man asked with offense.

"Pardon, Monsieur Duponte!" I said, also protesting the insult.

Duponte ignored this. "I shall demonstrate the conclusion," he said. We two waited at the very edge of anticipation. But Duponte simply stood there. After a space of three and a half minutes, roughly, a regular stampede of hurried noises was heard nearby and there— I must reveal— came a piece of cake from around the corner, floating in the air, right near the nose of its rightful owner!

"The cake!" I pointed.

The confection was attached to a short string of some sort, and followed behind two small boys running headlong through the gardens. The man chased down the boy and untied his cake from its thief. He then ran back to us.

"Why, remarkable monsieur, you were entirely right! But how have you recovered my cake?" For a moment the man looked at Duponte suspiciously, as though he had been involved in some scheme. Duponte, seeing he would have no peace without explaining, offered this simple description of what had transpired.

Among the most popular attractions in the natural collections of the Jardin des Plantes was the exhibition of bears. Before being accosted by the cake-widower, Duponte had casually noticed that it was near the time in which the bears usually stirred from their sleep. This was also known by the many local devotees to these animals, and it was a daily occupation to try to make the waking bears perform various antics and climb the pole provided for them, an effort that often involved dangling some item of food into their pit by twine or string. Indeed, the vendors at the gates to the gardens sold as much of their wares for these purposes as for human nourishment. But since among the lovers of the bears who would come from miles away for this sport were many young boys, and since most of these *gamins* had no spare *sous* in their pockets for such delicacies, Duponte reasoned that as the man had turned to secure his umbrella at the sign of rain, one of these boys had snatched the cake on his way to the bears. Because the bench was quite high, and the boy short, the man, on turning around again, saw no one nearby and thought the source of the theft fantastic.

"Very well. But how did you know the cake would return, and at this very spot?" the man asked.

"You may have noticed," continued Duponte, seeming to talk more to himself than to either of us, "that upon entering the grounds of the gardens, there was a larger group of officers of the garden in the vicinity of the zoological attractions than usual. Perhaps you remember reading of one of the bears, 'Martin,' having recently devoured a soldier who leaned over too far and fell into their domain."

"Indeed! I remember," said the man.

"No doubt these guards were stationed to prevent young men and boys from any longer climbing the parapets to get close to the monsters."

"Yes! You are likely right, monsieur!" The man stood open-mouthed.

"It might have been further essayed, then, that if a boy had in fact taken possession of your cake, the same lad would be turned away from his plan by these vigilant guardians within the first few minutes of the bears' stirring, and the bandit would return by the most direct path— a path which crosses the grounds where we now stand— to the attraction second in popularity only to the wells of the bears for this sort of spectator: I mean the wire house of the monkeys, who, at the delivery of a bright piece of cloth or item of food, could be made to chase one another in, presumably, a manner almost as enchanting as the bears' climbing of the pole. None of the other popular holdings, the wolves or the parrots, will make such an exhibition over one's cake."

As delighted by this explanation as if it had been his own, the grateful man, with a magnanimous air, invited us to share in his cake, even though it had been in the grubby hands of the boy and had since been made flat by the rain. I politely declined, but Duponte, after a moment of thought, accepted and sat with him upon a bench. They ate with great relish as I held the man's umbrella over them.

That evening, I met the same man at a crowded café near my hotel. The bright lights of the interior presented a dazzling effect. He was playing a game of dominoes with a friend, whom he dismissed when he saw me come in.

"Monsieur, bravely done," I said joyfully. "Quite well done!"

I had met this man the day before in the same Jardin des Plantes. He was one of the *chiffonniers* of Paris, men whose occupation was to search through the rubbish heaps put out from the houses of Paris. They would use sticks and baskets with great expertise to collect anything of remote value. "Bones, scraps of paper, linen, cloth, bits of iron, broken glass, broken china, corks of wine bottles . . ." he explained. These men were not vagrants; rather, they were registered for this activity with the police.

I had inquired of the fellow how much he collected each day.

"Under King Philippe," he said of the former monarch, "thirty *sous*' worth a day! But now, under the Republic, only fifteen." He explained, with a sad tone of nostalgia for the monarchy, "People throw away less bones and paper now! When there is no luxury we who are poor can do nothing."

I would remember his words strongly in the months to come.

Because he could legally ply his trade only between five and ten in the morning, and was bent on earning money, I thought he would be agreeable to the scheme I had conceived. I had instructed him that when he saw me walking with my companion the following afternoon, he should exclaim in our hearing over the loss of some object of value and beg Duponte for assistance. In this way, Duponte might be jolted into some small undertaking.

Now, at the café where we had agreed to meet, as my part of the bargain I informed the waiter that I would pay for the meal of my accomplice's choice. And what a meal! He called for the *tout ensemble* of the place: *poulet en fricassée*, ragout, cauliflower, bonbons, melons, cream cheese! As was the practice in France, each new item of food came with a new plate, for the French abhorred the American practice of mixing tastes— for instance, vegetables and the sauces of meat— on one plate. I watched his feast happily, for his performance at the gardens had pleased me greatly.

"I did not think, at first, cake would work," I admitted to him. "I thought it a strange choice! Yet you managed quite well with that boy."

"No, no, monsieur!" he said. "I had nothing to do with that boy. The cake was truly stolen from me!"

"What do you mean?" I asked.

The *chiffonnier* said that he had planned to position his umbrella in some concealed spot and report the missing umbrella to Duponte to fulfill our agreement. It had been during the time he searched for a hiding place for the umbrella near the bench that his cake had vanished.

"How did he know what happened to it?" he asked. "Had you told your friend to watch me that whole time?"

"Of course not!" I shook my head. "I wanted to see if he would solve the mystery, and that would spoil the experiment, wouldn't it!"

The incident had clearly weighed on his mind. "He is an odd stick. Yet I suppose when a body is hungry, he shall do what he must."

I reflected on this axiom after parting from the man. I had been too excited about Duponte's promising behavior to consider *why* Duponte had performed his task of analysis. Perhaps Duponte, who had skipped dinner, had just been hungry for the cake, his share of the spoils, all along.

This was hardly the end of that line of attempts on my part to provoke Duponte into renewing his abilities. I had brought from America the pamphlet of *The Prose Romances of Edgar A. Poe.* I marked the first page of "The Murders in the Rue Morgue" and left it for Duponte, hoping that his interests would be captured. I rejoiced when it seemed that all my tactics were having an impact. The first true indication that Duponte was changing in some extraordinary way came one evening when I followed him to Café Belge. Two or three times a week he would sit on a bench, ignoring the billiards games and the chatter, comfortably lost in the ugly bustle and brawls around him. I had followed him here before. Something seemed different as soon as I saw him this time. His glance had already become less vacant.

I lost sight of him after he turned into the small, narrow café. Mirrors lining the walls exaggerated the confusion of people inside. This was where the best billiards players in the city congregated to play. There was one roguish fellow who was said to be the best of all the players. He was wildly *red* all over— his hair, his brow, his irritated, picked skin. He almost always played his game alone, I suppose because he was too good for the others who came only for leisure and gaiety. He shouted encouragement to himself on a good shot, and cursed himself mercilessly when he fell short.

Café Belge was the only billiards café in the city to allow women to play— though, it will surprise many who have not visited Paris, it was not the only café to permit the smoking of cigars by ladies. True, the unsuspecting American might blanch just by walking past many of the illustrations displayed in the windows of print-shops, or after witnessing scenes of maternal activities, usually confined to the nursery, displayed for all the world to see in the middle of the Tuileries gardens.

As I searched for Duponte, a young lady threw her hand on top of mine.

"Monsieur, you wish to play a game with us?"

"Mademoiselle?"

She pointed to the three other nymphs at her table. "You wish to play billiards, I suppose. Come, here is a stick. You are an Englishman?"

She propelled me in front of the table. "Do not fret. Nobody plays for money in Paris, only for drinks!"

"You see"— I leaned in to speak as quietly as possible— "I am not married." I had learned that in France unmarried women were to be seen with single men at great risk to their reputation; the compensation was that married women could freely be seen doing all manner of things.

"Ah, that is all very well," the damsel reassured me in a loud, smoked whisper. "I am." She and her companions laughed, and their French grew too rapid for me to follow. I struggled to cross the room, colliding with the elbows of a few of the men surrounding the billiards tables.

After a few moments, I noticed another young woman in the room, standing apart from the others. Although she looked to be of the same modest class, she held herself up with elegance unknown to her peers in the café. And unknown, for that matter, to the "unrivaled beauties" that paraded themselves along Baltimore Street. She was shorter than me, and her deep-set eyes seemed almost to anticipate my path through the crowd. She carried a basket with blooming flowers and stood quietly. A man would raise his hand and she would walk close, where the man would toss a copper coin or two into the basket.

As I searched my own pockets for a coin to contribute to this lovely vision, I bumped into the next table, knocking a player as he shot at a ball.

"What in hell?" It was the roguish red-haired fellow. The best player in the arrondissement. Standing near him was a beautiful, but pale woman, with dark hair, who consoled him by stroking his arm.

The other nymphs I had encountered pointed and giggled at me from across the room. "Monsieur Englishman!" they kept repeating.

"You've ruined my game," he said. "I'll crack your skull into two! Get back to England."

"Actually, monsieur, I come from America. Accept my apologies."

"A 'Yankee Doodle,' are you? Maybe you think you're back with the Indians then? What do you want here, stirring trouble?"

He shoved me hard several times. I nearly fell backward, barely regaining my balance. Somewhere during this ordeal— whether here or in the more dire later stages— my hat disappeared. With the next shove, I lost my balance, falling against a table, and watched myself sink to the floor in the café's mirrors.

In my next bit of memory, I was flat on my back. I thought it best to remain low, looking up to the ceiling where the old smoke of the place peacefully collected and continued forever in the mirrors like a fog rolling over the ocean.

A pair of arms broke through the cover of smoke and yanked me to my feet. The room seemed hotter, louder, smaller. Shouts and laughter floated in the background— though part of the raucousness was directed to one of the nymphs, who was now on top of a table and tripping the light fantastic with a dance. These shouts emboldened the Red Rogue. His sloppy mouth formed a sickly grin right against my face.

His breath was painfully sharp. "My best game ever," he said threateningly. Or at least whatever it was he was saying, it had a threatening ring, as I cannot be sure of the words— he was, naturally, speaking French and, for the moment, that language was all but lost to me. I hoped the elegant girl with the flower basket was not watching.

Then a voice came from behind me. "Monsieur, if you please!"

The rogue looked over my shoulder.

"I challenge you in a game of billiards, monsieur," said the same voice behind me. "And we shall wager whatever amount you choose."

Red Rogue seemed to forget me altogether, and pushed aside his girl, who wheeled around anxiously at the scene and pulled at his elbow.

"At my table?" said the rogue, pointing to the billiards table where we had collided.

"None other would be as suitable," replied Duponte, bowing precisely.

An amount of money was called out. This scene quickly attracted an audience, not only because an unknown player had dared to take on the champion, but because there was money— rather than the customary drinks— at stake, and significant money.

As though this might be a second Duponte, I looked around the café to make sure he was not somewhere else. Though overwhelmed with relief at my escape from harm, I instantly felt Duponte's mistake. In the first place, I knew from my observations of Duponte that he had no money should he lose. Secondly, there was the matter of this fellow's talent for the game of billiards. As if to remind me of this, one of the bystanders behind me whispered to his friend, "Red Rogue is one of the best players in Paris." Except he used the fellow's real name, which, from the mayhem of events, I no longer remember.

Red Rogue slapped his money on a chair. Duponte was busy selecting his stick.

"Monsieur?" the rogue demanded, banging three times on the chair.

"The money is my reward," explained Duponte. "Not yours."

"And what if I win?!" shouted his opponent, the red in his face turning purple.

Duponte motioned a hand at me. "If you are the winner of our game without forfeit," replied Duponte, "then you may resume your business with this gentleman unhindered."

Much to my despair, the rogue turned to me and seemed to savor the barbaric license that would be afforded by a victory. He even offered Duponte the honor of beginning the game. I tried desperately to think if Poe's stories had ever mentioned skill in billiards on the part of the analyst hero; on the contrary, Dupin professed a dislike for mathematical games like chess and pronounced the superiority of simple matches of whist in showing the real skills of ratiocination.

Duponte opened with a shot so terrible that several onlookers laughed.

Red Rogue became perfectly serious, even graceful, as he struck the ball with ease turn after turn. If I had ruined his best game ever, surely this was his second best. I held on to the hope that Duponte would suddenly grow skilled, or reveal that his ineptness was but an act of trickery. Not so; he became worse. And then there were only three or maybe four turns left on the part of Red Rogue before the game would be finished to his advantage. I was searching my pockets, with the thought of replacing my part in the wager with silver, but I hadn't brought more than a few francs with me.

This was most remarkable: through all of this, Duponte remained utterly composed. With each awful turn, his expression stayed perfectly untroubled and confident. This was increasingly upsetting to his opponent, though it did not in the least affect his excellent play. One reward of triumph is to watch the loser deflate. And Duponte was refusing to comply with this. I believe Red Rogue even slowed his victory in order to attempt to induce the proper degradation.

Finally, the villain turned to the table with renewed speed and a flash of anger at Duponte. "Here we finish," he said, then directed a boiling gaze of hatred at me.

"Yes? Very well then." Duponte, to my horror, shrugged.

In my state of fear, I did not at first even hear the commotion at the street door. In fact, it did not gain my attention until there were several people pointing in our direction. Then there burst in a man with a bushy orange beard who, other than the beard and a much larger frame, looked similar to Red Rogue. I saw Red Rogue's greedy, flushed face whiten pathetically and I knew something was wrong. My French had returned enough to make out the fact that Red Rogue had, according to this enraged newcomer, directed his romantic passion toward this man's lover, the girl standing nervously near the table. She now screamed at the larger man to forgive her, and Red Rogue fled into the streets.

Duponte had already collected the money from the chair and was departing by the time I regained my bearings.

If you are the winner without forfeit . . . The words circled my head. Forfeit. He had known— from the beginning— how this would turn out. I followed Duponte into the street.

"Monsieur, I might have been killed! You could have never won the game!"

"Certainly not!"

"How did you know that man would come?"

"*I* didn't. The girl on Red Rogue's arm had earlier been peering out the window every few moments but, if you observed, always keeping herself away from view of someone outside the window. Moreover, she did not merely hold Red's arm; she *squeezed* it, as though to protect him, and upon my challenge pleaded with him to leave— certainly not because she thought anyone could defeat him at this child's game. *She* knew— from having encountered him earlier in a state of anger, or having carelessly left one of Red Rogue's letters on her dresser, perhaps— that her other lover was looking for her. I merely observed her, and counted on the fact that he would soon enough come. When someone else knows something, it is usually unnecessary to discover it for yourself. There was nothing to worry about."

"But what if he had come only after you had lost the game?"

"I see you are of a very sensitive constitution."

"Would he not have committed some monstrous violence against me?"

"Agreed," Duponte admitted after a moment, "that would have been quite troublesome for you, monsieur. We should be grateful it was avoided."

One morning soon after, my knocking at Duponte's door met with no reply. I tried the handle and found it open. I entered, thinking he had not heard me, and called out.

"A walk today, monsieur?" I paused and glanced around.

Duponte was hunched over his bed as though in prayer, his hand gripping his forehead like a vise. Stepping closer, I could see he was reading in a troubling state of intensity.

"What have you done?" he demanded.

I stumbled back and said, "Only come to look for you, monsieur. I thought perhaps a walk by the Seine today would be pleasant. Or to the Tuileries to see the horse-chestnuts!"

His eyes locked straight on mine, the effect unsettling.

"I explained to you, Monsieur Clark, that I do not engage in these avocations you imagine. You have not seemed to comprehend this simplest of statements regarding this matter. You insist on confusing your literature and my reality. Now you shall do me a good turn by leaving me alone."

"But Monsieur Duponte . . . please . . ."

It was only then that I could see what he had been reading so attentively: "The Murders in the Rue Morgue." The pamphlet I had left for him. Then he pushed me by the arm into the hall and closed the door. My heart sank fast.

In the hall, I pressed my eye against the space between the door and the frame. Duponte was sitting up on the bed. His silhouette was surprisingly expressive as he continued to read. With each page he turned, it seemed his posture improved by just that much, and the shadow of his figure seemed to swell.

I waited a few moments in bewildered silence. Then I knocked lightly and tried to appeal to his reason.

I knocked harder until I was pounding; then I pulled on the handle until the concierge appeared and pried me from the door while threatening to call for the police. Monsieur Montor, back in Washington, had warned that under no circumstances should I allow the police to find me in some act of disturbance. "They are by no means like the police here in America," he said. "When they set themselves against someone . . . Well!"

I surrendered for the moment and allowed myself to be removed down the stairs.

❖   ❖   ❖

Speaking through keyholes and windows, rapping the door, pushing notes into the apartment . . . these were activities in the long painful days after this. I trailed Duponte when he took walks through Paris, but he ignored me. Once, when I followed in Duponte's steps to the door of his lodging house, he stopped in the doorway and said, "Do not allow entrance to this impertinent young gentlemen again."

Though he was looking at me, he was speaking to his concierge. Duponte turned away and continued upstairs.

I learned when the concierge tended to be out, and that his wife was content to let me through with no questions for a few *sous*. *There is no time to lose,* I wrote to Duponte in one of my unread notes to his door that would invariably be slipped back into the hall.

During this time, another letter arrived from Peter back home. His tone had noticeably improved, and he urged that I should return immediately to Baltimore and that I would be welcomed back having finished with my wild oats. He even sent a letter of credit for a generous amount of money at the French bank so I could arrange my trip back without delay. I returned this directly to him, of course, and I wrote back that I would accomplish what I had come to do. I would, at length, successfully deliver Poe from those who would destroy him, and I would do all credit to the name of our legal practice by achieving this promised goal.

Peter wrote subsequently that he was now very seriously considering coming to Paris to find me and bring me back, even if he had to drag me home with his two hands.

I still collected articles on Poe's death from the reading rooms that carried American papers. Generally speaking, newspaper descriptions of Poe had worsened. Moralists used his example to compensate for the lenience shown in the past toward men of genius who had been praised after death despite "dissolute lives." A new low came when a merciless scribbler, one Rufus Griswold, in order to make a penny off this public sentiment, published a biography malevolently brimming with libel and hate toward the poet. Poe's reputation sank further until it was entirely coated in mud.

Occasionally amid this mad fumble to dissect Poe, a new and important detail arose illuminating his final weeks. It had been shown, for instance, that Poe had planned to go to Philadelphia shortly before the time he was discovered in Ryan's hotel in Baltimore. He was to receive one hundred dollars to edit a book of poems for a Mrs. St. Leon Loud. This information, however, was met with the usual mystification of the press, as it was not known whether Poe did go to Philadelphia or not.

Stranger still was the letter shown to the press by Maria Clemm, Poe's former mother-in-law, which she had received from him directly before he left Richmond, telling her of his plans regarding Philadelphia. It was Poe's last letter to his beloved protector. "I am still unable to send you even one dollar— but keep up heart— I hope that our troubles are nearly over," read Poe's tenderhearted letter to her. "Write immediately in reply & direct to Philadelphia." Then he went on: "For fear I should not get the letter, sign no name & address it to E. S. T. Grey Esqre. God bless & protect you my own darling Muddy." It was signed "Your own Eddy."

E. S. T. Grey Esqre? Why would Poe be using a false name in the weeks before his death? Why did he have such fear that Muddy's letter would not reach him in Philadelphia? E. S. T. Grey! The papers that reported this seemed almost to be grinning at the apparent madness of it.

My investigations seemed more urgent than ever, yet here I was in Paris, and Duponte would not even speak with me.

8

HAD THIS ALL been a tremendous mistake, a product of some deliri-ous compulsion to be involved in something outside my usual scope and responsibility? If only I had been content with the warmth and reliabil-ity of Hattie and Peter! Hadn't there been a time in childhood when I needed no more than the swirling hearth of Glen Eliza and my trusted playmates? Why turn my heart and my plans over to a man like Duponte, encased alone in a moral prison so far from my own home?

I determined to combat my gloominess and occupy myself by visiting the places that, according to the advice of my Paris guidebook, "must be seen by the stranger."

First, I toured the palace at the Champs-Élysées, where Louis-Napoleon, president of the Republic, lived in rich splendor. At the great hall of the Champs-Élysées, a stout servant in laced livery accepted my hat and offered a wooden counter in its place.

In one of the first suites of rooms in which the public is permitted, there was the chance to see Louis-Napoleon himself— Prince Napoleon. This was not the first time I had glimpsed the president of the Republic and nephew of the once-great Emperor Napoleon, who was still the people's favorite symbol of France. A few weeks earlier, Louis-Napoleon was riding through the streets down Avenue de Marigny, reviewing his scarlet-and-blue-clad soldiers. Duponte had watched with interest, and (as he had still tolerated my companionship then) I had accompanied him.

Crowds on the street cheered, and those dressed most expensively yelled out with passion, "Vive Napoleon!" At these moments, when the president was but an indistinct figure on his horse surrounded by guards, it was easy to see a resemblance, though faint, to the other sovereign Napoleon parading through the cheers of forty years earlier. Some said it was Louis-Napoleon's name alone that had recently elected the president-prince. It was reported that illiterate laborers in the poorer countryside of France thought they were voting for the original Napoleon Bonaparte (by now dead some three decades)!

But there were also twenty or so men, with faces, hands, and throats stained in black soot, repeating, in frightful chants, *"Vive la République!"* One of my neighbors in the crowd said they were sent by the *"Red* party" to protest. How shouting "Long live the Republic" was considered a protest or insult in an official Republic was beyond my understanding of the current political state. I suppose it was their tone that made the words threatening, and that made the term "Republic" fearful to the followers of this president, as if they were saying instead, "This is no Republic, for with this man it is a sham, but one day we shall overthrow it and have a true Republic without him!"

Here at his palace he seemed a more contemplative man, quite pale, mild, and thoroughly a gentleman. Napoleon was flushed with satisfaction at the crowd of mostly uniformed people around him, many of whose breasts sparkled with impressively gilded decorations. Yet, I observed, too, a painful sense of awkwardness elicited by the reverence with which the president-prince was treated— one moment a monarch, the next an elected president.

Just then, Prefect of Police Delacourt came in from the next chamber and conferred quietly with President Napoleon. I was surprised to notice the prefect glaring quite impolitely in the direction in which I stood.

That unwanted attention expedited my departure from the Champs-Élysées. There was still the palace of Versailles to see, and my guidebook advised leaving first thing in the morning when traveling there, but I decided that it was not too late in the day to enjoy a full visit to the suburbs of the city. Besides, Duponte had advised me to visit Versailles— perhaps if he knew I had he would be more inclined to speak to me.

Once the railroad tracks exit Paris, the metropolis abruptly disappears, giving itself over to continuous vast open country. Women of all ages, wearing carnation-colored bonnets and laboring in the fields, briefly met my gaze as our train rattled by them.

We stopped at the Versailles railway station. The crowd nearly picked me up and carried me into a stream of hats and trimmed bonnets that ended under the iron gates of the great palace of Versailles, where the running water of the fountains could be heard at play.

Thinking back, I suppose it must have begun while I was touring the palace's suites. I felt the sting of general discomfort, as when wearing a coat a bit too thin for the first winter day. I attributed my uneasiness to the crowds. The mob that had driven away the Duchess d'Angoulême from these walls was surely not as boisterous as this one. As my guide pointed out which battles were depicted in the various paintings, I was distracted by feeling so many sets of eyes on me.

"In this gallery," said my guide, "Louis the Fourteenth displayed all the grandeur of royalty. The court was so splendid that even in this enormous chamber the king would be pressed round by the courtiers of the day." We were in the grand gallery of Louis XIV, where seventeen arched windows overlooking the gardens faced seventeen mirrors across from them. I wondered whether the notion of a monarch was more attractive now that the late revolution had vanquished it.

I think my guide, whom I had hired at a franc an hour, had become tired of my distractedness over the course of the afternoon. I fear he thought I was ignorant of the finer qualities of history and art. The truth was, my distinct sense of being observed had been growing steadily— and in that hall of mirrors prodigal gazes were everywhere.

I began to take note of those people who recurred in the different suites. I had convinced my guide to modify our path through the palace— an alien idea to him, clearly. Meanwhile, he did not help my mental state when he turned to the topic of foreigners in Paris.

"They would know much about how you're spending your time here— you being a young energetic man," he mused, perhaps looking for a way to vex me.

"*Who* would know about me, monsieur?"

"The police and the government, of course. There is nothing that happens in Paris that is not known to someone."

"But, monsieur, I fear there is nothing so interesting enough about me."

"They would hear all from the masters of your hotel, from the *commissionnaires* who watch you leave and return, from fiacre drivers, sellers of vegetables, wine-shop masters. Yes, monsieur, I suppose there is nothing you can do that they cannot discover."

In my current state of nervousness, this commentary did not endear me. I paid him what I owed and dismissed him from his service. Without my guide I could now move faster, weaving through the slow gatherings of mobs in each chamber. I noticed behind me some commotion, men huffing and women exclaiming over some disturbance. It seemed some of the tourists were complaining about someone who was rudely pushing through the crowd. I turned into the next chamber, not waiting to see who had been the culprit of the strife. Meanwhile, I dodged every figure and expensive furnishing in my path until I reached the palace's immense gardens.

"Here he is! He's the one plowing through the place!"

As I heard this voice, a hand caught my arm. It was a guard.

"I?" I protested. "Why, I was not pushing anyone!"

After it was reported to the guard that the man rudely pushing through was spotted behind us, I was released into the gardens and quickly created distance between the guard and myself in the event he changed his mind. I would soon wish I had not left the safety of being at his side.

I thought back to Madame Fouché warning me about the dangerous areas of Paris. "There are men and women who will rob you and then throw you over the bridge into the Seine," she had said. It was from this population that the revolutionaries in March 1848 drew most of their "soldiers" to force out King Louis-Philippe and establish the Republic in the name of the people. A hackney cab driver told me that during that uprising he saw one of these villains, surrounded by police and about to be shot, yell, *"Je suis bien vengé!"* and remove fifteen or sixteen human tongues from his pockets. He tossed them into the air before dying, and they landed on the shoulders and hats of the police, and even in one policeman's mouth, which had dropped open in disbelief at the disgusting sight.

I was in the plush sanctuary of Versailles's immaculate gardens, not in one of these neighborhoods of tongue-cutters. Still, I had the sensation that each step I made was being marked. The sharp hedges and trees of the gardens revealed fragments of faces. Passing rows of statues, vases, and fountains, I came to a standstill at the God of Day, a hideous deity rising up from a splashing fountain of dolphins and sea-monsters. How much more secure I might have been inside the suites of the palace, surrounded by hordes of visitors and my busybody guide! It was then that a man appeared in front and snatched my arm.

*   *   *

Here is what I remember after that. I was inside a rickety carriage riding over loose stones. Next to me was the face I last saw before losing consciousness in the gardens of Versailles— a thick, rigid face carved below an emotionless frown. A face I had also noticed in several of the suites of the palace at Versailles. This had been my shadow! I licked my teeth and gums and found it was still present; my tongue, I mean.

Did I think before I reached for the door of the carriage? I cannot recall. I threw myself onto it and tumbled to the road. When I pushed myself to my feet, another coach was barreling at me. It swerved and narrowly squeezed between me and the vehicle that had been carrying me. *"Gare!"* growled its driver, who seemed to me only a large set of yellow teeth, a slouched hat, and a floppy collar. A lean dog howled from that carriage's window.

I ran for the fields that sloped down from the road. Beyond that was open country.

Then my captor was out of the coach and starting toward me, terribly fast for so bulky a man. I felt a quick, decisive blow to my head.

My hands were stiff behind my back. I was looking around— or should I say *up*. Upon waking, I found myself in a wide trench indented some twenty feet into the earth. Above that were towering walls; they were nothing like the petite rows of buildings and homes on every Paris street. It was as though I had been brought to another world, and a monstrous silence stretched around us as in the widest desert.

"Where am I? I demand to know!" I shouted, though I could see no one to shout to.

I heard a voice mutter something in French. I craned my head but could not move enough to see behind me. Only a shadow fell over me, and I believed it was that of my captor.

"Where are we, you blackguard?" I demanded. He made no indication of hearing. He just stood, waiting. Only when the villain in question came from the other side did I realize that this shadow belonged to someone else.

Finally, the shadow moved and he came around to face me. But it was no man.

Here she was, wearing a fresh white bonnet and a plain dress, she who could have been in one of the Parisian gardens. She stopped in front of my chair and leaned over me with what seemed to be caring protectiveness, looking at me with deep-set eyes— in fact, eyes so deep they seemed to reach to the back of her head. She seemed no older than a girl.

"Stop squeaking."

"Who are you?" I whispered, hoarse from hollering.

"Bonjour," said the girl, who then turned her back and walked away.

I returned the greeting, though thinking any attempt at cordialness odd under the circumstances.

"You fool," admonished my first captor, seeming to wish she not hear, as though he would be blamed for my error. "That is her name. Bonjour!"

"Bonjour?" I repeated. Then I realized I had seen her before, another time I was in jeopardy. "At Café Belge! I saw you there, holding a basket! Why were you there?"

"Here we are!" a new voice boomed in English, tinged with a French accent but otherwise perfectly fluent. "Is it very necessary to have our welcomed guest from the great United States so restrained?"

The answer was demure enough to identify the latest arrival as the leader. My captor moved closer to him and spoke confidentially, as though I had suddenly lost the power to hear. "He swooned at Versailles, and then he ran from the coach, leaping out the door like a madman. He nearly killed himself— "

"No matter. Here we are all safe. Bonjour, please?" The girl agilely untied the ropes and released my wrists.

I had not up to this point been able to see this new arrival, only glimpses of a long white cloak and light pantaloons. With my hands free, I stood and faced him.

"My apologies for going to such lengths, Monsieur Clark," he said, waving his bejeweled hand at our surroundings as though the whole thing was an accident. "But I am afraid these unfortunate fortresses are among the few places within the environs of Paris where I can still travel with some tranquillity. Most importantly— "

I interrupted. "Now see here! Your rogue has ill-treated me and now— But in the first place, I would like to know where exactly you have had me taken and why. . . !" I choked on my words, staring at him through a spark of sudden recognition.

"Most importantly, as I say," he continued warmly, a grin pressing out the olive skin of his face, "we finally meet in person."

He took my hand, which fell limp when the truth struck me.

"Dupin!" I cried out in disbelief.

9

YOU WILL RECALL that there were five or six other men that I seriously examined as potential inspirations for the Dupin character before eliminating them in favor of Duponte.

A Baron Claude Dupin was one of these— a French attorney who, it was said, had never lost a single case, and who boasted distant royal lineage, wherein derived the dubious title of "Baron." He had been among the most prominent jurists of Paris for many years, thought of as a hero for successfully advocating in favor of many accused but sympathetic wrongdoers. He was even a candidate for advocate-general at one time, and almost sent to the chamber of representatives by his district during one of the upheavals in French government. He was alleged by some to employ unsavory tactics and, soon, relinquished his work altogether in favor of biding his time with other enterprises in London. While there, he was sworn in as a special constable during a period of fear of an uprising, and acted bravely enough in that capacity to continue with that title in an honorary capacity.

All of this information had been collected piecemeal during my careful searches of French periodicals. There was a time before I went to Paris when I was quite certain that Claude Dupin was the basis for C. Auguste Dupin, and I had sent several letters to Baron Dupin inquiring into further details of his history and describing the pressing situation at hand in Baltimore. Soon enough, however, I had stumbled upon the articles concerning Auguste Duponte and altered my theory. When Claude Dupin had replied to me, I had mailed him an apologetic letter explaining my mistake.

One of the French periodicals I had seen included an illustrated portrait of Baron Dupin, which I had studied closely. Thus, I knew the man who was pressing my hand as though we were old friends. That's when I yelled in alarm and astonishment: "Dupin! . . . You're Claude Dupin!"

"Please," said he magnanimously, "call me Baron!"

I yanked my hand away. I looked for my best chance at immediate escape. The carriage that had brought me there was now waiting in a temporary passage in the masonry, but I had no thought of being able to commandeer it, as my first captor had returned to the vehicle and was waiting there.

The trench around Paris was part of the impenetrable fortification built to provide against future assaults on the city. A continuous enclosure surrounded the outskirts of Paris, with embankments for artillery, surrounded by ditches and trenches.

In these daunting surroundings, Dupin now assured me of my complete safety and began explaining that his colleague Hartwick— that was the name of my captor, who'd nabbed me at Versailles and put me in his carriage— had merely wished to ensure my safe presence for this interview.

"Hartwick can outswear Satan, and he has almost bitten a man's arm clean off once, but taken together he's not badly made up. Do forgive him."

"Forgive? Forgive this assault? I'm afraid, Dupin, I shall not do that!" I cried.

"You see, it is already a great relief to know you," said Claude Dupin. "After so much time living in London, I'm afraid it's been a while since a soul has pronounced my name correctly, like a Frenchman!"

"Listen, monsieur," I reprimanded, though I liked the rare compliment to my French. "Do not butter me up. If you wished to speak with me, why not choose some civilized place in the city?"

"It would have been my pleasure to share a *demi-tasse* of coffee, Monsieur Clark, I assure you. But shall I call you Quentin?" He had a dashing way of talking that conveyed a high degree of ardor.

"No!"

"Be easy, be easy. Let me explain myself more, good Quentin. You see, there are two types of friends in this world: friends and enemies. In Paris, I possess both. I am afraid one of those groups would like to see me a head shorter. I may have been involved with the wrong sort some years ago, and promised certain amounts of money that, at the end of a thorough and unforgiving mathematical evaluation, I failed to possess. I was as poor as Job's turkey. Fortunately, though I was in a bad box, I have enough protection in London to prevent too much worry when I am there. You see where I am reduced to meeting when I wish to visit Paris," he added, waving his hand around at the fortifications. "You have luck enough to have some fortune of your own, I believe, Brother Quentin. Business? Or born with a silver spoon? No matter, I guess."

It was surprising, and a bit troubling, to see Dupin remove my letters from his coat. Should I describe the physical appearance of the Baron here, you would see how difficult it was to deny him conversation despite the inexcusable treatment for which he had been responsible. He was expensively dressed, in a gaudy, almost dandyish white suit and gloves of the flash order, with a flower out of his button-hole, and very well groomed, wearing an orderly mustache. There were brilliant studs in his shirt-bosom and some glittering jewels on his watch-guard and on two or three rings on his fingers, but to his credit he seemed to take no pains to show them. His boots were polished so voluptuously they seemed to absorb all the warmth of the sun. He was dramatic and inviting; he was, in short, magazinish.

Most of all, his mannerisms exuded an excess of civility and philanthropy— I mean by philanthropy the sort that would rescue prostitutes off the street by bringing one or two home with him. Although he had abducted me to a deserted fortress, I found myself worrying that I not appear rude in his presence. I calmly asked how he had found me in Paris.

"Among those I still count as friends in Paris are several members of the police who survey visitors from abroad quite closely. Your final letter mentioned you would be searching for Auguste Duponte— and I only supposed you might look for him here. Bonjour confirmed you were indeed in the area." He smiled at the beautiful nymph, now smoking a cigar; she had previously followed me to Café Belge the evening of Duponte's risky billiards game.

"How is it she is called Bonjour?" I asked quietly, as though to avoid her hearing. I confess that even in the midst of all this, the question distracted me. I was presently ignored, however.

I wonder if it was just the name that fascinated me. No, I do not think so. She was quite beautiful in the expressiveness of her small mouth and large eyes. She showed no particular interest either in me or in our proceedings, but this did not lessen my own fascination.

"I am quite confident we can now complete our arrangement, Brother Quentin," the Baron said, knocking me from my trance. He unfolded my letters and showed them to me.

"Arrangement?"

He rebuked me with a frown of disappointment. "Monsieur. The arrangement by which we shall together solve Edgar Poe's death!"

The forcefulness of his announcement almost made me forget why this was not possible. "There is a mistake here," I said. "I am afraid you are not, in fact, the model for Poe's tales of Dupin as I had once speculated. I have found the true one— Auguste Duponte. You did read that in my last letter?"

"Was that what it meant to say? I only thought it was a jest for you to speak of Duponte. Monsieur Duponte has begun his analysis of the beloved Poe's shocking and wrongful demise then, I suppose? He is determined to sift it to the utmost?"

"Well . . . we have entered rather deeply into secret examinations. More I cannot say." I spun around with renewed restlessness, but there was still nowhere to go. I admit that, perversely, I did not entirely want to escape from the predicament. It was thrilling to hear someone speak impassionedly of Poe's death. It had been a long time of me talking of it to Duponte, with nothing granted in return.

"I can tell, Monsieur Quentin, you have got yourself in an awkward position," Dupin said. He pressed his hands together as though in prayer, then let them curl into a double fist. "But I am the real Dupin— I am the one you have sought all along."

"What a claim!"

"Is it? I am a special constable for the English. What is that but the preserver of truth? I never lost a single case as an attorney— that record is as unbendable as iron. What is an attorney but an announcer of truth? Who is the real Dupin but truth's protector? You and I are attorneys, Monsieur Clark; the whole world of justice is our territory. If we lived at the time when Aeneas descended into hell, we would have gone underneath the earth with him just to be present at an audience of Minos, wouldn't we?"

"I suppose," I said. "Though I usually tend to mortgages and the like."

"It is time to enter the financial arrangements you suggest in your letter for my service and begin. We all will profit in this together."

"I will do nothing of the sort. I have told you: I am loyal to Auguste Duponte. It is him in whom I believe."

Bonjour directed a quick warning glance at me.

Dupin sighed and crossed his arms. "Duponte has flattened out long ago. He has the acute disease we may call *precision,* and throws a dead weight on all he does. Why, he is like the old, dying painter who can only pretend in his mind that he is the artist he once was. A puppet of his own brain."

"I suppose you are interested in this for the money so you may pay the debts," I said indignantly. "Auguste Duponte is the original 'Dupin,' Monsieur Baron, however much you dare to use him up with insults. You are fortunate he is not present here."

The Baron stepped closer to me, and his next words dripped out slowly. "And what would your Duponte do if he were here now?"

I wanted to tell him Duponte would crack his skull into two, but I could neither remember the French for it, nor convince myself it was true. Claude Dupin, mustache and jewels equally shining, grinned as he instructed Bonjour to bring me up to the carriage.

She took my arm with a grip as surprisingly hard as Hartwick's and led me ahead through the trench. In Paris, men are hardly needed at all for the operation of society. I had by this point seen women, unattended by any men, as hatters, drivers of huge carts, butchers, milkmen (or "milk-women"), intriguers, and money-changers, even waiters at the baths. I had once heard a female-rights orator in Baltimore argue that if women held the occupations of men they would be more virtuous. Here was a young woman who might be happy to disagree.

We had walked out of the hearing range of the Baron. I turned to Bonjour. "Why do you serve his wishes?"

"You were told to speak?"

I marveled to hear this from a lady who seemed a few years younger than Hattie, and with a voice as raspy as a decayed old man's and oddly mesmerizing. "I suppose I wasn't, but Bonjour— miss— mademoiselle. Mademoiselle Bonjour, you should ensure your safety from this man."

"You wish only to save your own bacon."

That would have been most wise, I suppose— but self-preservation had not been first on my mind. There had been in the gleam of her eyes a visible independence of spirit, to which I found myself instantly attached. The only blemish on the smooth skin of her face was a scar— or, properly speaking, more of a dent— that ran vertically over her lips, stretching above and below them and forming a rather enchanting cross with her smile.

"They are coming fast!" a voice shouted in French from above. Hartwick was running toward his master with an elongated spyglass in his hand.

"They've found us!" Dupin yelled. "Get to the carriage!"

Apparently, some of the Baron's less welcoming friends had come looking for him. All of my company began to run toward the carriage.

"Make haste, you ass, cut dirt!" Dupin said as he ran past me.

I saw Hartwick, standing closer to the carriage, fall at the sound of a shot, clumsily stumbling on the rocks. He had started to yell, "Dupin," but the word was lost. When he was rolled lifelessly upon his side by one of the others, it could be seen that his ear was gone, replaced by a circle of dark red.

As my eye caught the horror of this and the path to the carriage became steeper, I tripped and fell back down the side of the trench. I suppose this might have also been seen as strategic, so I could separate from my captors. In fact, it was the sight of the pistol drawn by the Baron Dupin that left my feet unbalanced. Bonjour swerved back for me.

"Leave him!" ordered Dupin. Then, to me: "Next time, perhaps, we shall meet somewhere more congenial to our mutual interests, without such flusterations! In the meantime, go and seek glory, Brother Quentin!"

Yes. I am aware it will seem fantastic to readers that these were Dupin's words even while he was presently being fired upon and his chief henchman had just now been killed and he was climbing up this ditch, but I report it only as it happened.

I raised my head to watch. All at once, I felt myself tackled and pulled down hard. My body crumpled to a heap, and I looked up to see that Bonjour had thrown herself over me. She held one of my arms down with her hand. Imagining Hattie watching me, and feeling a pang of guilt and temptation, I tried to wriggle away from under her but could not. I could not help shudder at the lightness but *immovability* of her body.

"Stay down," she said in English. "Even once I leave. Understand?"

I nodded.

She then pushed herself up and followed the Baron into their carriage without looking at me again. Their horses burst onto the path through the fortifications. After a few minutes, the trampling hoof-falls and rolling wheels of another carriage boomed along the fortifications. There followed more blasts of gunfire in the direction of the Baron's escaping carriage. I covered my head with my arms and did not stir as splinters of rock rained down from all directions.

My deliverance appeared in the form of a hired coach of German visitors who had come to see the fortifications; they kindly permitted me to ride back with them to Paris.

Of course, part of me wanted to run straight to Duponte and tell him all about what had happened. But it would be of no use. If my encounter with Claude Dupin made me realize something, it was that all had become jumbled. The true analyst would not help for any price, and a charlatan like this "Baron" was too willing to pretend to help for a little money. I would do just as well never to see Auguste Duponte again.

It turned out that the guide from Versailles had been correct about the police agents' monitoring my residence in Paris. Shortly after that episode, my supply of cash dwindled and I moved to a less expensive lodging house. Upon arriving, I found two police officers waiting very politely to record my new address.

It was only two days later that my decision to avoid Duponte changed, while I was sitting and having my boots blacked. With that distinct French politeness, the owner of the blacking shop had bowed slightly, alerting me to the fact that my boots were dusty. I had picked up a newspaper. There was a large looking-glass situated right behind the bench so the owner could see the paper as he blacked his customer's shoes. I had heard it said that a certain species of boot-blacker in Paris had over the years learned to read newsprint backward to keep away boredom. I did not believe that anyone could develop such a skill of understanding words so twisted around. Not until that day.

I hurried through the pages quickly but was interrupted by the bootblacker.

"Turn back a page, kind monsieur? Is it Claude Dupin in Paris again? He is dogged more fiercely in Paris than any animal in the forest. That is what they say."

On this word, I turned the pages back to an astounding item, a paid notice:

> Renowned attorney and solicitor Claude Dupin, having never lost a law case in his career, has been enlisted by some of the first citizens of America [*I suppose that meant me*] to solve the mystery surrounding the death of that country's most beloved and brilliant genius of many literary treats— Edgar A. Poe. Claude Dupin was the basis and namesake, furthermore, for the famous character of "Dupin" from the tales of Mr. Poe, including "Les Crimes de la Rue Morgue," a story known widely in both English and French tongues. Obligated to honor

this connection, Claude Dupin has left for the United
States and in exactly two months from this day in the
year 1851, he will have resolved the enigmatic circumstances of Poe's death completely and with all finality.
Monsieur Dupin will return to Paris, the city of his birth,
after being lavishly heralded and rewarded as a new
hero of the New World . . .

I felt a lump rise in my throat. I had to get back to Duponte immediately.

I could not leave the continent with Duponte believing I had betrayed
him by *enlisting* Claude Dupin, as he would surely think if he read that
notice. Indeed, he could not fail to connect the matter with me. Even
some of the language in the paper was my own, having been purloined by
the Baron directly from my letters. I only hoped he had not seen it. I directed my carriage driver to Duponte's lodgings and rushed through the
gates and past the concierge's chamber.

"Hold there! You!" The concierge swiped his hand at me but missed.
I took the stairs two at a time. I found Duponte's door open but nobody
inside.

The gaslight over his bed smelled as though it had just been lately
lighted, and there in the center of his bed was a newspaper. It was *La
Presse*— a different newspaper than the one I had read at the boot-
blacker's stand— but it was opened to the very same notice. Other objects, papers and articles, had been pushed to the bottom of the bed. I
imagined Duponte had sat down slowly, clearing the always-crowded
surface of his quilt with one hand and clenching the article in his
other, his eyes filling with— what would it have been to see this? Rage?
Bitterness?— as he read about the recruitment of Baron Dupin. He had
already convicted me of betrayal.

"Monsieur!" The concierge had appeared at the door.

"You! I will hear nothing from you!" I shouted, prodded by the anger
I felt at Baron Dupin. "I am leaving Paris today, but I must and *shall* find
Auguste Duponte first. You will tell me where he has gone at once, or you
shall have me to face!"

He shook his head no, and I almost flung my fist into his chin before
he explained. "He is not here," he panted. "Inside, I mean! Monsieur
Duponte has left, with his baggage."

. . .

After further questioning, I learned that the concierge had assisted Duponte only minutes before with bringing his baggage into the court-yard. This after Duponte had studied the poisonous newspaper notice of the devious Baron. The treachery Duponte surely imagined from me had driven him to a melancholy so overwhelming that he could no longer re-main in his place. I looked from the apartment's windows for any sign of him before descending.

Driving away from the boardinghouse was a carriage that I could see was loaded above with baggage. I cried out without success for the coach to return but could only throw up my hands limply as it passed into the street. What a surprise when I found no sign of my own coach and driver— whom I had ordered to wait. Stewing over this final insult, I was jarred by seeing that Duponte's coach was driving back— and that it was not Duponte's coach at all; well, he sat inside and his baggage wobbled on top, so now it was his, but it had been my driver and my carriage.

The horses stomped to a halt in front of me.

"Just wanted to turn the horses around to pull away easier, monsieur," the driver said to me, "so we'd not lose time."

He climbed down and opened the door opposite Duponte's, but first I had to see him. I walked to Duponte's side and opened his door. The an-alyst sat with a fixed gaze. Had the Baron Dupin's deceitful claims on C. Auguste Dupin's character finally affected him in a way none of my enticements or rewards could?

"Monsieur Duponte, does this mean . . . are you . . . ?"

"You'll be late," shouted the driver, "for the train to your ship, mon-sieurs. You'll lose your passage. Come in, come in!"

Duponte nodded to me. "Now it is time," he said.

10

THE CUNARD STEAMER *Humboldt* to America had seventy-eight officers and seamen aboard and a sufficient number of accommodations— narrow staterooms entered from the sides of the richly carpeted main saloon— for more than one hundred passengers. There was also a labyrinth of ancillary chambers— the library, the smoking rooms, and the sitting rooms, as well as the sheltered pens for cattle.

Duponte and I had been among the earliest passengers to arrive at this floating palace, and I brimmed with anticipation, gazing upon the ark that would carry us to the New World. Duponte remained standing in place as soon as he reached the upper deck. I froze too. I imagined he was experiencing some sudden doubt, a premonition, and would back out of our voyage.

"Monsieur Duponte?" I said attentively, hoping I could oblige him. "All right?"

"Do request, Monsieur Clark," Duponte said, taking my elbow, "that the steward inform our ship's captain there is a stowaway on board this ship. Armed."

My anxiety flitted away into utter astonishment. When I had sufficiently regained my calm, I commanded an interview with the steward in a private corner.

"Sir, there is a stowaway on board the ship," I whispered urgently, "possibly armed."

He lowered his brow at me, showing no concern. "How do you know that?"

"Whatever does that matter?"

"We checked all stowage and cabins already, sir, as always. Did you see someone on board?"

"No," I replied. "We have only just arrived!"

He nodded, persuaded that he had proven his argument.

I looked back at Duponte across the deck. I could not fail him so soon, not after all that had been required to secure him. I wanted him to feel that anything he asked was no sooner suggested than done. "Sir, what do you know of ratiocination?" I asked the steward.

"Aye. That is a new sea-beast, sir, with six hundred legs and a hunched back."

I ignored this. "It is the rare ability of knowing, by a process of reasoning not only using logic, but through the higher logic of imagination, that which is outside the mental function of most ordinary people. There is— I promise you— an armed and most villainous stowaway here. I suggest the captain be informed double-quick and that you look more carefully."

"I was going to have another look anyway," he said importantly. He walked with a deliberately slow step.

A few minutes later, the steward was calling— or, rather, *shrieking*— for his superior to come to the mail chamber. Soon the burly old captain and the steward had wrestled a struggling, shouting man from down below.

The stowaway thrust both his elbows out, breaking loose and shoving the steward flat on his back. The few passengers lolling about went immediately scurrying below in fear for their lives, or at least in fear for their jewels. Others, along with Duponte and myself, clustered together to watch the scene. There was a moment of stillness as the captain stood across from the intruder.

"Trying to steal our mail?" the captain barked out. Our steamer, like most crossing the ocean, supplemented its finances in large part by transporting mail.

The stowaway seemed for a moment a phantasm from another world, large and red in the cheeks. Perhaps the captain experienced a similar effect looking at him, as he put his hands in front of him in a soothing gesture. "Peace," said the captain.

"You shall want to know what I know!" warned the stowaway, looking beyond the captain toward the passengers, seeming to be assessing which one of us to take prisoner. We all took a step back, except for Duponte.

The captain did not jump at the man's declaration, but the foolish steward was intrigued by the bluff. "Like what?" he asked. "What could *you* know?" The stowaway lost his footing on some wet boards and the captain and steward charged again, overwhelming their victim. After a few awkward attempts and to the cheers of some passengers, they heaved him straight overboard.

The captain leaned over the side and observed the fellow, whose lost hat had left his baldness to shine in the sun. I rushed to the rails, too, and stood watching for a long while. I could not help feeling some pity for the shocked, flailing rogue. The captain, believing his own crew member responsible for the discovery, shook the steward by the hand probably more heartily than ever before.

Later that same day, after we'd pushed away to sea, the steward found me alone and said with a snarl, "How the deuce did you know about him?"

I held my tongue.

"How in the devil could someone know there was a stowaway here, just after stepping on deck? How in the devil? How did you get this *ration-sin-ation*?"

He would take his small-minded revenge by giving Duponte and me undesirable seats at the dining table. But that day I could not help but wear a peculiar grin, which reappeared whenever I saw the steward during all three weeks of our voyage to America.

-BOOK III-

BALTIMORE 1851

11

Ratiocination. NOUN. *The act of deliberate, calculated reasoning through the imagination and spirit; the intimate observation and fore-casting of the complexities in human activity, especially the frequent simplicity in that activity. Not interchangeable with mere "calculus" or "logic."*

❊   ❊   ❊

IN THE BEGINNING, I watched constantly for some error on my part that would divert the path of Auguste Duponte's ratiocination (the above being my own definition, which Webster and other publishers might use to correct their own, and which I compiled as I watched Duponte on our transatlantic journey). I wanted to assist without being an obstacle. As it happened, I had made my first mistake long before we had begun.

I was sitting across from him in my library on our third morning after arriving in Baltimore. He was settled in the most comfortable armchair. I saw the analyst in a state of complete leisure. To say "leisure" conjures an incomplete impression, since he was constantly busying himself. But his efforts were unhurried and peaceful.

Duponte read through all the newspaper articles I had collected about Poe's death. I also gave him other materials relevant to Poe— biographi-cal notices from journals and magazines, engravings, as well as my per-sonal correspondence with the author. Duponte read the papers like the governor of a state would read the news over breakfast, with that strong grip on the page that suggested mastery over it.

On this day, when he acknowledged me from across the room, it was with such a sudden movement of the head that I half expected him to pronounce his conclusion about Poe's death.

"I shall need the rest," he said.

"Yes." I hesitated. I thought I understood his reference, and its surprising error, but I did not want to appear discouraging. "Monsieur Duponte, from the vagaries of the press, it is unlikely many additional items have been published about Poe's death."

Duponte handed my memorandum book to me and then tapped the large portfolio of cuttings. "Monsieur Clark, I require not just these articles— but the *newspapers* from which they were excised. And, perhaps, the numbers of those newspapers for a week before and after each article."

"But I examined the entire newspapers whenever possible for the smallest reference to the poet in the most out-of-the-way column, even the simple mention of his name. I assure you these were all the items concerning Poe that could be found."

"Dunce!" he said, sighing.

It is impossible to convey, I suppose, without knowing him personally, but I had grown accustomed to Duponte's frequent exclamations of this kind, and they no longer seemed like insults.

Duponte went on: "The cuttings are not enough, monsieur. There is as much to reveal from what surrounds information as the information itself. Skip the columns that make the heart of the populace palpitate with excitement— read everything besides this, and much shall be learned. You have sacrificed a great portion of the intelligence in each article by divorcing it from its sheet."

To be perfectly honest, it was difficult to keep from showing restlessness at Duponte's pace. I suppose I should have predicted it. Poe had recognized the requirements of an intelligence this sophisticated. In his tales, C. Auguste Dupin undertakes meticulous reviews of newspaper reports of the respective crimes before he ventures to resolve the cases.

But here was the difference, in the line of timing, between those literary tales and our undertaking: we were not alone. In the back of my mind at all times there stood the ghostly image of my kidnapper, Dupin. (Looking at that sentence, I see I must not write "Dupin" like that, or I shall think automatically of the C. Auguste Dupin of Poe's tales. Though it costs more in ink, "Claude Dupin" or "Baron Dupin" it shall be.) Sometimes, I even thought I saw his face, in the open window of a building, in a crowd on Baltimore Street, grinning cunningly at me. Had the Baron truly come to America, or had his announcement been a hoax to confuse his creditors in Paris?

I began to collect all the newspapers Duponte had requested. The imposing *Baltimore Sun* building had been the first iron structure in Baltimore. Although some judged the five-story edifice beautiful, that was the wrong sort of term. Impressive: that's what you thought while walking through the newspaper offices, the presses and steam engines whirling below in the basement, heating your boots; the cracking of telegraph machinery raining onto the ceiling from the second floor above. You were in the middle of something powerful, something demanded by the mass of our citizens.

Visiting also the *Sun*'s competitors, the Whig papers *Patriot* and the *American,* and those known for Democratic leanings, the *Clipper* and the *Daily Argus,* I gradually furnished Duponte with everything he had asked for from Baltimore. Then I started for the athenaeum to search for more from other states and any new reports about Poe.

I had not yet sent word to Hattie or Peter of my return. Auntie Blum's prohibition on Hattie writing to me had remained for the balance of my time in Paris. Peter, in his last few letters, had said little of Hattie or anything else of interest, but had alluded to certain sensitive matters of business he needed to speak with me about. I had a strong desire to commune with both of them. But it was as though the world outside my involvement with Duponte was suspended; as though I had been caught in a universe made only from Duponte's mind and his ideas and could not return to my usual place until the task at hand had been achieved.

Though I had been abroad for only a season, I noticed every change in Baltimore acutely. The city was growing bigger by the day, so it seemed. There was the rubble, ladders, joists, and tools of construction in every direction. Warehouses five stories high had overtaken old mansions. All that was brand-new, like the dust of the construction, cast a dull pallor over the city. There was something else, I know not what to call it. An unrest. A cheerless restiveness. This is how it seemed passing through the street.

At the reading room, I situated myself at a table with my memorandum book and opened a newspaper. I scanned the columns, stopping several times to study some interesting bit of news that had transpired in my absence. Then I saw it. My heart quickened with— surprise, exhilaration, fear. I could not have said which. I switched to the next paper, then another. There was not just a chance mention in the back sheets of one paper. No. There were mentions everywhere! Each paper featured some item about the death of Poe! There were many details yet to learn in the mysterious circumstances of the late poet's death, wrote the *Clipper*. "The prominent topic of conversation in literary circles, has been the death of that melancholy man Edgar A. Poe," said a weekly dollar magazine. "He was altogether a strange and fearful being."

The articles provided almost no factual details. Instead, each page was like a newsboy who shouted *ad infinitum* of some sensational hanging without saying how it had come to be.

I rushed to the front of the room, where the ancient clerk sat. Another patron of the reading room stood across from the desk, but as he was not yet addressing the clerk, I felt free to proceed.

"What is all of this about Edgar Poe? How has this come about?" I asked.

"Mr. Clark," replied the clerk, with a look of great interest, "you have been away quite a while!"

"My good sir, not many months ago," I said, "there was hardly any concern for the death of Edgar Poe. Now it forms a topic in the columns of every paper."

The clerk appeared ready to answer when we were interrupted.

"Yes, yes!"

We both turned to the other patron, whose spot I had taken. He was a bulky man with wiry eyebrows. He blew his large nose into a handkerchief before continuing.

"I have read of it, too," he said collegially, nudging me, as though we had shared snuff from the same box.

I looked at him blankly.

"Of Poe's death!" he said. "Isn't it wonderful?"

I studied this stranger. "Wonderful?"

"Certainly," he said suspiciously, "you think Poe a genius, sir?"

"Of the greatest degree!"

"Certainly you think there is no better prose written in the world than 'The Gold-Bug'?"

"Only 'A Descent into the Maelström,'" I replied.

"Well, then, it is wonderful, is it not, that it is finally receiving the attention it deserves from the editors of the newspapers? Poe's sad sorrowful death, I mean to say." He touched his hat to the clerk before leaving the reading room.

"Now, you say . . . what is it that has come to your attention?" the clerk asked me.

"The newspapers, why . . ." My thoughts were lost in the memory of what the other man had just said. I pointed to the door. "Who was that gentleman standing here before, who has just bid us farewell?"

The clerk did not know. I excused myself and hurried to the corner of Saratoga Street, but there was no sign of him.

I was so struck by these combined phenomena— the newspapers, the strange Poe enthusiast, the restiveness that seemed to have overtaken the city— that I did not initially direct much attention to a woman, with puffed cheeks and silver hair, on a bench not too far from the athenaeum. She was reading *a book of poems by Edgar A. Poe*! Here, I should say, I was in command of a unique advantage of observation. Having purchased every volume of Poe's writings published, I could recognize the editions from great distances by small attributes of appearance, size, and engravings unique to each of them. I suppose my boast is lessened by the fact that there were not many collections. Poe did not like the few that were published. "The publishers cheat," he lamented in a letter to me. "To be controlled is to be ruined. I am resolved to be my own publisher." This would not happen, though. His own finances were in disarray, and the periodical press remained miserly in what they would pay him for his writings.

I stood over the woman's bench and watched her propping her finger to turn the dog-eared and spotted pages. For her part, she did not notice me, so rapt was she in the tale's final pages, the sublime collapse of "The Fall of the House of Usher." Before I realized it, she had closed the book with an air of deep satisfaction and scurried away as though fleeing from the crumbled ruins of the Ushers.

I decided to inquire to a nearby bookseller to see whether he had followed the new public discussion of Poe. It was one of the booksellers less likely to fill his shelves with cigar-boxes and portraits of Indians and anything else *other than books,* which had become a growing trend among these establishments since more people were buying books through subscriptions. I paused inside the front vestibule when I saw another woman, this one committing the most peculiar crime.

She was standing on one of the store's ladders used to examine the higher shelves. The crime, if it qualifies as that, was not the theft of a book, which should be noteworthy and strange enough, but the placement of a book from the folds of her shawl onto the shelf. Then she

moved to the next higher rung of the ladder and added yet another book
from her shawl to the store's selection. The sight of her was obscured to
my view by the rays coming through the large skylight, but I could see
she was wearing a fine dress and hat; she was not one of the gaudy but-
terflies to be found promenading on Baltimore Street. Her neck hinted at
golden skin, as did the sliver of arm beneath her glove. She descended
the ladder and turned down a row of bookshelves. I walked down the
next aisle in a parallel line and found her waiting at the end.

"It is impolite," she said in French, the scar-crossed lips posed in a
frown, "for a man to stare."

"Bonjour!" My former captor in the fortress of Paris, the Baron Dupin's
compatriot, stood before me. "Many apologies— you see, I seem to be
staring sometimes in a sort of haze." But this had not been one of my
staring spells. Her killing beauty rushed back to me at first sight, and I
looked elsewhere to break her hold on me. After recovering myself, I
whispered, "What in the world are you doing?"

She smiled as though it were self-evident.

I ascended a few rungs of the ladder that I had seen her climb and removed the book that she had placed on the shelf. It was an edition of
Poe's tales.

"It is opposite from my custom. Putting valuable things *into* a place."
She laughed with child-like enjoyment at the idea. When she smiled she
had the air of a little girl, particularly now, as her hair had been cut
shorter.

"Valuable? These are only valuable for readers who can appreciate Poe!"
I said. "And why place them so high up, where they are difficult to find?"

"People like to reach for something, Monsieur Quentin," she said.

"You have done this under the direction of the Baron Dupin. Where
is he?"

"He has begun the work of resolving Poe's death," Bonjour said. "And
shall end it in triumph."

My head was pounding. "He has no business with that! He has no
business here!"

"Consider it fortunate," she replied cryptically.

"I do not consider his using this serious matter for his entertainment
fortunate."

"Still, he has found an activity more useful than murdering you."

"Murdering *me*? Ha!" I tried to sound cavalier. "Why should he do that?"

"When you wrote your letters to Baron Dupin, you spoke at length of the urgent assistance needed to decipher the beloved Mr. Poe's death. 'The greatest genius known to American literary journals, who will be endlessly and forever mourned,' and so on."

This was a true rendition of my sentiments.

"Imagine the Baron's surprise, then, when we arrived here to Baltimore some weeks ago. No ladies weeping in the streets for the *post-mortem* of poor Poe. No riots demanding justice for the poet. Few people we could find knew, with particularity, who Edgar Poe was other than to say a writer of some queer and popular fantasies. Indeed, most didn't know that Monsieur Poe had gone to his long home."

"It is true," I said defiantly. "There are many, mademoiselle, who will greet genius with jealousy and indifference, and Poe's uniqueness made him an especial target for that. What about it?"

"Baron Dupin had come here to answer the demand to understand Poe's death. And here no demand at all could be found!"

I fell silent. I suppose I could not argue against the Baron's frustration, as I had experienced the same kind.

"He blamed me," I muttered.

"Well, do not imagine my master felt very forgiving toward you. In fact, finding we had traveled so far and at great expense without purpose, the Baron grew very warm very quickly."

I think I must have shown apprehension, because she smiled.

"Nothing to fear, Monsieur Quentin," she said. But her smiling, somehow, made me feel less safe. Perhaps it was the scar that divided her mouth into two. "I do not think you are in the shadow of any harm— at the moment. You have no doubt seen what has happened, since that time, to the awareness of Poe in your city."

"You mean, in the newspapers?" I began to put it together. "You have something to do with all that?"

She explained. First the Baron had placed notices in all the newspapers in the city, offering substantial rewards for "vital information" in the "mysterious and untoward death" of the poet Poe. He did not expect to actually hear from witnesses at once. Rather, the notices served their real purpose— to stir questions. The editors of the papers sensed excitement, and they followed its path. Now the people were clamoring for more and more Poe.

"We are helping to enliven the public's imagination," Bonjour said. "I believe Poe's books are met with a ready sale now."

I thought back to the woman in the park . . . the Poe enthusiast in the reading room . . . and now Bonjour planting books for more people to find.

She turned to leave, and I grabbed her. If anyone was watching us, my hand wrapped around the gloved wrist of a young woman, it would occasion a small scandal and would travel with the speed of a telegraph to Hattie Blum's aunt. In Baltimore, the cold breezes of the North met the hard etiquette of the South, and the gossip that came along with it.

It was a twofold compulsion that made me reach for her hand. First, being seized once again by her careless beauty, so strikingly relocated in Baltimore, so distinct from the normal lady's-magazine appearance of local girls. Second, she might know something of Poe's death already. Third— for I suppose the compulsion should be called threefold— I knew that where she came from in Paris, touching the hand of a lady was hardly a noticeable act, and this emboldened me. But her eyes burned at me, and at a breath I pulled my hand away.

I find it difficult to describe the sensation that passed through me upon touching, even for a moment, this lady. It was the sensation that at any moment I could be transported anywhere in the world, into anyone's life, almost that I was not restricted to my own body— it was a spiritual feeling, in a sense, feeling as light as a star in the sky.

Much to my surprise amid the bookstalls, as soon as I released her, both her hands sprung toward me and gripped me far more firmly than I had seized her. I could not pry her fingers off my hands, and we stood facing each other for a long moment.

"Sir! Remove your hand, if you please!" she burst out in an outraged, virginal voice.

Her cry prompted the Argus-eyed inquisitiveness of everyone in the store, at every table and bench. After she released me, I attempted to appear occupied by commonplace interest in the nearest books. By the time the stares dissipated, she was gone. I raced into the street and spotted her, the back of her head now covered by a striped parasol.

"Stay!" I called out, hurrying to her side. "I know you are well intentioned. You kept me safe from the shooting at the fortifications. You saved my life!"

"It seemed you wished to assist me when thinking the Baron forced my service to him. This was"— she tucked her lip under her small front teeth to consider this— "unusual."

"You must know that this is far too important a matter to cheaply excite the periodical press. No good shall come of that. Poe's genius deserves more. You must stop this now."

"Do you think you can shuffle us off from our task so easily? I have read some of your friend Poe. It seems it consists chiefly of him saying plain things in a fashion that makes them hard to understand, and commonplace things in a mysterious form which makes them seem oracular." Bonjour checked her speed momentarily to look at me. I also came to a stop. "Are you in love, Monsieur Clark?"

I had lost my concentration on Bonjour. My gaze had landed nearby, where a woman was striding along the sidewalk. She was a woman of around forty, attractive enough. My eyes followed her path down the street.

"Are you in love, monsieur?" Bonjour repeated gently, following the object of my gaze.

"That woman . . . I saw her with Neilson Poe, a cousin of Edgar's, you see, and she looks remarkably like— "

I had not meant to blurt this out.

"Yes?" Bonjour said. Her softer tone compelled me to finish the sentence.

"Remarkably like a portrait I've seen of Virginia Poe, Edgar's deceased wife." The fact was, even seeing this woman seemed to bring me closer to the life of Edgar Poe.

My view of her was soon blocked by the rest of the crowd. I then realized that Bonjour was no longer standing by my side. Looking around, I saw that she was approaching the woman— that Virginia Poe copy!— and I felt angry at myself for having revealed what I had.

"Miss!" Bonjour called. "Miss!"

The woman turned and faced Bonjour. I stood aside, not believing that the woman had seen me at the police station house, but wishing to be safe.

"Oh, I'm sorry," said Bonjour, in a convincing southern accent that she must have imitated from some of the belles she had heard around the city. She continued, "You looked so much like a lady I used to know— but I was mistaken. Perhaps it was only that lovely bonnet. . . ."

The woman gave a kind smile and started to turn her back to Bonjour.

"But she looked so much like Virginia!" Bonjour now said as though to herself.

The woman turned back. "Virginia?" she asked with curiosity.

I could see a look of enjoyment spread across Bonjour's face, knowing that she had achieved her object. "Virginia Poe," Bonjour said, adopting a somber aspect.

"I see," the other woman said quietly.

"I met her only once, but Lethean waters will never erase it from my memory," gushed Bonjour. "You are as beautiful as she was!"

The woman lowered her eyes at the compliment.

"I am Mrs. Neilson Poe," the other woman said. "Josephine. I am afraid no one shall ever be as beautiful as my darling sister was when she was still alive."

"Your sister, ma'am?"

"Sissy. Virginia Poe, I mean. She was my half-sister. She was all courage and confidence even at her weakest. Whenever I see her portrait . . . !" She stopped, unable to continue the thought.

So that was it! Neilson was married to the sister of Edgar Poe's late wife. After a few words of condolence, they walked together and Josephine Poe quietly answered Bonjour's questions about Sissy. I followed behind to listen.

"One evening while Edgar and Sissy were residing happily in Philadelphia on Coates Street, darling Sissy was singing at her beloved piano when a blood vessel ruptured. She collapsed in the middle of her song. There was an almost hourly anticipation of her being lost. Especially by Edgar. The winter of her death, they were so poverty-stricken that the only thing that could keep Sissy warm in their badly heated rooms was to be wrapped in his great-coat with a tortoise-shell cat lying on her bosom."

"What happened to her husband since?"

"Edgar? The oscillation between hope and despair for so many years had driven him insane, I believe. He needed womanly devotion. He said he would not live another year without true and tender love. People say he ran about the country looking to find a wife several times since Sissy's death, but I believe his heart still bled for Sissy. He was engaged to be married again only a few weeks before his death."

The women exchanged a few more words before Josephine departed with a graceful farewell. Bonjour turned back to me with a girlish giggle.

"It is too bad for you, that you must be against the Baron in one of his plots, Monsieur Clark. You see, we do not hide in the shadows, lingering over small details."

"Mademoiselle, please! Here, in Baltimore, in America, you do not have to retain your association with the Baron and his schemes! I would flee him at once. There are no bonds here!"

Her eyes widened with interest. "Is there not slavery?"

She was clever.

"Just so!" I said. "There are no bonds for a free Frenchwoman. You do not owe any duty to the Baron."

"I do not have duty to my husband?" she said. "This is useful to remember."

"The Baron. Your husband?"

"We have full swing over this, and beginning now there will be no letup. If I were you, Monsieur Clark, I would try not to get in our way."

❖ ❖ ❖

Wherever you travel in the world, you are sure to find the same limited number of species of lawyers, as surely as a naturalist finds his grass and weeds in every land. The first sort of lawyer views the intricacies of the rules of the law as profound and unshakable idols of worship. There is a different species of attorney, a carnivorous one to whom the first is prey, who instead treats rules as the principal barriers to success.

The Baron Claude Dupin was such a good specimen of the latter category that his skeleton might be hung in the Tuileries Cabinet of Comparative Anatomy. The legal codes were the weaponry he utilized to wage battle; they were his pistols and knives, nothing more hallowed. When he required a delay to his advantage, the Baron was known to have ended an appointment or even a trial by sneaking out an anteroom window. When such sinister methods were not sufficient, the Baron Dupin employed actual pistols and knives through his networks of rogues to secure the information or confession needed. The Baron was a lawyer, yes, but only secondarily; he was a heartfelt *impresario*, first, who worked as a lawyer. A showman on his box, a huckster of the law.

Duponte had told me one day, during our transatlantic journey, the story of Bonjour, though he had neglected to mention her marriage. In France, Duponte explained, there is a type of criminal known as the *bonjourier,* whose method entails the following: in fashionable clothing, the lady or gentleman thief will enter a house, moving past the servants as though present for an important appointment, take whatever objects they can quickly seize, and then walk right out the street door. But if a servant or other member of the household notices them between entrance and exit, they bow, say "Bonjour!" and ask for the resident of the house *next door,* having researched that name. They are, of course, assumed to merely have come in at the wrong door, and are directed away without suspicion and with as many stolen valuables as they'd managed to collect. The young woman who had stood before me in the fortifications was the best *bonjourier* in Paris and so had eventually become known to all simply as Bonjour.

Bonjour was said to have been raised in a rural village of France. Her mother, a Swiss woman, died a few months before the child had reached one year. Her French father, a hardworking baker, cared for his daughter. He spent most nights wailing, however, and the young girl soon had little patience for her father's endless grief. This, in combination with the lack of a maternal instructor, forged a young girl who was as fiercely independent as any Frenchman. Soon, the father was arrested and taken away before her eyes in the chaos of one of the country's smaller revolutions. She made her way to Paris to live on her own and survived through cleverness and physical strength. There were many assaults against her as a young thief, and one of these resulted in the prominent scar on her face.

"But how is it such a beautiful woman persists as a common thief?" I had asked Duponte one evening as we sat at the long dining table of the steamer.

Duponte raised an eyebrow at my question and seemed to consider leaving it unanswered. "She has not remained a thief, in fact, and has not been common. She has for many years been an assassin of the most efficient character. It is said that, because of her former practice, in her role as assassin it is her habit to call out 'bonjour' before sending a knife through a man's throat. However, this is mere speculation, for nobody living can confirm it."

"Yet she was womanly and courageous enough at the fortifications on my behalf," I said. "I believe poor health and environments create such lapses in character in women."

"She has been most poor then," replied Duponte.

It happened one winter that Bonjour, brought in by the Parisian police after a botched theft that left one gentleman dead in his parlor, was
threatened with execution to be made an example to the growing race of
female thieves. The Baron Dupin, at the height of his eminence, represented her with overpowering zeal. He demonstrated with skill that the
police of Paris had quite mistakenly victimized Bonjour, a delicate and
angelic creature whose physical appearance, petite girlish form, and
comeliness added not a little to the general effect for observers.

You shall not now wonder, considering this example, how the Baron
accumulated faithful rogues. When he secured their release from prison,
as he did Bonjour's, their loyalty accrued to him as a matter of honor.
You shall think this a contradiction, but all people need rules to live, and
criminals can only have a few— loyalty is one they favor. The Baron had
been married before, but the women were said to have motives ranging
from simple love to, at one time in his life, his great wealth. It remains
anyone's guess whether with the loyalty of Bonjour also came love, or
one superseded the other, or they mingled together in some heartless
combination.

BACK AT GLEN ELIZA, Duponte, when he heard all that Bonjour had told me, mused only that the Baron Dupin's tactics would complicate matters. I had of course arrived at the same conclusion, and this made me more eager to continue tracing the fruits of the Baron's campaign I had begun to witness around the city. I was now out all through the city on errands a good deal and Duponte was almost always sitting in my library. He was usually silent. I sometimes found myself unconsciously imitating his posture or an expression on his face, whether out of monotony or in an attempt to assure myself he was really there.

One day, Duponte, reviewing some newspapers, exclaimed, "Ah, yes!"

"Found something, monsieur?" I asked.

"I have only this moment remembered the thought I was having when your caller arrived yesterday, while you were out."

"Caller?"

"Oh yes, her visit was monstrously disruptive, and I have recovered my line of reasoning only *now*, if you believe it."

When Duponte would say little more on the subject, I surveyed my chambermaids. They had not thought to inform me of the caller since Duponte had been here to receive her. It was clear from their varied descriptions that the visitor was in fact Auntie Blum, who came with a male slave holding an umbrella over her head. Though my domestics differed on some of the particulars, this was the fullest narrative I could re-create of the conversation that occurred in my library.

Auntie Blum: Is not Mr. Clark here?

Auguste Duponte: Right.

AB: Right? What do you mean, "right"?

AD: You are correct. Mr. Clark is *not* here.

AB: But I did not— Who are you, then?

AD: I am Auguste Duponte.

AB: Oh? But—

AD: Mademoiselle—

AB (alarmed by the French): Madem-mois . . . ?

AD (now looking up for the first time): Madame.

AB: Madame?

AD (Duponte said something in French that, after much reflection, neither servant could recollect, and that unfortunately must be imagined).

AB (newly alarmed): You do know you are in America, sir!

AD: I have noticed that people put heels on chairs and carpets, pour eggs into glasses, and spit tobacco-juice upon windows. I know I am in America, madame.

AB: Now just— Who are you?

AD: The answer of my name has not seemed helpful to you before. Though I am quite occupied and have little desire to render myself at your service, madame, I shall attempt this in Monsieur Clark's stead. Perhaps, rather than asking who I am, it would be more enlightening for you to ask *who is Mr. Clark.*

AB: Mr. Clark! But I know Mr. Clark quite well, sir! Have known him practically from his infancy! Indeed, I have just heard of his return from Europe and wish to see him.

AD: Ah.

AB: Very well. I shall play along at this game, though you are a stranger, and *insolent.* Who is Mr. Clark, sir?

AD: Mr. Clark is my associate in this present matter.

AB: You are an attorney then?

AD: Heavens!

AB: Then what *matter* do you speak of?

AD: You do mean the present matter occupying me quite well, until you came in?

AB: Yes— Yes, but— Are you going to light that cigar, sir, indoors? While I am standing here before you just so?

AD: I suppose. Unless I cannot find a match-box; then I shall not think of it.

AB: Mr. Clark shall hear of this treatment! Mr. Clark shall—

AD: Here! Here is a match after all, madame.

I left word for Peter, spurred in part by the awful account of Auntie Blum's visit, and after several times missing each other we had a meeting arranged in his chambers. He was quite brotherly. He looked around his office once we were seated, with a sudden pang.

"Perhaps this is the wrong place to discuss— well, but, Quentin, I suppose we must talk openly." He blew a windy sigh. "In the first place, if I have ever grown warm with you, it was in the hopes that I have been helping you, and doing as your father would have wanted."

"Impudent!"

"What, Quentin?" Peter was utterly startled.

I realized Duponte's odd habits of speech had infected me. "I mean," I said quickly, "that I understand the matter perfectly, Peter."

"Well, just so. Because you were away from Baltimore, and things change, by the bye. Quentin . . ."

I leaned forward with interest.

"I must tell you, though it is not comfortable . . ."

"Peter?"

"I have begun speaking with another fellow from Washington about taking your place here," he managed to blurt out. "He is a good lawyer. He reminds me of you. Understand, Quentin, that I am simply overwhelmed with all the work."

I sat in silence and surprise— not surprise that Peter would be engaging another attorney, but surprise that, after all my yearnings to leave these chambers, this would stir something sad in me.

"This is good news, Peter," I said after a moment.

"The practice is in peril— there have been some financial hitches, and we are hard pushed. It is all knocked into a cocked hat and could crumble in the next year if something isn't done. The firm your father built for us."

"I know you will manage," I said with a slight waver in my voice that seemed to invite Peter to plead his case.

"You must realize, Quentin, that you can have your position back. Today, any hour, if you wish! We are all quite glad to hear of your return. Hattie especially— you must address that situation immediately, you know. Her aunt has practically built a fortress around her to prevent you from seeing her."

"Of course, she is merely trying to guard her welfare. Now that you mention the topic, there is a matter of Auntie Blum calling at my house. . . . I am certain I can sway her away from any bitterness, though."

Peter glared in a manner that suggested he did not agree.

Indeed, I knew that while I was so immersed in my undertaking, any attempt to reconcile with Hattie's family, even if successful, would only reverse its course once the demands for attention to the various questions of the future could not be met. I would have to wait a bit longer before repairing those relations. I adjourned my interview with Peter, promising to explain more later.

Meanwhile, I was now frequenting the athenaeum reading rooms, where the very same loquacious gentleman whom I had encountered before, the mysterious Poe enthusiast, continued his regular appearances, reading the newspapers and gushing over the inept articles appearing in print on Edgar Poe.

One morning, I took a seat on the stone steps of the athenaeum before it opened and waited for the doors to be unlatched. Once inside, I chose a chair across from the place where I knew the gentleman preferred, so I could watch him more closely. When he arrived, though, he, seemingly oblivious to my motives, found a different table. I did not want it to seem like I was following him, so I kept a distance. The next day, I loitered near the clerk's desk, to see where the other gentleman would situate himself. I claimed a nearby place. I could now observe his every movement.

He was most galling in the joyfulness he exhibited at reading about the circumstances of Poe's death.

"Ah, did you see this one now?" He turned to a woman at the neighboring table, holding up a newspaper. "They're wondering what happened to all the money he scraped together from lecturing in Richmond. If it had been on Poe's person, where is it now? That's a question. The editors of the press *are* shrewd." There he laughed as if at an infinitely witty jest.

Shrewd, he says! "Sir, how is it you laugh in such a manner?" I asked, knowing I should instead keep to myself. "Do you not think this a subject of the most serious gravity, deserving higher decorum?"

"It is most serious," he said, his unruly eyebrows straightening on command. "Serious as a judge. Yet most critical, too, that we shall be told in full what happened to him."

"And do you not take these reports with a considerable modicum of salt? Do you think every item you read proclaims the truth, as some prophet of a Gospel?"

He gave the idea of his credulity strenuous thought. "Why else would they waste fine ink on it, dear man, if it weren't true? I should not think like the Hebrews, and not believe that newer testaments are also smarter, instead chasing all false Messiahs with 'lo here, lo there!' "

In my agitation, I left the athenaeum for the remainder of the day. I suspected that the pest's desire to gawk would expire quickly, and was relieved when there came days he failed to appear; but then he would be resurrected the following day. Sometimes, given some reminder to a certain poem by Poe, he would rise and spontaneously recite verses to the room. For instance, one afternoon a church bell tolled outside for a funeral. He jumped up with Poe's words on his lips:

> Oh, the bells, bells, bells!
> What a tale their terror tells
> Of Despair!

He would usually sit among the papers, interrupting himself only to blow his nose ferociously into his handkerchief, or one he borrowed from an unlucky patron. I became excessively friendly with strangers I happened to meet at the reading room, based only on their virtue of not being that sneezing, supercilious man.

I complained to the clerk, pacing in front of his table. "Why should he be so concerned with articles about Poe?" I asked.

"Who, Mr. Clark?"

I blinked at the kind old clerk. "Who? Why that man who comes in nearly every day— "

"Ah, I thought you were speaking of the man who had given me those articles about Edgar Poe some time ago," he replied, "which I ordered delivered to you."

I brought my pacing to a stop as I thought of the package of cuttings the clerk had sent me before I left for Paris— a selection that included the first mention I had seen of a real Dupin. "I had naturally assumed you had collected those yourself."

"No, Mr. Clark."

"But who was it that gave them to you?"

"It must have been some two years ago now," he meditated. "Which pigeon-hole of my brain did that go into?" he laughed.

"Please try to recall. I should be most interested." The clerk agreed that he would tell me if he was able to remember. Someone, I presumed, who cared about Poe *before* the morbid sensation and vulgar curiosity that had been caused by the Baron's manipulation. Before men like this enthusiast who was now forever stationed across the room from me.

Duponte advised me to ignore the man. Now that I had met Bonjour at the bookseller's, he said, the Baron Dupin would have many eyes looking for me— just as he had in Paris— to determine the nature of our activity. I must pretend he was not even there, as though he did not exist.

"Oh, look here. We shall hear more soon." That was the shaggy-haired man's commentary one morning at the athenaeum.

I tried exceedingly hard to keep away before finding myself replying from the next table over. "Sir? How do you mean we shall hear soon?"

He squinted as though never having seen me before. "Ah, right here, dear man," he said, finding his spot on the page. "There. They say there are whispers in the very first circles of society that the 'real Dupin' *has come to Baltimore* and will sort out what it was happened to Poe. Do you see?"

I looked over the paper and found the notice.

"The editor heard of it first-hand. C. Auguste *Dupin* was . . ." the man went on, then paused to blow his nose. "C. A. *Dupin* was a most winning genius in some of Poe's tales, don't you know? He solves some rather knotty puzzles. He's the real china, and no mistake."

I wanted to report all this to Duponte, primarily to give voice to my vexation, but did not find him in his accustomed place in my library that evening. The newspapers were scattered over the desk and table as usual, indicating that he had been at his labors earlier.

"Monsieur Duponte?" My voice traveled upon Glen Eliza's long halls and up the stairwells in an aimless echo. I questioned my domestics, but none had seen him since earlier that day. An ominous fear seized me. I shouted loudly enough to be heard by neighboring houses. Duponte probably had come to feel confined by his reading for so long. He might still be near my house.

But I found no traces of the analyst on the property or in the valley below the house. Soon I walked to the street and hired a carriage.

"I am looking for a friend, driver— let us ride around, with all steam on." Given that Duponte had not left the grounds of Glen Eliza since our arrival, I'd begun to suspect he'd happened on something exciting to investigate.

We passed by the avenues around the Washington Monument, through the Lexington Market, through the crowded wharf-side streets watched over by the clipper ships. The affable coachman tried several times to start a conversation, once along the stretch of road as we drove past the Washington College Hospital.

"Do y'know, your honor," he shouted back to me, "that is where Edgar Poe died?"

"Stop the carriage!" I cried.

He did, happy to win my attention. I stepped up to the driver's box.

"What is it you said before about that place, driver?"

"I was just pointing out the sights to you. Ain't you a stranger here? Can whip you up to a nice culinary establishment in no time, if you wish, rather than riding in circles, your honor."

"Who told you about Poe? You read it in the newspapers?"

"It was a fellow who rode in my coach who was telling me about it."

"What did he say?"

"That Poe was the greatest damned poet in America. Yet he heard tell Poe been left to die on the dirty floor of a rum-hole by some rough circumstance. He said he read of it all in the newspapers. A sociable man, he was— I mean he who rode in my carriage."

The driver could not call to mind what this man looked like, although he was clearly nostalgic for what an easy conversationalist he had been, compared to his present passenger.

"Not three days ago I had him in my coach. Do y'know, he did sneeze something awful."

"Sneeze?" I asked.

"Yes, borrowed my handkerchief and used it up something *awful.*"

I watched the afternoon sink into twilight, knowing that with sunset I would lose any hope of spotting Duponte. Baltimore's street lighting was among the poorest of any city, and sometimes walking home after dark was difficult even for the native citizen. I had concluded that the wisest course would be to return and wait for him at Glen Eliza.

Swine now filled the street. Though there had been increasing calls for public carts to be established to remove garbage and refuse from the streets, these ravenous creatures were still the primary method, and at this hour they filled the air with contented squeals as they devoured whatever offal they could find.

Soon after I had instructed the driver to bring me back home, I saw through the carriage window a glimpse of Duponte walking at his customarily measured pace. I paid my coachman and bolted out, as though the Frenchman might dissolve into the air.

"Monsieur Duponte, where are you going?"

"I am observing the spirit of the city, Monsieur Clark," Duponte told me, as though the fact were obvious.

"But monsieur, I cannot understand why you left Glen Eliza on your own— surely I could be your best guide to the city." I began, by way of demonstration, to describe the new gasworks that could be seen in the distance, but he raised his hand to silence me.

"Regarding certain facts," he said, "I shall readily welcome your trained knowledge. But do consider, Monsieur Clark, that you know Baltimore as a native. Edgar Poe lived here for a time, but many years ago— fifteen, if I am not very far mistaken. Poe, in his last days, would have come here as a visitor, seeing the city and its people as a visitor and stranger does. I have already stopped into some stores of special interest and a wide variety of markets, knowing only what strangers would from signs and the behaviors of the native people."

I supposed he had a reasonable argument. As we walked for the next hour, progressing far eastward, I explained what I had found in the newspaper at the reading rooms, and what I had heard from the coachman. "Monsieur," I asked, "should we not do something? Baron Dupin has placed notices offering money for informants to provide information regarding Poe's death. Surely we must counter him before it is too late."

Before my companion could respond, both of our attentions were caught by a figure stepping down onto the sidewalk across from us. I narrowed my eyes— a lamp furnished a glare so dim that it almost made it harder to see than if there were no lights at all.

"Monsieur," I whispered, "why, I should not believe it aright, but that is him; that is the fellow who has been planted in a chair at the reading room nearly every day! Across the way from us!"

Duponte followed my gaze.

"That is the man whom I've met at the reading room!"

Just then I could see the dark gaze of Bonjour. Her hands were hidden in her shawl, and she was trailing menacingly behind the unsuspecting man. I thought of the stories of ruthlessness Duponte had enumerated to me about this woman. I thrilled at the sight of her, and trembled for the man walking in front of her.

The Poe enthusiast had turned suddenly and was approaching our position.

Duponte nodded at him. "Dupin," he said, touching his hat.

The man replied loudly with a blowing of his nose; this time the bulbous front of his nose came off in the handkerchief. Then the Baron Claude Dupin removed his false eyebrows. His charming English-French accent reappeared. "Baron," he said, correcting my companion. "Baron Dupin, if you please, Monsieur Duponte."

"Baron? Ah, yes, so it is. Perhaps a bit formal for Americans though," said Duponte.

"Not so." The Baron showed his brilliant smile. "Everybody loves a baron."

Bonjour joined her master in the circle of light. The Baron spoke some orders to her, and she disappeared from view.

My shock at the true identity of the Poe enthusiast was instantly surpassed by a second realization. "You and Baron Dupin have met before?" I asked Duponte.

"Many years past, Monsieur Clark, in Paris," the Baron said with a quaint smile, as he shook his wig and lifted it off with his hat. "Under much less promising circumstances. I hope your voyage from Paris, gentlemen, was half as pleasant as our own. Nobody bothered you on the seaworthy *Humboldt,* I hope?"

"How did you know which . . ." I stood aghast. "The stowaway! You had us followed by that bald-headed rogue, monsieur? He was in your pay?"

The Baron shrugged playfully. His long black hair, which was slightly wet and waxy looking, fell into curls. "What rogue? I merely stay informed of the lists of passengers arriving to port. I do read newspapers, as you know especially well, Monsieur Clark."

The Baron removed the shaggy, stuffed coat he had worn, which with the now liberated nose, wig, and eyebrows had completed his crude costume. I felt disgusted that I could have been fooled by the disguise.

Yet, I am not merely defending myself by adding that there was far more to it— there was a sort of metamorphosis difficult to impress upon someone who has never met Claude Dupin. The Baron possessed an uncanny ability to modify his voice and gait and even, it seemed, the shape and appearance of his head to a degree that would have embarrassed the most respected phrenologist; and through complex positioning of the jaw, lips, and neck muscles, he was able to obscure himself better than with a mask. Each face seemed made of steel, with the soul of a hundred human beings waiting beneath. His voice was flexible, too, in unnatural ways; it seemed to change completely depending on what he was saying. As much as Duponte could control what he observed of others, the Baron Dupin seemed capable of controlling others' observation of him.

"I wish to know all other deceptions you have enacted in this matter, monsieur!" I demanded, trying to conceal a rush of mortification.

"When I take up the case of a downtrodden defendant on behalf of the suffering class, I make the world care. That defendant's bad luck is the world's bad luck; his fate, its fate. This is why I, the Baron Dupin, have never lost a case. Not one case of the lowliest man or woman. The louder we shout in advocating justice, the more insistent the people will be for it to arrive.

"The primary method," he continued, "is not to tell the public what should concern them, but to make it seem you are answering the concerns already burning in their breasts. I have done that for Poe now, too. The editors of the newspapers have begun to seek more on Poe, as you have seen. The booksellers find a need for new editions, and Poe shall one day be on every shelf in the land, in every family library, read by the old to the young and kept by the young next to their Bibles. I have walked the street . . . or, sometimes, *I* walk the street." He held the false nose to his face and, with stunning alacrity, was now talking in a counterfeit Americanized voice. "And whisper about Poe's death in restaurants, churches, markets, hackney cabs"— he paused— "and athenaeum reading rooms . . . Now the suffering classes all believe, they all doubt, and in city and country they shall all be clamoring for the truth. Who shall give it to them?"

"You wish only to stir up a spectacle for your own gain. You have no concern for finding the truth, Monsieur Baron; you've come only to try your fortune in Baltimore!" I replied.

He mocked being hurt— but mocked it, I should add, with a most sincere and guilt-provoking face. "Truth is my *only* concern. But— truth must be hauled and carted from people's heads. You have a quixotic sense of the honorable, Brother Quentin, I admire that. But truth does not exist, my misguided friend, *until you find it*. It does not thunder down from the benevolent gods, as some people believe." Here he put his arm on Duponte's shoulder and looked askew at my companion. "Tell me, Duponte, where have you been these years?"

"Waiting," Duponte answered evenly.

"I suppose that we have all been, and grown tired of it," said the Baron. "But it is too late for your assistance here, Monsieur Duponte." He paused. "As usual."

"I think I should like to stay, nonetheless," said Duponte calmly, "if there are not presently objections."

The Baron frowned patronizingly, but apparently could not help being flattered by the deference. "I must suggest you stay away from this matter and keep your handsome American pet on a leash— for he seems to have all the loyalty of a versatile monkey. I have already begun to gather the true facts of what befell Poe. Hear me now, Duponte, and you will remain safe. I must admit, my dear wife will slice the neck of any who try to inhibit me— isn't this love, though? Do not speak with any of the parties with information on the subject."

"What are you driving at?" I exclaimed, feeling my face redden, perhaps in defiance at his demand or perhaps in embarrassment at being called a pet. "How do you dare to talk to Auguste Duponte in this manner? Do you not know we have more mettle than that?"

Duponte's reply to the Baron, however, shook my nerves more than the threat itself.

"I'll exceed your wishes," said Duponte. "We shall not speak with any witnesses."

The Baron was insufferably pleased with his victory. "I see you do finally understand what is best, Duponte. This will be the greatest literary question of our day— and it will be my role to be its judge. I have begun a try at my memoirs. It shall be titled *Memories of Baron Claude Dupin, the upholder of justice for Edgar A. Poe and the true life model for the personage of C. Auguste Dupin of the Rue Morgue Murders.* Being a literary appreciator, I should be interested in whether that seems fitting— Brother Quentin?"

"It is '*The Murders in the Rue Morgue*,'" I corrected him. "And here before you, Auguste Duponte, is the true source for Poe's hero!"

The Baron laughed. There was a hackney carriage now waiting for him, and a young black servant held the door for the Baron as though he were an actual royal personage. The Baron ran a finger across the door of the carriage and the spirals along its woodwork.

"A fine coach. The comforts of your city, Brother Quentin, are hardly to be surpassed, as is the case in all the wickedest cities in the world." As he said this, his hand shifted to grasp that of Bonjour, who was already sitting comfortably in the coach.

The Baron turned back to us. "Let us not be filled with so much friction. Let us at least be civil. Have a ride somewhere, rather than stumbling through the dark. I would take the reins myself, but since my London years I cannot remember to stay to the right side of the road. You see, we are not villains; you need not nullify fellowship with us. Come aboard."

"How about," began Duponte suddenly, in the tone of a revelation, drawing the Baron's full attention. "How about *Duke*? Think of it: if they love a baron, they should love a duke to a correspondingly greater degree. 'Duke Dupin' has a certain glorious ring to it in its double sound, doesn't it?"

The Baron's expression hardened again before he slammed the door.

For several minutes after their carriage rolled away, I stood bewildered. Duponte gazed with downcast eyes in the direction we had first seen the Baron approaching us.

"He was angry we did not go. Do you think he planned to take us somewhere to do us harm?" I asked.

Duponte crossed the street and studied an old building with a rudely constructed, plain brick façade. As he did, I realized that we were on the same block of Lombard Street as Ryan's hotel and tavern, where Poe was discovered and brought to the hospital. Muted sounds of nighttime gatherings could be heard from that building. Duponte now stood across from Ryan's. I joined him there.

"Perhaps the Baron was angry not because he wanted to take us somewhere, but because his aim was to take us away from somewhere," he said. "Is this the building where the Baron and the young lady came from?"

It was, but I had no answer when Duponte inquired about the ownership and character of that address. After having offered my expert services as guide to Baltimore! I explained that the building adjoined an engine house for one of the city's fire engine companies, the Vigilant Fire Company, and said perhaps it was part of the company.

The street door of the place from which the Baron and Bonjour had emerged was stiff but unlocked. It opened onto a dark corridor that slanted down to another door. A heavy-set man, perhaps one of the firemen from the adjoining company, opened the door from the other side.

From the long stairwell behind him came down fleeting shouts of joy. Or of terror, it was hard to decide which.

The doorkeeper's sheer width was impenetrable. He stared menacingly. I thought to remain quiet and still. Only when he motioned with his hand did it seem necessary to move closer.

"Pass-word," he said.

I looked anxiously at Duponte, who was now peering down at the floor.

"Pass-word to go upstairs," the doorkeeper continued in an undertone that was meant to frighten— and did.

Duponte had entered a sort of trance, letting his eyes glide over the floor, around the walls, up the stairs, and to the doorkeeper himself. What a moment to lose attention! Meanwhile, from the doorkeeper's throat there could be heard a canine grumble as though at the slightest movement from us he would strike out.

With an explosive thrust, the doorkeeper grabbed my wrist.

"I'll ask you jack-dandies for the last time, 'cause I ain't joking. *The pass-word!*" It felt like the bone would snap if I tried to move.

"Release the young man, good sir," said Duponte quietly, looking up, "and I shall provide you with your pass-word."

The doorkeeper blinked dryly a few times at Duponte, then cranked open his grip. I pulled my arm to safety. The man said to Duponte, as though he had never pronounced the words before, and would certainly not pronounce them again without murdering someone, "Pass-word." The doorkeeper and I both stared at my companion doubtfully.

Duponte squared his body to his confronter and spoke two words. *"Rosy God."*

13

EVEN WITH MY unshakable faith in Duponte's analytic talents; even with the breathless tales I had heard of his achievements from newspapers, *commissionnaires,* and policemen in Paris; even remembering what I had witnessed in the Parisian gardens and in the revelation of the stowaway on the steamship; even remembering that Poe himself had pointed in his direction through his tales as a genius separate from all others; even with all this, still I could not believe what happened in the damp corridor of this building. The doorkeeper glared, stepped aside, then motioned us forward to the threshold behind him. . . .

The signal that had admitted us— as in some nursery tale of magic— this "Rosy God," I had heard occasionally on the street as a low phrase for red wine. What extraordinary cipher could have been seen in the floors, in the walls, in the stairs, in the doorkeeper's countenance or dress, that had led Duponte to decipher the call of entrance— a password that might change with the season or every hour— into this private and well-guarded den?

"How did you," I said, stopping midway on the creaking stairs. "Monsieur, the pass-word— "

"Aside! Aside!" A man lurching over the stairs from above squeezed past us. Duponte accelerated our climb. The raucous shouts from above became clearer.

The upper floor was a small room filled with smoke and noise. Firemen and tottering rowdies sat at gaming tables and called for more drinks from thinly clad bargirls, dresses only barely covering the milky white of their necks. One rogue sprawled out flat on a bed of sharp oyster shells, while one of his comrades kicked him over to the left for a better place to stand for a billiards game.

Duponte found a small, broken table more or less right at the center, where we were conspicuous. Heated stares followed us into our rickety chairs. Duponte sat and nodded to a waitress as though entering a respectable café on the sidewalks of Paris.

"Monsieur," I whispered, taking a seat, "you must tell me directly— how is it you knew the pass-word to admit us?"

"The explanation is rather simple. I did not give the pass-word."

"My dear Duponte! It was like an 'open sesame'! If this were two centuries earlier, you would have burned as a witch. I cannot stand to continue without being enlightened as to this point!"

Duponte rubbed one of his eyes as though just waking up. "Monsieur Clark. Why have we come here to this building?" he asked.

I did not mind playing the student if it would provide answers. "To see if Baron Dupin had also come in here, and if so what he was looking for tonight before we happened upon him."

"You are right— all right. Now, if you were the proprietor of a secret or private association, would you be most interested in talking with a visitor who gave the correct pass-word, as was given by every simpleton and sot you see in this rum-hole"— this he said without lowering his voice, causing some heads to swivel— "or talking with that one peculiar person who arrives out of place and, quite brashly, provides an absolutely incorrect pass-word?"

I paused. "I suppose the latter," I admitted. "Do you mean to say that you invented a phrase, knowing plainly it was wrong; and that *because* it was wrong we would be as readily admitted?"

"Exactly. 'Rosy God' was as good as another. We could have chosen almost any word, as long as our demeanor was equally interested. They would know we were not part of their usual community, and yet be aware that we seriously desired entrance. Now, these suppositions accepted, if our intent was thought to be possibly aggressive, even violent, as they must initially consider, they would rather us inside here, surrounded by their rather large-sized allies and whatever weapons are kept here, than downstairs, where, they might imagine, our own friends could be hiding outside the street door. Would you not think in the same way? Of course, we seek no violent confrontation. Our time here will be brief, and we need no more than a few moments to begin to understand the Baron's interest."

"But how shall you be led to the proprietor here?"

"He shall approach us, if I am right," Duponte answered.

After a few minutes, a paternal man with a white beard stood before us. The menacing doorkeeper lumbered to our other side, closing us in. We rose from the table. The first man, in tones harsher than seemed possible from his looks, introduced himself only as the president of the Whigs of the Fourth Ward and asked why we were there.

"Only to aid you, sir." Duponte bowed. "I believe there was a gentleman trying to enter here in the last hour, probably offering money to your doorkeeper for information."

The proprietor turned to his doorkeeper. "Is it true, Tindley?"

"He waved some hard cash, Mr. George." The doorkeeper nodded sheepishly. "I turned the blockhead away, sir."

"What was it he was asking?" Duponte inquired. Though my companion had no authority here, the doorkeeper seemed to forget that and answered.

"He was all agog to know if we had been interfering in the elections in October of two years ago, laying pipe with voters and such. I told him we were a private Whig club and he would do well to give the pass-word or lope."

"Did you take his money?" asked his chief sternly.

"Course not! I was on the sharp, Mr. George!"

Mr. George glanced peevishly at the doorkeeper at the use of his name. "What do you two have to do with this? Are you sent by the Democrats?"

I could see Duponte was satisfied with what had been so readily revealed: what sort of club this was, what the Baron had wanted, and the name of the leader of this society. Now Duponte's face lit up with a new idea.

"I live far from America, and could not tell a Whig from a Democrat. We have come merely to proffer a friendly caution," said Duponte reassuringly. "That gentleman who called earlier tonight will not be satisfied with your doorkeeper's answer. I think I can put you in the way of detecting the villain of this rascality. He means to quarrel with you over the moral principles of your club."

"That so?" the proprietor said, contemplating this. "Well, thank you kindly for your concern. Now you two cap your luck before there are any more quarrels here."

"Your servant, Mr. George," Duponte said with a bow.

14

THE NEXT DAY, I pressed Duponte on why he had so easily agreed to the Baron Dupin's demand that he refrain from talking to witnesses. It would now be a race to gather information, and we could afford no encumbrance. I was anxious to know Duponte's plans to combat the Baron.

"You intend to deceive him, I suppose? You will, of course, speak to persons who know something of Poe's last visit?"

"I shall remain quite faithful to my pledge. No, I will not interview his witnesses."

"Why? Baron Dupin has done nothing to merit your pledge. He has certainly done nothing to claim any witnesses as *his* alone. How shall we possibly understand what happened to Poe if we cannot speak to those who saw him personally?"

"They will be useless."

"But would their memories not be fresh from the time of Poe's death, which was but two years ago?"

"Their memories, monsieur, hardly exist at present, but are subsumed by the Baron's tales. The Baron has infected the newspapers and the whispers of Baltimore with his sophistry and craft. All actual witnesses will have become tainted, if they are not already, by the time we would be able to locate them."

"Do you believe they would lie?"

"Not purposefully. Their genuine memories of those events, and the stories they can tell from them, will irrevocably reshape themselves in the image of the Baron's. They are as much his witnesses now as though he has recruited them into a trial and paid them for testimony. No, we cannot gain very much beyond the most basic facts provided by those witnesses, and I suspect we will gather that information through the natural course of events."

You'd probably guess that Duponte was a formal sort of person. You are right and wrong. He did not subscribe to rules of manners and meaningless pleasantries. He smoked cigars inside the house, regardless of who was in the room. He was inclined to ignore you if he had nothing to say, and answer with a single word when he felt it was sufficient. He was in a way a *fast friend*, for he was your companion without any of the usual rituals or demands of friendship. However, he always bowed and sat with absolutely correct posture (though upon standing there was a noticeable slant of the shoulders). And in his labors he was most strict and serious. In fact, it made you quite uneasy to interrupt him when he was at all occupied. It could be the least important task imaginable, it could be stirring oatmeal, but it would seem leagues more critical than anything you might have to say to break his concentration were the house burning down around his ears.

Yet he grew attached to some of the strangest frivolities. When he was out on the city streets, a distinguished gentleman with a fancy cravat fastened in voluminous folds exclaimed aloud that Duponte was the queerest specimen of man he had ever seen. Duponte, taking no offense, invited the man, who was a painter of some renown here in Baltimore, to share a table with us at a nearby restaurant.

"And tell me your story, dear sir," said the man.

"I would gladly, monsieur," replied Duponte apologetically, "but then there is the likely danger that I would have to hear yours."

"Fascinating!" said the man, unruffled.

The man expressed his eagerness to paint Duponte. It was soon arranged that he would call at Glen Eliza to begin a Duponte portrait. This seemed to me quite absurd considering our other occupations, but I did not object since Duponte was fervent about it.

Rather than coming to find me in the house when he had something to say, Duponte would often send one of the servants to me with a note. Glen Eliza was large and rambling but not so terribly mammoth as to require a messenger through its corridors! I did not know what to think when a servant first handed me the note, whether it was done out of the height of sloth or an excess of concentration.

The times when we ventured out of the house and into public establishments, Duponte refused to be waited on by slaves without paying them some small amount. I had seen instances of this over the years when visitors from Europe came to Baltimore, though during extended stays custom would soon wear down their finer sensibilities and the habit would gradually cease. Duponte's action, however, was not out of any sentimentality, I believe, nor a point of principle, for he had said that more people are slaves than realized it and some far more enslaved than the blacks of our South; rather than sentimental reasons, Duponte did this, he said, because service without payment would never be as valuable to either party. Many of the slaves would be extremely grateful, others timid, and some strangely hostile to Duponte's subsidies.

At Glen Eliza, we had difficulties with the domestics I had hired upon my return from Paris. No doubt, our peculiar practice of sending letters from the parlor to the library made extra work for them, though this was not the only source for discontent. Many of my servants immediately rebelled against Duponte. One colored girl, in particular, a free Negress named Daphne, occasionally refused to wait on him. When I asked Daphne for the reason, she said that she thought the houseguest most cruel. Had he ever abused her? Scolded her for a mistake, perhaps? No. He had hardly addressed her at all, and when he did he was very polite. Something was not right, she said, nonetheless. "He is cruel. I can see it."

In between household duties, I called on Hattie's house more than once without success. Peter's pessimistic remarks about rectifying that situation had rendered me quite anxious. Her mother, who had always been of delicate health and in her bed when not away recuperating in the country or at a spring, had been further debilitated over the summer. After a stay by the seaside, she was now largely confined, which meant more duties for Hattie. It also gave Auntie Blum fuller swing over the household. Each time I called, a servant would inform me that neither Miss Hattie nor Auntie Blum was present. Finally, I was able to speak with Hattie one day as she was ascending a carriage outside her house.

"Dear Hattie, have you not received my notes?"

Hattie glanced around and spoke stealthily, leading me away from the gates. "You must not be here, Quentin. Things are quite different here, now that Mother has been worse. I am needed by my sisters, my aunt."

"I understand," I said, fearing that my endeavors had only added to the strain that had fallen on poor Hattie's shoulders. "Of our plans . . . I need only a bit more time . . ."

She shook her head, silencing me. "Things are different," she repeated. "We cannot speak about it now, but we will. I will find you when I can, dear Quentin— I promise. Do not speak to my aunt. Wait for me to find you."

Noises came from the house. Hattie directed me to return to the street and make a hasty exit. I did so. I could hear Auntie Blum (and could almost hear the wide bird feathers I pictured in her hat ruffling, too) ask in her big tones, "Who was that, dear girl?" I kept my back to them and quickened my stride, having the distinct feeling that if I turned to look back, the older woman inside the carriage might direct her driver to flatten me.

At Glen Eliza, the portraitist, Von Dantker, sat across from Duponte with his array of canvas and brushes spread on a table. Duponte remained giddy about the prospect of this artistic creation. The hotly temperamental Von Dantker sternly admonished Duponte to remain still, and so only the analyst's mouth moved when we conversed. When I commented that this was not a very polite manner of holding a conversation, Duponte claimed he was all attention and that he wished to see if he could divide his mind into compartments of concentration. At times it was like speaking to a living portrait.

"What would you say truth is for the Baron, Monsieur Clark?" Duponte asked pointedly one evening.

"How do you mean?" I asked.

"You asked him whether he seeks the truth. Surely truth is not the same for everyone, as most people think they have it, or desire to have it, and yet there are still wars, and there are professors who daily overthrow each other's hypotheses. So what is it for him, for our friend the Baron?"

I considered this. "He is a lawyer. I suppose in law, truth is a practical matter, thus one finds the practice of indiscriminate advocacy on either side in which one is retained."

"Agreed. If Jesus Christ had kept a lawyer by his side, Pontius Pilate might have been swayed that his judgment could be reversed for defect of form and so settled on a lighter sentence, and the restoration of the human race would have been interrupted. Very well. Then if it is in the language of the law that Baron Dupin speaks, truth is not that which is likely to have happened, but that for which he can present *proof* as likely having happened. These are not the same. In fact they are hardly related and should never be introduced to one another."

"How should we know if the Baron is inventing his proof in relation to Poe's death?"

"He might try to manufacture it, indeed, but likely with some small basis in reality. If he intends to publish a popular account of his dealings on the matter of Poe's death, as suggested, and intends to gain by lecturing on the subject, he cannot afford to be so easily discredited by using lies out of whole cloth, Monsieur Clark. After all, we saw from the Parisian newspapers that he wished his creditors to know his plans to return with enough financial resources to free himself from their attention. He is relying on this to protect him from their plots against him. He shall require facts— even if he compels some portion of them into existence."

Duponte continued to remain on the grounds of Glen Eliza most of the time, often engaged in disagreements with Von Dantker over whether he remained sufficiently still. Duponte displayed for the artist the strangest sort of half smile, with points sharp as knives carved out at the corners of the mouth.

Sometimes I excused myself from the house on an errand; these excursions were most of all sacrificial offerings to my nerves. Earlier that year, the post office had begun delivering the mail, for an extra fee of two cents, and so I had no need to call at its offices. I described the operation of our postal services to Duponte and for a few moments he seemed acutely interested in the topic, before quickly settling back into his air of distraction. I always looked first at the mail for something unexpected: perhaps, even, a last letter written to me by Poe, if it had been misplaced or lost, and now recovered. Duponte did not receive any letters.

But one morning of note, as I started out, a messenger delivered a trunk. It had the same shape and color as one of the trunks Duponte had brought from Paris. This surprised me, for I had believed Duponte's baggage all at my house. But he seemed to expect the object's arrival and waved his acceptance to me.

I explored the newspapers myself each morning before adding them to Duponte's collection. Despite all the sudden attention to Poe's death, there was nothing like any real scrutiny in the newspapers, only rumors and anecdotes. In one, there was a new explanation about the loose-fitting and ragged clothes in which Poe had been discovered.

"This newspaper says that it has been suggested to the editor— by Baron Dupin, I have no doubt— that Poe's clothing, which were not his own, had constituted some sort of a *disguise!*"

"Of course, monsieur," said Duponte, using his eyeglass but hardly reading the article.

I was startled. "You have already thought that?"

"No."

"Then how is it you respond to me by saying, 'Of course'?"

"I mean to say, 'Of course *the paper is quite mistaken.*'"

"But how do you know that?" I asked.

"Newspapers are almost always quite mistaken about everything," he said. "If you should find one of the tenets of your religion in type on the sheet, it is likely time to reconsider your form of God-worship."

"But, monsieur! You have spent the better part of every day reading the newspapers at my library table! Why waste all that time?"

"You must notice their errors, Monsieur Clark, in order to advance to the truth."

I stared at him until he continued.

He arched his eyebrows in a particularly French fashion. "A demonstration. Take this matter of Monsieur Poe's garments that your paper mentions. The Richmond *Observer* has lately written that Poe had, some days before his arrival in Baltimore, inadvertently switched his own walking stick with the Malacca cane of a friend in Richmond, one Dr. John Carter. In the same paper we read— in a burlesque error somewhat different from the equally erroneous *disguise* camp— that Poe's clothes were stolen and had been replaced in a robbery during his time in Baltimore. To place the garments in the central position of importance, because they are easily visible to those who found Poe, is to subdue reason to fancy."

"How do you know, without further information, that the clothes were not stolen in this way?"

"Have you ever heard of a thief stealing one's clothes— rare enough— and then replacing the clothes of a victim with other dress? An idea only someone who is not a thief could devise. The editors have merely taken the most common scenario against a visitor, a robbery, and altered it to match the end results without regard to likelihood. At all events, the special quality of the borrowed cane alone tells us it is most unlikely."

In the newspaper article to which Duponte had referred, the *Observer* reported that Poe had visited Dr. Carter and, after playing with the latter's new Malacca cane, took it with him by accident. Carter also speaks of the fact that Poe left an 1819 volume of Thomas Moore's *Melodies* in his office. "But this says nothing more in detail about the cane than that it is 'Malacca.' How, from that, do you determine that it has any special quality?"

Duponte had already moved on to a new topic. "Would you," Duponte said, "bring me the trunk that arrived just this morning?"

I was perplexed, and a bit irritated, that this request would interrupt our discourse, particularly since I had already stored the trunk in Duponte's chambers. I went upstairs and then wheeled the trunk from there down into the library where we sat. Duponte instructed me to open the lid. I did. My eyes widened at what I saw.

I bent down and reached in with reverence. It contained one object lying at the bottom of the trunk. "Is this . . . ?"

"Poe's cane. Yes."

I picked it up cautiously in both hands and said, with wholly renewed wonder at my guest, "Duponte, how in the world— ? How has Poe's cane come to appear in your trunk?!"

Duponte explained. "Not the actual one carried by Poe at the time of his death, but the very same kind, we can be sure. That the cane Poe borrowed was identified as 'Malacca,' as you have just read, revealed quite more than its wood. I guessed that a finite number of canes were sold in America from that specific palm, which grows on the coasts of the Malay Peninsula, out of the beaten track. On my walk the other day, you will remember I said I stopped at some stores. I found from speaking with sellers of walking sticks that my guess was correct: there were but four or five chief selections of canes available made from Malacca in Baltimore, and likely in Richmond, as well. I purchased one of each. Then I emptied one of my trunks and sent the canes with a messenger to the Washington College Hospital, where Poe died, along with a note to Dr. Moran, the physician who attended to Poe. It explained that a shipment to Richmond had been mixed up with other canes, and kindly requested him to identify the one cane that had been held by Poe and return it here."

"But how did you know Dr. Moran would have sent such a shipment to Carter?"

"Oh, I did not suppose he had, which is why he would not have found my request odd. More likely, Dr. Moran sent all the effects to one of Poe's family members— possibly your acquaintance Neilson. He, in turn, would have attempted to return articles to their respective owners. As gratitude for the favor, my note to Dr. Moran made a gift of the other three Malacca canes I sent him. As I hoped, Moran has sent me one back. Do you find anything special about the cane, Monsieur Clark?"

"If Poe were assaulted in a robbery," I said, realizing its significance, "the thieves would surely have taken a stick this fine!"

"You have come closer to the truth by finding what is false." Duponte nodded approvingly. "And now this cane is yours."

❊   ❊   ❊

My next errand in the city— to where, I cannot now remember— was also a good excuse to make use of my new walking stick. It was a very handsome ornament. It even inspired me to lend more attention to my dress, and I employed the deliberation of a statesman in selecting a hat and a vest that complimented the new accessory. Several representatives of the kinder sex, both younger ladies and those who watch after them, looked upon me with visible approval as I went through Old Town.

Oh yes, the errand— it was to two dronish men who had left word for me to call on them about various investments I held through my father's will. With a delay in the planned expansion of the Baltimore & Ohio Railroad to the Ohio River, various interests were affected, and they passed on to me a thick portfolio of papers that required my review. Naturally, I'd had little time during all else that was happening to peruse these papers very meticulously.

I found myself that afternoon again in the neighborhood where Poe was discovered on the third of October 1849. I decided to walk to the establishment, Ryan's hotel, where Poe had turned up in poor condition. I thought about what might have been done or said at that time— to save Poe, or at least to reassure him— in those crucial moments now two years ago.

My melancholy reverie was interrupted with shouting from around the corner. There was nothing of much consequence about stray noise in the streets of a city like Baltimore, where rattling fire engines and hollering continued through the nights and sometimes erupted into riots between rival fire companies or against groups of foreigners. But this lone scream, crackling like the death aria in an opera, sent chills straight through me.

"Reynolds . . . !"

"*Reynolds!*"

It was the word Poe had cried out in the hospital as he died.

Now, remember where this cry found me. Standing before the spot where Poe was removed to his hospital deathbed. Think of my disorientation, as though I had suddenly been lifted into someone else's life— someone else's death.

I crept forward. It rang out once more!

I turned onto the next street and stepped into the shadows of a narrow passage between two buildings, closing in on the sounds. A short man wearing spectacles and a morning coat walked right by, sending me jumping back, and now I recognized the voice of the man chasing him.

"Why, Mr. Reynolds!" the pursuer boomed out.

"Leave me be, won't you," replied the man— well, now we are free to say *replied Reynolds.*

"Good sir," protested the Baron Dupin, "I must remind you that I am a special constable."

"Special constable?" Reynolds repeated doubtfully.

"For the British crown itself," the Baron said patriotically.

"British crown!" Reynolds exclaimed. "Why would it harass me? To hell with their crown then!"

"Is deep concern a sort of harassment? One is the very opposite of the other. I wish only to know the full story, for your protection." The Baron Dupin grinned. He spoke in his usual dashing fashion; he was not in his shaggy disguise this time.

"But I haven't a story to tell anyone!"

"You don't realize you have one yet. My dear Reynolds, there are parties who are quite interested in how events came off that day, as you have seen lately in the newspapers. Your public reputation, your livelihood as a carpenter, your family's good name could be in jeopardy if the truth is not sufficiently extracted first. You were there that day at Ryan's. You saw— "

"I saw nothing," said Reynolds. "Nothing out of the ordinary. It was an election day. There was debauchery, of course! The year before, there was a large fuss over the election of sheriff— both sides with their supporters. Election days are rather wild in Baltimore, Mr. Baron."

"Just 'Baron,' dear fellow. Poe called urgently for 'Reynolds' as he lay dying in his hospital room." So the Baron had discovered that, too, "Do you not think that is out of the ordinary? Shall we say *extraordinary?* Was there some reason he would remember your part in his last hours?"

"I do not remember meeting any *Poe* there. You may ask the other judges. I insist you pardon me."

I leaned out far enough from behind the wall that hid me to see the Baron's face after Reynolds walked away. The Baron remained standing in place. His smile was contorted, as though he had tasted something sour or had just stolen Reynolds's wallet. (Would it have been surprising if he had?) In all his activities, the Baron looked smugly victorious. Though he was a disgraced attorney fleeing from creditors— and though now Reynolds wanted nothing to do with him— the Baron was generally confident in his prospects.

Standing alone in the street, the Baron ran his tongue over his lower lip several times, as if to slick up for future eloquence. His face and bearing looked dead when he was not barking, or cooing, at someone. His gears and pumps had to move constantly. The glimmer of his intellect shined out as he muttered one word to himself. This word:

"Dupin!"

He grinded out the word "Dupin" as though it were a curse. It no doubt seems strange for a man to jeer his own name in this way, much like punching oneself in one's own chin. It is less strange, perhaps, if you think about it not as his name, but his heritage and legacy that he admonished. The Baron, however, was the type to see himself as culminating rather than offshooting all that had come before him. When asked who were his ancestors, he might, like Emperor Napoleon to the royal potentates, reply: "I am an ancestor."

No. His imprecation of "Dupin" was directed at neither himself nor his family. The Baron meant to conjure up none other than the figure of C. Auguste Dupin. The persona over which he sought to prove paternity, authority. Why did he murmur in this way about the literary Dupin? This deception to which he had clung since my first meeting with him in Paris, that he could be the real Dupin, was now a specter too powerful for him— and this he could only admit, if at all, when completely alone, as he thought he was now on the street. He could not argue or intimidate or mask himself as the real Dupin, as he was used to doing in life and law. He either was, or was not. There was a desperation to the scene, a vulgarity to it. I thought perhaps he was conceding something there, preparing to cave in. I was wrong.

I leaned against a post supporting the awning of a daguerreotyping establishment. Soon, a carriage that I recognized drove up the street. It was the same hackney cab that had been waiting for the Baron and Bonjour the other night. I could only imagine how the Baron had cajoled or threatened the original coachman to gain private use of the carriage. Bonjour stepped down. The same lean, light-skinned black man sat in the driver's seat. I learned later that the Baron had secured the service of this slender slave still in his teen years, whose name was Newman, to drive and deliver messages for them. He had told Newman that if he performed well, he would purchase the slave's freedom from his master.

Bonjour quietly reported to the Baron, in French, that at nightfall "we meet him at the Baltimore Cemetery." That was all I could hear.

I returned to Glen Eliza and pulled the city directory from the shelf. The Baron Dupin had revealed that the "Reynolds" in the street with him was a carpenter. In the directory, the entry for the beguiling surname with that occupation and an address close to where I saw the two men read thus:

REYNOLDS, HENRY, CARPENTER, CORNER FRONT AND LOW

What could this inconspicuous carpenter I had seen in the street have had to do with Poe? The one sort of person who never employs a carpenter, after all, was someone traveling, as Poe had been in Baltimore. *That* I could know without the aid of ratiocination. And this particular Mr. Reynolds himself had denied seeing the poet.

I thought more about the Baron Dupin's comments on the street. He had implied that Henry Reynolds had been with Poe in Ryan's, had *witnessed* something. I sat thinking gravely about why this Reynolds might have been with Poe in his hour of misery, and how the Baron would know . . .

There was mention of the election. "Election days are rather wild in Baltimore, Mr. Baron." And the "other judges." Reynolds had been at Ryan's, perhaps, in some connection to the elections, since Ryan's was used that day as the Fourth Ward polling station. I burrowed through our collection of newspapers. I stopped when I found the *Sun* from October 3, 1849. That was the day when Poe was discovered in Baltimore in "shocking condition," as one of the papers had said, at Ryan's.

There, in the political department of the newspaper, was the name "Henry Reynolds," on a page with a long list of Baltimore's election judges, men who administered the oaths to voters and oversaw the polls. Reynolds was one of the election judges for the Fourth Ward's polling place, Ryan's hotel. This was Reynolds's local poll. That explained why the Baron had been hounding him so close to Ryan's— it was right near where the carpenter lived.

I was burning to speak aloud about my discovery. But if I told Duponte, I would certainly be reproved. He would repeat, philosophically, his previous pronouncement that we not speak to witnesses. "We can ascertain everything we need obliquely," he would say. Besides, the Baron Dupin had already spoken with Reynolds, he would reason; the Baron had contaminated him, not to mention most other persons in Baltimore.

I repeated silently to myself that Duponte was the world's most eminent analyst, that my contribution should be nothing more ambitious than providing for his needs. Yet, now I could not stop myself from thinking who *him* might be— the man the Baron and Bonjour were to meet on the dangerous grounds of the Baltimore Cemetery tonight according to what I had overheard. I could not help but wonder this, and wonder whether their rendezvous touched the subject of Reynolds. When darkness fell, I excused myself for some air.

I secured a coach and rode through the streets into a northeastern quarter of the city where one would prefer to have daylight. Closing in on the Baltimore Cemetery, my carriage came to a choppy halt. The horses pulled and quivered.

"Driver, do you not have control over the horses?" I asked.

"No, sir, I suppose I do not."

"Stop here! I will walk the rest of the way."

"*Here,* sir? You'll walk here?"

I would have asked myself the same question if I were not so guided by a need to know more about the Baron. I stepped hesitatingly through the gates of the graveyard and stayed at the perimeter, as close as possible to the nearest light at Fayette and Broadway.

I spotted the Baron's carriage ahead and kept enough of a distance to be safely concealed by the night. I could see that a heavy package was being transferred into the vehicle, and then another figure disappeared into the dark of the cemetery. Though I was careful not to be noticed by them, I was taken with a rush of panic when their carriage started to drive away from the cemetery. I had no wish to be alone in this kingdom of the dead after dark (no Baltimorean would), and I scurried along with the grace of a rodent.

Now hurrying to the right of the graveyard, I followed the sounds of the carriage toward the Washington College Hospital— the hospital where Edgar Poe had been brought from Ryan's hotel, and where he had died. This large brick building, with its two severe towers hovering above, was hardly less dismal than the neighboring burial yard. In fact, not long after Poe's death, the faculty of the college had decided the location was too inconvenient to the center of Baltimore, and there was now only sporadic use of the building as a hospital. The college, overstraining its financial resources with new locations, was now attempting to sell the barren edifice and its property.

The Baron's carriage was parked nearby. I found the gates to the hospital yard locked.

"No more bodies!" a voice shouted at me, from a front window of the building.

I ignored this strange pronouncement and was testing the gate again when the caretaker appeared once more in a state of agitation.

"We don't need no more bodies! We got a fresh one in!"

Newly deceased corpses were used by the doctors to instruct their students in the practice of surgery. The resurrection men would furtively sneak into cemeteries and use an iron rod with a hook on the end to pierce a hole in a coffin. These fishermen of bodies would catch the corpse under the chin and pull it up from the ground, sometimes only hours after it had received a respectful burial. The proximity of this cemetery to the college hospital made it an especial target for the theft of bodies. Few persons even of the bravest constitution would venture near the Baltimore Cemetery and Washington College Hospital at night, for it was said that sometimes, when no fresh corpse was to be found, passersby would be kidnapped and made to suit the purpose— earning the kidnappers the usual ten-dollar award from the doctors.

"You heard me now? No more bodies." The face squinted from its place in the window.

"My apologies, sir," I said.

He retreated inside. I paced along the fence until I found a section lying flat in the mud and stepped over this. The street door to the hospital building was still unlocked from the recent entry of the Baron Dupin and Bonjour.

This division of the hospital seemed empty. It was much colder in here than outside, as though the old building congealed and chilled the air. I jumped every time there was a noise, thinking the caretaker had heard me come in and would nab me, but soon I realized that the windows and doors up and down the giant structure were slamming from the wind.

I climbed the stairs cautiously and upon reaching the third floor heard garbled voices from above. It sounded like the Baron and Bonjour were speaking with someone in a fourth-floor lecture room. However, the stairs curved right past that room, and as the door to that lecture room was open, I could not ascend the stairs without them seeing me. Meanwhile, I could hear their conversation only faintly.

I have told you, said an unfamiliar voice.

I surveyed my surroundings. If I could not raise my position quickly by some means other than the stairs, my aim would be lost. There did not seem to be a rear staircase. There was, however, a closet filled with barrels. Removing two of the lids in search of some helpful tools, I gasped to find them filled to the top with human bones.

Growing despondent at having come so far to no avail, I soon found a hollow shaft in the wall that seemed like a sort of oversized dumbwaiter. Though it was pitch-black in the shaft except for the light that dripped in from each floor, I reached inside and, fortunately enough, could feel there was a hoist and pulley. It rose up from below and continued above— right up to the lecture room. A stroke of great luck, it seemed.

Finding that my body fit with surprising ease into the passage, I placed my hat on the ground and then wrapped my legs as tightly as I could around the rope and inched upward by pulling on the opposite end of the rope. The air was noxious and stale. I tried my best not to look down at the three stories below as I approached the fourth floor. The conversation became clearer with each small advance upward toward the lecture room.

The man who was with them had a loud voice, almost as theatrical as the Baron's.

"And now the newspapermen have been dunning me about it. Why we must speak more of this, I cannot see."

"The particulars," Bonjour said calmly. "We need all your particulars."

"You see," Baron Dupin continued Bonjour's thought, "we are close to understanding exactly what happened to Poe on that singular day he was brought to you. You, Brother Moran, shall be the hero in a tale of injustice."

An intrigued pause in the exchange. Meanwhile, I looked around at the narrow and dark tunnel enclosing me. When I groped the wall for balance, it was slimy and cold. Then a pair of red eyes appeared in a crevice along the wall and a rat, alarmed by my hand on its hiding place, extended itself toward me. "Choo, choo," I pleaded with the rodent. Its horrific blood-red stare nearly caused me to slide back down, but my determination to hear more allowed me to climb closer to the voices.

The bit about being a hero seemed to enlarge Moran's voice as he continued. "Edgar Poe was brought in the afternoon of a Wednesday, around five, sent by hack. The driver assisted me in lifting him out. I paid him myself."

"Was there nobody else in the coach other than Poe and the driver?" asked the Baron.

"No. There was only a card from Dr. Snodgrass, the magazine editor, informing me that the man inside was Edgar Poe and required assistance. We gave him a very comfortable room on the second-floor tower with a window facing the courtyard. He was unconscious of his condition— who brought him or with whom he had been associating."

"What did Mr. Poe say? Did he mention the name Grey or E. S. T. Grey?"

"Grey? No. He talked, but it was vacant conversation with imaginary objects on the walls. He was pale, I remember, and drenched in perspiration. We tried to induce tranquillity. Naturally, I tried to get more information from him. He was able to mention that he had a wife in Richmond. I have since come to understand they were not yet married; no doubt he was confused mentally. He did not know when he had come to Baltimore or how he came to be here. That is when I said we would make him comfortable enough to soon enjoy the society of his friends."

As Moran was speaking, I climbed nearly even with the lecture room. My outstretched hand groped the dark and landed on some solid material. Canvas, it seemed. I squinted for a better view. This must have been the bag that was placed in the Baron's carriage at the cemetery. Its lower portion was now even with my head. Patting it with my hand, I struck upon the realization that I was grasping a lifeless human foot. Suddenly, I realized what the Baron had brought from the cemetery and knew that this was no dumbwaiter. The shaft I had climbed was used to hoist corpses to the various floors' dissection rooms.

The body had been moved from the rope on which I was clinging to a hook in the shaft, and by peering into the lecture room, I could see why it had not yet been transferred inside. There was already the body of a dead man, or part of a body, salted and covered with a white cloth on the examination table in the middle of the room. Aprons, both clean and bloody, were hanging nearby. They could not move in this new subject until the old one was disposed of.

I shuddered at this sight and my closeness to this fresher corpse. I breathed quicker to try to calm myself, but that let in a horrific stench I hadn't noticed before. My grip loosened.

I slipped down fast— and down more— nearly an entire floor down. Scrambling my legs into the side of the shaft, I attempted to regain my balance so I would not drop four stories to a certain demise in the eternal blackness below.

"What was that?" I heard Bonjour say. "That noise? It's from inside the wall. The hoisting shaft."

I steadied my grip and made myself as still as the corpse now several feet above me.

"Perhaps our little gift to you has woken up, Dr. Moran." The Baron laughed in a way perhaps no man had ever done in the immediate vicinity of two dead bodies. The Baron leaned through the opening and peered down into the shaft. I was now in the dark center of the passage and, miraculously, was blocked from the Baron's view by the bag with the corpse. He returned his head to the room.

"Never mind," said Moran, "we secure the windows and doors with ropes in this building, and the place still seems to make more noise than any of the patients ever did."

I then saw Bonjour trade places with the Baron at the shaft opening, and I became more anxious. She leaned fearlessly inside the horrible compartment.

"Take care, miss!" Moran said.

Bonjour now launched herself fully into the shaft, and for a moment I was certain she would land on top of me. Instead she caught the rope with one hand and then between her knees to steady herself. Moran must have been protesting above, since I could hear the Baron trying to placate him. I clung to my position for my life and prayed for a miracle. I could almost feel Bonjour's eyes pierce the darkness directly onto my uncovered head.

She lowered herself inch by inch toward me, raising my side of the rope so that I was involuntarily moving nearer to her.

Eyes closed tight, ignoring the drops of cold perspiration, I waited for my discovery. A terrible inhuman shriek broke my concentration— at a breath, an army of voracious black rats rushed up the walls of the shaft. They ran *en masse* toward Bonjour, as though involuntarily attracted by her. Several propelled themselves onto my shoulders and back, their wiry claws attaching to my coat and daring me not to scream.

"Only rats," Bonjour murmured after a moment, then kicked some of the creatures off the walls, sending them dropping down. The Baron extended a hand and helped her back into the lecture room.

"For goodness' sake," I gasped in gratitude to the beasts. I brushed off two that had remained perched on my back.

Since I could still hear most of the conversation, I decided to pull myself back up only a few inches and stay at that safer position.

"If you will go on with the details, Doctor," said the Baron. "You told Poe you would bring his friends to him."

Moran paused in hesitation. "Perhaps I should consult with Mr. Poe's family and friends before speaking with you further. There were some cousins of his, when we were treating him— if I remember right, a Mr. Neilson Poe and a friend, a lawyer, Mr. Z. Collins Lee . . ."

The Baron sighed loudly.

"Let us see what is on the doctor's table," Bonjour said playfully. I could hear her rustling the white blanket on the naked cadaver.

"See here!" Moran gasped with obvious embarrassment. "What are you doing?"

"I have seen men before," Bonjour replied happily.

"Do not shock the young doctor, my dear!" the Baron cried.

"Perhaps we should take this deceased gentleman home for our study," Bonjour said, rolling the table away. Dr. Moran protested vigorously. Bonjour continued: "Come now, Doctor. No halves— finder keeper. Besides, I wonder, Baron, if the family of that young woman we have hoisted up in that shaft would be interested to know her body's missing from the grave and could be found here, waiting to be diced to pieces by the dandyish doctor."

"Most interested, I'd think, sweetheart!" said the Baron.

"What? But we do this to learn to save lives! You brought that other body here yourselves!"

"On your request, Doctor," said Bonjour, "and you have accepted it in exchange for the information my master asks for."

The Baron, *sotto voce*, leaned in to Moran: "You can see you had the wrong sow by the ear, Doctor."

The heroism of the doctor's voice deflated. "I see the gist now. Very well. Back to Poe then. I told him, in trying to comfort him, that he would soon enjoy the society of his friends. He broke out with much energy and said, I remember, *The best thing my best friend could do would be to blow out my brains with a pistol.* When he beheld what had become of him, he was ready to sink into the earth, and so on, as one talks when depressed in spirits. He then slipped into a violent delirium until Saturday evening, when he began calling for 'Reynolds' again and again, for six or seven hours until the morning, as I have told you the other day. Having enfeebled himself from exertion he said, 'Lord help my poor soul' and expired. That is all."

"What we wonder now," said the Baron, "is whether Poe had been induced to have taken some sort of artificial stimulus, a drug— opium, perhaps— that put him in this condition?"

"I do not know. The truth, sir, is that Poe's condition was quite sad and strange, but there was no particular odor of alcohol on his person, that I can remember."

During this exchange, I alternated between careful attentiveness to their words and desperate attempts to calm my pounding heart and breathing from my near discovery by Bonjour. When they closed the interview to the Baron's satisfaction, and I felt convinced by listening for footsteps they had left the fourth floor, I climbed past the body and heaved myself through the opening in the wall. I checked that the coast was clear and dropped into the lecture room. Flattening myself on the floor, I coughed out the air of the dead and gulped in rapid, grateful bursts.

You will perhaps judge me harshly for not immediately relating my adventures to Duponte, and yet you have seen yourself the frequent inflexibility of his philosophies. I am not of a particularly philosophical cast. Duponte was born an analyst, a reasoner; I, an observer. Though it may occupy only a lower rung of the ladder of wisdom, observation requires practicality. Perhaps Duponte, and our investigations generally, needed a light shove toward the pragmatic.

I should have explained above, when I was searching for the mention of Henry Reynolds, how it was I had free access to the newspapers we kept in the library without Duponte taking notice. Since the first day we had disembarked in Baltimore, Duponte had inhabited the library and oversaw all the contents of his sanctum. However, when he was reading other things he would remove himself from the increasingly cramped library to different chambers and bedrooms of Glen Eliza I had forgotten existed. He would choose the odd book that I had on my shelf; or one of my father's atlases of an obscure province of the world; or a pamphlet in French that my mother had brought from abroad. Duponte also read Poe, a practice that did not escape my interest.

At times the concentration with which he read Poe reminded me of the sheer nourishment the tales had provided me for so many years. But usually it was far more scholarly than that. Duponte read mechanically, like a literary critic. The critic never lets his reading overtake him; he never pulls the pages promiscuously close to his face and never wishes to be brought into the crevices of the author's mind, for such a journey would relinquish control. Thus, often a reader will read a magazine critic's notice of a book, after having already read the book himself, eager to compare perspectives, and think, "This cannot be the book I read! There must be another version, in which everything has changed, and I shall have to find it, too!"

I thought a dispassionate survey of Poe's works by Duponte quite fitting. I believe it allowed Duponte crucial insights into Poe's character and into the mysterious circumstances that we had begun to examine.

"If only it was known which ship Poe arrived to Baltimore on," I said one afternoon.

Duponte became instantly animated. "The local papers speak of it as the unknown details of his arrival. That *they* do not know, monsieur, certainly does not confine it to the bounds of the *unknown*. The answer is plainly presented in the articles from the Richmond newspapers published in the last months of Poe's life."

"When Poe was lecturing on various subjects of poetry and literature."

"Precisely. He was doing so in order to raise money for his proposed magazine *The Stylus*, as he mentioned also in his letters to you, Monsieur Clark. We may not know on which ship Poe sailed from Richmond to Baltimore, but this is hardly what is important, and hardly qualifies as making the *purpose* of his trip unknown. His reason for coming to Baltimore is quite knowable to any person employing thought. From the rumors in the newspapers over the last two years before his death, Poe had been involved in various romantic unions since his wife's death. In this last period, he had just engaged himself to a wealthy woman in Richmond, and so his trip to Baltimore would likely not have been for the purposes of any romantic interlude. Now, in view of the fact that his intended, one Mrs. Shelton, was known as wealthy by all periodical editors, and thus naturally by everyone else (for editors rarely know something the mob does not know first); in view of this fact that her wealth was widely known, Poe might properly feel the need to deflect any perception by the public that he was set to marry her because she was 'bankable.' "

"He would certainly never marry someone for money!"

"Whether or not he would, and your indignation on the question is quite beside the point, the result is exactly the same. This makes it easier for our review. If Poe *were* marrying her for money, it would be all the more reason to deflect the perception of it in order to avoid ruining the engagement if she suspected it. If his motives were pure ones, as you believe, his goal would remain identical— to raise money, this time in order to provide for his own expenses rather than rely unjustly on hers. Either way, finding he had not earned as much as he hoped in Richmond, he would come to Baltimore to gain professional support and subscribers for *The Stylus*, and thus bolster his financial prospects independently of Mrs. Shelton's."

"Which explains why he went first to see Nathan Brooks, for Dr. Brooks is a well-known magazine editor. Except," I said grimly, "that, as I saw for myself, Dr. Brooks's house had caught on fire."

"Poe came here with plans, Monsieur Clark, to remake his life. I think we shall find that he died in a state of hope, not in despair."

But I remembered Dr. Moran's statement about Poe: he did not know when he had come to Baltimore or how he came to be here. How did this conform to the other particulars now before us?

The above conversation with Duponte occurred a few days after my secret call to the hospital. Meanwhile, in my visits to the reading rooms and my various errands around the city, I felt an increasing number of eyes on me. I thought that perhaps it was an unconscious product of my guilt at hiding my previous discoveries from Duponte, or my distraction whenever I remembered Hattie's distressed behavior in my last encounter with her at the gates to her house.

There was one man in particular, a free black of about forty years old, whom I observed near me on more than one occasion in crowds on the street or from the window of a carriage I was riding in. He had sharply angled features and was of solid physical dimensions. It was usually easy to differentiate between the free and enslaved blacks by the superior and often quite fashionable dress of the former, although certain city slaves— slave dandies, as they were known— were provided exquisite clothing to fashionably match that of their owners.

I thought of the Phantom who had followed me once, long before I had dreamed of finding a man like Duponte or hiding from a man like the Baron Dupin; I thought, too, of the dead stare of the Baron's man Hartwick as he trailed me through the halls of Versailles, preparing to grab me. Once, I saw this new stranger standing across from where I was walking on Baltimore Street. I was not surprised to see this presumed freeman speaking quietly with the Baron Dupin. The Baron took his arm enthusiastically.

That same evening, Duponte was reading Poe's tale "Ligeia" on a sofa in the drawing room. Von Dantker had left with his brushes some hours before in a state of high irritation. Duponte had announced that he no longer wanted to see Von Dantker's staring face whenever he looked up, and had informed the artist that he would have to sit behind him. Von Dantker had naturally protested on the basis that he could not paint Duponte's back, but Duponte had refused to argue, and a system had soon been devised whereby a mirror was placed in front of Duponte and Von Dantker sat behind the analyst. He had positioned another large mirror by his easel, facing the first mirror, to transfer the original reflection back to the correct orientation. I thought both men quite mad. But Von Dantker, taking bites from the "olycoke"— a strange cake fried in lard— he always brought with him, had continued on with his project.

I busied myself reading a copy of Thomas Moore's *Irish Melodies,* which I had procured from a book-stand. Dr. Carter, Poe's friend in Richmond, had told the newspaper there that Poe had been reading Moore's poems when he visited his office. It was also said that during his stay in Richmond Poe quoted this verse of Moore's to a young lady he befriended: "I feel like one / Who treads alone / Some banquet hall deserted."

My thoughts floated to the distracting subject of Hattie. "I wonder," I said, interrupting Duponte's reading.

"Yes?"

"Well, I am wondering whether a woman who says that things are 'different' means to say that her emotions, that is, *affections*, have changed, or rather refers to other, less profound matters."

"Are you," Duponte asked, putting aside the book, "soliciting my opinion on the subject, monsieur?"

I hesitated, hoping he would not believe that I was attempting to misdirect his skills of ratiocination at a purely personal concern, although that was precisely what I was doing.

He continued without an answer from me. "Do you, Monsieur Clark, believe it is the larger or smaller concern that her words refer to?"

I considered this. "Well, which is the larger and which the smaller of the concerns?" I asked.

"Exactly the quarrel, monsieur. To persons who are not the direct recipients of her affections, the question of her emotional state would be the *smaller* one; the state of the roof of her house, or a loan she may have secured from the bank, and whether these are *different* from some previous state of affairs would be the larger and most crucial question. To the person who seeks or has sought her affections, those emotions would be by far the more significant question to unravel, whereas if her roof were sinking entirely it would make little difference to that suitor. Therefore, your answer is that the meaning of her words would vary depending very much on whom she is addressing."

I was quite flabbergasted by the coolness of Duponte's advice on love, if that is what this was, and I did not pursue the subject any further.

At length the doorbell rang. The servants had left for the day, and I had gone downstairs. After several moments, Duponte clapped his book closed, rose from his place with a sigh, and descended to the street door. There on the other side stood a short, bespectacled man peering inside expectantly.

"What is it you wish for me, sir?" the man asked politely.

"Is it not you who has come to the door?" replied Duponte. "I should think I would have asked you that very question, had I any interest in the answer."

"Why— ?" said the visitor, flustered. "Well, I'm Reynolds. Henry Reynolds, may I come inside?"

I watched this from the kitchen corridor. Mr. Reynolds found a place for his hat. He showed Duponte the card he had received from me earlier that day.

I had planned that Duponte might have a greater degree of interest if he were to unexpectedly greet Reynolds at the door, and thus be the proprietor of the discovery and, finding the opportunity irresistible, pursue all information that could be extracted from the visitor.

This was not to be. Duponte, his hand cupping his book of Poe tales, bid a polite good evening to the guest and walked past me to the stairs. I rushed after him.

"But where are you going?"

"Monsieur. You have a caller, a Monsieur Reynolds, I believe," Duponte answered me. "I suppose you gentlemen wish to talk together."

"But— !" I fell quiet.

"Someone did call for me?" asked Reynolds loudly and impatiently from the bottom of the stairs. "I have other appointments too. One of you fellows is Clark?"

I caught up to Duponte with a sheepish shrug. "I know I should have told you about leaving word for Reynolds to call. I saw the Baron Dupin speaking with this fellow, and found out that he was an election judge at the voting place where Poe was found. But this man wouldn't give the Baron any information. Just hold for a moment! Come to the drawing room. I thought you might refuse at first, and this is why I have done this secretly. I believe it is a matter of utter importance that we interview him."

Duponte remained impassive. "What do you wish me to do?"

"Sit in the room. You needn't say a single word."

Of course, I hoped that Duponte, incited by whatever knowledge was held by the carpenter, would not only say a single word; I hoped he would intervene with extensive interrogatories once I began the dialogue. The analyst assented to come with me to the drawing room.

"Well, how are we today?" The carpenter forced a friendly smile as he looked around the gigantic room and up at the impressive dome that rose to the height of the third floor. "Planning on bettering the structure of your home, Mr. Clark? Its beauty is a bit in decay, if I may take the liberty to say. I've appreciated not a few mansions this year with betterments."

"What?" I demanded, perturbed, forgetting for a moment his profession.

Duponte sat in the corner armchair by the hearth. He propped his head in his hand, and his fingers spread in a web over the side of his face. He sucked his tongue, as was his habit.

Instead of feeling compelled by the situation to speak, Duponte directed his glare beyond Reynolds and me to some indefinite point of the room's horizon, and yet betrayed a look of distant enjoyment at how the conversation progressed.

"I am in no need of carpentry," I said.

"Not carpentry? Why have I been requested to make this visit, gentlemen?" Reynolds frowned and then fed himself some chewing tobacco, as though to say that if there was no carpentry, there might as well be tobacco.

"Well, Mr. Reynolds, if I may . . ." My mouth felt dry, and my words dribbled out uncertainly.

"If I made this visit for you gentlemen's amusement— " he said indignantly.

"We require some information," I said. This seemed like a good start to me. Duponte's mouth twitched, and I waited for him to speak, but it was a yawn. He crossed his legs at a different place.

Reynolds was speaking over me. "— well, because I shouldn't like to think I have wasted my time. I am a key figure to the future dignity of Baltimore. I have helped erect the athenaeum, have lent my hand to raising the Maryland Institute, and directed the first iron building in the city for the Baltimore *Sun.*"

I tried to pull him to the primary subject. "You served as a ward judge for the Fourth Ward polling station at Ryan's hotel in 1849, is that true?"

Duponte was now most fixedly looking at absolutely nothing. Sometimes a cat coils into such a careless, comfortable position as to fall soundly asleep but forgets to close her eyes. This was Duponte's current appearance.

"As I say," I babbled on, "the information I seek, about that night at the polls, I mean, at the Fourth Ward, there was a man named Poe— "

"Now, see here," Reynolds interrupted. "You're something to do with that fellow, Baron Whatnot, who's been bothering me, leaving me letters and notes, aren't you?"

"Please, Mr. Reynolds— "

"Talking of Poe, Poe, Poe! What is all this about Poe anyway?"

"It is true," said Duponte philosophically to me, "as Mr. Reynolds implies, that the decease of a person of some interest to the public will be looked at for the person rather than the death, and thus will obtain larger holes of error and misperception. Very good, Reynolds."

This helped nothing except to confound our guest's line of thought.

Reynolds wagged his finger at me, and then at Duponte, as though the analyst was an equal culprit in this attempted interview. "Just see here." Black tobacco juice was sent flying around the room by the venom of his speech. "This bangs all things! I do not care that the other fellow's a baron, or that you are lords and kings. I don't have nothing to say to 'im, and I have much to do! I don't have a word to say to you two! Is that it? Well, my good princes, please *never* call for me again or I shall send for the police."

When I came down for breakfast, there was a note from Duponte that I should find him in the library at noon. He had not said a word to me before parting for the night. To my surprise, he was more interested in the fact that I had seen the Baron Dupin than that I had surreptitiously sent for Reynolds.

"So," he said when I met him in the library, "you found yourself following the Baron Dupin."

I recounted all that had passed between the Baron and Reynolds and what I had seen at the cemetery and hospital. I pleaded my side for leaving my card for Reynolds. "Understand, monsieur. Poe called out for 'Reynolds' again and again when he was dying. That Henry Reynolds was one of the election judges that day in charge of overseeing the Fourth Ward polls, which were held in Ryan's— where Poe was found! Do you not think this was too remarkable a connection?" I answered for him: "It is too remarkable to ignore!"

"It is, at most, incidental, and to a lesser and more forceful degree co-incidental."

Incidental! Coincidental! Poe calling for Reynolds at his hour of judgment, and here one Henry Reynolds had been in the very same place as Poe days before. But you see, Duponte was a persuasive personality, even when he said little. If he had said Baltimore's cathedrals were incidental to its Catholics, one would be inclined to find reason to agree.

He agreed to my suggestion of a walk. I hoped it would render him more willing to consider my latest suppositions. I had fallen into a rather concerned state about our inquiry, and not only because of Duponte's refusal to consider Mr. Reynolds as the Baron had. It seemed to me there was much else we could be missing, insulated as we were— for instance, the probability that Poe had traveled from Baltimore to Philadelphia and was in that city before his death. I made reference to this point as we walked.

"He was not."

"Do you mean he was not in Philadelphia that week he was discovered?" I asked, surprised at his certainty as to the point. "The newspapers have been throwing their hands up wondering about it."

"It is easily in front of their eyes, too accessible to such frantic minds as the public press, who never lose confidence that they are able to find some true detail, as long as it is at all times far from them. They are surprised at everything, when they should be surprised at nothing. If a fact is said once, we may pay attention, but if a fact is fixed in four places, ignore it, for along the way its replication has stopped all thought."

"But how could we know positively? After his attempt to visit Dr. Brooks, we hardly possess a solitary fact about Poe's days in Baltimore until he was nearly five days later seen at Ryan's. How do we know Poe did not, sometime between these times, board the train to Philadelphia, and, further, if he did, can we dismiss the possibility that there, in that other city, lie all the chief keys to the right understanding of the events that followed?"

"Let us settle your worries on this point. You do recall the reasons Monsieur Poe had planned to visit Philadelphia, I suppose," said Duponte.

I did, and repeated them to Duponte. Poe had been asked to edit the poems of Mrs. Marguerite St. Leon Loud for publication, for which her wealthy husband, Mr. Loud, would pay a sum of one hundred dollars. It had been reported by the newspapers that Poe had agreed to this lucrative arrangement in his last weeks when Mr. Loud, a piano manufacturer, visited Richmond. Poe had even instructed Muddy Clemm to write him there, in Philadelphia, under the strange pseudonym of E. S. T. Grey, Esquire, adding, "I hope that our troubles are nearly over."

"One hundred dollars would be an enormous difference to Poe, for he was quite pushed for money for himself *and* his magazine," I said. "One hundred dollars, to edit a small book of poems— for Poe, who had been the editor of some five periodicals, for which he was hardly rewarded enough to supply bread to his family, this was a task that could be done while sleeping. But how, with no evidence to the contrary, should we know when Poe made his visit to Philadelphia?"

"Through Mrs. Loud, of course."

I frowned. "I'm afraid that has not been helpful. I penned a few letters to this woman, but have received no reply."

"You misunderstand my meaning. I would not think to write to Mrs. Loud. By the nature of her circumstance, aspiring poetess and wife of an affluent husband, she would likely in this season be in the country or on the shore, so correspondence would be rendered inefficient. We need not bother the poor woman herself in order to listen to her."

Duponte removed a thin, handsomely printed volume from inside his coat. *Wayside Flowers: A Collection of Poems, by Mrs. M. St. Leon Loud,* published by Ticknor, Reed, and Fields.

"What is this?" I asked.

"Here is the very book of poems, we may presume, that Poe had agreed to edit, and that has been recently published with little attention— thankfully."

I opened up to the page listing its contents. I hesitate to print a sample. "I Wooed Thee," "To a Friend on the Birth of a Son," "The Dying Buffalo," "Invitation to a Prayer Meeting," "It Is I: Be Not Afraid," "On Parting with a Friend," "On Seeing a Monument," "The First Day of Summer," and, of course, "The Last Day of Summer." The contents list alone went on for pages. Duponte explained that he had ordered this book from one of the local booksellers.

"We know Monsieur Poe never arrived at Philadelphia to edit Madame Loud's poems," said Duponte.

"How, monsieur?"

"Because it is quite clear *nobody* has edited these poems, judging from the terrific numbers of them here included. If *somebody* had edited them, heaven forgive them, it was not a poet of experience and strong principles regarding the brevity and unity of verse, as we know Monsieur Poe to have been."

This did seem a fact. I saw now the practical gains that Duponte had made by spending hours in the parlor with Poe's poetry.

I had a doubt about his conclusions, however. "What if, Monsieur Duponte, Poe did go to Philadelphia and begin to edit the poems, and simply had a disagreement with the poetess, or balked at the quality of her work, and returned to Baltimore?"

"An intelligent question, if also an unobservant one. It would be possible that Poe arrived at the Louds' estate in order to fulfill his obligation, and once there could not agree on some final term of compensation or other fine point of the arrangement. However, we need only consider this possibility briefly before discarding it."

"I do not see why, monsieur."

"Search again through the book's contents. I am confident this time you will know where to stop."

By this point we had taken a table at a restaurant. Duponte leaned over and looked at the title where my finger was pointing. "Very good, monsieur. Now, read the verses from those pages, if you would."

The poem was entitled "The Stranger's Doom." It began:

> They gathered round his dying bed,—
> His failing eye was glazed and dim;
> But 'mong the many gazers, there
> Were none who wept or cared for him.
>
> Oh! 'tis a sad, a fearful thing,
> To die with none but strangers near;
> To see within the darkened room
> No face, no form, to memory dear!

"It sounds rather like the scene, as we know it, at the college hospital when Poe was dying!"

"As our romancer imagines it, yes. Continue, please. I rather like your recitation. Spirited."

"Thank you, monsieur." The next verses spoke of the man's lonely demise with "no clasping hand, no farewell kiss." It continued with the scene of death:

> Yet thus he died— afar from all
> Who might have mourned his early doom!
> Strange hands his drooping eyelids closed,
> And bore him to his nameless tomb.
>
> They laid him where tall forest trees
> Cast their dark shadows o'er his bed,
> And hurriedly, in silence, heaped
> The wild-grass turf above his head.

> *None prayed, none wept, when all was o'er,*
> *Nor lingered near the sacred spot;*
> *But turned them to the world again,*
> *And soon his very name forgot.*

"*His nameless tomb* . . . the *wild-grass turf* of the grave that should be *sacred* . . . the quick burial, in which *none lingered* . . . surely this is Poe's funeral at the Westminster burial yard! Described very much as I saw it!"

"We have already surmised that Madame Loud is a traveler of some frequency, a probability supported by the subjects of several of her poems, and so we now assume from the details here that she has visited Baltimore sometime in the last two years since Poe's death. Taking a natural interest in the death of a man she had been set to meet right around his demise, she has gathered this description of the funeral— so close to your own remembrance— by visiting the burial yard and questioning its sexton or grave digger, and perhaps individuals at the hospital, as well."

"Outstanding," I said.

"We may read closely and come to several conclusions. We may say she shares your own perspective, Monsieur Clark, faulting those who failed to honor him. The poem speaks with no special knowledge of Poe's whereabouts or demeanor prior to his death. We know, then, that Madame Loud followed the tidings of Poe's death from afar, not as one who had only just been separated from Poe with the privilege of hearing any of his plans. Moreover, his doom is that of a *stranger*, as declared in the poem's title, *not* of one whom she has known. So we obtain even greater certainty that he did not meet Madame Loud, as he hoped to do, in Philadelphia. This shall only be our first document of proof of Poe's failure to reach that city."

"Our first, Monsieur Duponte?"

"Yes."

"But why would Poe direct his mother-in-law to write him with a false name, E. S. T. Grey?"

"Perhaps this shall be our second proof," Duponte said, though he seemed content, for the moment, to close the topic there.

Duponte had been taking more walks outside. He was liberated from Glen Eliza when, after many arguments and much ranting by Von Dant-

ker over Duponte's queer demands, the artist decided he could finish the
painting without further sittings. Not wishing for any more distractions
from the man, I sent word that I would make payment for his labors, but
he replied that he was to be paid by another party that afternoon. Because this made no sense whatsoever, I went to Von Dantker's chambers,
only to witness the Baron Dupin exiting. The Baron touched his hat and
smiled.

I frantically related this information to Duponte, who only laughed at
the notion of Von Dantker as spy.

"Monsieur Duponte, he could have been listening to every word we
would have said, even as he sat there pretending to be concerned with
the painting!"

"That simpleton, Von Dantker? Listening to anything! Ha!" That was
all I could induce Duponte to say on the matter.

In making himself an observer of the "spirit of the city," Duponte proceeded with strides as slow as they had been around Paris. I usually accompanied him on these walks, not wanting to lose him, as had
happened before. Often these excursions were in the evening. I could almost say, as the narrator of "The Murders in the Rue Morgue" said of
C. Auguste Dupin, that we sought our quiet observation "amid the wild
lights and shadows of the populous city." Except for the wild lights. You
have seen already that Baltimore, unlike Paris, is quite hard on the eyes
after dark.

Indeed once, I remember, in the poor lighting, I collided headlong
with a smartly dressed stranger. "Many apologies," I said, looking up at
him. The man was muffled in an old-fashioned black coat. His response
stayed in my mind the rest of that night: he looked down and walked
away without a word.

Duponte did not mind the bad lighting in Baltimore. "I see in the daylight," he would say, "but I see *through* in the night." He was a human
owl; his mental outings were nocturnal hunts.

On two occasions during these meanderings, including the one in
which I collided with that stranger, we happened upon the Baron Claude
Dupin out with Bonjour. Baltimore was a large and growing city of more
than one hundred and fifty thousand; therefore, the odds of any two parties intersecting paths at the right time must have been mathematically
modest. There was a magnetism of purpose that brought our groups

together, I suppose. Or the Baron went out of his way to taunt us. The Baron had begun to look different, around the face and a bit in the eyes— I wondered whether he had gained weight? Or perhaps lost some?

The Baron liked to demonstrate the "enormous" amount of knowledge he had accumulated about Poe's death.

"A very fine walking stick," the Baron said to me once. "Is that all the go these days?"

"It is Malacca," I replied proudly.

"Malacca? Like Poe's when he was found. Oh yes, anything you have discovered we already know, my dear friends. Like why he used the name E. S. T. Grey. And of his clothes that did not fit? You have read in the papers they were his disguise? True, but not by Poe's own choice— " And then the Baron would end enigmatically in mid-sentence, or share a laugh with Bonjour. She stared toward Duponte and me, not subscribing to the policy of false politeness shown by her husband. Then the Baron would say, "What enormous discoveries are at hand, my friends! We shall find our passport to glory in this!" He liked to do everything on a big figure.

"My good Brother Duponte," the Baron greeted my companion on an after-breakfast stroll, grasping his hand vigorously, "it is awfully good to see you in fine health. You shall have a quiet voyage returning to Paris, I can assure you. We have made *enormous* strides, and are about to complete all the work needed here."

Duponte was polite. "I shall have had a very fine visit to Baltimore, then."

"Indeed! I do believe," the Baron said in a loud whisper, swiveling his head in a showy fashion, "that nowhere else have I seen so many beautiful women at one glance as in Baltimore."

I winced at the tone of his comment. Bonjour was not with him on this occasion, but I wished she were.

After we parted from the Baron, Duponte turned to me. He put a heavy hand on my shoulder and stood for a while without saying a word. A chill went through me.

"What are you prepared for, Monsieur Clark?" he said quietly.

"How do you mean?"

"You are treading closer to the center of the examination, extraordinarily closer each day."

"Monsieur, I wish to assist any way I might." The truth is, I did not feel

I was treading anywhere near the center of Duponte's labors or plans, in fact hardly at its circumference, and I certainly had not yet felt us anywhere but at the outskirts of detecting the truth of Poe's death.

Duponte shook his head fatally, as though giving up on the possibility that I could understand. "I want you to look further in on his affairs, if you are agreeable."

Taken by complete surprise, I asked for elaboration.

"It would aid us to know the tactics being employed by the Baron," said Duponte. "Just as you discovered Monsieur Reynolds."

"But you disapproved forcefully of my contact with Reynolds!"

"You're right, monsieur. Your discovery of Reynolds was utterly meaningless. But as I have said before, one needs to know all that is meaningless, to know just what meaning we have found."

I did not know exactly what Duponte imagined when he asked what I was prepared for. I did not know and I knew. There was the obvious fact that by following the Baron, I would be exposed more directly to the possibility of harm.

But I do not think that was all of it. He meant to ask whether I would want to reclaim the life I had before when this was finished. Would I have sent him back on the next steamer to Paris, would I have turned around and chosen the quiet sanctuary of Glen Eliza, had I known what was about to come?

-BOOK IV-

PHANTOMS CHASED FOR EVERMORE

15

THAT IS HOW I became our secret agent.

The Baron Dupin changed his hotel every few days. I presumed his movements were spurred by constant fears that his enemies from Paris would trace him here, though this seemed far-fetched to me. But then I began noticing two men who seemed to be regularly observing the Baron. I was observing the Baron too, of course, and so it was difficult for me to watch them closely at the same time. They dressed as though in uniform: old-fashioned black dress coats, blue trousers, cocked derby hats hiding their faces. Though they did not resemble each other physically, both had the same unconscious stares, like the disdainful eyes of the Roman statues of the Louvre. These orbs were always trained on the same object: the Baron. At first I thought they might be working for the Baron, but I noticed that he strenuously avoided being in their proximity. After several times crossing their paths, I remembered where I had seen one of them. It had been on one of my walks with Duponte. I had tripped into him around the site of one of our encounters with the Baron. Perhaps that had been near the time they had first located their object.

They were not the only people in Baltimore now interested in the affairs of the Baron Dupin. There was also the doorkeeper from the "Rosy God" club— the den of the Whigs of the Fourth Ward where we had met with Mr. George, the president of that group. This massive doorkeeper began to harass the Baron while the Baron was in disguise— the disguise that I had first seen in the athenaeum reading room. Not even the Baron would openly challenge this Whig agent, Tindley— far too pretty a designation for a monster. Everyone seemed a dwarf next to him.

"What is it you want, good man?" the Baron asked his tormenter.

"For you dandies to stop talking about our club!" Tindley answered.

"Dear fellow, what makes you think I am concerned with your club?" the Baron asked magnanimously.

Tindley's mouth remained open, as he placed his finger into the folds of the Baron's flowing black cravat. "We've been warned about you, after you tried to palm me to enter the club! Now I'm watching."

"Ah, you have been warned, have you," said the Baron lightly. "Then I am afraid you have been terribly misled by this warning. Now," he inquired with desperately concealed worry, "who in the wide world would have warned you?"

Tindley didn't have to say Duponte's name— he didn't know it, regardless; the Baron could guess. "Tall, unelegant Frenchman with an oval head? Was it him? He is a fraud, dear sir," the Baron said of Duponte. "He's more dangerous than you can imagine!"

What a futile flash of anger in the Baron's eyes, as he stood there, all the while silently damning the triumph of Duponte! Obstructed by Tindley wherever he went, the Baron soon had to retire that disguise of the sneezer and the informants he had established through it. . . . A small victory for us, I thought to myself vengefully, after the Baron's successful infiltration into Glen Eliza by the Dutch portraitist.

Speaking of how our Baron Dupin looked these days, what changes he was affecting before our eyes! I have mentioned in a past chapter his facility for altering his physical appearance with singular effectiveness. On recent occasions seeing the Baron on the streets, I had noticed a new transformation about his face and general person, without being able to identify what exactly had changed. This was no matter of a falsely bulbed nose and wig— that former costume belonged with the third-rate summer performers in the Rue Madame in Paris. His entire countenance now seemed to have become altogether different, and at the same time eerily, breathtakingly familiar.

One night I was adding some kindlers to the fire in the living room hearth. Duponte commented that he was comfortable enough. On this topic, I ignored him. In Paris, it's said there is hardly a smoking chimney even on the worst nights of winter. We Americans are rather too sensitive to heat and cold, while in the Old World they seem hardly aware of it at all— but I would not sit wrapped in blankets like a Frenchman would insist on doing. This same evening, I received a note.

It was from Auntie Blum. I opened it with some hesitation. She said she hoped that my unmannered French pastry cook (meaning Duponte) had been discharged. Chiefly, she wished to inform me, out of courtesy to her longtime friendship with the household of Glen Eliza, that Hattie was now engaged to marry another man, who was industrious and trustworthy.

At first, I fell under a spell of shock at the news. Could Hattie really have found someone else? Could I have managed to forfeit a woman as wonderful as Hattie, while at the same time doing what seemed right and necessary?

Then I realized. I thought back to Peter's sage warning that it would not be easy to appease Auntie Blum, and recognized this letter as a ploy by that cunning woman to torment me into apologies and excessive confessions of my wrong toward her niece.

I was not above this tactic, or beneath it, as the case might be.

I sat upon the sofa, thinking whether I had by nature of my present endeavor given up all proper intercourse with society. I was, after all, now in the company of men of great intensity like Duponte and the Baron, who defied any social customs and sought action that could not be obtained by ordinary politeness.

When the flames began running terrifically along the log, and I was contemplating these matters, I had a sudden thought about the Baron Dupin as though his face had been reflected back to me from the fire. It came to me while I was trying to picture the man without having the original present.

No portrait-maker or Daguerrean artist could do the Baron any justice because of the changes that constantly befell his features. In fact, if it were attempted, the Baron would likely grow more like the portrait canvas rather than the other way around. One would have to catch him asleep to see his true form.

"Monsieur Duponte," I said, with a leap to my feet, as the fire cracked and popped to life. "It is you!"

He looked up at my dramatic pronouncement.

"He is you!" I waved my hands in one direction, then the other. "That is why he schemed to have Von Dantker here!"

It took me three or four tries to express the meaning of my realization: the Baron Dupin had appropriated the form of Auguste Duponte! The Baron had tautened the muscles in his face, had weighed down the ends of his mouth, had— for all I could say— used some spell of magic to sharpen the very contours of his head and adjust his height. He also selected his dress like Duponte's, in the loose cut of the cloth and dull colors. He left behind the jewelry and rings with which he was formerly adorned, and smoothed the wilderness of ringlets in his hair. The Baron had subtly, using observation and the study of Von Dantker's sketches and portraiture, remade himself into a version of Duponte.

The reason, I presumed, was simple. To irritate his opponent; to avenge the provocation of Tindley; to sneer at the nobler being who dared to compete with him in this endeavor. Whenever he saw Duponte around the streets, the Baron could hardly speak without breaking into laughter at the brilliance of his newly instituted taunt.

An abomination, a conjurer, a swindler: masquerading as a great man!

He had also— somehow— I vow to you— he had also transmogrified the very timbre and pitch of his voice. To parrot with precision that of Duponte's! Even the accent was adjusted to perfection. If I had been in a dark chamber, and had been listening to a monologue by this falsifier, I would have happily addressed the fiend as though he were my accustomed and true companion.

The Baron's petty masquerade dogged me. It haunted me. It ground down my teeth. I do not think it bothered Duponte half as much. When I complained about the Baron's ploy, Duponte's mouth lengthened into an enigmatic arch, as though he thought the taunt amusing, child's play. And when he met his competitor, he bowed at the Baron all the same as before. The sight was astounding, particularly at nighttime, seeing them there together. Eventually, the only certain way to distinguish them was by the identity of the devoted associates, me on one side and Mademoiselle Bonjour on the other.

Finally, one day, I confronted Duponte. "When this fiend scoffs at you, mocks you, you allow it to continue unchallenged."

"What would you counsel me to do, Monsieur Clark? Propose a duel?" asked Duponte, more mildly than I probably deserved.

"Box his ears, certainly!" I said, though I do not suppose I would have personally done so. "Become quite warm with him, at least."

"I see. Should that help our cause?"

I conceded that it might not. "Just so. It would remind him, I should think, that he is not alone playing this game. He believes, in the infinite deception of his brain, that he has already won, Monsieur Duponte!"

"He has subscribed to a mistaken belief, then. The situation is quite the opposite. The Baron, I am afraid for him, has already lost. He has reached the end, as have I."

I leaned forward in disbelief. "Do you mean . . . ?"

Duponte was speaking of our very purpose, the unraveling of the entire mystery of Poe . . .

But I see I have jumped too far ahead of myself, as I tend to do. I will have to retrace my steps before I return to the above dialogue. I had begun to describe my life as a spy, stimulated by Duponte's desire to know the Baron's secrets and plans.

As I noted before, the Baron changed hotels frequently to elude pursuers. I maintained my knowledge of their lodgings by following as one tired hotel porter moved their baggage from his hotel to the custody of a brother porter. I do not know how the Baron answered questions about the peculiar practice of moving hotels when he signed each new register. If I ever found myself doing the same, and could not give the actual reason— "You see, sir, my creditors are looking to make me a head shorter"— I would have claimed I was writing a guidebook for strangers to Baltimore, and required a basis to compare lodging choices. The proprietors would shower you with advantages. This was such a good idea, I was tempted to write of it as an anonymous suggestion to the Baron.

Meanwhile, Duponte instructed me to find out more information about Newman, the slave the Baron had engaged, and so I insinuated myself into a discussion with him in the anteroom one afternoon.

"I gonna leave Baltimore after he spring me," Newman said to my questions about the Baron. "I got a brother and sister in Boston."

"Why not run away now? There are northern states that will protect you," I commented.

He pointed to a printed notice in the entrance hall of the hotel. It stated that no colored person, "bond or free," could leave town without first depositing his papers and taking a white man to be his surety.

"I ain't no dumb nigger," he said, "to be hunted down and dead. I'd as good as go to my owner and beg to be shot."

Newman was right; he would be traced even if his owner did not especially care about the loss.

I should include an additional note, to avoid any perplexity, about the language of the young slave. Among the Africans, both slaves and free, in the southern and in northern states, the use of the word "nigger" was not about race. I have heard blacks talking of a mulatto with that term and even calling their masters "them white niggers." "Nigger" was used by blacks to mean a low fellow of any sort, color, or class. This rather ingeniously redefines the ugly word, until it will no doubt be removed from our language altogether. For those who ever doubted the intelligence of that mistreated race, I point to this linguistic stroke and wonder if whites would have thought of the same.

"And what of the other Negro?" I asked.

"Who?"

"The other black engaged by the Baron," I replied. I had become sufficiently convinced that the stranger I had seen once before with the Baron had been assigned by him to watch me— spying on me even as I spied on him.

"There ain't no other, sir, black or white. Baron D. don't want too many people to know him real close."

With my new proximity, I was surprised, and not a little pleased, to find a diminishment in the bluster the Baron displayed. On several occasions in my hearing, Bonjour would pose a rather elementary question about the Baron's conclusions regarding Poe; the Baron Dupin would demur. This brightened my hopes at our own success. But I suppose this also placed something of a negative and unsettling fear over me that Duponte would also be at a loss, as though there was a mystical connection between the two men. Maybe this was a subtle consequence on my mind of the new and startling resemblance between Claude Dupin and Auguste Duponte, as though one were real and one an image in the mirror, as in the doomed last encounter of Poe's own William Wilson. Other times it seemed both were mirror images of the same being.

Their behaviors, though, were different enough.

In the public eye, the Baron continued his loud, obnoxious proclamations. He began raising a subscription for a broadsheet he proposed to publish, and a lecture series he would give, on the true and sensational details of Poe's death. "Come, fly around, fly around me, gentlemen and gals, you shall never believe what happened under your noses!" he proclaimed in taverns and public houses, like a showman or mountebank. I must own, he was convincing, superficially; nearly another Mr. Barnum. You half expected him to announce to some street crowd that he would now transform this container of bran into a . . . live . . . guinea pig!

And the money that followed him wherever he went! I could not fathom the number of Baltimoreans who willingly forked over hard money into the hands of this storyteller; Baltimoreans, I sadly say, who exhibited no signs of doing the same for a book of Poe's poetry. Yet a veritable fortune was lent to the notion that the Baron Dupin would unveil the events of the same poet's last and darkest hours on this earth. Culture was enjoyed as long as it came with conflict. I recalled the time two actors simultaneously played Hamlet on nearby stages in Baltimore and everyone argued with passion about his own favorite Hamlet, not for the play itself but for the competition of it.

The lyceum lecture would be held at the Assembly Rooms of the Maryland Institute. The Baron began sending wires to repeat the same announcements of lectures to be subsequently held in New York, Philadelphia, Boston. . . . His plans were expanding, and ours seemed to fall more and more in his shadow.

The Baron, along the way, had further pried open Pandora's box of rumors in the newspapers.

Some samples: Poe was found robbed in a gutter by a watchman; or the dying Poe was lying across some barrels in the Lexington Market covered entirely with flies; no, said another, Poe met with former cadets from West Point, where the poet had learned musket and munitions, dealing now in some private governmental operation that introduced Poe to a dangerous intrigue and probably related to his reported roles in his wild youth fighting for the Polish army and with the Russians; not so: Poe's vain end had been a debauch at an acquaintance's lively and intemperate birthday party; or he had been guilty of suicide. One female acquaintance claimed that as a ghost Poe had sent her poems from the spiritual world about being fatally pummeled in an attempted theft of some letters! Meanwhile, a local paper had received a wire from a temperance newspaper in New York that claimed to have met a witness to Poe's raging debauchery in the day before he was discovered at Ryan's, proving for the recorder at Judgment Day that all was Poe's own fault.

While I sat surveying these articles in the reading room, that reliable, ancient clerk came over to me.

"Oh, Mr. Clark! I am still thinking of who had given me those articles on your Mr. Poe. Indeed, I *have* remembered distinctly how he asked me to give the articles to you."

Suddenly, I lost all attention to the papers before me. "What, sir?" It had never occurred to me that those cuttings had been given to the clerk with specific instructions that they be delivered to *me.* I asked if I understood him correctly.

"Right."

"This is startling!" I cried, thinking of how that single extract alluding to the "real" Dupin had completely changed the course of events.

"How so?"

"Because someone— " I did not finish the statement. "It is a matter of moment that you tell me more of this person, whoever he is. I am much occupied these days, but will call on you again. Try— please do try— to remember."

My imagination was fired by this new revelation. Meanwhile, I found a less speculative distraction in determining to settle matters with Hattie. I wrote her a long letter, acknowledging that Auntie Blum's cruel though well-meaning tactic had encouraged me, and proposing that upon my receiving word from her we should commence again the plans for our union.

16

TRACING THE ACTIVITY of the Baron Dupin, through covert observation and interviews, I learned that nearly a week earlier, Bonjour had insinuated herself as the chambermaid at the home of Dr. Joseph Snodgrass, the man whom Dr. Moran remembered had ordered the carriage that brought Edgar Poe to the hospital from Ryan's on that gloomy October day. The Baron Dupin had paid a visit to Snodgrass earlier to find out the details of that stormy October afternoon. Snodgrass adamantly declined an interview. He insisted he would not contribute to the industry of gossiping about the worthy poet's death.

Soon after, Bonjour had secured the position among the help in Snodgrass's house. Remarkably, she did this with no position open. She had appeared in neat, unostentatious dress, on the doorstep of the fashionable brick house at 103 North High Street. An Irish servant girl opened the street door for her.

Bonjour said that she had been told the house was looking for a new upstairs girl (assuming, rightly, that this was the downstairs girl— and imagining it likely she had a rivalry with the current upstairs girl).

Was that so? replied the servant. *She* had not heard about this. Bonjour apologized, explaining that the upstairs girl had told a friend about her plans to leave without proper notice to her employers, and Bonjour was eager to present her desire for the post.

Soon after this, the downstairs girl, who had a straggly figure and a jealous tendency toward comelier females, reported the dialogue to the Snodgrasses, who felt obliged to dismiss the protesting upstairs girl. Bonjour was the heroine of the household drama for uncovering the imminent loss to their domestic operations and, appearing again at the opportune time, was the natural choice as replacement. Though Bonjour was far more handsome than the jealous downstairs girl, the fact that she was too thin for the popular taste and had an unseemly scar down her lip made her more acceptable.

All this was easily discovered later from the former upstairs girl, who after her departure was eager to speak of her unfair treatment. But once Bonjour was installed behind the walls of the house, there was little chance at gaining any further intelligence about her enterprise.

"Leave her to the Snodgrass family then, and confine your observations on the Baron," Duponte suggested.

"She would not remain this long unless there was information to gain. It has been better than two weeks, monsieur!" I said. "In all events, the Baron is mostly occupied selling subscriptions to his lecture on Poe's death."

"Perhaps the information mademoiselle gains is not so large," Duponte mused, "but simply slow."

"I could inform Dr. Snodgrass that Bonjour is no chambermaid."

"Why do so, Monsieur Clark?"

"Why?" I replied incredulously. It seemed obvious. "To stop her from gaining intelligence for the Baron!"

"What they find, we shall inevitably learn," he replied, though I did not see the track of this reasoning.

Duponte, during my reports, regularly asked me to describe Bonjour's demeanor and mood toward the job and the other servants.

Bonjour would leave the Snodgrass home every day to meet with the Baron. On one of these evenings, as she made her way to one of these rendezvous, I followed her into the harbor area. Not infrequently, a man would be expelled out the door of a public house, and one would have to take a high step over his body or trip into a pile with him. The streets there were filled with bar-rooms and billiards-rooms and stale, human smells. Bonjour was dressed accordingly: hair disheveled, bonnet crooked, and dress in comfortable disorder. She changed costume often— depending on whether an errand for the Baron Dupin required the appearance of one class or another— but there was no demonic transformation as with the Baron's disguises.

I watched as she neared a group of low men, who were laughing and yelping riotously. One pointed at the passing figure of Bonjour.

"Look there," he said gruffly, "a star-gazer! What a pretty bat!" "Stargazer" and "bat" were equally vulgar terms; heard among the lowest classes, they connoted a prostitute who came out only at night.

She ignored them. He stretched out his arm as a barrier. He was almost twice Bonjour's size. She stopped and looked down at his bloated forearm, on which the sleeve was rolled up indecently.

"What's this, gal?" He yanked a piece of paper out of her hand. "A love letter, *I'd* guess. What's this now? 'There is a gentleman, rather the worse for wear . . . ' "

"Hands off," said Bonjour, taking a step forward.

The man held the paper up high and away from her reach, to the exaggerated amusement of his compatriots. A chunky little fellow among his companions guffawed and sympathetically said to let it go, at which point the ringleader punched his arm and declared him a positive gump.

Bonjour eased closer with a light sigh, the plane of her eyes hardly coming up to the large man's neck. She placed one finger along the muscle of his upstretched arm and followed the line. "The strongest arm I've seen in Baltimore, mister," she said in a whisper, though projected distinctly enough for the others to hear her.

"Now, I ain't going to lower this arm, my dear, on a little soft-soaping."

"I don't want you to lower it, mister, I want you to raise it higher—there, like that."

He did as instructed— perhaps despite himself. Bonjour leaned almost into the crook of his neck.

"Oh, oh, look," he said jovially to his companions, "the *bat* is going to fly at me for a kiss!"

They laughed. The man himself was giggling as nervously as a girl.

"Bats," Bonjour said, "are awful blind." In one gesture, swifter than lightning, she drew her hand behind her head and across the side of the gentleman's neck. His arm, raised high on that side, could make no attempt to block her.

The man's shirt and sack-coat collars, cleanly sliced at the buttons, both dropped to the ground. His clique fell into a grave silence. She returned a blade thin as a pin into the crown of her disordered hair. The man patted around his neck— making sure all his flesh was still there— and then, finding not a scratch, stumbled backward. Bonjour picked up the piece of paper where it had dropped and went on her way. Perhaps I imagined it, but before her departure, it seemed she glanced at me, across the way, and her face seemed to wear a look of bemusement at my stance of readiness to come to her aid.

I continued to frequent the area of the Snodgrass house. One morning after I arrived I saw Duponte approaching, dressed in his usual black suit and cloak and cape.

"Monsieur?" I greeted him inquisitively. It was something of an extraordinary event of late to see him in the daylight. "Has something happened?"

"We have an excursion today, in the interests of our investigation," he commented.

"Where shall we go?"

"We are here already."

Duponte walked through the gates and up the front pathway to the Snodgrass house. "Go ahead," Duponte said when I came to a halt.

"Monsieur, the Snodgrasses are not home this hour. And, you must know, Bonjour may see us here!"

"I fully rely on it," he replied.

He took the silver-plated knocker in hand, which promptly brought to us the downstairs girl. Duponte glanced around and saw with satisfaction that Bonjour was peering from the staircase high above, as likely she did with any guest calling for Dr. Snodgrass.

"Our business, miss," said Duponte, "lies with Dr. Snodgrass. I am"—here he paused, with a slight nod up to the landing of the stairs— "the *Duke Duponte*."

"Duke! Well, the doctor is not at home, sir." She passed a slow gaze over my outer garments, which prompted me to remove my hat and coat.

"I should think not, for he is a man of extensive business. But he has left word, I believe, with your upstairs girl that we are to wait for him in his study at this hour," said Duponte.

"Likely! How queer!" exclaimed the girl, whose jealousy for Bonjour seemed to rise like a visible object before our eyes.

"If the young woman is present, miss, perhaps she shall be able to confirm the particulars of our invitation."

"Likely!" the downstairs girl repeated. "Does this have truth, in fact?" she called up to Bonjour. "The doctor said nothing to me."

Bonjour smiled, and then said, "The doctor tells you nothing of what occurs upstairs, of course, miss. And his study *is* upstairs."

Bonjour approached us and curtsied a greeting. I was quite startled to find her compliant in Duponte's scheme, but as that first moment of surprise passed I came to understand. If Bonjour exposed Duponte's scheme as a false one, we could quite as easily demonstrate Bonjour's own falsehoods in securing her position. It was an automatic and unspoken bargain.

"Dr. Snodgrass asked that you follow me," she said.

"Into the study, I believe he suggested," Duponte replied, accompanying her up the stairs and gesturing for me to come.

Bonjour seated us in the study with a smile and offered to close the door behind us for our comfort. "You gentlemen will be most happy to know that the respected doctor will not be long before his return," she said. "He returns early today. I shall be certain to bring him *straightaway* when he comes home."

"We would expect nothing less, dear miss," said Duponte.

When we were alone, I turned to Duponte. "What shall we be able to learn from Snodgrass? Shall he not object strenuously to our pretending to have an appointment? And, monsieur, have you not said a hundred times we haven't any call to speak with witnesses?"

"Do you think that is why we've come? To see Snodgrass?"

I chafed a bit and made a point of not answering.

Duponte sighed. "We are not here to see Dr. Snodgrass; we shall be able to *read* what we wish to know among the doctor's papers. This is no doubt why the Baron has sent Bonjour here, and why she cleverly ensured she would become the upstairs servant, to have a free hand in his study without observation. She seemed rather amused with our presence, and quite loose with the more established servant, which suggests she is nearly finished with her purpose here. Nor does she believe we have enough time to discover anything of importance among all these papers."

"She's correct then!" I said, noticing that Snodgrass's study was awash in papers, in piles and stacks upon and around and inside the drawers of his office desk.

"Rethink your conclusions. Mademoiselle Bonjour has spent several weeks here now, and though she is a practiced thief, she would have no desire to risk that Dr. Snodgrass would notice the removal of any papers, which would foreclose any further search she might have wished to make. Thus she would have secretly copied in her own hand any items of interest and returned the originals to their place here for us to discover."

"But how shall we be able to discover in a matter of minutes what has taken her weeks to compile?"

"Precisely because she has discovered them first. Any document or paper that has attracted a high degree of interest will have commanded her to remove it from its place, perhaps more than once. Certainly one would not casually notice this difference, but once knowing to look for it, we should have no trouble selecting and copying these particular documents."

We went to work immediately. I took one side of the desk. Guided by Duponte, I searched for bent and misaligned corners, smudged ink, slight tears and folds, creases, and other indicators of recent handling among the various assortments and collections of documents and newspaper articles on all subjects, some with dates as much as twenty-five years old. Together we located many mentions of Poe that apparently had been examined by Bonjour in her time in this house, including a wealth of articles on the death of Poe that, if not quite as comprehensive as my own collection, was not unimpressive. Exhilarated and appalled, I found some rather more unique documents, three letters— the handwriting on which I recognized right away— from Edgar Poe to Dr. Snodgrass, dating from several years earlier.

In the first, Poe offered Snodgrass, then editing a magazine called *The Notion*, the rights to publish the second of the Dupin tales. "Of course I could not afford to make you an absolute present of it," wrote Poe firmly, "but if you are willing to take it, I will say $40." Yet Snodgrass turned him down, and Poe was declined by *Graham's*, too, before publishing "The Mystery of Marie Rogêt" elsewhere.

In the second letter from Poe, the writer asked Dr. Snodgrass to place a favorable notice of Poe's work in a magazine then being edited by Neilson Poe, hoping that the latter would oblige him as his cousin. The attempt seems to have failed, and Poe wrote back in disgust. "I *felt* that N. Poe would not insert the article," he said. "In your private ear, I believe him to be the bitterest enemy I have in the world."

I rushed to share this. "Neilson Poe, monsieur! Edgar Poe calls him his bitterest enemy. . . . Didn't I guess at his position in all this!"

Our time being too short to discuss each item, Duponte directed me to quickly copy into my memorandum book all items about Poe that seemed important to me and, for that matter, he said after thinking it over, items that seemed unimportant to me as well. I duly noted the date of Poe's letter about Neilson: October 7, 1839— exactly ten years to the day before Poe's death!

"He is the more despicable in this," wrote Poe of Neilson, "since he makes loud professions of friendship." And did Neilson not profess the same fables, when I met him? *We were not only cousins, but friends, Mr. Clark.* Neilson Poe, with his heart beating for his own literary fame, his hand holding a wife who was sister and near copy to Edgar's— had he wanted the life of the very man he so outwardly denigrated?

This was not all I found in letters from Poe to Snodgrass about his Baltimore relatives. Poe had declared Henry Herring (the first Poe relation to arrive at Ryan's) "a man of unprincipled character."

Dupont paused in the midst of opening every possible drawer in the room.

"Survey the streets from the other side of the house, Monsieur Clark. Watch out for Dr. Snodgrass's carriage. When he arrives, we must leave immediately, and ensure the Irish chambermaid says nothing of our visit."

I studied Duponte's face for any hint at how we would accomplish the second objective. I walked to a chamber at the front of the house. Looking from the window, I found that a carriage was passing nearby, but after it seemed to check its speed briefly, the horses continued down High Street. Turning back toward the study, I found myself facing Bonjour, leaning upon the hearth so that her black dress and apron radiated with the flame of the fire.

"All right, mister? Anything that I can help you with while you wait for Master Snodgrass?" she asked, in imitation of the downstairs chambermaid's voice, and loud enough that she might hear. In a quieter tone, she commented, "You see now that your friend is only a vulture on my master's investigation."

"I am quite well here, miss, thank you, only looking out at these dreadful rain clouds," I said in my loud voice, and then quietly: "Auguste Duponte imitates no man. He shall resolve this in a manner deserving of Monsieur Poe. He can help you, too, if you wish, more than that thief, mademoiselle, your so-called husband and master."

Bonjour, forgetting the necessities of her charade, slammed the door closed. "I think not! *Duponte* is a thief of true measure, Monsieur Clark— he steals people's thoughts, their faults. The Baron is a great man because he is himself in all things. The most freedom I can have is by being with him."

"You believe that by ensuring the Baron's victory here you will have repaid the debt you owe him for releasing you from prison, and will be free from this marriage he has compelled."

Bonjour threw her head back in amusement. "Well! You are firing into the wrong flock. I'd suggest you not judge me by mathematical analysis. You are becoming too much like your companion."

"Monsieur Clark!" Duponte called hoarsely from the study.

I shifted my weight anxiously from one foot to the other.

Bonjour moved closer and studied me. "You do not have a wife, Monsieur Clark?"

My thoughts darkened. "I will," I replied without confidence. "And I will treat her well and ensure our mutual happiness."

"Monsieur, the French girl possesses no freedom. In America a girl is free and honored for her independence until she is married. In France, the tables are turned. She is only free once she marries— and then with a freedom never to be imagined. A wife can even have as many lovers as her husband."

"Mademoiselle!"

"Sometimes, a man in Paris is far more jealous of his mistress than his wife, and a woman more true to her lover than her husband."

"But why remain a thief for him, mademoiselle?"

"In Paris you must get what you want from others by hook or crook, or others will get what they want from you first." She paused. "Your master is calling, monsieur."

I started for the door. Bonjour lingered a moment before stepping aside with a mocking curtsy. As I re-entered the study, Duponte said, "Monsieur, here is the note that perhaps tells us more than anything else, the one you heard read in part at the harbor. Write *every word and every comma* in your memorandum book. And quickly: I believe I hear the wheels of another carriage coming up the path. Write then: 'Dear Sir, There is a gentleman, rather the worse for wear, at Ryan's . . .'"

Upon the completion of our transcriptions, Bonjour led us downstairs rapidly.

"There is a back entrance?" I whispered.

"Dr. Snodgrass is just in the carriage house." We all turned around. It was the downstairs girl, who had appeared among us suddenly. "The Duke shan't leave now?"

"I'm afraid my schedule has become conflicted," said Duponte. "I shall have to see Dr. Snodgrass another time."

"I shall be certain to tell him you were here, then," she replied dryly, "*and* sitting in his study *alone* among his private things for nearly half of an hour."

Duponte and I froze at this warning, and I glanced over questioningly at Bonjour, who would no doubt be implicated as well.

Bonjour stared at her fellow domestic almost dreamily. When I turned back to Duponte, I saw he had entered into a private conversation with the Irish girl, whispering somberly to her. At the end of his comments, she nodded slightly, a faint crimson blush splashed on her cheeks.

"The other door, then?" I asked, noticing that she and Duponte seemed to have reached some accord.

"This way," said the maid, motioning to us. We crossed through the rear hall even as we could hear the boots of Dr. Snodgrass on the steps to the street door. As we climbed down to the pathway, Duponte turned back and touched his hat to the two ladies in farewell. "Bonjour," he said.

❖   ❖   ❖

"Monsieur, how did you persuade the doctor's chambermaid to cooperate so Bonjour would not be caught?" I asked as we walked up the street.

"First, you are on the wrong scent. It was not for Bonjour's sake, as you assume. Second, I explained to the chambermaid that, in all honesty, we were not in fact leaving for another appointment."

"Indeed? You told her the truth then," I said with surprise.

"I explained that her interest, or infatuation, with you was highly inappropriate, and I wished to leave discreetly and quietly before her employer returned and might notice it first-hand."

"*Infatuation with me?*" I repeated. "Wherever did such an idea come from, monsieur? Had she said something I did not hear?"

"No, but she certainly contemplated it upon my mention and, thinking something must have shown to that effect in her expression, she *thought* it must indeed be true. She will remain quiet about our visit, I assure you."

"Monsieur Duponte! I cannot begin to understand this tactic!"

"You are the model of the handsome young man," he replied, then added, "at least by Baltimore standards. That you are hardly aware of it only allows it to enter more decidedly in the eyes of a young female.

Certainly the chambermaid noted this upon our entrance; indeed, her eyes flitted, as it were, immediately. Even if she did not consider it directly— until I mentioned it."

"Monsieur, still— "

"No more talk of this, Monsieur Clark. We must continue our work in relation to Dr. Snodgrass."

"But what do you mean by 'it was not for Bonjour's sake'?"

"Bonjour hardly needs our assistance, nor would she hesitate to cross us for her purposes when given the opportunity. You would be especially wise to remember this. It was for the sake of the other girl I did that."

"How do you mean?"

"If the chambermaid had attempted to allege misconduct against Bonjour, I do not suppose the poor girl would have fared well against mademoiselle. Certainly, it is wise to save lives whenever you can."

I reflected a moment on my naïve understanding of the situation.

"Where shall we go next, monsieur?"

He gestured to my memorandum book. "To read, of course."

Meanwhile, a new obstacle awaited us. While we had been occupied, my great-aunt had arrived at Glen Eliza. Her purpose here was no mystery: word had reached her of my return to Baltimore and she came to see why I had not yet been married after my notorious lapse. She had a long fellowship with Hattie Blum's aunt (a conspiracy of these creatures!) and would have heard the odd bits of half-truth that the other woman had collected about my goings-on.

Nearly two hours passed after we returned home before I learned of her presence. After our endeavors at the Snodgrass home, we had adjourned to the athenaeum to match some of the records we had discovered with articles from the press. We continued on at Glen Eliza in fastidious conversation regarding our various discoveries made there. Because Duponte and I were organizing the intelligence we had gathered at the Snodgrass house, I gave firm orders that we were not to be interrupted. The table in the library had grown thick with newspapers, lists, and notes, and therefore we remained in the massive drawing room, which stretched out over half of the second floor of the house. At length, around twilight, I went to the other side of the house to consult something, but was stopped by Daphne, my best chambermaid.

"You must not go inside, sir," she said.

"Not go in my library? But why?"

"Ma'am insists she must not be disturbed, sir."

I obediently released the handle of the door. "Ma'am? What 'ma'am'?"

"Your aunt. She arrived with her bags at Glen Eliza while you were out, sir. She has been exhausted by her trip, as it was frightfully cold and her baggage nearly lost by the railroad men."

I was confounded. "I have been sitting in the drawing room without knowing this. Why have you not told me?"

"You declared in great hurryment you must not be disturbed even before stepping through the street door, didn't you, sir!"

"I must greet her properly," I said, straightening my neck-cloth and smoothing my vest.

"Well, go about it quietly— she needs strict quiet to cure her sick-headache to which she is subject, sir. I'm sure she was quite displeased at the other disturbance."

"Daphne, the other disturbance?" I then remembered that, not more than an hour earlier, Duponte had retrieved a book he had remembered was in the library. Surely my faithful maid had instituted my great-aunt's domineering orders against Duponte as well?

"The gentleman would not heed my words! He went right in. . . ." Daphne explained with heated disapproval and a fresh revival of her Duponte misgivings.

I thought about Duponte and Auntie Blum's encounter some weeks earlier, and imagining my great-aunt's reaction to any similar conversation made my own head throb. I now thought better of my desire to greet her— especially given the humor any woman of her advanced age was likely in, between the delayed train and Monsieur Duponte. I returned to the drawing room. Great-Aunt's presence would be no small disruption. Indeed, I could not guess the influence that elder relation would ultimately have over all this.

The next vivid memory I possess of that evening was when I stirred awake. I had fallen into an uncomfortable sleep on one of the drawing room's long sofas. The papers I had been reviewing had scattered on the carpet below. It was an hour or so past nightfall and Glen Eliza was eerie with silence. Duponte, it seemed, had retired to the third floor to his chambers. A loud bump jolted me to a greater state of consciousness. The wind was blowing through the long curtains, and a feeling of great anxiety flitted inside my stomach.

The corridors on this side of the house were deserted. Remembering my great-aunt, I ascended the winding stairs and crept past the chambers where she would have been placed by the servants, but found the door open and the bedclothes undisturbed. Walking back down directly to the library, I quietly pushed open the doors to the dimly lighted room.

"Great-Auntie Clark," I said softly, "I hope you are not still awake after such a difficult day."

The room was unoccupied— but not undisturbed. It was all but ransacked, papers overturned and books scattered around the room. No trace of the old woman was to be seen. In the corridor, I saw a darkly cloaked figure race past at a strong pace. I gave chase to the figure's shadow through the long halls of Glen Eliza. The figure dove through an open window near the kitchen on the first floor and ran toward a trail in the wooded area behind the house.

"Burglary!" I cried. "Auntie," I gasped to myself in sudden dread.

Following the little glen that ran along the house toward the gravel street, the burglar slowed to decide which way to run, leaving himself entirely vulnerable. I pounced, and wrestled him down with a giant leap and a groan.

"You shall not get away!" I yelled.

We fell together into a heap and I turned his body to face me, locking his wrist in my hand and struggling to throw off the hood of his velvet cloak. But this was no man.

"You? How? What have you done with Great-Auntie Clark?" I demanded. Then I realized my own stupidity. "It was you the whole time, mademoiselle? My aunt hasn't come?"

"If you wrote more frequently, perhaps she would," Bonjour scolded me. "I daresay there is reading in your library far more interesting dredged up by your master Duponte than in all your Monsieur Poe's tales."

"We saw you still at the Snodgrass house upon our departure!" Then I recalled our stop at the athenaeum.

"I was faster. That is your flaw— you hesitate always. Do not be angry, Monsieur Quentin. We are now even. You and your master wished to be in my territory in the Snodgrasses, and now I have entered yours. This is familiar, too." She writhed a bit under my grip, as I had done at the Paris fortifications in opposite positions. The velvet of her cloak and the silk of her dress rustled against my shirt.

I quickly released my grip. "You knew I could not send for the police. Why did you run then?"

"I like to see you run. You are not half slow, you know, monsieur, without a proper hat to hinder you." She passed her hand playfully through my hair.

My heart wild with bewilderment, I jumped up from our entangled position on the ground.

"Heavens!" I cried, looking ahead at the street.

"Is that all?" Bonjour laughed.

There was a small conveyance lurking on the hilly side of the street. Hattie stood calmly in front of it. I did not know when she had arrived, and could not imagine what she thought she saw before her.

"Quentin," she said, taking a cautious step forward. Her voice was unsteady. "I asked one of the stablemen to drive me. I have managed to get away from my house a few times but, until now, have not found you at home."

"I have been away much," I replied dumbly.

"I thought nightfall would provide us privacy to meet." She glanced at Bonjour, who lingered on the cold grass before hopping up. "Quentin? Who is this?"

"This is Bon— " I stopped myself, realizing her name would sound like a queer invention on my part. "A visitor from Paris."

"You met this young lady in Paris, and now she has come to call on you?"

"Not to see me in particular, Miss Hattie," I protested.

"You are in love after all, Monsieur Quentin. She's beautiful!" Bonjour tossed her head. She leaned forward as though peeping at a new litter of kittens. Hattie flinched at the attention of the stranger, wrapping her shawl tighter.

"Tell me, how did he pop the important question?" Bonjour asked Hattie.

"Please, Bonjour!" When I turned my back to Hattie to admonish Bonjour, Hattie climbed into her coach and ordered it away. "Hattie, wait!" I cried.

"I must go home, Quentin." I chased the carriage and called out to Hattie before losing too much ground as they passed into the forest. When I turned back to Glen Eliza, Bonjour had vanished as well, and I was alone.

The next morning, I firmly rebuked the chambermaid who had acted as guard to Bonjour's fraud.

"Say, Daphne, that you truly thought that young woman, hardly old enough to be my wife, was my great-aunt!"

"I did not say *great*-aunt, sir, but aunt only, as she said. She was in her shawl and the finest hat, sir, so I did not judge her age. Nor did the other gentleman question her on the matter when he entered there. And more so, sir, in large families one can have many aunts of all ages. I knew a girl of twenty-two whose aunt was not yet three years old."

I turned my attention to her most salient point, Duponte. It was possible, perhaps, that in the midst of his usual unbreakable concentration and with the library's stained glass keeping it dim even in the day, he had noticed no more than a feminine silhouette at the library table when he had gone inside for his book. Still, this seemed unlikely. I confronted Duponte on the issue. I could not restrain my anger.

"The Baron shall now possess nearly half, if not more, of the information we have gathered! Monsieur, did you not notice Bonjour *right in front of you* when you walked into the library yesterday?"

"I am not blind," he replied. "And to a very beautiful girl! It is a dim room, but not so dim as that. I saw her plainly."

"Why didn't you call for me, for God's sake? The situation has been much damaged!"

"The situation?" Duponte repeated, perhaps sensing that my frenzy went beyond her infiltration of our investigation on the case. Indeed, I wondered if I could ever look the same again in Hattie's eyes.

"All the intelligence we had possessed that they had not," I said more calmly and with decision.

"Ah. Not so, Monsieur Clark. Our hold on the events surrounding the time of Monsieur Poe's death is dependent only in very small part in possessing the details and facts, which are the blood of the newspapers. That's not the heart of our knowledge. Do not mishear me: details are elemental, and at times trying to acquire, but not in themselves enlightenment. One must know how to read them properly to find their properties of truth— and the Baron Dupin's reading of them has nothing to do with ours. If your concern is that we shall give the Baron some advantage over us, worry not, for it is the opposite of what you think. If his reading is incorrect, than the more particulars he must read, the farther we move ahead of him."

17

*Dear Sir,– There is a gentleman, rather the worse for wear, at Ryan's
4th Ward polls, who goes under the cognomen of Edgar A. Poe, and
who appears in great distress, & he says he is acquainted with you,
and I assure you, he is in need of immediate assistance.*

❋   ❋   ❋

A LOCAL PRINTER named Walker had signed this note in an urgent scrawl that had almost sent the pencil through the coarse paper. It
was dated 3 October 1849 and addressed to Dr. Joseph Snodgrass, who
lived close to Ryan's, which on that election day when Poe was found
also served as a polling place for the Congressional and state election.

A few days after Duponte and I occupied the study of Dr. Snodgrass,
and Hattie stood dazed as I lay entangled with another woman, the Baron
Dupin called on Snodgrass again.

I had been watching the Baron when he suddenly idled at a corner of
Baltimore Street as though he had forgotten that he had any cares in the
world. I was across the street, remaining inconspicuous among the crowds
of people heading to hotels and restaurants for supper and the high baskets balanced on the heads of laborers and slaves. After a seemingly unending time waiting for the Baron to do something, I was distracted by the
rumble of a carriage that swerved suddenly to the side near me.

From inside the carriage, I heard a voice:

"What are you doing? Driver! Why are you stopping here?"

Confirming that the Baron had not moved from his position, I decided
to investigate the identity of the perturbed passenger. When I was near-
ing the carriage, I came to a standstill. I knew him instantly as a man I'd
first seen at the burial ground on Greene and Fayette. He'd stood restlessly that day, shifting from foot to foot, at the funeral of Edgar Poe.

"Do you hear me, driver?" continued his complaint. "Driver?"

Here, by some strange ordering of the universe, the mourner had left that dark dream-land, a place of fog and mud, and had been driven right to me in the clear of day. After my meetings with Neilson Poe and Henry Herring, I was now with the third of the four mourners. Only the fourth remained, Z. Collins Lee— a classmate of Poe's from college who, as I'd recently heard, had been appointed a United States district attorney.

I stepped to the side of the coach. But the man had now wriggled to the other side, shouting out at the driver and fidgeting with the handle to open the door. I was about to speak, to call his attention through the window. Then his door opened.

"Isn't it Dr. Snodgrass!" a voice bellowed.

I wheeled away from the window and hid myself near the horses.

It was the Baron Dupin's voice.

"You again," Snodgrass said contemptuously, stepping down. "What are you doing here?"

"Nothing at all," the Baron said innocently. "You?"

"Sir, I beg your leave. I have another appointment. And this rascal driver— "

Leaning over, I could see the Baron's light-skinned slave Newman on the driver's seat and I understood. The Baron had not been idling across the street; he had been waiting for this very man to be delivered to him. No doubt he had stationed Newman in a place where he had known Snodgrass would look for a hackney coach. The first time I had eavesdropped on Snodgrass with the Baron I had seen Snodgrass's face only obliquely. Now the Baron removed the Walker note from his coat; the few sentences written by Walker the day Poe was found, recorded above. He showed it to Snodgrass.

Snodgrass was astonished. "Who are you?" he asked.

"You were involved that day," said the Baron, "in tending to Mr. Poe's well-being. If I chose, this note could be printed in the papers as proof that you were responsible for him. Some people, not knowing better, will assume you were hiding something both by not coming forward honestly with more details and, worse, by sending Mr. Poe alone to the hospital."

"Balderdash! Why would they assume that?" Snodgrass asked.

The Baron laughed good-naturedly. "Because I shall tell the newspapers just that."

Snodgrass hesitated, wavering between compliance and anger. "Did you enter my house, sir? If you stole this, sir . . ."

Bonjour now joined the Baron's side.

"You! Tess!" This had been Bonjour's assumed name at the Snodgrass home. "My chambermaid?" Now Snodgrass could not help choosing anger. "I shall call for the police this moment!"

"There may be evidence of a small theft you can present them with. But there is also evidence . . . well, should I mention?" the Baron said, putting a finger to his lips in restraint. "Yes, should I mention there were other private papers of yours we have happened upon . . . ? Oh, the public and all of your blessed committees and societies and so forth would be most interested if we were to kick up a dust . . . ! Do you not think so . . . *Tess,* my dear?"

"Blackmail!" Snodgrass stopped himself again, outraged but also hesitant.

"Unpleasant business, I agree." The Baron waved it away. "Back to Poe. You see, that is what really interests us. If the public knows your story— if they believe you tried to save his life . . . that would be different. But *we* must have your story first."

Baron Dupin had a sly talent for shifting effortlessly from badgering to dandling. He had performed the same dance with Dr. Moran, at the hospital where Poe died.

"Come now. Back into the carriage, Doctor— let us visit Ryan's!"

At least that is what I imagined the Baron said next as the defeated Snodgrass contemplated a reply, for I had already started away to find an unobtrusive place to wait at the tavern, knowing that was where they would be headed.

❊   ❊   ❊

"Once I received that letter from Mr. Walker, I repaired to this drinking-saloon— tavern is too dignified a name— and, sure enough," Snodgrass continued as he escorted the Baron inside, *"there he was."*

I sat at a table in a sunless corner of the room, obscured and further darkened by the shadow of the stairwell that led up to the rooms available for hire, which were often taken by those customers not sober enough to find their way home.

"Poe!" interjected the Baron.

Snodgrass stopped at a dingy armchair. "Yes, he was sitting over here with his head dropped forward. He was in a condition that had been but too faithfully depicted by Mr. Walker's note— which, by the bye, you have had no business to read."

The Baron only grinned at the reproof. Snodgrass continued dejectedly.

"He was so altered from the neatly dressed, vivacious gentleman I knew, that I hardly would have distinguished him from the crowd of intoxicated men, whom the occasion of an election had called together here."

"This whole room was a polling place that night?" the Baron asked.

"Yes, for the local ward. I remember the whole sight well. Poe's face was haggard, not to say bloated," said Snodgrass, unbothered by the contradictory adjectives. "And unwashed, his hair unkempt, and his whole physique repulsive. His forehead, with its wonderful breadth, and that full-orbed and mellow yet soulful eye— lusterless and vacant now."

"Did you have a good look at his clothing?" The Baron was scribbling at a railroad pace in his notebook.

Snodgrass seemed to be dazed by his own memory. "There was nothing good to see, I'm afraid. He wore a rusty, almost brimless, tattered and ribbonless palm-leaf hat. A sack-coat of thin and sleazy black alpaca, ripped at several of the seams, and faded and soiled, and pants of a steel-mixed pattern of cassinette, half worn and badly fitting. He had on neither vest nor neck-cloth, while the bosom of his shirt was both crumpled and badly soiled. On his feet, if I remember aright, there were boots of coarse material, with no sign of having been blacked for a long time."

"How did you proceed, Dr. Snodgrass?"

"I knew Poe had several relatives in Baltimore. So I ordered a room for him at once. I accompanied a waiter upstairs and, after selecting a sufficient apartment, was returning to the bar-room to have the guest conveyed to his chamber so he could be comfortable until I got word to his relatives."

They stepped toward the stairwell, Snodgrass pointing up to the chamber he had selected for Poe on the other side of the stairs. At my table, I tried my best to lose myself in the darkness.

"So you selected Mr. Poe's room, and then sent for his relations?" asked the Baron.

"That is the peculiar thing. I did not need to. When I reached the bottom of the stairway again, I was met by Mr. Henry Herring, a relative of Poe's by marriage."

"Before you had called for him?" the Baron asked. I thought the detail strange, too, and strained to hear Snodgrass's reply.

"That's right. He was at the spot— perhaps with another one of Poe's relatives; I cannot recall."

This was another peculiarity. Neilson Poe had told me he first heard of Edgar Poe's condition when the latter was in the hospital. If there was another relative with Henry Herring, and it was not Neilson, who was it?

Snodgrass continued. "I asked Mr. Herring whether he wished to take his relation to his house, but he strongly declined. 'Poe has been very abusive and ungrateful on former occasions, when drunk,' Mr. Herring explained to me. He suggested a hospital as a better place for him than the hotel. We sent a messenger to procure a carriage to the Washington College Hospital."

"Who accompanied Mr. Poe to the hospital?"

Snodgrass looked down uncomfortably.

"You did send your friend there alone, then," the Baron said.

"He could not sit up, you see, and there was no room in the carriage once he was lying flat on the seats. He was past locomotion! We carried him as if he were a corpse, lifted him into the coach. He resisted us, muttering, but nothing intelligible. We did not think he was fatally ill then. He was stupefied with drink, alas. That was his final demon." Snodgrass sighed.

I had known already what the doctor felt of Poe's purported drinking. Among the papers in his study, Duponte had come across a few verses on the subject of Poe's death. "Oh! 'twas a saddening scene to find," read Snodgrass's refrains,

> *Thy proud young heart and noble brain*
> *Steeped in the demon draught— thy mind*
> *No longer fitted for the strain*
> *Of thought melodious and sublime.*

"So much for the death of Edgar Poe," Snodgrass now remarked sullenly to the Baron. "I should hope you are satisfied and do not aim to put further light onto Poe's sin. His failings have been mourned enough in public, and I have done everything I can not to say more of it for the time."

"In that, Doctor, you have nothing to worry about," said the Baron. "Poe took nothing to drink."

"Why, what do you mean? I have no doubt. It was a debauch, sir, that killed Poe. His disease was *mania a potu*, even as the papers reported. I am a possessor of the facts."

"I am afraid you witnessed facts," said the Baron with a grin, "and may even possess them, but you fail to possess the *truth*." The Baron Dupin put up his hand to silence Snodgrass's protest. "You need not trouble to defend yourself, Dr. Snodgrass. You did your best. But it was not you, sir, nor was it any manner of alcohol that brought Edgar Poe low. There were forces quite more devilish turned against the poet that day. He shall yet be vindicated." The Baron's speech was now more to himself than to Snodgrass.

But Snodgrass still shook his hand in the air as though he had been meanly insulted. "Sir, I am expert in this area. I am an officer with standing of the Baltimore temperance committees! I know a . . . a . . . drunken sot, don't I, when coming face to face with one? What are you attempting to do? You may as well try to outstorm the sky!"

The Baron repeated his words slowly, turning around in a circle, his nostrils flaring like a warhorse's. "Edgar Poe shall be vindicated."

18

"POE *HAD NOTHING* to *drink,* the Baron said, and drinking did not cause his death, as the press reported."

I was sitting opposite Duponte in my library now, perched at my chair's edge.

Naturally, I did not wish to appear overly pleased about the Baron's conversation with Snodgrass. I did not intend to praise the Baron *too* highly. He, after all, was our chief rival and obstacle.

"Oh, the look across Dr. Snodgrass's face!" I accidentally continued. "Dupin might have punched him hard in the jaw." I laughed. "Snodgrass— that false friend— deserved it, if someone were to ask me."

An extraneous thought came into my mind, or a question really. Had there been suggestions, in the text of Poe's tales, I asked myself, that C. Auguste Dupin had been a lawyer? I could not help it. The question chimed in my head without offering me a choice to reject it.

"And anything further?"

"What?" I stirred, realizing there had been an awkward interval of silence.

"Did you observe anything further today, monsieur?" asked Duponte, rolling his chair halfway back to the desk of newspapers.

I explained the other points of interest, particularly the sudden and inexplicable presence of Henry Herring at Ryan's before Snodgrass had a chance to call for him, and the detailed descriptions of Poe's disheveled dress. I was careful not even to say the name of Baron Dupin again, as much for my benefit as for Duponte's.

"Neilson Poe, Herring! Now Snodgrass!" I exclaimed in distaste.

"What do you mean, monsieur?" Duponte asked.

"They were all at Poe's funeral— men charged with honoring him. Instead, Snodgrass delivers a vision of Poe as a drunken sot. Neilson Poe takes no action to defend his cousin's name. Henry Herring arrives quickly at Ryan's, before he is even called for by Snodgrass, only to push his relative off alone into a hack to the hospital."

Duponte passed a hand thoughtfully over his chin, sucked at his tongue, and then turned his chair so his back was toward me.

Around this time, the idea had begun to forcefully develop in my mind that, in encouraging my role as spy, Duponte had chiefly wished to keep me occupied. After the disquieting conference recorded above, I hardly spoke to him but to report the particulars of my latest findings, which he usually received with easy indifference; some evenings, if he had already retired by the time I returned to Glen Eliza, I would leave a concise letter detailing all I had observed on that day. I could not forget, moreover, that his somber inaction after discovering Bonjour's prank had led to the great embarrassment between myself and Hattie in front of Glen Eliza. I suppose Duponte took notice of my cooler demeanor, but he never commented about it.

Over breakfast one day I said, "I'm thinking of composing a letter. To that temperance newspaper in New York that claimed knowledge of Poe having a debauch. It has been much on my mind. Someone should demand that they produce the name and account of this so-called witness."

At first Duponte did not reply. Finally he looked up in a cloud of distraction.

"What do you think of the temperance periodical's article, Monsieur Duponte?"

"That it is a temperance periodical," he said. "Their stated desire is the universal elimination of the use of spirits, yet they have a different, in fact most contradictory need, monsieur: a reliable supply of well-regarded people ruined from drink to prove to their readers why their temperance periodical should remain in existence. Poe has become one of these."

"So you do not think the magazine's witness is real?"

"Doubtful."

This raised my hopes and, for an instant, fully restored my fellowship with my companion. "And you have acquired the evidence, monsieur, which we might use to refute them. Can we prove yet that Poe did not drink when he was here?"

"I have never said that I believe he did not."

I could not reply, so fixed was I in momentary shock. His implication was not absolutely certain, but I feared I understood it too well as the exact opposite of the Baron's declaration at Ryan's. My thoughts turned to changing the topic. . . . I did not want to hear him. . . .

"In fact"— Duponte talked over me, preparing to confirm my dread— "he almost certainly did."

Had I heard this correctly? Had Duponte come all this way only to affix Poe's condemnation?

"Now, do tell me more about the subscriptions the Baron has been raising. . . ." he said.

In my turmoil, I welcomed any other subject. Baron Dupin had continued to amass his fortune in subscription moneys around Baltimore. In one oyster tavern alone, he had gleefully received payment from twelve eager fellows. The proprietor, bothered by the Frenchman's interruptions, had related to me the substance of his visits. "In two weeks, folks," the Baron would say, "you shall hear the first true account of Poe's death!" To Bonjour, he once added, "when they hear of my success in Paris, then, then . . ." His comment trailed off there; to the Baron Dupin's hungry imagination, there was every possibility opening from this success. . . .

A few days later, the Baron Dupin showed himself a bit distressed in the anteroom of his hotel. Afterward, I bribed a nearby porter and asked what had transpired. He said the Baron Dupin had called for his colored boy and found that he was gone. After much shouting and fussing, it was discovered through the civil authorities that Newman had been manumitted. The Baron knew he had been humbugged, and by whom. He laughed.

"Why do you laugh?"

"Because, my dear," he said to Bonjour, "I should be smarter than that. Of course he has been freed."

"You mean that Duponte has done this? But how?"

"You do not know Duponte. You shall yet know him better."

I smiled at the Baron's reported frustration.

On Duponte's instructions, I had a day earlier found the name of Newman's owner. He was a debtor who required quick funds, and thus had made the arrangement with the Baron to hire out Newman for an indefinite period of time. He had not known of the Baron's promise to Newman to purchase his freedom. He was also appalled to hear that Newman had not gone to work for "a small family," as had been advertised. New-man's owner became angry when I told him of the deception. Not angry enough, though, to refuse my own check to him to secure the slave's free-dom. In my law practice I'd had extensive experience dealing with per-sons in great debt in a manner that neither offended their self-esteem nor overlooked their pressing needs.

I even escorted the young man to the train depot myself to send him on his way to Boston. When manumitting a slave, it was dictated that the former slave be quickly removed from the state so he would not nega-tively influence blacks who remained slaves. Newman was overjoyed as we walked, but seemed filled with worry, as though the ground might collapse beneath our feet before he was safely outside the state. He was not far off. We had only a few yards before reaching the depot when an enormous rumble came from behind and cleared the street of all who were on foot, including us.

Approaching were three omnibuses filled with black men, women, and children. Behind these conveyances were several men on horseback. I recognized one man, tall and silver-haired, as Hope Slatter, the most powerful of the city's slave-dealers, or *nigger-traders.* The practice of the larger slave-traders in Baltimore was to house the slaves they purchased from sellers in their private prisons, usually a wing of their homes, until a ship could be sufficiently filled to merit the expenses of delivering a shipment to New Orleans, the hub of the southern trade. Slatter and his assistants were now driving to the harbor with approximately a dozen slaves in each bus.

Along the sides of the omnibuses waited other blacks, perpetually stopping to put their arms up to the windows of the omnibuses, and then running to keep up with them, to touch or speak with the occupants one final time. It could not be determined whether a greater amount of weep-ing occurred inside or out. From within, a voice shouted hysterically, loud enough for anyone who would listen. She tried to make clear that she had been sold to Slatter by her owner with the express provision that she not be separated from her family, as he was now doing.

I steered Newman away from this whole scene, but he was dangerously transfixed by the sight, perhaps the last of its kind he would see before leaving for the North.

The slave-trader and his assistants held up their whips and warned those surrounding the vehicles not to delay their pace. One man had climbed up to a window of the omnibus and was clinging to it, calling for his wife, whom he could not see. She pushed her way through other slaves in the bus to the window.

Slatter, spying this, pressed his horse around from the other side. "Do not continue!" he warned the man.

The climber ignored this, reaching inside to embrace his wife.

Out came Slatter's cane, its strap wrapped closely around his wrist. He knocked the man in the back and then the stomach and left him writhing on the ground. "Away, little dog, before I call for your arrest! You do not wish what would follow that!"

As Slatter steered his horse to step around from the fallen man, his eyes drifted to my position— or, rather, to the young black standing with me.

"Who is this?" he asked gravely from his high saddle as he approached us. He pointed his cane down at Newman.

Newman's lips trembled terribly; he tried to speak but failed. I hoped the man would simply continue on with his other horrid task, but that was not to be.

He pointed his cane at Newman's mouth, and then across his body as though he were lecturing at the medical college. "A likely Negro, aren't you. Fine mouth, generally good teeth, no broken bones to be seen. Good coachman, I'd bet, or a waiter, if he can be careful and honest." Addressing me, he said, "I could sell him for at least six hundred dollars, with a commission to me, my friend."

"I am not his owner," I replied. "Nor is he for sale."

"Then perhaps he is your bastard child?" he said sarcastically.

"I am Quentin Clark, an attorney of this city. This young man you see is manumitted."

"I'm a free man, boss," Newman finally said in a tiny whisper.

"Oh?" Slatter asked musingly, reversing his horse and peering down again at Newman. "Let us see your certificates then."

At this Newman, who had received all the necessary papers that morning, merely trembled and stammered.

"Come on now." Slatter prodded Newman in the shoulder with his cane.

"Leave him," I cried out. "He is freed by my own hand. A man with more freedom than you, Mr. Slatter, for he knows what it is not to have it."

Slatter was about to hit Newman in the shoulder harder when I raised my cane and blocked his instrument with it. "Tell me, Mr. Slatter," I said. "I wonder, if you are so interested in papers, if you should like to have the authorities inspect your slaves on the bus and ensure that all are being sold in accordance with their particular deeds."

Slatter grinned darkly at me. He withdrew his cane with an air of courtesy and, without saying another word to us, dug his heels into his horse's sides to catch up with the train of vehicles heading down into the harbor. Newman was breathing rapidly.

"Why not show him your papers?" I asked insistently. "You do have them on you?"

He pointed to his head, where he wore a ragged hat— he had sewn the papers into the brim. Newman then told of the many traders like Slatter who asked to inspect their certificates of freedom and, once they had them in hand, destroyed the documents. They'd then conceal the rightfully free men and women in their pens until they were sold as legal slaves to another state, far away from any evidence to the contrary.

19

"MONSIEUR DUPONTE, I must ask something at once."

I said this after one of our many recent silent suppers in the large rectangular dining room of Glen Eliza.

Duponte nodded.

I continued. "When the Baron holds his lecture on Poe's death, it may irrevocably pollute the truth. Perhaps, when he delivers his speech, I should cause some distraction to him outside the hall, and you could claim the stage and reveal the truth to the people!"

"No, monsieur," said Duponte, shaking his head. "We shall do nothing of the kind. There is more here than you realize."

I nodded sadly, and did not touch another morsel of food. That had been my experiment. Duponte had failed. He went on with his undisturbed silence.

I was entirely absorbed in distraction. To my visible displeasure, the dronish fellows who were overseeing some of my father's investments came to the door and I sent them away at once. I could not think about numbers and annual accounts.

"The Purloined Letter": the second sequel to "The Murders in the Rue Morgue." That's what I was thinking about with such a wistful air. C. Auguste Dupin has discovered the secret location of the letter stolen by Minister D––– , hidden most ingeniously by being placed *right in front of everyone's eyes.* It was the ordinary aspect of the spot that eluded all but one man. The analyst uses an unnamed collaborator to fire a gun in the street and raise a commotion. The collaborator's distraction allows C. Auguste Dupin to retrieve the letter, and put a false one in its place.

I relate this to bring out a point. C. Auguste Dupin trusts his collaborator there; and, besides, puts increasingly great trust in the work of his faithful assistant in all of Poe's Dupin trilogy.

Yet Auguste Duponte, my own companion, hardly gave credence to my role as collaborator and quietly dismissed my numerous ideas and suggestions, whether it was questioning Henry Reynolds, for which he made a mockery of me, or my latest design regarding the disruption of the Baron's lecture. On the other hand, Baron Dupin in all he endeavored constantly favored employing accomplices!

Then there was the interesting fact to consider of Baron Dupin's gift for disguises and alterations. A similarity might be noted, that the literary Dupin uses his green spectacles as another way to dupe his brilliant opponent, Minister D— — — , in "The Purloined Letter."

And how about Baron Dupin's profession as a lawyer? I had begun in the last few days to underline certain lines in the trilogy. "The Mystery of Marie Rogêt" implies to the careful reader, in certain key passages, that C. Auguste Dupin was deeply acquainted with the law, perhaps hinting for us at *his past practice as a lawyer.* Like Baron Dupin.

Then there is that initial, so uninteresting to the uninformed eye: C. Auguste Dupin. *C.* Dupin. Could it not remind the reader of one *Claude* Dupin? And is not Poe's character of the genius analyst known by the time of the second tale by the dignified title of "Chevalier"? Chevalier C. Auguste Dupin. Baron C. Dupin.

"But what of the Baron Dupin's cold penchant for money?" I asked myself. Alas, recall that C. Auguste Dupin profits monetarily, and most *deliberately,* from the employment of his skills in each of the three tales!

Above all, here was the Baron Claude Dupin confronting Snodgrass, boldly denying the notion of Poe expiring through a disgraceful debauch. While on that same day in Glen Eliza *Auguste Duponte was allowing for the merits of that shameful position.* His nonchalant comment about Poe's drinking resounded in my mind again and again until bitterness and regret reigned over me. "I had never said he had not."

I acknowledged the seeds of my idea and allowed it to germinate: what if the Baron Dupin, all this time, were the *real Dupin.* And would not Poe have enjoyed this jolly, philosophical, hoaxing rogue, who had so thrilled and plagued me? Poe had written in a letter to me that the Dupin tales were ingenious not just for their method but their "*air* of method." Didn't the Baron understand the importance of appearance in gaining the awe of those around him, whereas Duponte ignored and alienated to no end? What a great, strange relief these thoughts suddenly provided me. I had miscalculated all along.

Though it was late at night when these ideas culminated in me, I descended the stairs soundlessly and stole out of Glen Eliza. I reached the

Baron Dupin's hotel room a half hour late and stood at the door. I was breathing deeply, too deeply, my breathing an echo of my frantic thoughts. I knocked, too exhilarated and fearful to be articulate. There was a rustle from the other side of the door.

"I've possibly been mistaken," I said softly. "Some words, please, just a few moments." I looked behind me to make sure I had not been followed.

The room door nudged opened, and I put my foot in front of it.

I knew I would have only a brief hearing to state my position. "Baron Dupin, please! I believe we must speak at once. I believe— I know you are the one."

20

"BARON! IS THERE a real baron staying in this hotel?"

A thickly bearded man in nightclothes and slippers stood at the door, holding up his candle.

"This is not the room of Baron Dupin?"

"We have not seen him!" replied the man with disappointment, looking over his shoulder as though perhaps there was a baron in his bedquilt he had neglected to notice. "But we've only arrived this afternoon from Philadelphia."

I mumbled my apologies and returned hurriedly through the hall and to the street. The Baron had changed hotels again and, in my distraction, I had missed it. My thoughts ran quick and conflicting as I emerged from the hotel. Immediately I felt eyes upon the back of my neck and slowed my walk. It was not merely the intensity of my mood. There was the handsome black whom I had seen before, hands deep in his coat pockets, standing under the streetlamp. Or was it? He remained within the scope of the light only momentarily; then I could find him no more. Turning to the other side, I thought I saw one of the two men in the old-fashioned dress I had seen following the Baron. My heart thumped violently at the vague feeling of being surrounded. I marched away as quickly as possible, jumping nearly headlong into a hackney coach, which I directed back to Glen Eliza.

After a night of sleeplessness, images of Duponte and the Baron Dupin alternating and mixing in my mind with the sweeter sounds of Hattie's sonorous laugh, a messenger arrived in the morning with a note from the athenaeum clerk. It concerned the man who had handed him those Poe-related articles— that first hint of the existence of the real Dupin. The clerk had indeed remembered or, rather, had seen the very man himself, and when doing so had requested his calling card to send to me.

The man who had passed along the articles was Mr. John Benson, a name meaningless to me. The enameled calling card was from Richmond but had a Baltimore address written in a man's hand. Had someone wanted me to find the real Dupin? Had someone possessed a motive in seeing him brought to Baltimore to resolve Poe's death? Had I been chosen for this?

To say sooth, though, my hopes for elucidation were dim. It seemed to me likely that the ancient clerk, however well-meaning, may have simply mistaken this fellow as the man he had met so briefly two years ago.

I thought of the figures who'd seemed to creep from the shadows around me the night before. Prior to venturing outside on this day, I had secured a revolver that my father had kept in a box to bring on his business visits to the less cultivated countries that traded with Baltimore. I placed the weapon in the pocket of my coat and started for the address printed on Benson's card.

Walking through Baltimore Street, I saw, from a distance, Hattie standing in front of the sign for a fashionable store. I signaled her halfheartedly, not knowing if she would simply walk away without addressing me.

With great abruptness, she ran ahead and embraced me warmly. Though I thrilled at her affection, and the comfort of being close to her again, I imagined with true torment and anxiety that she would brush against the revolver in my coat and develop again the doubts about my behavior that had plagued her. She pulled back as quickly as she had reached for me, as though afraid of spying eyes.

"Dear Hattie," I said, "you do not abhor the very sight of me?"

"Oh, Quentin. I know that you have found new worlds for yourself, new experiences outside the ones we could have together."

"You do not understand who that was. She is a thief, a burglar! Please, I must make you understand. Let us talk together somewhere quiet."

I took her arm to lead her. She gently pulled away.

"It is far too late. I had only come to Glen Eliza that night to explain. I have told you things are quite different."

This could not be! "Hattie, I needed to follow what seemed right. But soon all will be returned to normal."

"Auntie wishes that I never say your name again, and has instructed all of our friends that they are never to mention our engagement with a single living breath."

"But surely Auntie Blum can be readily convinced. . . . What she wrote in her note to me about you finding someone else . . . it is not true?"

Hattie gave a small nod. "I am to be married to another man, Quentin."

"It is not because of what you saw at Glen Eliza."

She shook her head no, her face motionless and ambivalent.

"Who?"

Here was my answer.

Peter stepped from inside the store where Hattie stood, counting out some coins given to him by the shop-girl. Seeing me, he turned away guiltily.

"Peter?" I cried. "No."

He let his gaze drift aimlessly. "Hello, Quentin."

"You are . . . engaged to marry Peter!" I moved forward and whispered to Hattie so that he could not hear. "Dear Miss Hattie, Hattie, just tell me one thing— are you happy? Just tell me."

She paused, then nodded brightly, putting out her hand to me.

"Quentin, let us all talk together," Peter said.

But I did not wait. I rushed forward, passing Peter without so much as touching my hat. I wished that both of them would disappear.

"Quentin! Please!" Peter called out. He followed me for a few feet, but he gave up when he saw I would not stop— or perhaps when he saw the anger that flashed in my eyes.

I almost forgot the gun hidden in my coat, considering the mortal weight of this new discovery. On my way to Mr. Benson's address, I passed through some of the finer, most well-appointed streets of Baltimore.

After explaining that I was a stranger with some brief business to discuss with the gentleman of the house, and apologizing for possessing no letter of introduction, I was ushered inside by a colored servant to a sofa in the parlor. The rooms were sparser than was the fashion of the day, with rather exotic paper of an Oriental flavor on the walls, the background for several small silhouettes; the only large portrait loomed behind the sofa, and at first it did not strike me as anything worth noticing.

I do not know, scientifically speaking, if one's senses can detect the eyes of a painting looking upon them, but as I waited for the master of the house, a curious sensation arose in me that made me crane my head. The position of the lamps threw a vivid light around the picture. I rose to my feet as the painted eyes met mine. The face was full, wearied but still alive with vivacity, as though from some idealistic past. The eyes, though . . . No, how foolish of me. It was an excitable spell at work from the strains of the last days. The shadowy face was older, the hair whiter, the chin thick, whereas *his* was gaunt and almost pointed. Yet the eyes! It was as though they had been transplanted from the dark orbs of the Phantom, the man whose image still invaded my mind at regular intervals, telling me not to meddle and having started, almost single-handedly, the quest that had taken me this far. I quickly shook away this unhealthy notion of recognition, yet remained in a bothered state. As I waited longer, I remembered how little faith I had in the use of the present visit, and felt the formal setting of the receiving room to be suffocating. I decided to leave my calling card and return to Glen Eliza.

But upon hearing someone coming, I halted.

Slow steps led down the stairway, and from around its bend Mr. Benson appeared.

I gasped. "The Phantom!"

There he stood. The singular man who so many months earlier had warned me away from the case of Poe. A younger version of the eyes on the wall behind me. The man who had seemed to dissolve himself into smoke and mist as I pursued his shadows through the street. Without thinking about it, without considering what I might do next, my hand plunged into the pocket of my coat and my fingers found the handle of my revolver.

"What's that?" he asked, turning one ear toward me doubtfully. "Fenton, do you say? Benson, sir. John Benson . . ."

I imagined myself pointing the gun at his mouth. That, after all, was the mouth that provoked me to investigate Poe, that had led to all this, to all these decisions, to the neglect of my friends, to Hattie and Peter's irreversible betrayal of me!

"No, not Fenton." I do not know what perverse urge led me to correct a man into knowing he was my long-sought foe. I clenched my teeth around the word: *"Phantom."*

He studied me carefully, lifting a finger to his lips in thoughtful contemplation of my reply. "Ah." Then, raising his eyes in the operation of remembering some lines, he recited:

> *"That motley drama— oh, be sure*
> *It shall not be forgot!*
> *With its* Phantom *chased for evermore,*
> *By a crowd that seize it not.*

"Mr. Clark, isn't it? This is a surprise."

"Why did you give me that article? Did you want me to find him? What sort of madman— Was this some sort of plan all along?" I demanded.

"Mr. Clark, I confess confusion," answered John Benson. "If I may ask a question in return, what brings you here?"

"You warned me not to meddle in the business of Poe's death. You cannot deny it, sir!"

Benson leaned back with a sad grin. "May I suppose from your manner that you did not listen to me?"

"I demand you explain!"

"Happily. But first . . ." He extended his hand. Hesitating for a moment at the gesture, I removed my hand from its pocket, yielding the ready grip on the revolver, and watched his hand as though he might throttle me. "Pleased to properly make your acquaintance, Mr. Clark. I'll certainly explain how you came to my personal attention. But tell me something I had been wondering at the very time we first met: what is your interest in Edgar Poe?"

"To protect his name from the vermin and false friends," I replied, looking him over suspiciously for a reaction.

"Then we did indeed have some common interest, Mr. Clark. When we spoke that day near Saratoga Street, I was visiting Baltimore. I live in Virginia, you see. In Richmond I am an officer of the Sons of Temperance. Edgar Poe was visiting Richmond that summer, as you may know, and had met some of our members at the Swan Inn, where he was lodging, including a Mr. Tyler, who invited the writer to tea."

I thought of the clipping from the Raleigh newspaper describing Poe joining the temperance men. *We mention the fact, conceiving that it will be gratifying to the friends of temperance to know that a gentleman of Mr. Poe's fine talents and rare attainments has been enlisted in the cause.* That was only a month and three days before he'd turn up in distress at Ryan's.

"Mr. Poe took our pledge never to sip the juice again. He stepped up to the desk and attached his signature with unusual firmness. He was the newest son, and one we took pride in among our 'children.' There were those who were skeptical. I was not among them. I heard that after the vigilance committee secretly followed him for a few days in Richmond, they found him honest to his word. Not long after Mr. Poe's departure from Richmond late the next month, we were shocked to hear of his death at a hospital here, and more shocked to read that it was the result of a spree he commenced on reaching this city. We of the temperance order tried to reach the facts from Richmond, and the consensus had been he was not drinking. But we were too far from the facts to try to change the public opinion.

"Being as I was only a few years younger than Poe, and had met him on occasion and had greatly admired his writing, our council suggested that I travel here to inquire after the circumstances of what happened to him. You see, I was born in Baltimore, and lived here until I was twenty-one, so it was thought I would have the better chance of discovering what had happened than any other of our members. I was determined to make a careful investigation, and bring back the truth about Poe's death to Richmond."

"What did you find, Mr. Benson?"

"First, I spoke to the doctor at the hospital where I heard Poe had died."

"John Moran?"

"Yes— Moran." Benson looked me over, perhaps a bit impressed by my knowledge. "Dr. Moran admitted that he could not say that Poe had been drinking, but that Poe was in such an agitated and insensible state Moran could not prove that he *was not.*"

It was the same comment I had heard Moran say, which made me trust Benson's account more. "When did you make this visit, Mr. Benson?"

"A week after Poe's death, perhaps."

It began to settle upon me that this man, the devious Phantom of months past, had entered the mystery even before I had.

"The newspapers," he sighed. "The way they cut up Poe. Those fictions they were printing! The temperance unions here and in New York were keen on using him up. You have seen the articles, perhaps. As though to defeat a dead man to teach a lesson was a triumph. Well, Mr. Clark, believing that Poe was innocent, and knowing his genius, I felt rather— "

"Enraged," I completed his thought.

He nodded. "I am by habit a man of calm and reserve, but yes: I was *enraged.* I left word in many quarters that I wished to discover the details of Poe's final days as corroboration that he had held his pledge to the Sons of Temperance. It happened, while doing some researches, that I overheard you one afternoon, in the athenaeum, request the reading room clerk to reserve for you all articles about Poe's death. I presumed you were among those taking pleasure in reading these venomous reports of Poe's supposed demoralization and sin. I asked the clerk your name, and I learned from others that you were a local lawyer, gifted with a bright mind but known to be under the thumb of people more assertive than yourself. And that you had represented some local periodicals before. I suspected, at that point, that you were engaged by the Baltimore temperance press, who wished to portray Poe as a drunkard as a moral lesson against drinking. I imagined that perhaps you had been paid by them to counter my own mission and to disrupt the aim of the Richmond Sons of Temperance. And so, when I observed you on a different day coming toward the athenaeum, I proffered to you a caution not to meddle in it."

"You thought I was part of the ruin of Poe's name?" I asked, astounded.

"It seemed at the time I was the only one who was not, Mr. Clark! Do you know what that feels like? I tried to visit the offices of the editors of some of the city's newspapers. They would not hear of correcting the misleading information they were printing. I compiled a selection of positive extracts and articles on Poe from years past— praising him, praising his writings— and handed these to the editors to try to persuade them that the late Mr. Poe deserved more honor. Some of these articles I left in the care of the athenaeum clerk for you, as well, with the same purpose. I believe this is one of the articles you referred to earlier."

"Do you mean you selected the articles at random?" I asked.

"I suppose," he said, unclear at the source of my utter disbelief.

"They were not intended to cause or provoke any particular action?"

"I hoped the praise included about Poe from less bloodthirsty times would cause more consideration of the value of Poe and his literary productions. Soon after that, I returned to Richmond. Having presently come back to stay here with my Baltimore relatives for a while, I had the occasion to come upon the clerk from the athenaeum, and the clerk excitedly requested my calling card so he could pass it along to you, Mr. Clark."

"When you spoke to me on the street, you said I must not meddle 'with your lowly lies.'"

"Did I?" He blinked thoughtfully, then developed a trace of a smile.

"It comes from Poe's poem of a woman half in death and half in life, Lenore, 'that now so *lowly lies.*'"

"I suppose it does" was Benson's maddening answer.

"Didn't you mean something by this? Some sort of message or cipher? Do not say, Mr. Benson, that this too was only randomly selected?"

"You are a man with a highly nervous character, I see, Mr. Clark." He did not seem inclined to answer my questions beyond this observation, yet he continued. "When you have taken to reading Poe, it is difficult, nay, impossible, to stop his words from affecting you. Indeed, the man or woman who reads Poe too much, I'd suggest, will believe themselves eventually to be in one of his astounding and perplexing creations. When I came to Baltimore, my mind and every thought was engraved with Poe; I could read only words that had passed through his pen. Every sentence I said might be at risk to be his voice, no longer belonging to my own speech or intelligence. I reveled in his dreams and in what I believed was his soul. It is enough to crush a man who is liable to the trap of discovery. The only answer is to cease reading him at all— as at length I have done. I have banished him from memory, though perhaps not entirely successfully."

"But what of your investigation into Poe's death? You were among the first, perhaps the very first, to make any sort of examination— you were in the best position to learn the truth!"

Benson shook his head.

"You must have learned more!" I cried.

He hesitated, then began as though I had asked something different. "I am an accountant, Mr. Clark. I had forgotten this for a moment. I had begun to damage my business interests by remaining here, away from my proper work in Richmond. Imagine, a man who has kept perfect account books since age twenty, losing all sense of his finances. Indeed, the decline was to such a degree that I must now depend on working for part of each year in my uncle's business here in Baltimore, as I am doing at present." It was this uncle of the Benson family who was pictured in the portrait above us showing the strong resemblance to Benson. "Your city is fine in many respects— though far more coachmen drink spirits while they are meant to be in control of their horses."

Seeing my lack of interest in the point, the temperance side of the man became more adamant. "It is an appalling danger to society, Mr. Clark!"

"There is still much more to be done, Benson," I reasoned with him. "In relation to Poe, I mean. You can help us— "

"Us? Are there others involved?"

Duponte? The Baron? I was not confident of an answer. "You can help.

We can do this work together, Mr. Benson; we can find the truth you sought following Poe's death."

"I can do nothing more here. And you, a lawyer, Mr. Clark, do you not have quite enough to keep you occupied?"

"I have taken a leave from my situation," I said softly.

"I see," he replied knowingly and with a tone of some satisfaction. "Mr. Clark, the most dangerous temptation in life is to forget to tend to your own business— you must learn to respect yourself enough to preserve your own interests. If pursuing the causes of others— even in charity— prevents your own happiness, you will be left with nothing.

"The populace wishes to see Poe how they wish to see him, martyr or sinner; nothing you do prevents that," he went on. "Perhaps we do not care what happened to Poe. We have imagined Poe dead for our own purposes. In some sense, Poe is still very much living. He will be constantly changed. Even if you were somehow to find the truth, they would only deny it in favor of a newer speculation. We cannot sacrifice ourselves on an altar of Poe's mistakes."

"Surely you have not come to believe those temperance men who fought you? That Poe caused all this by some petty vice?"

"Not at all," said Benson with weak defiance. "But had he been more cautious, had he used his passions to address the claims of the world rather than only those of his high order of intellect, all this might not have had to happen— and the millstone around his neck would never have become ours."

I felt a type of relief after my interview with Benson— relief that someone else had attempted to find the truth behind Poe's death. Benson's undertaking had proven Peter Stuart and Auntie Blum wrong. I had not embarked on the quest of a madman. Here was another; an accountant.

Relief flooded me from another direction, too, regarding the Baron and Duponte. I had stopped just short of betraying my allegiance to Duponte in favor of a criminal, a false showman. For what, a series of narrow coincidences between the Baron and Poe's tales? I had lost Hattie forever and would never find a person in the world who knew me as she did. The law practice that my father's good name helped build was sinking into extinction. My friendship with Peter was no more. At least I'd not made a horrible mistake with Duponte, too. I felt, returning home from Benson's, as if I had just awoken from a deep sleep.

How much trust, how much confidence, how much time I had placed in Duponte and his own confluences with Poe's tales! If he were but more confrontational against the Baron Dupin's activities; if he but provided more reason to think he progressed as well as the Baron Dupin; if only he did not stand idly by while the Baron Dupin spouted his own claims; if he were to take these measures upon himself, I would naturally be able to eject these dangerous revolutions in my thoughts!

I watched Duponte as he sat in my living room. I looked directly at him and questioned him as to his ongoing submission to the Baron Dupin's aggressiveness. I asked him why he stood by as the Baron Dupin all but claimed victory in our contest. I had begun to recount this conversation prematurely at an earlier chapter. You remember. You'll recall I suggested boxing the Baron's ears, to which Duponte noted that it might not assist our cause.

"Just so," said I. "It would remind him, I should think, that he is not alone playing this game. He believes, in the infinite deception of his brain, that he has already won, Monsieur Duponte!"

"He has subscribed to a mistaken belief, then. The situation is quite reversed. The Baron, I'm afraid for him, has already lost. He has come to the end, as have I."

That is when my other fears suspended themselves. "What do you mean?"

"Poe drank," said Duponte. "But he was not a *drinking man*. In fact, he was quite the opposite. On average, we can be confident he took less stimulus than any common man on the street."

"Yes?"

"He was not intemperate, but he was *intolerant*, constitutionally, to spirits, to an extreme degree never witnessed by most ordinary persons."

I sat upright. "How do you know this, Monsieur Duponte?"

"If only people would *see*, rather than just look. You will no doubt remember one of the few obituaries written by an acquaintance, rather than by a reporter. Therein was a report that, with a *single glass of wine*, Monsieur Poe's 'whole nature was reversed.' Many would understand this to mean that Poe was habitually intoxicated, a reckless and constant drunkard. In fact, it is just opposite. The detractors have proved too much in this arena, and therefore prove nothing. It is likely— nay, almost certain— that Poe possessed a rare sensitivity to drink that would almost at an instant change and paralyze him. In a state of mental disarray, and in the company of low fellows, no doubt Poe sometimes followed this with further drinking, especially when in the midst of your aggressive southern conviviality, which requires that one not refuse such offers. But this last fact is irrelevant to us. It was the first drink, almost the first sip, that would send him into an attack of insensibility. Not madness from excessive drinking, but temporary madness from not being able to drink as does the next fellow."

"So, on the day he was discovered at Ryan's, monsieur, you believe he had taken some drink?"

"Perhaps one glass of indulgence. Not as the temperance writers would have it, who look upon human actions for their morality. I shall show you how they operate— indeed how they were operating at the *very time* that interests us."

Duponte rummaged through one of his incomprehensibly organized piles of newspapers and brought out an issue of the *Sun* from October 2, 1849, the day before Poe was found.

"Do you know the name John Watchman, Monsieur Clark?"

At first I responded that I knew no one by that name. A vague memory recurred, and I corrected myself. The day I had been chasing after the Phantom— Mr. Benson of the Richmond Sons of Temperance— I had looked for him under the street in one of the city's popular rumholes. "Yes, I thought this Watchman was the Phantom because of a similar coat. Watchman was pointed out to me by another patron as one dangerously deep in the cups."

"Not surprising. Monsieur Watchman's hopes, his ambitions, for notoriety had been dashed not long before that. Here: a notice that would have interested you little two years ago, but may be of great value now."

Duponte pointed to an article in the October 2 newspaper. The temperance Sunday law had been a prominent issue in that state election, though, as Duponte had surmised, I'd had no particular feeling about it at the time. I had seen examples enough of the effects of drinking to sympathize with the ideas of the temperance cause. But it seemed hard to squeeze together one's energies into a single issue like temperance, to the exclusion of all other moral principles.

The Friends of the Sunday Law, an organization comprising the Baltimore temperance leaders of most consequence, had announced their own candidate for the House of Delegates to support their push for a Sunday law restricting the sale of alcohol: Mr. John Watchman. But

Watchman was soon seen drinking at various taverns around town, and on October 2 the Friends withdrew their support of Watchman. Most interesting was the man who spoke in this column for the Friends of the Sunday Law committee: Dr. Joseph Snodgrass!

"This was only *one day* before Snodgrass would be called to Poe's side at Ryan's!" I said.

"Now you see the state of mind Snodgrass would possess. As a leader of this temperance faction, he had just been personally humiliated by his own candidate. Monsieur Watchman had been weak, no doubt. However, there is little doubt that the Friends of the Sunday Law suspected that Watchman had been purposely tempted by enemies of their political endeavor. Now, I should ask you also to look at the *American and Commercial Advertiser* from one week earlier to get a better view of Ryan's inn and tavern in the days before Snodgrass and Edgar Poe met there."

The first cutting Duponte pointed out to me spoke of

> a large and enthusiastic meeting of the Whigs of the
> Fourth Ward of the city, held at Ryan's Hotel.

"Then Ryan's was not only a polling station," I said, "it was also a place for Whigs of that ward to gather. And the place," I sighed, "fated to be Poe's last passage outside a hospital bed." I thought of the group of Fourth Ward Whigs Duponte and I had observed at the den above the Vigilant engine house, near Ryan's. That was their private place; Ryan's, it appeared, their room for more public gatherings.

"Let us step backward even further," said Duponte, "looking at several days before . . . when this meeting by the Fourth Ward Whigs was advertised. Read aloud. And note most of all how it is signed below."

I did.

> A Mass Meeting of the Whigs of the Fourth Ward will
> take place at Ryan's Hotel, Lombard Street, opposite the
> Vigilant Engine House, on Tuesday. Geo. W. Herring, Pres.

Another extract advertised a meeting for October 1, two days before the election, at 7½ *o'clock,* again at *Ryan's Hotel, across from the Engine House,* with *Full attendance earnestly requested;* this one was also signed *Geo. W. Herring, Pres.*

224 THE POE SHADOW

"George Herring, president," I read again. I remembered Tindley, the burly doorkeeper, obsequiously answering his superior at the Whig club: Mr. George . . . Mr. George. "The man we saw, that president, it was his Christian name that was George, not his surname . . . George Herring. Surely he is a relation to Henry Herring, Poe's uncle by marriage! Henry Herring, who was the very man who came first to Poe's side after Snodgrass and refused to board him in his own home."

"Now you see that whatever Poe drank was a small part only of what transpired in his final days, but still is of importance to us to place all else in order. It helps now that we are able to comprehend the whole sequence of events."

"Monsieur Duponte," I said, putting down the newspaper, "do you mean that you *do* comprehend the whole now? That we are ready to share it with the world before the Baron Dupin speaks out?"

Duponte rose from his chair and walked to the window. "Soon," he said.

21

IT WAS SURPRISING, considering the Baron's recent frantic activities, how quiet he had become. He was not to be seen; presumably he was preparing for the lecture in two days' time— it was all Baltimore talked about. I took several circuitous walks around the city, trying to discover which hotel he had moved to.

While I was engaged in this way, my shoulder was tapped.

It was one of the men whom I had seen so many times following the Baron Dupin. Another man stood near him in a similar coat.

"Account for yourself," said the first one, with a concealed accent. "Who are you?"

"Why is that your concern?" I replied. "Shall I ask you the same?"

"This is not a time to be bold, monsieur."

Monsieur. They were French, then.

"We have seen you in past weeks. You seem always to be outside his hotel," he said with suspicion, his eyebrows gesturing in that peculiar French manner Duponte sometimes exhibited.

"Yes, well, there is hardly anything extraordinary about that. Does not one visit his friend often?" A man who had in the past kidnapped, deceived, and intimidated me— to call that a friend!

Caught in their silence, I worried about the implications of my hasty statement. My spying on the Baron, it seemed, had made enemies of these enemies of the Baron! I added, "I know nothing of that man's debts or his creditors, and have not the slightest interest in such matters."

The two men exchanged a quick glance.

"Then tell us which hotel he's putting up at now."

"I do not know," I said honestly.

"Do you have any idea, monsieur, the scope of his troubles? They shall become yours if you try to guard him. Do not protect him."

I turned quickly and began walking away.

"We are not finished with you, monsieur," he called out from behind me.

I looked over my shoulder; they were following. I wondered if I ran, whether they would do the same. Testing this, I accelerated my steps.

Crossing Madison Street, I neared the Washington Monument, where a small assembly of visitors was gathered. The massive marble column, twenty feet in diameter, rose up from the base and supported the grand statue of General George Washington at the summit. The pure white marble stood out not just for its massiveness, but as a contrast to the brickwork of the street. It seemed the safest place in Baltimore right now.

Entering the base of the monument, I joined others waiting to begin the passage on the stairwell that ascended in a spiral up the long, hollow column. After I'd climbed the first flight of steps, I paused at one of the curves, illumined by only a small square opening, and watched a few young boys race past me. I smiled to myself, satisfied that the men had let me be or not seen me enter— but just as I expressed this silent delight to myself, I heard the heavy steps of two pairs of boots.

"*Il est là!*" came a voice.

Without waiting for a glimpse of them, I turned and dashed up the stairs. My only advantage was that I had known the vast interior of the monument from the time I was young. The Frenchmen may have been stronger and quicker, but they were strangers here. Indeed, I imagine they'd compare this narrow flight to the wider compass of their Arc de Triomphe in Paris. Both places had the same reward for the sturdy climber— an unrivaled view of each city at the summit— but honored opposite achievements. The Parisian arch, Napoleon's empire. The marble column, Washington resigning his commission as commander of the army, refusing to use his position to seek the permanent power of a despot.

I suppose none of this occurred to these men, who seemed to prefer thinking of throwing me off the top of the monument. They ran faster even than the group of young boys, who, chasing each other upward, had wearied by the middle of the ascent. The two men finally reached the observation gallery at the top, and walked around the circular platform, pushing past the visitors who stood looking across the Patapsco River to the Chesapeake in the distance. Though the two men inspected the face under the brim of each man's hat, and peered around widely flounced dresses, they did not see their subject anywhere.

But I could see them. I'd already hidden 120 feet below: near where a narrow, unmarked door in the lower portion of the stairs opened onto a lower ledge used by those whose task it was to keep every crevice of the monument clean. It was a passage used also by persons who needed a bit of air on their journey upward. I waited on that ledge to ensure that both men appeared on that gallery platform far above, thus confirming that neither was lying in wait for me below.

Realizing they had been deceived, they now leaned upon the railing and found me standing below them. I smiled and saluted them before rushing back to the door.

My celebration was short. The door back to the stairs would not budge. "For God's sake!" I kicked at it.

The latch on the inside of the door had somehow fixed itself after I had closed it. I pounded at the heavy door for someone to open it from inside.

Observing my situation from their all-seeing view, one of the men started back to the stairwell, while the other waited and watched me from that omniscient perch. If the first made it down the stairs and to my door, I would certainly be trapped. I craned my neck and watched with faint hope that the band of older ladies emerging above from the stairs would delay his descent long enough for me to arrive at some miraculous plan for my deliverance.

The second man stood guard by leaning over the rail and keeping his eyes fixed on me. After another fruitless attempt to attract attention from the other side of the door, I returned to the railing and looked down below to assess my chances of jumping into the trees. Then I was met with a familiar face from below!

"Bonjour!" I exclaimed.

She looked up at me, then looked to the sky where that blackguard was peering down at me. "Back up toward the door," she said.

"It is bolted from the other side. You must open it for me, mademoiselle!"

"Back up! More . . . more, monsieur . . ."

I did as instructed, moving away from the railing. The man above leaned farther over the railing so he could still watch me.

Bonjour took a breath and then shrieked, "He's going to jump!" She pointed with hysterical gestures to the Frenchman, who was now nearly hanging from the railing 180 feet above the ground. The Frenchman's face went pale as screams erupted from the gallery. The gallery-goers, in an effort to aid him, swarmed the man on the rail so forcefully as to almost push him off. Meanwhile, those sightseers rushing up from below to witness the human tragedy now herded the second Frenchman, who had just managed to enter the stairwell for his descent, back onto the gallery platform.

"Mademoiselle, ingenious! Now, if you can open this door!"

Bonjour entered the stairwell, and soon enough I could hear the door to the base unlatch. I gleefully swung the door open to thank my savior, perhaps the one woman left who cared about me.

She stepped through the doorway, the end of a small revolver pointed at me. "Time to come with me, monsieur."

❊   ❊   ❊

Bonjour did not say another word on the way to the hotel. She untied my hands and legs— which she had bound— upon our arrival at Barnum's Hotel and rushed me through the anteroom without attracting notice. Upon reaching their rooms, where the Baron awaited, she spoke. "He was with them, very hand and glove together," she said to the Baron. "I separated them, but they may have been signaling each other."

"Who?" I asked confusedly. "Those two blackguards? I would never have anything to do with men like that."

"Very cozy, going into that monument together."

"They were accosting me, mademoiselle! You rescued me!"

"I had no such intention, monsieur!" she assured me. "Perhaps Duponte leads *them* by a leash, too."

The Baron had an agitated manner. "Make yourself scarce, my dear."

Bonjour gave me a pitying glare before leaving us alone.

The Baron held up a glass of sherry cobbler. "The proportion of sherry is decidedly smaller at this hotel than the proportion of water. Still, at least the beds have curtains, a rare enough luxury in America. Do not mind mademoiselle. She believes she depends on me because I saved her, when in fact it is just the opposite. If she were ever to give me the bag, or to be harmed, I would go to pieces. Do not underestimate her arts."

I had noticed on the writing-desk stacks of paper with widely scribbled notes on them.

"There," said the Baron with a proud, mischievous grin, seeing my interest. "There lie all the answers you have been looking for, Brother Quentin, put down in black and white. Of course, I have not perfected my presentation yet, but I will, be sure. But I am afraid"— here he leaned close— "that in the meantime I have the burden of ensuring that nobody troubles me before it is brought into the light of day. Now, who are they, the men Bonjour saw you with? Why are they working with you and Duponte?"

"Baron Dupin," I said with exasperation, "I do not know them, do not wish to, and certainly am not leagued with them in any way."

"You have seen them though, as I have," he said loftily. "They have been watching me. There is death upon their eyes. It is dangerous. You have noticed them, surely, while you yourself have acted the spy on me?"

I opened my mouth to speak but was caught off guard.

"I know," he said, taking my silence as an admission. "Since I heard Bonjour happened upon you at the wharves, watching her quite closely. I hardly think that would be your usual place of leisure, among the drunkards and the slave-traders. Or perhaps"— he broke into laughter— "you will surprise me yet, Quentin Clark."

"Then why not stop me, if you knew?"

He swirled his drink. "Isn't it quite obvious to you? Haven't you learned from your master? It was a desperate measure— Duponte knew he was losing, so he sent you out. The very fact made it clear that I need not defend myself against him. Besides, seeing what you were trying to spy on permitted me to know what Duponte was most interested in— to be a spy is always to be *spied upon*, monsieur."

"If you are all-knowing, Baron, I would guess you have already discovered who those two Frenchman are and who sent them."

He paused, his agitation stirred. "They are French, then?"

"From their accents, their words, yes. You could coax them to your purposes perhaps, as you did with Dr. Snodgrass." I wanted to regain some balance in the interview, and make it clear I was not without my own sources of knowledge.

"If they serve certain powerful factions against me for my pecuniary interests back in Paris, I am afraid it is not so simple."

He spoke in that open tone of his, as though you were firmly on his side of affairs, which made you temporarily forget you were anything but. He had to push aside strands of his hair from his eyes; his hair now looked thin and soapy.

"You see, Brother Quentin, how a man can be pushed to live behind masks. Never able to freely be myself. And I am quite good as myself, yes, monsieur. Thundering good! In the courtroom, all eyes, even those of the lawyers opposing me, would look to me for the truth. I am happy there. I am not ready to hang up my fiddle, not yet."

"Yet you carry on your cheap charade to bully us," I protested. "You mimic Auguste Duponte."

I noticed a painting of Duponte leaning in the corner of the room. I had seen Von Dantker's work at various stages of progress, and recognized this canvas as his. I could not help remarking on how complete the finished portrait seemed— as though it had completed Duponte himself. It captured his exact likeness but also *more* than his likeness.

The Baron laughed good-naturedly. "Has Duponte appreciated the humor of it, Brother Quentin? My small jest among serious business, that is all. Duponte does not know about wearing masks. He believes that if he does not, he will be attached to reality. In fact, without any masks, he is— we are— nothing."

I thought about that singular pointed grin that Duponte had innovated for his sittings with Von Dantker, which could be seen creeping onto his face in the portrait. A smile that was not really his . . . Perhaps Duponte did know about wearing masks, after all? I grabbed hold of the portrait and placed it under my arm.

"I shall take this, Baron; it is not your property."

He shrugged.

I continued, perhaps hoping to induce a bigger reaction, "You know— you must know— that Duponte shall resolve this. He *is* the real basis for Dupin."

"Do you believe that is important to him?"

I cocked my head with interest. It was not the reply I'd expected.

"Has Duponte told you how he and I came to know each other?" The Baron looked at me with a serious air. "Of course the answer is no," the Baron went on, shaking his head knowingly. "No, he too much lives inside himself. Duponte needs to feel people are interested in him, but finds the act of speaking of himself too tiring. We were both in Paris. There was a lady named Catherine Gautier accused of murder, a woman most important to your friend."

I called to mind the policeman at the café in Paris who said changes had come over Duponte when the woman he loved was hanged for murder and he could not stop it. "Duponte loved her, didn't he?"

"That is nothing! I loved her too. Oh, do not look at me so, like we are in some light novel; I do not mean what you think. No, Duponte and I were not rivals for her affection. But she was attractive enough, and brilliant enough, for any man who knew her to love her. You ask, how could we live in a world where such a woman could be accused of bludgeoning her own sister to death? The idea is absurd."

Catherine Gautier, the Baron said, was of the poorer class, but virtuous and known as very intelligent. She was Duponte's closest and (some said) only companion. One day, this woman's sister was found murdered in a vile fashion, and Duponte's lover was suspected at once. Because the police were Duponte's enemies after he had embarrassed them by solving crimes they could not, many believed that the accusation represented their reprisal against Duponte by turning against Catherine.

"She was innocent then?"

"Innocent enough" came the Baron's peculiar answer after a pause.

"So you were acquainted with her?"

"Dear friend, has he really never said anything about it? Your companion for so many long months now. Yes, I knew her." He laughed. "I was her lawyer, dear man! I defended her against that terrific charge of murder."

"You?" I asked. "But she was executed. You *never* lost a case."

"Yes, that is true. I suppose that record was somewhat knotted up by Mademoiselle Gautier."

I looked down, thinking of Duponte's failure. "Duponte failed to free her. He will return to his *glory*, though," I asserted, using the Baron's favorite term, "now, with Poe."

"Failed to free her!" the Baron laughed. *"Failed to free her?"*

His taunting angered me. I knew Duponte had tried examining the affair himself when Mademoiselle Gautier was arrested, but had given up in despair. I repeated this history to the Baron.

"He tried to examine, is that what you have been told? Why, monsieur, Brother Duponte *did* examine the matter. He never gave up. He was as successful as always."

"Successful? How? Do you mean she was not executed after all?"

"I remember vividly," the Baron began, "my first visit to the apartments of Auguste Duponte in Paris."

The Baron Dupin found a place for his hat and stick himself, since Duponte did not offer. The Baron wished for better light. The lawyer found brightness an advantage when demonstrating through the eager motions of the hands and large expressions of the face why cooperation should be offered to him. He did not relish relying on any ordinary routine of persuasion with Auguste Duponte, of course— but circumstances were dire. His career was at a treacherous crossroad. Also, a woman's life was at stake.

The Baron had never been to see Duponte before. He had, like all informed persons in Paris, and like all the criminal-minded, known of Auguste Duponte. The Baron had devised one strict rule as an advocate. He would not accept the case of an accused criminal who had been arrested through the ratiocination of Duponte. The reason for this was not the obvious one: that the Baron presumed a person accused by Duponte automatically guilty. Instead, it was that Duponte's reputation was too strong in that day— once it was known by a judge that Duponte had brought down the charges, it would be almost impossible to obtain an acquittal.

Now the Baron saw an opportunity. He could use Duponte's blind affection for Catherine Gautier to win his most important case. The Baron convinced himself that each case was the most important, but this one was special— it was a case that seemed to every other lawyer quite impossible. That made him all the more determined.

"We are mounting a steady defense," the Baron told Duponte. "We aim to give mademoiselle her liberty," he said in a brave tone. "Your assistance, Monsieur Duponte, would be most valuable— most critical, in fact. You will be the hero in absolving her." The Baron did not actually believe this, for he knew he would be the hero.

Duponte was fixed in an armchair by the unlit hearth. "My assistance will confirm that she is doomed," he answered almost absently.

"It need not be so, Monsieur Duponte," the Baron said excitedly. "You are reputed to see what others cannot. If others see only her guilt, you can use your talents, your genius, to see her innocence. The Holy Bible says we are all guilty, monsieur, but does it not follow that we are also all innocent?"

"I had not heard you were a religious scholar, Monsieur Dupin."

"It is 'Baron,' if you please."

Duponte stared at him unblinkingly.

The Baron cleared his throat. "I bring a choice, monsieur, that surely will appeal to your wisdom. You can employ your genius to rescue a person you love, a person who has loved you, from a fate of the blackest die. Or you can sit idly here in your luxurious rooms, and let yourself perish forever in solitude. It is jackassable— I mean, any ass could see what to decide. Which will be your destiny?"

The Baron was not usually inclined to argue in profound terms, but he was not above it. Mademoiselle Gautier had salvaged her life after being a mistress to a wealthy Parisian student who had tossed her aside. In her circumstance, most girls fell into prostitution, but Catherine Gautier had managed to avoid that. Not so for her sister, however, despite Catherine's pleas. Her sister's ruin would be hers as well, for they shared not just a surname but also appearances similar enough to be confused on the street by acquaintances, shopkeepers, and policemen. This was ample motive for Catherine to eliminate this stain on her own identity. Still, the Baron had learned much that suggested the accused was quite unlikely to act in any foul deed, and had found the names of many villains that the sister had consorted with in her new profession who could quite easily be shown culpable with the most minor evidence.

"If I do examine the affair of her sister's death," Duponte began, and the Baron thrilled at those words, "if I do so, I would not wish others to know of my involvement."

The Baron promised not to talk to the press about Duponte's assistance.

Duponte did investigate the Gautier sister's death, as promised. He promptly discovered, with no trace of a doubt, the chronicle of events that led to the murder. His conclusions pointed indisputably at his lover, Catherine Gautier, as the perpetrator. He passed on his information to the prefect, producing a witness undetected by the police and ruining all of Baron Dupin's chances to win by other means. This turn made the Baron more desperate. He was too proud to accept defeat gracefully. He expended many favors, and many thousand francs beyond what was already a deepening debt, to manipulate the case. But it was to no effect. Duponte's evidence was too strong to be tarnished. The Baron was now ruined in his finances and reputation.

Meanwhile, Officer Delacourt, ambitious to advance in the prefecture, assured Duponte and Gautier that with the new evidence, which painted the young woman as confused and deluded but by no means demonic, and taking into account her sex, there would be leniency in her sentencing. And yet, a few months later she was executed, with Dupin and Duponte, along with three-quarters of Paris, attending.

❖   ❖   ❖

"First of all," I said, "it was Duponte more than you who suffered in this matter. Not only did it sap him of an ability to pursue the work of his genius, he also lost the one woman he loved— at his own hands! You shall not avenge yourself for your disgrace by plaguing Duponte now. You cannot use Poe's death for that purpose. I shall not stand by!"

The Baron retorted, "Recollect that fine legal axiom *super subjectum materiam:* no man can be held professionally responsible for opinions which have been founded on the facts submitted to him by others." The Baron stood over my chair. "I didn't start this, monsieur. *You* did. You prompted me to look into Poe's fall. You stand in your own light, do you realize it? Feel your oats, Brother Quentin! You made me see that I could renew myself. My name was crushed by detractors and defamers because the shadow of my genius grew too large and refused to conform to their small lives, so the eyes upon us make every small peccadillo into a mortal sin to stop me— why, it is like our dear Poe."

"Will you compare yourself to Poe?" I asked, openly aghast.

"I do not have to, because Brother Poe *has already*. Why do you think he chose the character of Dupin as his finest hero? He saw in the genius of the decipherer his own divine abilities to understand what gods and men could never fathom. And with what credit? The prefect of the police, not the hero Dupin, receives the praise of all parties. Even as other writers half as good as Poe found themselves winning gold from the magazines, Poe struggled one last time to overcome adversity, struggled until the end, until finally cut— from existence."

"Do you truly believe, monsieur, that you are worthy as the model for Dupin?"

"You did, before having the misfortune to find Duponte, seduced by talents that he uses only for his own interests. Duponte is an anarchist. Have you ever, since meeting him, had any doubts that . . . perhaps . . ." He stretched out the words. "Perhaps you know there was another reason I gave you leave to act the spy on us, my friend. So you might see first-hand, Brother Quentin, that you passed something up in Paris, at the fortifications, when you chose him over me."

I wondered if he knew— if the Baron had had someone observing me when I had come to what I thought was his hotel that night. That free black standing under the lamp? "Duponte is the one. You cannot hold a candle to him," I said. I could not let him have the mental victory of knowing how close I had come to giving up hope in Duponte only a few days earlier. I think my expression might have been transparent, though.

"Well," he said, smiling a little, "only Edgar A. Poe could answer who the original Dupin is, and he is gone. How does one solve something when the solution is unreachable? The real Dupin is whoever convinces the world of it; he shall be the remaining one."

22

I FOUND MYSELF fearing Duponte for the first time. Wondering if— indeed— his talents, when released unrestrained and unharnessed, could turn disastrous, as they had against Mademoiselle Gautier. I could not help calling to mind the finale of "The Gold-Bug," Poe's rousing tale of a hunt for treasure— it had always seemed to me, rumbling beneath the surface, that in the triumphant ending there was the clue that Legrand, the master thinker, was about to murder his servant and his friend now that their mission was achieved. The last ominous words of that story— "Who shall tell?"— reverberated in my head.

I called to mind one peculiar evening during my stay in Paris. I was walking behind Auguste Duponte into an area of the city Madame Fouché had warned was not safe at night. Your cries, Madame Fouché had said, would bring no police, who are often in league with the bad people. I remember I was stopped by an object inside a store window that seemed to shift as though on its own power. There was a circle of artificial jaws representing every state of the human mouth: one with bright gums and spotless milky teeth, another with decayed and wilting gums, and so on. Each rotated and opened and shut at different speeds through some unseen mechanical ingenuity. Above the jaws were revolving wax heads showing a toothless, collapsed face and then one boasting a fresh and sturdy mouth with shining teeth, presumably repaired by a dentist with his office behind this window.

Before I could pull myself away from the mesmerizing sight, I felt a tightness around my ears. Everything went black. My hat had been thrust down over my eyes to blind me, and I could feel hands burrowing into my coat from behind. As I cried out for help, I managed to knock the narrow portion of my hat up from my eyes. I saw an old woman with a threadbare dress of rags and blackened teeth. After having tried to blind me with my hat to rob me, she had stepped back and now only stood staring. I followed her gaze to Duponte, standing a few feet from the attacker.

Once she had run off, I turned gratefully to Duponte. What had so frightened her away? If he knew, he never shared it with me.

I now considered that the wretched being must have recognized Duponte from a former era. A criminal enterprise that Duponte must have spoiled— perhaps she had once been part of some grand assassination plan (for it was said of Duponte that in his time he had uncovered more than one plan to kill the head of France) and, in consequence of his acumen long ago, was in the interim reduced to animal desperation. It was no physical fear of Duponte that had prompted her flight from me. She could have thrust a blade through my heart ten times before Duponte stopped her (if stopping her was his intention). It was not fear of his strength or agility. It was raw, impulsive fear of his pure intellect— a fear of his *genius*.

Who shall tell?

After leaving the Baron's hotel, I found Duponte sitting by the large window in the drawing room of Glen Eliza, intently facing the door. I began to tell him all that had occurred at Barnum's Hotel.

"Take this," Duponte interrupted, holding up a leather bag. "Bring it to the address on this paper." He handed me a slip of paper.

"Monsieur, have you not listened to the intelligence I bring? Baron Dupin— "

"You must go out at once, Monsieur Clark," he said. "It is time."

I looked down at the address and did not recognize it. "Very well. . . . What should I say once I arrive?"

"You shall know."

Such was the extent of my distraction that I did not notice that it was three times as dark as it should have been for that hour. By the time it was starting to rain I was already too far on my walk to return for an umbrella. The water grew deeper along the way until it was lapping at my ankles. I trudged ahead, the brim of my hat sheltering my face as much as possible.

I took an omnibus part of the way to the address Duponte had written down. Still, I was drenched walking through the downpour. The address was a small office where a man behind a desk dispatched telegraph messages. "Sir?" he turned to me.

Not knowing what to say, I merely asked whether this was the address I sought.

"Downstairs," he said blandly.

I walked down the steps, to the next sign, which was dripping with streams of water. It was a clothier. Well! This was the urgent mission, perhaps to hand over a coat that needed mending for Duponte— perhaps he had some supper party to attend. I walked in, overcome by my impatience.

"Ah, you've come to the right place."

It was a man with a large belly stuffed into a bright satin vest.

"Me? Are we acquainted, sir?"

"No, sir."

"Then how do you know I'm at the right place?"

"Look at you!" He put his arms out dramatically, as though I was the prodigal son returning to him. "Wet to the bone. You shall have a chill and fall sick. Now, I have just the suit." He rummaged behind his desk. "You have found the right place to trade your clothes."

"You are mistaken. I have brought something for you."

"Truly? I am not expecting it," he said greedily.

I put the bag down on a chair and opened it, finding only a folded newspaper— a number of the Baltimore *Sun*. Drops of water blotted the page from my hair and brow.

He snatched it from me while his friendly face sharpened. "Blame me! I daresay I can purchase my own newspaper, young man. This isn't even from this *year*. Do you come here to jest? What shall I do with this, I ask you?" He glared at me reprovingly. I had dropped from "sir" to "young man." "If you have no business for me tonight . . ." He waved his hand.

At the word "business" he pointed to one of the signs on his wall to demonstrate his own. *Fashionable Clothing and Outfitting Establishment. Shirts, Collars, Under-shirts and Drawers, Cravats, Socks, Hosiery— Warranted in every respect equal to the best custom work.*

"Hold on a minute! Apologies, sir," I said eagerly. "I should like very much to make that exchange of clothing, after all."

He brightened. "Excellent, excellent, a wise choice. We shall put you in a suit of *finest* quality and fit."

"That is what you do, sir? Trade clothing?"

"When there is the need, of course. It is a necessary service for stranded gentlemen like yourself, dear sir. So many forget umbrellas even in the fall and bring but one suit in their trunk. Especially strangers to Baltimore. You are a visitor, I suppose?"

I made a noncommittal gesture. I began to better understand the work of this man; and of Duponte . . .

The clothier brought me a handful of garments— what a costume it was! He repeated his assessment that they were of the finest quality, though they were quite shabby, and they did not fit in the least. The coat and its drab velvet collar almost matched one leg of the pants— the less faded one— and neither were intended to match the vest. All were several sizes too small for me, yet the clothier had an expression of deep pride as he declared me very "finefied" and held up a looking-glass so I might glory in the sight of myself.

"There, snug and dry! It is quite a fair shake for you, this trade," he said. "Now this"— he picked up my cane— "this is as fair a specimen as I have seen. Heavy thing, though, for a pilgrim like yourself. A burden. Looking to part with it? I may pay well for this, and my prices are not cut under by anyone in the neighborhood."

I almost forgot, before leaving his store, the newspaper Duponte had sent with me. I looked at the date at the top of the page. October 4, 1849. The day after Poe was discovered with ill-fitting clothes at Ryan's. I scanned the pages, stopping at the reports of the previous day's weather. The day, I mean, when Poe was found. "Cold, raw, and misty." "Damp and rainy." "A steady, heavy blow from the northeast."

Just like today. When I'd entered the library, Duponte had been waiting at the window, looking not absently into the air, as it seemed, but into the sky and clouds. He was waiting for a day fitting the description of that fateful third of October to send me into.

"I'll take that, sir," I said politely, removing the Malacca cane from his grasp. "This I shall never part with." Before leaving, I fished out some half-dimes and took an umbrella the clothier had sitting behind his table.

Outside, I found my steps were uneven, with my legs constrained by the irregular pants. I stood under the awning while testing the flimsy umbrella.

"The heavens are splitting tonight."

I jumped, startled by the coarse voice. In the dark covering of rain I could hardly make out the figure of a man.

I screwed up my eyes as he turned and faced me. Another shape appeared near him.

"You would try to hide from us, would you, Monsieur Clark?"

The two French thugs.

"Clothes like this," said the other one, bowing his head down at my scrubby dress, "will still not conceal you."

"Gentlemen— monsieurs— I know not what to call you. I do not wear this to conceal myself from you. I know not why you should continue to bother me."

It was not the time for this, I know. But my eye, which somehow felt free of the concerns of my brain, was drawn inexplicably to a flyer on the lamppost, which was flapping from the pressure in the air. I could not read it, but I suppose by some instinct I knew it contained something of great interest.

"Look here when we speak!"

The man slapped me against my cheek. It was not particularly hard, but the extreme abruptness left me standing in shock.

"You cannot long protect a man marked for death. We have been handed our orders."

His partner pulled a pistol from his coat. "You're in for it now. You should select a friend more carefully."

"My friend? It is untrue!"

"Then his wench assisted you for her mere pleasure at the Washington Monument?" he replied.

"I vow it! He is no friend!" I shouted, my voice trembling at the sight of the weapon.

"No . . . not any longer."

23

"SIR! SIR! YOU FORGOT—"

The clothier had come out with the bag I had left inside. He stopped when he saw my company in their unfriendly postures. One of them had wrapped his arm around mine.

The clothier gesticulated angrily at my assailant. "What is this about? Let that suit be!"

When the clothier took a step forward, the other assailant turned around and slapped the clothier across the face with more force than a punch. It sent him spinning down hard beyond the awning.

As the clothier met the ground, he let out a high-pitched, cat-like groan. Making use of the distraction, I pulled my arm free. I flung my new umbrella behind me and ran against a sheet of rain that felt like a brick wall against my body. The two assailants bolted after me.

I swerved onto the first street, hoping the darkness of the storm would cloak me. But the pair of men trimmed the distance almost at once. My head twisted around to watch them, and I tripped over some uneven ground. Though I caught myself, they were now dangerously close, one of them brushing my coat with his hand. I dared not look back again.

Ahead a party of pigs was devouring the evening's garbage. Our chase disturbed them, sending them scattering. A flash of light hit the sky and illuminated all of us. I found myself panting and sucking at the air for breath. They were coming nearer to my heels, and I would certainly be tackled within a few rods. I noticed the street we were coming to and heard faint bells. This gave me an idea. I quickly turned around and ran toward my pursuers. The Frenchmen, running fast as they were, took a moment to halt themselves on the slippery ground.

In Europe, I knew, the railways began on the periphery of the city, and I had met in my life many visitors from other countries surprised that our trains began right in the center of town— first drawn by a span of the strongest horses and then latched onto an engine. When the men started back toward me, I led them right past the sign: LOOK OUT FOR THE LOCO-

MOTIVE. The two Frenchmen, perplexed at it, did just that, looking every-where they could think.

I ran like mad. Finally I slowed down, surveying the trail behind me. Not a soul. The rain was a bit lighter, too. I came to a stop. I was safe.

Then there came the pair of them, side by side, like devils appearing from the great Abyss.

Just when I fell into a terrible despair, another figure appeared in front of me. As he came closer, I was shocked to realize it was the older black man I had previously seen with the Baron and eyeing me watchfully on the streets. Indeed, since the Baron's young slave had insisted the Baron had no other blacks in his employment, I had come to consider that this man might be in collusion with the French rogues. And here he was run-ning toward me!

I had nowhere to turn without making myself vulnerable either to the two men behind or the one in front of me. I decided my chances were better against one man and plunged myself toward him. As I attempted to pass, he grabbed my arm and pulled me.

"This way!" he said against my struggling.

I allowed myself to be led onto a darker, narrower avenue; we were now running side by side. He moved his hand to my back, helping me to keep up.

The men still followed us. My companion suddenly began crossing back and forth in front of me as we ran.

"Do the same!" he shouted.

Understanding his scheme, I followed his example. In the rain and darkness, the two rogues would not be able to see who was who.

He now darted away from me, and after a moment's hesitation and confusion, one of the rogues followed him. The other stayed on my trail with renewed vigor. At least the number of hands that could strangle me at any moment had been cut by half. I hadn't even time to think why that stranger whom I thought an adversary had assisted me against these killers.

A window of advantage had opened, but I had to act quickly. I looked back and saw the rogue stop in mid-run and raise his pistol. The dis-charge broke like thunder. The bullet went right through my hat, which flew off. The rage in his eyes and his loud, seething grunts frightened me more than the pistol. My Malacca cane repeatedly slipped in my hand from its coat of water and almost fell, but I would not let it drop.

· · ·

The rain lessening, all the earth turned muddy. I slipped and slid through the streets while the solitary pursuer followed. I tried to cry for help, but my power of speech died in the back of my throat, and although both of us had been hobbled by our rough paths, if I stopped I would be at great risk. Besides, in my wet and disheveled clothes, with my head bare, I looked like a wild vagrant— the very fear of the city residents. Nobody would come to aid me this time. Searching for sanctuary in the business part of the city, I spied the door to a large warehouse that had been blown open by the wind. I rushed inside and located a stairwell.

Bursting onto the upper floor, I bumped into a single wheel, freshly painted, that stood nearly up to my neck. I realized where I was.

Wheels, chaises, straps, and axles were all around me: I had come upon Curlett's carriage factory on Holliday. On the first floor, there was a room where the latest carriages were shown and sold. Along with the piano works a few blocks away, the building represented a new idea: to manufacture, warehouse, and sell all in the same location.

"Your flint is fixed, brave fellow," said a voice, now speaking in French. The rogue appeared at the door. A smirk emerged through a wheezing pant, and he peered over at me savagely. "There is nowhere else to run. Unless you want to jump out the window."

"I want no such thing. I wish to speak like civilized men. I care nothing of preventing you from collecting your debts from the Baron."

He stepped closer and I backed away. He looked at me inquisitively. "Is that what you believe, monsieur?" He snickered very unpleasantly. "Do you think we're here to dun some dead-head for a few thousand francs?" he asked with offense. "There is far more. There is the very future peace of France at stake."

The Baron Dupin? A disgraced lawyer? Affecting the future of France?

My face betrayed my utter bafflement, and he looked over at me with angry impatience.

With an abrupt swipe, I grabbed the gigantic wheel next to me and pushed it with all my remaining strength. He put out his hand and boot to stop it, and it toppled on its side, limp and harmless.

I dashed farther into the room but knew he had been right— there was nowhere to go. Even if I had not been dead tired and soaking wet, the warehouse was just one gigantic space littered with carriage parts. I tried to leap over the half-completed chaise of a carriage, but it snagged my boot and I went tumbling down, to the echoing of brutal laughter.

I had not, in tumbling, fallen to the floor— it was much worse than that. I'd become tangled in a rope around the back of the carriage tying together certain components that were not yet fixed to the vehicle. As I pulled and kicked through the rope, I found my neck entangled inside a narrow loop. I held my cane in one hand, using its tip to cling to the back of the carriage, and tried desperately to loosen the snarled confusion of knots around the area of the rope pressing my neck. Still, it pulled tighter with my every movement.

The man's unhurried steps came closer. He entered the coach, which as yet had no roof. Standing above me smiling, with a sudden and bold motion he kicked my cane away from the coach. Though I still had a grip on one end, the other end, which I'd been using to cling to the carriage, was displaced, and now I found myself dangling. Each time I tried to grasp the back of the carriage, with cane or hand, my pursuer joyfully kicked harder. Feeling the knots of this horrid lasso tighten fatally around my throat, I propped the hook of the cane into the widest spot between the rope and my neck. Meanwhile, I flailed with my feet; but the few inches between the bottom extremity of my body and the floor simply could not be reduced.

To be hanged to death, by a carriage! I could almost share my murderer's ghastly smile at my fate.

As I hung suspended there, I gripped my cane tightly with both hands in a sort of hapless, hopeless prayer. I held it so tightly that the pores in the wood would later leave a white trail on my moist palms. Squeezing my eyes shut, I was surprised to suddenly feel the cane giving way, as though in my hands were the strength of four men. The middle section had jerked out of its place. The cane, as I quickly appraised, was actually made as two separate parts, joined together in the middle. In the gap I could see the gleam of shiny steel.

I pulled harder and found that the entire top half of the cane was a sheaf, slipping right off. There, hidden underneath, was a sword. A sword two, no, a full two and a half feet long when unsheathed!

"Poe," I whispered, with what might have been my last breath.

At once I sliced the bond off my neck, swinging as I was freed onto the back of the carriage, which I grabbed with my free hand.

The first thing I saw when I looked up was the Frenchman perched on the top of the carriage chaise, peering curiously. In his confusion at the sight of my weapon, he had let his pistol dangle at his side. With a powerful yell, I swung the sword above me. It caught the side of his arm. Then, my eyes closed, I pulled the sword back and plunged the weapon forward again. He released a shrill scream.

I fell to the ground, landing on my back. My boots were propped against the back of the chaise. The rogue, wild and pale, hollering terribly from his wound, widened his eyes as I pushed hard with both legs. The half carriage went rolling across the room and, one of its loose wheels slipping off its axle, spilled over on top of him like a giant tomb. A piece of the carriage severed one of the nearby pipes, sending a burst of steam sizzling into the chaos.

✻ ✻ ✻

I pushed myself to my feet and returned the sword into its sheath. But the violent thrill of the triumph could not lift me home or sustain me; my exhaustion and my aching leg combined to inhibit me from moving hardly ten feet from the building before falling down. I leaned heavily on the cane that had saved my life, worried that one of the rogues I had escaped would find me in this weakened condition.

There was a rattling at the door of the warehouse, which I had just closed a few moments before, and a frightful moan.

"Clark!" I heard my name shouted from within my daze. It sounded like it was coming from a great distance, but I knew it was near.

Perhaps it was terrible fear, or the throbbing in my body, or the utter fatigue coming over me; perhaps it was from a combination of everything. As a hand reached me, I surrendered almost peacefully, feeling a heavy blow strike the side of my head.

24

NOISES OF INFORMAL conversation merged into one faraway hum. The scene grew clearer in my vision. Men drank wine and beer, and the smell of chewed tobacco filled my nostrils with an unpleasant sting. Trying to sit straight, I felt myself restrained around the neck. The room seemed identical to the tavern in Ryan's hotel, as it might have looked the afternoon Poe had arrived there. I thought about the unfriendly stares of the Whigs of the Fourth Ward across the street from Ryan's, and sat straight up despite a wave of dizziness.

As a small group of men walked past some candles, I saw they were all colored— indeed, the groggery was populated with black men and a few brightly clothed young women, and I now could see that the windows were in a different arrangement than at Ryan's. The easy intermingling of the sexes called to my mind Paris more than it did Baltimore. Around my shoulders, which had felt as though they were in some sort of immovable straitjacket, was actually a stack of heavy, warm blankets.

"Mr. Clark. You look better."

I turned and saw the black man who had diverted one of the rogues during the chase.

"Who are you?"

"My name is Edwin Hawkins."

My temples throbbed. "Was it one of them who hit me?" I asked, stroking the side of my head.

"No, you weren't hit just now, but it probably felt like you were. As you ran from the carriage warehouse, you keeled right over before you made it more than a few yards. You hit the side of your head on the pavement before I could catch you. I brought you here so they wouldn't find you. The one chasing me had given up after we passed under a streetlamp and he could see he was after the wrong man, but I'd wager he could still be searching."

"Did I kill that man in the warehouse?" I asked, remembering the events with chilling horror.

"He came out looking for you, and he fell down too. He looked cut pretty bad. I sent word for a doctor to treat him— you don't want murder on your head."

I looked around the room guardedly. The grogshop was in the rear of a black grocery. It was the sort of place, in Old Town localities like Liberty Alley, that the press often complained should be prohibited for its evil influences on the poorer classes and its instigation of riotous conduct. Two light-skinned black men were conferring confidentially in the corner, one occasionally throwing a glance in my direction. I looked on my other side. I did not wonder when I saw more suspicious gazes. I was not the only white man here, as there were several whites of the poorer classes sharing tables with black laborers. But it was quite obvious I was in some sort of trouble.

"You are safe, Mr. Clark," Edwin said with remarkable tranquillity. "You need to be out of the rain for a while."

"Why did you put yourself at risk for me? You do not even know me."

"You're right, Mr. Clark. But I did not do this for you. I did it for someone I did know," he replied. "I did this for Edgar Poe."

I looked over the hard angles and handsome features of the face before me. He was perhaps a few years past forty and had enough lines in his face to be older, but there was a younger, or at least more restless, gleam hidden in his eye. "You knew Edgar Poe?"

"Before I was freed, yes."

"You were a slave?"

"I was." He studied me and nodded thoughtfully. "Mr. Poe's slave."

❧   ❧   ❧

More than twenty years earlier, Edwin Hawkins had been a house slave for a relative of Maria Clemm's. Mrs. Clemm, called Muddy, was Edgar Poe's aunt and later, when Poe married her young daughter Sissy, would become his mother-in-law. Upon the death of Edwin's owner, the slave's deed and title had fallen to Muddy, then a resident of Baltimore.

Around the same time, Edgar Poe had recently withdrawn from his position as sergeant major in the army at Fortress Monroe, Virginia, certain now that he would be a poet after having completed an epic lyric, "Al Aaraaf," from his army barracks. The struggle to secure his military discharge had been long and frustrating, as Edgar Poe had needed consent from two equally strict parties: John Allan, his guardian, and his military superiors. Having finally accomplished this, Poe was now residing temporarily with Aunt Muddy and their extended Baltimore family. Eddie, as he was called by most people then, had enlisted in the army as Edgar A. *Perry* (the young slave had overheard Poe tell Muddy to watch for mail addressed to that name), initially having hoped to end all ties with Mr. Allan, who refused to support Poe's desire to publish his poetry.

Now, though freed from Allan's demands and from his army service, Edgar Poe had no money and no help to earn his place in the world.

Muddy, a tall, nurturing woman of forty, opened her home to Eddie Poe as though he were her son. He seemed to Edwin the style of man who liked exclusively to be around women. Overwhelmed with family illnesses in the household, Muddy asked her nephew to take the newly inherited slave and act as her agent in Edwin's sale. Soon Poe made an arrangement to sell Edwin to the family of Henry Ridgeway— a black family— for forty dollars.

I expressed my interest in the details of this arrangement. For a strong young male slave, Poe might have received five or six hundred, possibly more.

Edwin explained: "Our legislature tries hampering the freeing of slaves by making the process costly, so they don't look like they're disturbing our domestic economy. Mr. Poe and his aunt did not have that sort of money. But there is no law to prevent a free black family from purchasing a slave, and no law requiring a minimum sale price. Selling a slave cheap, maybe for the price of the lawyer's fee, to a free black owner was another way to free a slave— a way to free me, as Mr. Poe did in this arrangement. It also meant I could stay in Baltimore: not a perfect city, but my home. There are men among my people who own their wives and children as slaves, for the same reason."

"Poe did not write much about the slavery question," I said. "He was not a writer for any abolitionist causes." In fact, it had always seemed to me that Poe had never liked causes at all, automatically believing them hypocritical. "Yet he did this in your situation, forgoing hundreds of dollars, at a time when he was entirely poor and without support."

Edwin replied, "It is not a question of what a man writes. Especially a man who writes to earn his dollar, as Poe was beginning to do then. It is a question of what a man *does* that says who he is. I was only twenty years old. Mr. Poe was twenty, also, only a few months older. Whatever he

thought on slavery, he was quiet about it in the little time I was acquainted with him. He was quiet altogether, actually. He was a man with
few associates, and if he had associates, they were not friends. He saw
something of himself in me, and he decided right there that he would
free me if he could.

"I never saw Mr. Poe again, but I'll never forget what he did. I loved
him for it and love him still, even though I knew him a short time. I
began employment for several of the local newspaper offices when I was
freed. Now I assist in wrapping the papers to be delivered to various
points around the city. It was in one of those offices that I overheard your
complaints to the editors, around the time Poe died, that Poe had been
used up by the press, and that even his grave was unmarked. I had not
known where he was buried until then. After finishing work that day, I
walked there and left a token at the place you described."

"The flower? Was that *you* who left it?"

He nodded. "I remember Eddie was always neatly dressed, and sometimes wore a white flower like that one in his button-hole."

"But where did you run to once you left the flower?"

"It is not a Negro cemetery, you know, and it would attract suspicions
to loaf there in the evening. While I knelt at the grave I heard a carriage
coming fast and made haste exiting."

"That was Peter Stuart, my law partner, out looking to see where I was."

"Every day after that as I readied the newspapers for delivery, I saw
another ungentlemanly article about Poe's character— having long ago
been taught to read by the Ridgeways and their Webster's spelling-book,
I could decipher all of this unkindness. The living like to prove they're
better than the dead, seems to me. Much time had passed when another
fellow, a foreigner, began coming around to the newspaper offices, filled
with blusteration about Poe. He claimed he wanted justice for Poe, but to
my eye he wanted to spread base excitement."

"That is Baron Dupin," I explained.

"I talked to this man, more than once, asking that he should respect
Poe's memory. But there is a saying he reminded me of: all sham-skin and
no possum. He merely dismissed me, or tried to persuade me there was cash
to be made for helping him." I remembered the day I'd seen the Baron with
his arm snaked around Edwin's and thought they were conspiring.

"It was around this time that I saw you again, Mr. Clark. I saw you and
this Baron, as you call him, arguing over Poe. I decided to learn more

about you, and I followed you. I saw you bring that young slave to the depot, and stand up to that slave-trader, Hope Slatter."

"Do you know Slatter?"

"It was Slatter who arranged my own sale to my second owner. At the time I did not blame Slatter in particular, for I was just a boy and it was the life I knew. He had his job. But I came back to his pen once years later to ask who my parents were— for he had sold them and had split us apart, though he had promised all the owners he would never separate families. Slatter was the one man who knew, yet he refused to answer, and drove me away with his cane. Since then, I can never look up when I see him with his rumbling omnibuses on the streets, bringing slaves to his ships. It is strange, but he sits always with Poe in my head— I knew neither man's heart, I guess, but I know one put me in chains and the other took me out of them.

"I saw you defy Slatter. It seemed as though you might need help— and so when I happened upon you out this evening in the storm, I followed again."

"You probably saved my life, Edwin."

"Tell me about those men."

"Villains of the first order. The Baron owes large amounts of money to powerful interests back in Paris. This is why he pursues the mystery of Poe— for money."

"And your involvement, Mr. Clark?"

"I have no involvement with those men who wished to leave me under the sod! Whatever ideas they have formulated in their minds, they're fables. They don't know me from a bull's foot."

"I mean your involvement in all of this. You say this Baron pursues the mystery of Poe to feather his own nest. Very well. What do you pursue?"

I thought of the past reactions, the disappointed gazes of my lost friends, of Peter Stuart and of Hattie Blum, and hesitated to reply. But Edwin did not seem to want to judge me. His open manner had put me at ease. "I suppose my reasons are not very different from yours for helping me tonight. Poe freed me from the idea that life had to follow a fixed path. He was America— an independence that defied control, even when being controlled would have benefited him. Somehow, Poe-truth is all personal to me, and all-important."

"Then brisk up, sir. There may still be more for you to do for the good cause." Edwin signaled the waiter, who placed a steaming cup of tea in front of me. I don't believe I'd ever tasted anything so marvelous.

25

MY WAY HOME was more leisurely than you would think after a night like this. I was filled with relief. I had left both of my pursuers far behind somewhere in Baltimore. Yet there was more than this, more even than Edwin's camaraderie, that brought me my new sense of relief.

The day had been long. I had been brought into the Baron Dupin's sanctum, had heard the painful secret of Auguste Duponte's past, had discovered something of Poe through revelations of dress and cane, the full meaning of which my mind was still receiving. Something else had happened, too. As I walked through the streets, through a rain that was now no more than an occasional mist, I saw that particular flyer— a yellow flyer with black print, hanging on boards and lampposts all over the city. Some were floating in puddles from the storm. There was a vagrant looking at one under the trickle of gaslight, with his hands deep in the pockets of his threadbare suit.

I stepped in front of him and touched the paper to ensure that it was real. I saw that he was shivering and removed my overcoat, which he wrapped around himself with a grateful nod.

"What does it say?" he asked. He took off his bent hat, which had the crown knocked in. I realized the pauper could not read. "Something remarkable," I commented, and read aloud with a vibrancy that would have rivaled any one of the Baron's presentations.

What a sight I must have been. In my shredded, drenched, untailored, unmatched suit, coatless, my hair uncovered and straggled down the middle, leaning my tired body on the precious but bruised Malacca cane. The glimpse of myself in the looking-glass inside the front hall of Glen Eliza seemed to be from another world. I smiled at this thought as I climbed the stairs.

"Poe was not robbed," I said to Duponte even before any salutation. "I see your drift now. The cane he had, this type of Malacca, has a sword concealed inside. He had 'played' with the cane at Dr. Carter's office in

Richmond, according to the press. That means he would have known of the sword. If he had been robbed of his clothes, or violently treated, he would have tried to use it."

Duponte nodded. I wanted to show him more.

"And the clothes. His clothes, Duponte, would have been soaked through from the weather the day he was discovered. There are clothiers across the city who would change his suit for another."

"Clothing is a unique commodity," said Duponte, agreeing. "It is one of the few possessions that can be worthless and valuable at the same time. When wet, a suit of clothing is quite worthless to the wearer; but, as experience teaches us it will inevitably dry, it is just as valuable as a comparable dry suit in the eyes of the clothier, for whom the value comes only when he sells it later."

On the table, there was a pile of the yellow flyers I had seen outside. I picked one up.

"You are ready," I said. "You are ready! When did you have these printed, monsieur?"

"There is more to do first," said Duponte. "In the morning."

I read the flyer again. Duponte was announcing that he would present to the public a lecture explaining the death of Edgar A. Poe. *The source for the celebrated character of Dupin,* it read. *The analyst of great fame in Paris, who sought out the infamous murderer of Monsieur Lafarge, the famous victim of poisoning, will present an exposition detailing all that happened to Edgar A. Poe on October 3d, 1849, in the city of Baltimore. All facts gathered by personal examination and reflection.*

Presented free to the public.

The next morning, the day of Duponte's lecture, I left before Duponte woke in order to distribute more flyers. I placed them on many stores, gates, and poles. I had sent for Edwin and, after hearing about Duponte, he agreed to help spread the notices around various quarters of the city while out and about for his newspaper jobs. I handed the flyers to passersby and watched their faces react with interest as they read.

As a hand reached for one, I looked up into the stern face before me. He grabbed for the flyer.

Henry Herring narrowed his eyes at me over the top of the flyer. "Mr. Clark. What is this all about?"

"Everything will now be understood," I said, "about your uncle's death."

"I hardly consider myself a relation, to speak the truth."

"Then you need not concern yourself," I answered, taking the flyer back. "Yet you were enough of a relation to be one of the few people to watch his burial."

Herring's lips compressed into a tight line. "You do not understand him."

"You mean Poe?"

"Yes," he grumbled. "Do you know that when he lived here in Baltimore, before marrying Virginia, Eddie courted my daughter? Did your friend Eddie tell you of that infamous conduct? Wrote her poems, one after another, declaring his love," he said distastefully. "My Elizabeth!"

Herring starting clucking in the hollow of his cheek. By this time, though, my attention had drifted. Filled with the excitement of the day that was about to occur, I had been imagining the face of the Baron Dupin upon seeing the flyer— assuming the French assailants had not yet caught him. Henry Herring said a few more words to the effect that it seemed unsavory to pull up the affairs of a dead man from a dishonorable grave.

I stared out at a tree bough weaving in and out of the wind. Looking around, I saw Duponte's flyers in glorious abundance at every corner. That is what filled me with alarm.

If the Baron did know about Duponte's lecture and the flyers, would he not be sending Bonjour and whatever rascals he might hire to tear them down, or cover them with his own notices? He would at least do that. It would only be fair, from his perspective. But not a single one of the notices had been removed. Would the Baron allow that? Would he back out so easily . . . ? Unless . . .

"The Baron!" I cried.

"Where in the deuce are you going?" Herring called out to me as I broke into a run.

※   ※   ※

"Monsieur? Monsieur Duponte!"

I called while still clutching the latch of my street door. I scurried through the front hall anxiously, climbed up the stairs, and rushed into the library. He was not there. I knew something had come to pass.

No, not Duponte.

I heard the light steps of Daphne in the hall with another servant. I ran after her and asked her where Duponte was.

She shook her head. She seemed frightened, or perhaps just bewildered. "His friends took him, Mr. Clark."

No, no, I thought, the words clutching my chest.

A young man had come to the door and said there was a caller for Mr. Duponte; but, he explained, the caller was lame, so Mr. Duponte would have to come to the gate to see him. The carriage was waiting there. Daphne replied that it would be better for the caller to come to the door, as was the custom. But the driver insisted. She informed Duponte and, after giving the matter some thought, he went.

"And then," I urged her to continue.

Daphne seemed to have softened her harsh stance against Duponte, as her eyes were blurred and she dabbed them before continuing. "There was a man sitting in the carriage like a king— I don't think he was lame at all, as he stood tall and took Mr. Duponte by the arm. And he— sir— "

"Yes?"

"He looked just like Mr. Duponte! As though exact twins, honor bright!" she vowed. "And Mr. Duponte went into the carriage, but with a quiver in his face that was sad. Like he knew he was leaving something behind, forever. How I wished you were here, Mr. Clark!"

I had been a simpleton, an ass! The Baron had not stopped our flyers for the lecture because he would stop the lecturer himself!

❆   ❆   ❆

There was no trace of the Baron at the hotels, which I began calling on myself. First, I went to the police to report that Auguste Duponte was missing and gave them Von Dantker's formal portrait, which I had taken from the Baron. I also gave them a drawing I hastily sketched of the Baron and his colleagues, including the various drivers, porters, and messengers who I had noted had at one time or another been engaged by him. Later, I received a message that I was wanted at the station house.

The same Officer White whom I had spoken with at the time of Poe's death was waiting at his desk. His hands were folded tightly together in front of him.

"Have you found him now? Have you found Duponte?"

"Or Dupin?" he asked. "These portraits you gave us help, Mr. Clark. But the hotel clerks we interviewed all recognize Duponte not as Duponte, *but as Dupin*. You do notice their similarities even in the sketch you made with the painting?"

I could barely suppress my agitation. "The reason they appear similar is because Baron Dupin has been flagrantly attempting to ape Monsieur Duponte, and the artist, Von Dantker— he was part of it!"

White repositioned his hands and cleared his throat.

"Duponte was pretending to be Dupin?"

"What? No, no. Entirely the reverse, Officer White. Dupin wishes to prove he was the real source for Poe's character— "

"Poe again! Now, what has this to do with him?"

"A great deal! You see, Auguste Duponte is the model for the character of C. Auguste Dupin. That is why he has come. To resolve the mystery of the death of Poe. He has been living in my house and has busied himself at his labor; that is why he has not been seen very much at all. Not to mention he walks mostly in the evening— well, Poe's Frenchman does the same. In the meantime, the Baron Claude Dupin has pretended he is also the model of Dupin, as well as imitating Duponte."

Officer White put his hand up to stop me. "You are implying Duponte is Dupin."

"Yes! Well, it is much more complicated than that, isn't it? The Baron Dupin is trying to be C. Auguste Dupin. The important point is simply to find the man before he comes to harm."

"Perhaps, if I may suggest, you have simply seen this one fellow, Dupin, and mistaken him for someone else."

"Mistaken him . . ." I said, reading his meaning. "I have not *imagined* the entire existence of Auguste Duponte, sir. I have not imagined someone living and supping and shaving in my house!"

White shook his head and looked to the floor.

I went on in a deep and serious tone. "Dupin is the wire-puller of this. He must be stopped at all costs! He is dangerous, Officer White! He has kidnapped a rare genius and may have already brought him to injury. He will spread his false version of events behind Poe's death. Does none of that concern you?"

It clearly did not; and there was nothing to do for the moment but keep on doggedly with my search.

. . .

I wondered what might have been had I been more aware of human malice in those days. Had I been able to posit the dismal, secret plans— had I known to stay near Duponte at all times, to carry him bodily to the lecture hall if necessary. For all of Duponte's strengths, he could do nothing faced with the Baron and Bonjour threatening his life, and I pictured him, as described by my domestic, accompanying them without even a struggle. What it would have meant to Poe's legacy for Duponte to have spoken on this night. But such a question is pure speculation.

The time for the lecture was growing near. Walking with a rueful air along that street, for I wished to brood at the appropriate site, I was startled to see a throng of people pushing into the entrance of the lyceum hall. I touched the arm of one of the men on line and asked him the occasion.

"Haven't the lyceum organizers canceled the lecture tonight?"

"No such thing!"

"This is the lecture that has been planned, you mean to say? On the true death of Poe?"

"Of course!" he said. "Perhaps you thought Emerson had come to town."

"Duponte," I breathed. "Has he escaped after all? He has come?"

"Only," the man interjected, "there has been a change of circumstances. They now must charge for each ticket of admission."

"Impossible!"

He nodded with resignation. "No matter. It is the original 'Dupin,' you know. It is worth one dollar and a half."

I stared at him. He proudly held up a copy of Poe's tales. "It is bound to be something," he said.

Running to the front of the mob, I shoved my way inside, past the objecting doorkeeper asking for my ticket.

There, behind the stage, sat the erect figure of Auguste Duponte, quietly waiting alone in contemplation. I looked on with renewed faith and triumph, and reverence.

"How— ?" I stepped closer.

"Welcome," he said, glancing up at me deviously, and then looking around as though waiting for something more important. "I am glad, Brother Quentin, you will be a witness to history."

It was not Duponte.

As remarkable as his imitation of Duponte had been at earlier times, the metamorphosis was now terrifyingly complete. Even the eyes contained something of Duponte's spirit.

"Baron! I will not let this come off, be sure of that." I gripped my Malacca in front of me.

"And what will you do?" His gaze fell leisurely over me. "You and Duponte have done me a favor, you know. I already have collected the subscription fees from my lecture to be held in a few days, and will receive those from today as well."

I was surprised, once my mind adjusted to the circumstance, to find no trace of Bonjour around him. Would the Baron leave himself so unprotected? I suppose someone had to guard Duponte, unless they had . . . no, not even the Baron. Not an unarmed man.

"I will tell you the truth, the real truth, Brother Quentin. There were times before this day when I thought the jig was up. That Duponte was too clever for me. I see by your face you can hardly believe it. Yes, I thought, by the bye, he would by some measure prevail. He has lost his last chance, and now he may lie down and die."

"Where is he?" I demanded. "What have you done to him?"

The Baron wore a devilish grin. "What do you mean?"

"I shall have the police on you! You shall not escape this!" I decided to try for any ace of information from him, and to loosen his confidence besides. "You know, wherever you have him, however you are holding him, Duponte will find a way out. He will come for you like all wrath. He will stop you at the last moment; he will prevail."

The Baron offered an intimate laugh. He revealed nothing, but his insecurity showed in a twitch of his lip. "Monsieur Clark, do you know the obstacles I have overcome to reach this day? The Baltimore police pose no problem to me. Today, I turn a corner. Today it is do or die to put a finale on all this. Unless you shall stop me, for you are the only one who can now— no, but clearly you will not. I shall no longer live in the shadows, not in the shadows of my enemies or of Auguste Duponte. There are times when genius, like Duponte's, must doff its hat to cunning. This day shall be my passport back to glory."

The Baron followed the lyceum director onto the platform and to the podium. I looked around desperately, trying to think of what to do, but found myself on a mental treadmill. Finally, I pushed forward onto the platform and attempted to at least divide the Baron from the podium. Then I saw the crowd— no, call it the mob, the endless, formless, hollering expanse of people's stares— and I understood why the Baron did not need Bonjour at his side to be protected. He was safe in a crowd. He was about to become legitimate again in the eyes of the world.

In the background, a lyceum clerk was fixing a light, causing it to sway disruptively, further confusing my senses in the dark hall. I could only shout for the lecture to be stopped and heard moans of displeasure in response.

I had lost all ability to articulate, all flow of logic. I shouted something about justice. I pulled and prodded, and was pushed in return. At some point in the fog of my memory, I can see there was the face of Tindley, the Whig doorkeeper, standing out in the crowd. A red parasol twirled in the horizon of my sight. I saw faces: Henry Herring, Peter Stuart, who pushed past the anxious crowd to come closer to the front. The old clerk from the athenaeum was there, too, squeezed into his seat, and newspaper editors from all the chief offices of the press. Sometime in all this, in the wavering light I saw it— the grin, the razor-sharp peculiar grin of mischief that Duponte had held for Von Dantker, now precisely plagiarized upon the face of the Baron. Then there was the noise, the only noise that could have risen above the excited clamor that my disturbance had now provoked. It was like a cannon burst. The first sent the stage lights crashing to the ground, drowning the whole place in darkness. And then there was another.

I jumped back amid the sea of screams and feminine shrieks at the sounds of gunfire. I trembled with a sudden chill, and from some macabre instinct put my hand to my chest. I remember only fragments after that:

The Baron Dupin above me and both of us falling together in a bloody tangle, upending the podium in the process . . . his shirt stained with a wide oval, the rim of which was a thick darkness the color of death . . . he groaning, gripping madly, passionately at my collar . . . a horrid weight over my body.

Then, both of us sinking, sinking into oblivion.

—BOOK V—

THE FLOOD

I feel like one
Who treads alone
Some banquet hall deserted

—THOMAS MOORE

26

I WAS NOT suspicious when Officer White took me in his coach from the lyceum to Glen Eliza. Think of it. I had more knowledge of the complex situation that had just occurred than anyone. Though I did not have unreserved confidence in the abilities of the police officers, I believed that with my assistance, Duponte could be found . . . and then he would find the truth the Baltimore police could not.

Officer White entered the drawing room of Glen Eliza with his clerk and several other police officers I had not seen before. I proceeded to transfer to White all the knowledge I possessed— from the arrival of Baron Dupin in Baltimore to the violent moment as I had just witnessed it. But from his interjections, I began to wonder how closely he was listening.

"Dupin is *dying*," White kept repeating with different emphasis. "Dupin *is* dying."

"Yes, at the hands of these two rascals," I explained once more, "who pursued me through the city earlier, thinking I was trying to prevent their petty vengeance against the Baron."

"Then you saw one of them shoot the Baron at the lyceum?" asked Officer White, who sat at the edge of an armchair. The police clerk was all the while standing dumbly behind me. I never liked feeling watched, and I looked back repeatedly with an unsubtle desire that he would at least be seated.

"No," I answered the officer, "I couldn't see anything from the stage, with the glare of the lights shining and then going off, and that mob of people. A few faces . . . But it is most obvious, it had to be their deed."

"These two rascals you mention— names?"

"I do not know. One of them nearly did me in the day before. I was shot through the hat! He would be injured, no doubt, from our struggle, as I managed to cut him. I do not know their names."

"Tell me what you do know, Mr. Clark." The police officer had a distant tone.

"That they were French, that is most certain. Baron Dupin was in great debt. A Parisian creditor will never quit his harassment and dunning— even as far as Baltimore." I did not know if this was true of all Parisian creditors, but thought it best under the circumstances to make an axiom of it.

To this, Officer White merely bobbed his head as one would do to a rambling child.

"Claude Dupin had to be stopped— for the sake of Poe," he said.

I was surprised at this turn in the conversation. "Precisely," I replied.

"You told me earlier he had to be stopped— 'at all costs.'"

"Indeed, Officer." I hesitated then began again. "Yes, you see, what I meant . . ."

"He was certainly laid out awful flat," commented the clerk from behind my chair, "Dupin was. Flat as a hog barbecued."

"A hog barbecued, sir?" I asked.

"Mr. Clark," Officer White continued, "you wished to choke off his speaking at the lyceum. You told me as much beforehand when you came looking for your French friend."

"Yes . . ."

"That portrait you passed along to us, signed by one Von Dantker, was of the Baron. It shows him to a hair. Why had you commissioned a portrait of him?"

"No, it was *not* the same man! I did not commission anything!"

"Clark, you may gas and blow all you have a mind to later, but no more fables today! It is said that the Baron had precisely the same fantastic smile upon his face right before being shot as the one shown in this portrait! Unusual smile!"

My skin grew warm, my body sensing danger before I could think about what was happening. I halted when I noticed my shirt stained with the Baron's blood. Then I realized that my servants were shuffling around nervously in the corridors, away from their posts. The three or four police officers who had come with Officer White were nowhere to be seen in the room— and other policemen were now parading through the room, enough to constitute a standing army. I could hear footsteps ascending the stairs and moving in the bedrooms above. Glen Eliza was being searched even as I sat there. I felt as if the walls were sinking around me, and the image of Dr. Brooks's burning house came into my mind.

"You grabbed the Baron, even as he began to address the audience— "

"Officer! What do you mean to say?" We were talking over each other now.

"No one could account for your presence— and there is no trace of your friend, this 'Mr. Duponte,' *anywhere.*"

"Officer, you are implying something . . . you may call me a story-teller if you like . . . !"

". . . Poe has done you in once and for all."

"What? What do you mean?"

"Your obsessive dalliances with Mr. Poe's writings, Mr. Clark. You would have done anything to stop Baron Dupin talking of Poe, wouldn't you? You have admitted you assaulted and 'cut' another Frenchman. You wished only for yourself to talk of Poe and nobody else. If someone indeed was involved with Mr. Poe's death, I wonder if that person would have exhibited signs of preoccupation with it— it's leading me to wonder about your own activities at the time Edgar Poe died."

As I strenuously objected, the police clerk came around and took my arm, asking in calm tones that I stand up and not struggle.

27

AT FIRST I was held in one of the cells across from Officer White's private rooms in the Middle District station house. At the sound of every footstep there rose in me a semi-desperate expectation. Imprisonment, I might interrupt myself to say, does not merely produce a feeling of being alone. Your entire history of loneliness returns to you piece by piece, until the cell is a castle of your mental misery. The memories of solitude flood over all other thoughts of the present or the future. You are only yourself. That is the world; no poet of the penal system could devise anything harsher than that.

Whom did I await with palpitating breast? Duponte? Hattie? Perhaps the sour but stalwart expression on the face of Peter Stuart? The Baron Dupin himself, escorted by the doctors, able to bear witness to the real culprit who shot him and to free me? I longed even for the clamor of my great-aunt's voice. Anything to remind me that there was another person concerned by my fate.

There was no word about Duponte, meanwhile. I feared for him an outcome worse than my own. I had failed him. Failed in my role to protect him in the operation of his genius.

Officer White circulated a selection of passable newspapers and journals as part of the jail liberties for the prisoners who were literate. I accepted them, but only pretended to read them while, in fact, I went about far more important reading, which I had smuggled in with me. When I had wrestled at the lyceum with the Baron Dupin, I had semi-consciously removed from his hands the notes he had brought for his speech. Hardly thinking of their significance, I had thrust these papers into my coat before accompanying Officer White to the station house.

As long as I had candlelight in my cell, I studied them, propped in a magazine. *Edgar Poe has not left, but has been taken away*, said the Baron's treatise. It was not on the whole inelegant, though at no time aspiring to literary merit. As I read, I committed it to memory. I thought of

Duponte reading over my shoulder. *Only through observing that which is mistaken can we come to the truth.*

One time while studying these pages, I was interrupted by the approach of a visitor. The slouching figure of a man came into the hall, escorted by the clerk. It was a man unknown to me, wearing an expressionless face. He leaned his umbrella on the wall and shook off the excess water from his gigantic boots, which seemed to take up half his height.

"The stink in here . . ." he said to himself, sniffing.

A woman sang drunkenly from the ladies' cells corridor. The visitor merely stood silently. Not finding any particular look of sympathy about him, I did the same.

I was surprised when the stranger was joined by a frightened young lady, wrapped tightly in her cloak.

"Oh, dear Quentin, look at where they've put you!" Hattie stared pityingly at me. She was near tears.

"Hattie!" I reached out and grabbed her by the hand. It hardly seemed possible that she was real, even with the warm leather of her gloves. Taking renewed notice of the stranger, I released her hands. "Is Peter not with you?"

"No, he would not hear of me coming. He will not speak of the situation at all. When he went to the lecture, he was quite angered, Quentin. He felt he had to do something to try to stop you. I do believe he is still your friend."

"He must know I am innocent! How could I have something to do with the shooting of the Baron? The Baron had kidnapped my friend to prevent him from speaking— "

"Your friend? Would that be the friend who has placed you into this *débâcle*, Mr. Clark?" said the man standing at Hattie's side, turning toward me with a frown not unlike Peter's.

Hattie motioned him for patience. She turned back to me. "This is my cousin's husband, Quentin. One of the finest attorneys in Washington in this sort of matter. He can help us, I'm certain."

Despite the despair of what was now my lot, I felt comfort at the word "us."

"And the Baron himself?" I asked.

"He lies without hope of recovery," my new lawyer blurted out.

"I have written to your great-aunt for her to come at once; she shall help rectify all this," Hattie continued, as though not having heard the terrible words. If what her cousin said was true, if the Baron was shortly to die, in the eyes of the world I would be condemned as a murderer.

A few days later I was moved from the district station house to the Jail of Baltimore City and County, on the banks of Jones Falls. The atmosphere duplicated my hopelessness; the surrounding cells were filled to capacity with some who'd been convicted of grave crimes along with those waiting, with small hopes, for their trial dates, or with perverse eagerness for their own hangings.

The morning before, I had been officially arraigned for the attempt to murder Baron Dupin. My declarations that the Baron must be stopped, combined with my appearance on the lyceum stage, were cited widely. Hattie's cousin shook his beard disapprovingly at the fact that a highly respected police officer was a witness against me. The police had also found a gun when searching Glen Eliza— the weapon I had brought as a safeguard when I'd visited John Benson, which, absentmindedly, I had left in plain view.

The tempests outside grew worse every day. The rain would not stop. Each time it slowed itself it followed on even harder, as though it had only been taking a breath. It was said that a bridge was swept away at Broadway near Gay Street and struck another bridge, so that the two bridges drove themselves downriver through half of Baltimore, knocking entire houses off the banks along their way. In the prison, meanwhile, the air itself seemed to change— full of pressure and discomfort. I saw one prisoner scream frightfully and squeeze his head with his hands as though something was burrowing through to get out. "It's come!" he cried apocalyptically. "It's come!" Confrontations between some of the more desperate prisoners and the guards also grew worse, whether from the air or from other causes of which I had not made myself aware. Through the bars of my window, I could see the shore of Jones Falls gradually surrender to the boiling layer of rainwater. I felt myself do the same.

My lawyer returned, each time with more bad tidings from outside. The newspapers, which I could read only listlessly, were quite giddy about my guilt. It was now written that the Frenchman dangerously wounded and lying in the hospital was the model for Poe's tales of analysis, and that I had done away with him because of jealousy, due to a diseased preoccupation with Poe. The Whig newspapers thought my action as assassin somehow heroic. The Democratic newspapers, perhaps in response against the Whigs, were convinced I was villainous and cowardly. Both, though, had decided I was certainly the killer. The newspapers known to be neutral, namely the *Sun* and *Transcript*, worried that the episode would do no insignificant damage to our country's relationship with the still young French Republic and its president, Louis-Napoleon.

I protested vociferously that the Baron Dupin was by no means the real Dupin, though I believe Hattie's cousin thought my choice of objection in the matter most strange. Edwin came to see me several times, but soon the police peppered him with questions, suspicious of any Negro having business with me, and I begged him to refrain from his visits to protect himself from their scrutiny. John Benson, my benevolent Phantom, came to call on me in this wretched place, too. I shook his hand warmly, desperate for an ally.

The cross-bar shadows fell over his haggard face. He explained that he was working nearly all hours on his uncle's account books. "I'm dragged out, no mistake. The devil himself was never so pressed with business," he said. He looked at me sidelong through the bars, as though at any moment we could exchange places if he were not careful with the words he chose.

"Perhaps you should confess, Mr. Clark," he advised.

"Confess what?"

"That you had been overtaken with Poe. *Overcome*, so to speak."

I hoped I could elicit more valuable assistance from him. "Benson, you must tell me if there was anything else you discovered about how Poe died."

He sat on a stool kicking his legs out, despondent and sleepy, and repeated his suggestion that I consider making a complete confession. "Don't think of the Poe predicament any longer, Mr. Clark. The truth behind his death is beyond discovery now. You see that."

Hattie visited me on the days she managed to avoid both her aunt and Peter. She brought me food and small gifts. In my anxious and confused state, I could hardly find words to express my gratitude to her.

She recalled many stories from our childhood to calm my nerves. We had frank discussions touching all subjects. She told me how she felt when I was in Paris.

"I could see yours were great dreams, Quentin." She sighed. "I know we do not have a life of mutual happiness ahead of us, Quentin. But I wish only to say that you mustn't think I was angered, or melancholy, for your having gone away, or because you have not told me more. If I have shown melancholy it is because you did not feel, you did not *know* decidedly, that you could say every detail and would receive in return my unblushing friendship."

"Peter was right. There was selfishness that began all this. Maybe I did all this not for what Poe's writings would mean to the world, but for what they meant to me alone. Perhaps that exists only in my mind!"

"That is why it is important," Hattie replied, taking my hand.

"Why couldn't I see?" I fretted nervously. "It has become all about his death to me, at the expense of his life. Precisely what I worried others would do. At the expense of my life, too."

The rains and flooding soon made it too difficult to travel to the prison from other quarters of the city. Separated from Hattie, there was no company outside the desolate prisoners. I had never felt quite so unaided, trapped, finished.

Once, during a night in which sleep had mercifully overtaken me, I heard light footsteps coming toward my cell. Hattie. She had come again, through the worst floods and rains yet. She came swiftly and elegantly through the corridor, closed off from the filth of the cells in her bright red cloak. Yet, strangely, there was no guard beside her and— I realized when coming to my senses— these were not hours in which visitors were admitted. As she emerged from the shadows of other cells, she reached in and grabbed my wrists so tightly I could not move. It was not Hattie at all.

In the weak light, Bonjour's golden skin now showed a ghastly pale tint. Her eyes widened into a gaze that seemed to look everywhere simultaneously.

"Bonjour! How did you get past the guards?" Though, I supposed, if anyone could arrange free entrance and exit into a prison, it was Bonjour.

"I needed to find you."

Her grip tightened, and I was suddenly consumed with fear. She had come to kill me for the Baron, to personally carry out an execution. Without hesitation, she could slice my neck and, upon finding me headless, nobody would know she had ever been here.

"I know you did not shoot the Baron," she said, correctly reading the frightened look in my eyes. "We must find out who did."

"Don't you know as well as I do? The creditors— those thugs who followed the Baron wherever he went."

"They were not sent by any creditor. The Baron settled with his creditors weeks ago, as soon as he was able after collecting subscriptions for
his lecture on Poe. The amounts he raised were beyond what we'd
hoped. Those assassins were not looking for his money."

I was shocked to hear this. "Then who were they?"

"I need to find out. I owe the Baron that. *You* need to for the woman
you love."

I looked down at my bare feet. "She no longer loves me."

When I raised my eyes I could see Bonjour's mouth linger open, forming a questioning circle. She let the topic pass. "Where is your friend? He
must help us find that answer."

"My friend?" I asked, surprised. "Duponte? How I have waited to ask
you that! I have thought the worst for him after you and the Baron kidnapped him!"

I learned that Duponte had not come to any harm— at least not at
Bonjour's hands. To my surprise, Bonjour had released Duponte shortly
after his capture from Glen Eliza. The Baron Dupin had instructed her to
free their rival at the hour the Baron's doomed lecture was to begin. The
Baron had not wished to murder Duponte; or, rather, he had wished to
murder his spirit. The Baron guessed Duponte would rush to the lyceum
and arrive in time to witness his rival's triumph, thus amplifying the
Baron's victory with Duponte's demoralization. But Duponte eluded this
defeat, for he did not appear— and if he did, nobody had seen him.

"Did Duponte fight you when you kidnapped him? Did he struggle?"

Bonjour paused, not sure whether I would be disappointed at the answer. "No. He was wise not to fight, as the Baron was determined to carry
out our plan. Where would Auguste Duponte go now, Monsieur Clark?"

"I have been locked up here, Bonjour. I haven't the remotest idea
where he is!"

Her eyes caught mine with uncomfortable intensity. I could not help
my thoughts: with Hattie to marry Peter, what hopes of love had I left?
For the strength it would give me— what wouldn't I give at the moment
for even a token of affection! Perhaps my thoughts were obvious, as she
now began to move closer to me. I looked away to break any improper in-
sinuation. But she placed her hand on my shoulder, and as I looked back
she pulled my face between the bars to hers, in a long moment that

thrilled me even more by its surprise than in the warmth of her mouth. The scar that I had seen on her lips seemed to form an indent in the same place on my own face, and the currents ran through my chilled body. I was remade. When the kiss ended, I felt she was somewhat captured by it, too.

"You must think of how to find Duponte," she said in a low, unwavering command. "He can find the assassin."

And for a few days, I did try hard to puzzle it out. But several nights after Bonjour's midnight visit, the gloom and unrelenting solitude of the prison cell conquered me again.

Once, when I woke from one of my long stretches of unconsciousness, I found a single book lying on my cell's small wooden table. I had no awareness of where it came from or who placed it there. At first sight of it I closed my eyes tightly and turned away, thinking it was part of some dream my brain had constructed to worsen my circumstances even further.

It was one of Griswold's volumes of Poe. It was the third— the latest volume— the one I could hardly suffer to look upon. The first two volumes contained a muddled though decent selection of Poe's prose and poetry, but for this third volume the reckless editor, Mr. Rufus Griswold, had composed a downright defamatory essay.

I had seen the advertisements in the press by Griswold the winter after Poe's death, asking for any correspondents of Poe's to send copies of their letters to Griswold for inclusion in this essay. However, having already been familiar with his obituary of Poe, with its manic lies, I hadn't had a thought of complying. I had written Griswold at once telling him of my possession of four letters personally autographed by Poe, and detailing the reasons I would never share them with him, ever, unless Griswold pledged a different approach to his solemn duty. He had not had the forthrightness to reply to me.

I had hoped, though, that Griswold would have grown to understand his responsibilities as a proper literary executor (not literary executioner!) after the publication of the first volumes. But upon this third volume originally coming into my possession— after opening to the page of Griswold's vicious memoir of his onetime friend— I had put the book down and not looked at it again. In fact, I had vowed to myself to burn it.

Duponte, however, had consulted the letters printed there in his examination. And now the volume had appeared in my cell. The stated reason given to me by a guard was that the officials were concerned for my health and, seeing that in my moral lethargy I would read no newspaper or magazine, and recalling my fondness for the writer Poe, this volume, which had POE printed in large letters on the boards, had been removed from my library and placed here.

I had no doubt, however, that the real reason it had come to me was Officer White. An attempt to torment me and force me to admit my crime, to bemoan my wretched position in life. In the minuscule cell, there was no escaping it; if I looked away from the book during the night, my hand would fall on it in the paroxysms of unhealthy slumber. When it was daytime, I would hide it under my sleeping board so I would not see it, only to find my foot kick against it when I moved to sit up, the maniacal volume revealing itself by sliding out the other side. I would throw the book through the bars into the corridor, rejoicing to be rid of it, but upon my next waking it would appear again, neatly positioned next to my pitcher of water or on the end of my sleeping board— placed there by a prison official or, for all I knew, another prisoner bent on plaguing me.

After all this, I could not help myself. I began to read. Skipping Griswold's worthless comments, I instead took in Poe's letters that he'd interspersed throughout his memoir of the author. I wondered, soon after, when I found what was there, whether Officer White had any secret inkling of the abyss into which this would sink me.

Deep within— I cringe to remember— I found Poe had listed me in a letter among several names of people who might support his magazine, *The Stylus*, in the city of Baltimore. Griswold had written to Poe in reply, asking for more details. Then came this, in a subsequent letter from Poe elaborating on my identity:

"The Clark you ask about is a young man of idle wealth who, knowing my extreme poverty, has for years pestered me with unpaid letters."*

Each day I would set aside a moment of my highest lucidity to read the page again in an effort to ensure that it was not merely an apparition of

---

* Since the above was in type, a scholar's preliminary comparison of Rufus W. Griswold's memoir with surviving manuscripts of Poe's letters has determined that this sentence, along with dozens of others, had been invented by the biographer as part of an effort to depict his subject as ungenerous to friends. Unfortunately, I had no means of acquiring this knowledge at the time I discovered the reference during my stay in the Maryland penitentiary.

mental fatigue. Unpaid letters! I could not believe it. Poe had— *but you have already seen!*— Poe *had insisted* I not pay advance postage on our correspondence, as if I would otherwise be offending our friendship. He had asked that I help him! *("Can you or will you help me?")* He had called for my commitment directly! *("Pestered"?)*

I could not stop repeating the words of Poe to myself and, worse yet, I could hear the words in the wearied voice of my father. *Young man of idle wealth!* The wealth that he had transmitted to me with so much industry and sense.

If only I knew how Poe's voice sounded, so my mind might abolish the other one! But at the moment, I could not even guess at how Poe might have talked. Perhaps he really did speak with my father's voice.

Pestered? . . . A young man of idle wealth.

I no longer found strength enough to leave my sleeping board. My feeble condition was obvious, and I could not bring myself to speak. After several days produced almost no sleep, I drifted off into continuous drowsiness, and I could not tell the difference between sleeping and waking states. I remember very little from this time except the undertone provided by the torrents of rain and regular claps of thunder that had been building now, on and off, for days.

There were no more visitors, no more faces to come to me except for indistinct police officers and guards. Although, once, I was certain I saw across from my cell a man whom I had seen before. The stowaway from the steamer *Humboldt,* the scene of Duponte's secret victory that made me feel as if a gift possessed by him had been bestowed onto me. There, in this dingy Baltimore prison, I thought in my dreamy hazes I saw him again, watching over me, but this time there was no sea captain to catch hold of his arms. There were also other strange moments, feeling every grain of my skin covered with bugs and flies, as one newspaper had reported Poe was found, only escaping this when waking up on my board in a cold perspiration.

With the probability of my own death by hanging gnawing at my bones, I would often rehearse the story in my mind that the Baron had told me about Catherine Gautier— only her face, as it gazed down with pale calm from the height of the gallows, sometimes looked like sweet Hattie, and other times like Bonjour, a wickedness creeping into the countenance. Meanwhile, the warden of the prison came through for inspections and, after determining that my senseless and speechless condition was authentic, ordered me to be moved to a cot on the first floor of the prison. When I was touched, I apparently gave only a cold shudder in response, and no pulling or shouting in my ear would make me stir.

I woke amid the new surroundings, and found myself the sole occupant of an apartment where not even the prisoners wanted to go— for though it was more comfortably appointed than the cells upstairs, here people were sent to die. The doctors detected nothing wrong with me physically, but concluded that my wavering sleep proved the die had been cast. Upon being asked some simple questions by agents of the police to test my consciousness, I remained silent or muttered unintelligibly. I was told later that when questioned as to my birthday, I repeated October 8, 1849, again and again— the date of Poe's funeral, which besides not being my birthday would have made me two years old.

For my part, I could call to mind only brief moments of myriad dreams. When news of my parents' death had first reached me, I had sat for many days in my chamber with a roving chill and illness. In my stupor, I had the clearest visions of speaking with my parents— conversations that had never occurred but were as real, or more so, as any that I had had in my life. In them, I repeatedly apologized for having given up so much, for not having heeded their years of advice as Peter did. Then I'd awake again. The book— the Griswold volume— had not followed me from my cell to the hospital chambers, and for this I was happy. I chuckled to myself, as though this were at last my great triumph.

There was not much light there in the penitentiary's hospital, the windows unscrubbed and filmy. Even on the morning the rain finally ceased, only a hint of daylight came through to the prison hospital rooms. The guards had been frantically moving prisoners around the building after flooding had begun to occur in some quarters. The hospital room had been safe from the flood so far, but that night I awoke with a shudder at a series of noises.

"Who's here?" I called out obliviously.

It was suddenly terribly cold and, as I swung my bare feet to the floor, a stream of cold water curled over my toes. I jerked back to the cot and groped for a candle. My eyes opened for what seemed the first time in years.

The floods had filled the sewer and had broken through the wall of the hospital chamber. I sat up and saw from the breach in the wall the darkness of the narrow passage open to me. The sewer, I knew, ran underneath the vast, high wall that surrounded the jail and passed into Jones Falls. There wasn't the smallest obstacle between here and there. Because I had not been exposed to light for days, my eyes were immediately able to assess the circumstances even in this darkness.

My mind turned rapidly, vivaciously. A new energy resurrected me from the funereal indolence I had been lying in. A half-formed idea, a certainty, propelled me forward to where the putrid water subsumed my ankles, my waist, reaching to my shoulders. Even as I became weighed down by the streaming water, it seemed I moved with greater swiftness, until I emerged where the gaunt towers of the prison could only be seen in the distant horizon.

This was my idea: *Edgar Poe was still alive.*

I was not ill, as you might think. There was no degradation of my mental acumen, despite the long ordeal of incarceration that led me to the realization— this half-formed idea. *Edgar Poe had never been dead.*

As my eyes turned to the outside of the prison for the first time in what seemed to be months or years (I would have believed either one if told so at this point), all knowledge related to the affair of Poe's death shaped itself in a new and startling way in my brain.

Perhaps I should have found aid, rest, sanctuary, at the moment. Perhaps I should never have left the confines of the prison, where, strange to say, I was safe from what awaited me outside. But what would you have done— remained there on your cot, staring out at the lights of the stars? Consider now what you'd have done, if you had known with sudden clarity that Edgar Poe was among the living.

(Had Duponte not seen it? Had he not considered it in all his analysis?)

We do not care what happened to Poe. We have imagined Poe dead for our own purposes. In some sense, Poe is still very much alive.

I remembered that Benson had said this in our first meeting, very nearly those words, at least. Benson had seemed to know more than he was telling me. Had he known *this*? Had he found something he could not reveal in his early investigation, and had he been giving me a suggestion, a clue to the secret truth?

I could see the faces of the men at the funeral, as though daguerreotyped on the mind, could still see them coming toward me with the hurried, muddied footsteps of that day.

Think of it . . . think of the *evidence.* George Spence, the sexton, had not seen Edgar Poe in many years, and had emphasized Poe's unfamiliar appearance when brought in for burial. Neilson Poe saw his cousin only through a curtain at the college hospital, and did he not tell me in his chambers that the patient *looked like another man altogether?*

Meanwhile, the funeral I witnessed had been performed hastily, lasting perhaps three minutes, with few witnesses and even a *canceled* oration— as inconspicuous, as quiet, as was ever seen. Even Snodgrass, intransigent Dr. Snodgrass, had exhibited anxiousness, misgiving, self-reproach over Poe's end and burial. I thought again of the poem we found in Snodgrass's desk that he had written on the subject, which spoke of his idea of Poe's drunkenness. It had also recalled that day of the funeral.

> *But haunts me still that funeral scene!*
> *In shame and sadness oft I trace*
> *Thy burial— sadder none hath seen—*
> *In that neglected resting place!*

Had any who knew him of recent years *seen* the lifeless form as it lay in the coffin before it was lowered under the earth? And most of those witnesses— Neilson Poe, Henry Herring, Dr. Snodgrass— wanted to say nothing about this funeral, as though there was something to conceal. Had they known more? That Poe, in fact, still breathed and still lived? Had he been hidden by outside agents concealing something? Or had he, Edgar Poe, perpetrated his ultimate hoax upon the world?

You see that the reasoning in my mind, produced in an admittedly highly excited state, was neither deranged nor insubstantial. I would demonstrate Poe was not yet dead, and all that had occurred would be thrown into an immediate reversal. I proceeded by foot after passing through the sewer directly to the old Westminster Presbyterian burial ground. Its place toward the center of the city, away from the larger bodies of water, had spared it and the surrounding roads the worst consequences of the flooding, though rivulets still streamed through the grassy burial yard, and certain crevices and corners contained deeper gullies of water.

I would speak to the sexton and insist upon full answers. But as I crossed through the gates, a different determination overtook me. Though it was dark, my eyes retained the exaggerated power of sight resulting from my prolonged stay in the dark cells of the prison. Indeed, with just a single burst of lightning from another storm that was gathering itself, I located precisely the spot of Edgar Poe's grave, which outrageously had remained unmarked. What was underneath?

I cleared the tree branches and other debris that covered it, and began digging with my bare hands into the grass. With each tuft of grass I removed from the center, a stream of water would appear from underneath. I tried around the periphery with no better luck. At certain places, the soil was so hardened that my fingernails cracked, staining the clumps of dirt and mud with blood.

Realizing I could make only incremental advancement in this fashion, I crossed the burial yard and, fortune on my side, located a small spade. With this instrument I began the labor of breaking up the earth in a circle outlining the grave. I drove the spade into the ground with zeal. Mounds of dirt soon surrounded me. The task was exhausting, and consumed me to such a degree that at first I did not pay attention to the sudden noise bearing down on me. I was distracted by what I saw below.

It was a common pine coffin. I reached my hand down and could touch the cold surface of the smooth wood. Clearing the soil from the top, my fingers found where the cover met the coffin but, just as I began to lift it, I was compelled to release it.

The sexton's mongrel dog was racing upon me ferociously. She pounced a few feet from me and I thought, for a moment, that she had paused because she remembered our having befriended each other. This was not the case. Or, if she remembered, she was all the more angered by my betrayal of our mutual trust. She was quite certain I was trying to steal a body from her domain (the opposite, brave canine! There is no body to steal!). She snarled and snapped her jaws among the graves, and in my state of intense excitement I thought I could see Cerberus's three jaws in that one. I tried waving her away with the shovel, but she only lowered her position and, at any moment, would launch herself onto my throat.

The sexton now emerged from within the underground tomb I had once found him in, holding up a lantern. The air was of a quality so dense and dark that I could hardly see him. He looked to be all of one color. I pictured him as the man who was found petrified to stone in that same vault.

"I am not a resurrection man!" I cried out. Although I suppose that as I was waving a shovel in the air, my hands and clothing covered in dirt and blood, with a partially revealed coffin below me, this proclamation was hardly convincing. "Look inside! Look inside!"

"Who is it? Who's there? Sailor, get 'em!"

I had no choice. I looked longingly at the wood below me, then dropped the shovel and ran. Man and dog chased at my heels.

I was not yet defeated. After leaving behind my pursuers in the cemetery, I located myself in a narrow alleyway for shelter. I spent nearly a half hour recuperating from the fatigue of my failed attempt at the burial yard before stirring myself with a renewed objective. Surely the sexton would now be guarding Poe's grave. But with wild determination, I made my way across the city, remembering along the way the address of Poe's last home in Baltimore, on Amity Street between Lexington and Saratoga, to which I had seen reference during my long researches into Poe's history.

I could ask him. *Why? Friend Poe, why write the letter? Why say I am an idle young man, a pest? Had you forgotten we understood one another?*

Poe had just withdrawn from his place as a cadet at West Point when, shunned by John Allan in Richmond, who refused to help rescue him from a series of debts, the twenty-two-year-old Poe came to this modest dwelling to live with his aunt, Maria Clemm, her daughter, Virginia— then eight years old— as well as Poe's older brother, William Henry, and his ailing grandmother. Poe searched for a position as a teacher in one of the local schools, without success. Each of his fellow cadets at West Point had given him a dollar for the publication of his first collection of poems, and with this volume he had great plans to make his name.

Certain I had found the correct address at a narrow house between Lexington and Saratoga streets, without any consideration of a more rational scheme, I burst up the steps through the street door and, finding myself at the foot of a narrow staircase, bounded upstairs. *Why? Oh, Edgar! Why write that of all things?* Perhaps, if Poe had lived, he would have returned here, to his last home in Baltimore, and left some sign for me of his next destination. I hardly noticed the two women, one with white hair and one young and fair, who screamed upon seeing me enter the tiny back room where they were sitting by a fireplace. (Perhaps I was a dreadful sight, my sackcloth uniform fitted to me by the prison now tattered and dripping, and spotted with soil and blood from my failed efforts at the burial yard.) In another bedroom, a garret room at the very top of the house, a lanky man leaned out the window overlooking Amity Street and began calling, *Robbery! Murder!* and other exclamations. The two women now scurried through the house, and the walls reverberated with unintelligible shouts.

I shrank from the commotion and, finding that the man was in the process of gripping a crowbar, I hastened down the stairs, past the frantic younger woman, through the front hall, back to the door. I ran at such velocity that I could not stop myself until I was in the middle of the street, where under the vague glow of a faraway streetlight I could see a giant horse and carriage coming right for me, leaving me without time to move in any direction where I would not fall directly under its mass of hooves and wheels. Having no chance to save myself from this gruesome fate, I merely blocked my eyes with my arms from the sight of death.

In a miraculous motion, I was pulled bodily to the curb, out of harm of the carriage. My wrist was held tightly. My deliverer struggled to move me closer. I had shut my eyes in lifeless surrender, and now opened them warily upon this person, as though to find a phantasm haunting me from beyond instead of a human. I looked and found I was gazing on the face of Edgar A. Poe.

"Clark!" he said quietly, gripping me tighter, his mouth contracting into a small, intense line under the dark mustache. "We must take you away from here."

I paused, I looked again, reached my hand to his face, and in that instant all things trembled and disappeared into blackness.

When I experienced a brief moment of consciousness, it was in a dark, moist chamber. I felt myself being lowered, and I fought a strange foreboding of mortal danger. As my eyes unclosed slightly, and I lifted my neck as high as it would move, I could see only one object with true clarity, for it loomed above, the very horizon of vision.

It was a rectangular tablet, with writing upon it: HIC TANDEM FELICIS CONDUNTUR RELIQUAE.

I gasped as I realized it was a gravestone marker, and with horror translated its morbid epitaph of my twenty-nine years . . . *Here at last he is happy.*

28

BLACKNESS OVERTOOK ME again. When I rose from my trance, I sat up in a sudden frenzy and gasped at the harsh thirst burning my throat. Though I could feel myself blinking, I could see nothing, and my thoughts shifted between persuading myself I had been blinded and assuring myself that I was only in a space or chamber with no light. A lamp now came on from across the room.

I heard a small voice near me: "He is awake." I could see a bowl of water and reached for it.

"No," another voice counseled sharply. "*That* is for the hand."

One of my hands had been hurt in my efforts at the burial yard.

"Here."

There was now a little circle of candlelight and two children, a boy and girl, whose fair complexions looked green to me, making them look like goblins under the conditions, and who stood around me in stocking feet. The gaslight was turned up now and I saw that the girl was holding forth a glass of water, patiently waiting for me with a look of perfect sweetness. I drank it feverishly.

"Where— " I began to say, then looked up again at the terrible grave marker! In the light, I could now see that it was a *large and detailed sketch* of a grave marker, and could read its full inscription. HIC TANDEM FELICIS CONDUNTUR RELIQUAE EDGAR ALLAN POE and, below that, OBIIT OCT. VII 1849.

I turned to the little girl, grateful for her kindness. I felt suddenly protective of the children. "You are not scared?"

"No," said the girl. "Only worried for you, mister. You were a frightful sight when Father brought you in!"

I breathed easily for the first time in months. I realized I had been changed into a clean suit of clothes, and was sitting on a flat board resting on two chairs, a makeshift bed I had been lying on.

"I'm afraid, Mr. Clark, there are rarely spare beds in a house with six

Poe children and one new Poe baby! I should hope this would afford you some rest nevertheless."

The man speaking was the one who'd rescued me from the street—only it was not Edgar, but rather Neilson Poe. He looked different than the last time we had met, at the police station house. He was thinner and wore a mustache that made him an almost perfect replica, at first glance, of the portraits of his cousin.

"William. Harriet." Neilson looked sternly to the children, who had remained loyally at my side. "To bed." The two children hesitated.

"You have been a great help," I said in a confidential voice to the boy and girl. "Now you must listen to your father."

They fled soundlessly from the chamber.

"Why am I here?" I asked my host.

"Perhaps you could answer the question better," Neilson said with concern, and sat across from me.

He explained that he had received word that there had been some attempt to dig out the coffin of Edgar Poe at the Westminster burial ground and, though the hour was late, he had hired a coach and started immediately for the cemetery. The streets, however, were in poor condition from the rains, and the drive necessitated a path across Amity Street, where Neilson Poe heard a great commotion that he thought was emanating from the old dwelling of his relation Maria Clemm, which— fifteen years ago— had been inhabited by Edgar Poe, as well.

Neilson, finding this coincidence most bizarre and disturbing, considering his current destination of Edgar's grave, had the driver return in this direction. Stepping down on the pavement, he began to investigate, but remembering that he should continue to the cemetery to inquire into those strange happenings, he instructed his driver to turn the carriage back around, facing the other direction, to save time. At this point, with the driver engaged in this task, I was seen emerging from the street door and, finding that I had placed myself in the immediate path of the carriage and would be crushed, Neilson pulled me down to the pavement, where I fainted.

Having seen the layer of dirt on my clothing as he lifted me into the carriage, Neilson Poe considered that the complaint he had received from the cemetery might not be entirely unrelated to my presence at Amity Street.

I remained silent, unsure how much to say. He went on.

"I transported you here at once, Mr. Clark, and my messenger boy assisted me in lifting you onto this board. The boy then brought back a
doctor from the next street, who examined you and departed only a short
time ago. My wife has been upstairs praying for you to recover your
strength. Had you been at the Westminster burial yard tonight, sir?"

"What is that?" I asked, pointing at the sketch of the grave marker. It
sat on a shelf harmlessly with other papers and books but, having initially been illumined by a little light in the chamber, had been the sole
and dreary object of my attention during my brief revival of consciousness earlier.

"It is a sketch by the man I have hired to build a suitable marker for
my cousin's grave. Perhaps we should speak of this later. You seemed excessively overtired."

"I will sleep no more," I said to him. Indeed, I felt my slumber had rapidly rejuvenated me. There was something more, too. Although Neilson
Poe had doubts about my affairs, and I had my own about him, he had
protected me— his children had protected me. I felt safe. "I am appreciative of your family's assistance this evening, but I'm afraid I know more
than you may realize. You have told me and the police that Edgar Poe was
not just cousin but friend. Yet I know what your cousin called you."

"What is that?"

"His 'bitterest enemy in the world'!"

Neilson frowned, stroked his mustache, and calmly nodded without
recoil. "It is true. I mean that he was known to make comments such as
that, about me as well as others who cared about him."

"What would lead him to think that of you, Mr. Poe?"

"There was a time, when his affections for young Virginia had just developed. I had married my wife, Josephine, who was Virginia's half-sister,
and, feeling that my sister-in-law at thirteen was too young to leave with
him, I offered to provide for her education and allow her to enter into society if she remained with us in Baltimore. Edgar saw this as an insult. He
said he would not live another hour without her. He felt that I was seeking to ruin his happiness and that he would never see his 'Sissy' again.
He could not bear himself under the pressure of any grief."

"What of his suggestion, made in a letter to Dr. Snodgrass, that you
would not help his literary career?"

"Edgar believed I was jealous, I suppose," Neilson answered forthrightly. "I myself attempted something of a literary career in my youth,

as I have said to you before. Because of this, he concluded that I was envious of the amount of literary notice he did achieve, both positive and negative."

"Were you?"

"Envious? Not in the way Edgar believed. I did not perceive myself equal to him. Rather, if I ever were jealous, it was from an observation that his writing carried a quality of *genius*, of naturalness, that my own lacked however meticulously I labored at it."

"I can't forget," I said firmly to my host, "that you hindered the chance for the police to investigate your cousin's death, Mr. Poe."

"Is that what you think?" He remained placid. "I understand why you would believe that. However, it was Officer White, before you arrived at the police station house, who was quite adamant that there should not be the least investigation made, for, you see, the Baltimore police are in the habit of fancying that there are no crimes in our city, particularly any crimes toward tourists. In my practice, I often represent those accused of petty wrongs, and depend much on the police to be reasonable to certain offenders, and felt I had little choice but to cooperate with Officer White's desires in the matter. I could see that he was wont to make an example out of those who tried to demonstrate more criminal acts in Baltimore than were already known, and so when I saw you at the police station house, I tried my best to dissuade you from any further pursuit for your own good. Sometimes I do not think our justice is so different from the days of witch-craft— crimes are seen only when it suits the accusers." He walked toward the door of the room. "I see that you believed me overly hostile toward my cousin in our first meetings. Follow me, Mr. Clark."

We moved into Neilson Poe's library. There was a row of books and magazines of Edgar Poe's writings that nearly rivaled my own. In my great surprise, I examined its contents, removing a particular volume or periodical from the impressive collection as I went.

Neilson could see that I was taken aback at his apparent devotion to Edgar's writings. He smiled and explained. "I had been angry at Edgar in his last years, and even after his death, for I knew he saw himself as su-perior to me all along. He saw my life as dilapidated in its artistic quali-ties. I knew, in short, that he had *hated* me for many years! Yet it occurred to me that I had never hated him. It has occurred to me, fur-ther, that Edgar was a man who represented himself through his literary productions— that was him, more than the physical form and character he presented in person, more than any letter he might write in a fit of anger, or some comment he might pass in an excited state to an acquaintance. His art was never meant to be popular, it was not meant to have a principle or a moral sense, but it was his true form of *being*."

As he spoke, Neilson situated himself in the corner of his library and, as he swiveled his chair for a volume of Edgar Poe's *Tales of the Grotesque and Arabesque*, there was a twitch at the side of his mouth that seemed a distinct quality of Edgar Poe's. To hide my observation of him, I removed from the shelf the April 1841 number of *Graham's*, containing the first tale of Dupin, "The Murders in the Rue Morgue." I held it reverently and thought of my own library, my own collection, my home, Glen Eliza, which no doubt had been disturbed and ruined by the police in their various searches for evidence of my guilt and obsessions.

"Do you know he was paid only fifty-six dollars for his first Dupin tale?" Neilson said, seeing the object of my interest. "In the time since his death, I have seen the press push and splatter him. I have seen that shameful and unjust biographer make Edgar whomever he would like. Remember, this is my name, too, Mr. Clark. Poe is the name of my wife, and my children are Poes— as my sons' children will be. I am *Poe*. In the last months, I have read and reread nearly all that my cousin wrote, and have felt with each turn of the page greater affinity with him, a closeness of the highest order, as though the same words might have come from me that he had managed to extract from our common blood. Tell me, Mr. Clark, you had met him?" he asked offhandedly.

"No."

"Good!" said Neilson. Seeing my puzzled reaction, he continued. "I mean only that it is better that way. Seek to know him through the words he published. His genius was of such a rare quality, hardly to be sustained in this world of magazinists, that he could not but believe all were against it and that, given time, even friends and relatives would turn into enemies. His perception, frightened and anxious on this point, was a result of a world harsh to literary pursuits— a harshness I discovered for myself in my youth. His life was a series of experiments on his own nature, Mr. Clark, that brought him far from the movements of our world into a knowledge only of the perfection of literature. We cannot know Edgar Poe as a man, but can know him well as the genius he was. This is why he could not be fairly read until after his death— by me, by you, and now, perhaps, by the world." He paused. "You are feeling better now, Mr. Clark?"

I found I could think more clearly and had been freed of a surge of wild emotions that had before consumed me. I could only remember my latest actions as one thinks of a dream, or a distant memory. I blushed a bit in embarrassment to think of how Neilson had found me. "Yes, many thanks. I fear I had been rather overexcited when you came upon me at Amity Street."

"Please, Mr. Clark," he chuckled in surprise, "you must hardly blame yourself for being poisoned."

"What do you mean?"

"The doctor who examined you was quite certain that you had been mildly poisoned. He found traces of the white powder still in the posterior of your mouth, an expert mixture of several chemicals. Do not worry. He was also rather certain the effects had quite exhausted themselves and were not permanently harmful in these doses."

"Poison? But who— " I stopped myself, knowing with sudden clarity the answer. The guards at the prison who, with great vigilance, constantly replaced the pitchers of water on my cell table. Officer White, frustrated with my continued denials in the interviews with him, had likely been the one to order it: to confuse my mind enough to extract some kind of statement of responsibility, to ensure a confession of my wrongs! Indeed, I now also possessed Neilson Poe's information about White's desire to suppress the inquiry I had demanded. He would have poisoned me until I confessed or *died*, or was driven to harm myself. My life had been saved through the means of my chance escape.

All the derangement of my mental state in the hours after leaving the prison became clear to me and stung my mind. Searching for Poe— digging his grave with the belief that he was alive— invading his former home from so many years earlier! That person had dropped from me and I stood taller now, seeing all that was happening with perfect vision.

Neilson seemed momentarily thoughtful and, perhaps, anxious. "Perhaps you do need more rest, Mr. Clark."

"The boy," I said suddenly. "The messenger boy of whom you spoke, the one who helped you carry me, and then who returned with the doctor. Where is he?" I had not seen anyone in the house other than the children.

Neilson hesitated. I could hear a new sound, unmistakable and increasing. Horses, high-stepping through the watery streets; a carriage's wheels splashing behind.

Neilson raised his head at the sound. "I am a member of the bar, Mr. Clark," he said. "You are a fugitive from justice, and I have done my duty by sending the police word of your presence. I have a responsibility. Yet, somehow, I cannot help but think that you, of all people, have the ability to vindicate the memory of my unhappy kinsman and my name. I would be pleased to serve as your defender in court, should you wish." I remained frozen in place. "Remember, Mr. Clark, you were an officer of the court, too. You have a duty to choose."

Neilson stepped slowly in front of the door, and in my weakened state he would have likely subdued me with ease until his messenger boy entered with the police.

"The children," Neilson said suddenly. "Do not think me too strict, Mr. Clark, but I must see to it that they are sleeping."

"I understand," I said, nodding with gratitude.

As he started into the hall toward the stairs, I dashed out of the room and did not look back.

"God watch over you!" Neilson called after me.

❖   ❖   ❖

My mission was clear. I would find Auguste Duponte. He alone could provide the definitive proof of my innocence. Now that Bonjour had revealed to me that no harm had been done to him, even thinking of how close he might be lent me an air of invincibility that moved me rapidly through the drowned streets of Baltimore. Indeed, perhaps Duponte had already begun to investigate the shooting of the Baron. Perhaps he had even come to the lyceum that evening, before it occurred, had witnessed it and fled in preparation for the troubles he knew would come from it.

It seemed the most necessary objective in the world to prove my name to Hattie, for she had persisted in her friendship to me throughout my stay in prison when others had abandoned me. It might seem small compared to the fact that my life could end as a criminal, and she was marrying another man anyway, but my goal now was to prove myself to Hattie.

I would not dry thoroughly for days; my ears, lungs, and insides were swimming long after I'd waded and splashed through the treacherous streets of Baltimore. It felt as though the Atlantic had broken over the shores and was moving across to unite with the Pacific. I was able to locate Edwin, and he secured me changes of linen and modest suits of clothing. He wished to assist me in obtaining a place safer from the eyes of the police. He had brought clothing in bundles to an empty packing-house, once belonging to my father's firm, where I took refuge by re-membering a loose door hinge from years ago that had never been repaired.

"You have helped me enough, Edwin," I said, "and I should not wish to risk your safety any further. I have called down enough trouble on everyone's heads for a lifetime."

"You have done what you believed right, you have bet your life on it," he said. "Poe is dead. A man has been shot. Your friend, disappeared. And enough people have been hurt. You must stay safe, at least, so there is someone sure of the truth."

"You must not be thought committing any crime, for aiding me," I said. This was a serious point. If a free black was convicted of a signifi-cant offense, he could be punished in the worst way imaginable for a freeman: by being entered by the authorities back into slavery.

"I was not born in the woods to be scared by an owl." Edwin laughed his reassuring laugh. "Besides, I think not even Baltimore has punished a man yet for giving some old duds to a man whose linen is out at the el-bows. Now, will you be able to rest here for the night?"

Edwin continued to lend his aid and searched me out at the packing-house at regular intervals. Although tempted to do so, I refrained from trying to make any calls on Hattie out of concern that they might endan-ger her. My outings were severely restricted, and I knew not to go any-where near the grounds of Glen Eliza for fear of being seen. I still had in my possession the issue of *Graham's* from 1841 that I was holding in my hand when I fled from Neilson Poe's house— the issue in which "The Murders in the Rue Morgue" first introduced Dupin. I was thankful for this as though it were a talisman. I would reread the tale and wonder what Duponte might have already discovered about the Baron's death. Yet this magazine was, for the time, *all* I had to read. So I read the other pages, too, though it was ten years old.

One time, Edwin came at an appointed hour and found me staring at the *Graham's.*

"All right, Mr. Clark?"

I could not stop reading these pages— reading and reading. I could hardly speak. I do not know how to describe my heart-wrenching discov-ery that night— I mean the truth about Duponte— or Dupin (you see I hardly know how to swallow all I understood, I hardly know where to begin)— that Duponte never was the real Dupin at all.

Once I had read the Baron Dupin's handwritten lecture notes several times in my cell at the Middle District station house, and had ensured that every word remained forged in my memory, I had thrown the pages to the fire that sizzled in the hall separating the men's and women's cells. I had not assassinated the Baron, of course, but I eagerly murdered his handiwork. After all that had happened, the possibility of his fictions about Poe's death spreading was a risk not to be borne.

It was not that his words were not convincing as to Poe's death. They were quite convincing, but not the truth— the opposite of Poe, who wrote only the truth even when many were not ready to believe. We shall come to the Baron's theories of Poe's death later. The Baron Dupin, in his notes, had also taken the occasion to defend his claim as the real Dupin.

Here is a sample: "You know the Dupin of these tales as forthright, brilliant, fearless. Those qualities, I must admit, Mr. Poe derived from my own humble adventures in truth-telling. . . . For that is what Dupin really does, isn't it? In a world where truth is hidden by the mountebanks and swindlers, by the lords and the kings, Dupin finds it. Dupin knows it. Dupin tells it. But those who tell the truth, my friends, shall always be met with ridicule, neglect, death. That is where we have found Edgar— no"— here I imagined the Baron shaking his head somberly, perhaps a leaden tear dropping from the corner of one eye— "that is where we have *lost* Edgar Poe. Edgar Poe has not left us, but has been taken away. . . ."

Now, before Edwin's arrival, as I sat in the empty warehouse's small splash of light, I picked up that April *Graham's,* that magazine containing the first appearance of Poe's Dupin. "How fortunate for *Graham's* to have Poe then," I thought, "for he not only contributed his tales but also he was their editor." Then my thumb stopped on a particular page. I strained in the light to see. It was not even a page I had meant to look at.

In the same number that "Rue Morgue" appeared, in that same April '41 number, the editor of the periodical— that is, Poe— reviewed a book entitled *Sketches of Conspicuous Living Characters of France.* This collection of biographical sketches, we find, includes a number of French persons of distinction. The one that attracted my eye was George Sand, the famed novelist. I should not know how it raced into my mind from some distant article or biography I had read about her— but I somehow recalled that her given name, which she changed to the masculine George Sand to allow her to publish without prejudice, was Amandine-Aurore-Lucie *Dupin*. Poe, in his review of *Sketches*, delights in an anecdote that involved Madame Sand/Dupin sitting dressed up in a gentleman's frock coat and smoking a cigar.

Another name in Poe's review arrested my attention: Lamartine. You may hardly know the name, for his reputation as a Parisian poet and philosopher I doubt will persist in memory. But look here. I turned back through our magazine to "The Murders in the Rue Morgue," that first tale of ratiocination.

> *We reached the little alley called Lamartine, which has been paved, by*
> *way of experiment, with the overlapping and riveted blocks.*

Was it a coincidence, that in the same number of the magazine that Poe published his first Dupin tale, he used the name of another prominent French writer in both the Dupin tale and this review he wrote? Do not stop there. Look at "Rue Morgue" further, and read about one of the witnesses to the beastly violence, as told by the narrator:

> *Paul Dumas, physician, deposes that he was called to view the bodies*
> *about day-break . . .*

Should this Dumas not make us all think of Alexandre Dumas, the inventive novelist of French romances and adventures? And there was this:

> *Isidore Musèt, gendarme, deposes that he was called to the house about*
> *three o'clock in the morning . . .*

Yes: a name much like Alfred de Musset, the French poet, intimate companion of George Sand herself.

You have probably already guessed at the conclusion now ready to be drawn. My mind spiraled down without warning. "The Murders in the Rue Morgue"— I can almost hear Poe chuckling cleverly at the real hidden mystery of this tale— was actually built as an allegory for the modern state of French literature. The references to George Sand (a.k.a. Dupin),

Lamartine, Musset, and Dumas were the most prominent of the network of quiet, clever allusions.

If this was so, as I was instantly certain it was, Poe had not drawn on a real investigator to invent this hero, not Auguste Duponte, not Baron Claude Dupin, but had worked wholly from his head and his thoughts on the various literary personages. When I first found all this, I made bold to walk openly to a book stall and pillage various books; I found that not only was my recollection correct about George Sand's real name, not only was her given name Dupin, but also that she had lost a brother in infancy named— yes, but you probably already guessed— Auguste Dupin. *Auguste Dupin.* Would Poe have known this detail? What was Poe's message to us? He re-created her lost brother in the form of a genius against death and violence. Had Poe thought of his own brother William Henry, taken from him while poor Edgar was yet a boy?

In frantically reading again through "Rue Morgue" I found new meaning in the narrator's description of his living circumstance with C. Auguste Dupin: "We admitted no visitors. Indeed the locality of our retirement had been carefully kept a secret from my own former associates; and it had been many years since Dupin had ceased to know or be known in Paris. *We existed within ourselves alone.*" Wasn't Poe trying to tell us? The astounding ratiocinator existed only in the imagination of the poet.

> We have been informed by a "Lady Friend" of the brilliant and erratic writer Edgar A. Poe, Esq. that Mr. Poe's ingenious hero, C. Auguste Dupin, is closely modeled from an individual in actual life, similar in name and exploit, known for his great analytical powers . . . &c.

I thought of that newspaper extract, the one given to the athenaeum clerk by John Benson and then to me, with blurry vision and brewing contempt. How vague it was, these sentences, this flighty rumor that had taken me in. Who was this "lady friend" of Poe's? How was it we could know she should be trusted? Had she ever existed at all? I searched my mind for answers to these singular questions, but all the while the larger reality possessed me like an unholy spirit— it seemed to say, "Duponte was nothing more than a fraud, Poe is dead, and you too will die, will walk the ladder to the gallows, will die for wanting more than you already had."

Duponte was no more.

"Clark, are you unwell? Perhaps I should bring you to a doctor." Edwin was trying to shake me from my spell.

"Edwin," I gasped, with just this peculiar phraseology: "I am nearly dead."

❈   ❈   ❈

I should say something more, by way of an interlude, about what began all this— Poe's death. For several chapters, I have mentioned knowing the Baron's full lecture on the subject, and it would be stingy of me to withhold it any longer from the reader. As I say, I remember every word of the Baron's notes. "'Reynolds! Reynolds!' This shall ring in our ears as long as we remember Edgar Poe, for it was his valedictory address to us. And he might have just said: 'This is how I died, Lord. This is how I died, friends and fellow sufferers of the earth. Now find out why. . . .'"

Though the Baron's account of Poe's death would have been ruinous to the truth, in some manner I regret that he did not deliver his words aloud. For now you cannot receive a full description of what it would have been like— the Baron marching back and forth on the stage as though it were his courtroom in his better days. Imagine the Baron, flashing his unmistakably shining teeth, spreading his hands wide and proclaiming the mystery solved:

29

POE HAD COME to Baltimore at the wrong time. It had not been his plan to visit Baltimore, for he was on his way to his New York cottage to fetch his poor mother-in-law and start his new life. But some ruffians on the ship from Richmond to Baltimore harassed the poet and probably stole his money, so Poe missed the train from Baltimore to travel north. This is shown by the fact that Poe had earned money lecturing in Richmond, but was not found with any just a few days later. Stranded in Baltimore, he noticed himself being followed by the thieves and attempted to take refuge in the house of a kind friend, the editor Dr. N. C. Brooks. However, Dr. Brooks was not home and these craven ruffians, not knowing this and worrying that Poe would report their actions to someone inside, recklessly started a fire that nearly burned down the Brooks home. Poe barely managed to escape with his life.

The poet had money enough left for a small room at the United States Hotel, but not yet enough to take another train to New York or to Philadelphia, where a lucrative literary task awaited him. His new literary magazine, to be called *The Stylus*, was about to trumpet a new era of genius in American letters— but his enemies wished to stop him from exposing the mediocrity of their own writings. Poe therefore had begun to assume a false name, E. S. T. Grey. He even directed his own sweet mother-in-law— his cherished protector— to write him by this name in Philadelphia "for fear I should not get the letter," for he worried that his adversaries would seek to intercept any letters of support or subscriptions to his daring enterprise. Nor did he wish them to know he was going to Philadelphia, certain that they would interfere with his task and destroy his attempt to raise money for his journal.

He found himself trapped in Baltimore during a heated election week. Poe was a literary man. He was above all this. He was above the petty and the grievous actions of politics and of ordinary man. But to the everyday rascal, the great genius is mere fodder.

Poe was easy prey. He had been traveling under his new alias,

E. S. T. Grey. On the evening before election day, in the dismal weather that had plagued the city that week, he was snatched from the street. Here began the murder of Poe, perhaps one of the longest murders in history, certainly the longest and most pathetic in the history of literary men. The saddest since the poet Otway was strangled by a few crumbs of bread, the most iniquitous since Marlowe was stabbed through the head, into the very organ of his genius; and all of this turned Edgar Poe into the most slandered man since Lord Byron.

Worse still, Edgar Poe's family— those very people in the world who should have protected him— were among those to make him a target and a victim. One George Herring, who may be sitting among us today, oversaw the Fourth Ward Whigs— and it was at the very place Poe was found, Ryan's Fourth Ward hotel, that these Whigs met. George Herring was a relation to Poe [here the Baron was barking somewhat up the wrong tree, as Henry Herring was an uncle of Poe's by marriage, and it was Henry, not Poe, who was related to George Herring, but to let him continue . . .] and as a near relation knew Poe was vulnerable. It was not a coincidence, ladies and gentlemen protectors of the names of genius, that Henry Herring was one of the first men to approach Poe when it was announced he was stricken— that Dr. Snodgrass was surprised to find Henry Herring there even before he sent word to him! For the Herrings had selected Poe as a victim— they knew him; he was not to them "E. S. T. Grey." George Herring knew from Henry that Edgar Poe was unpredictable when forced to take alcohol or other intoxicants, and determined that he was a vulnerable person to join the wretched voting "coop." Knowing that Poe was likely to have severe side effects, George later sent for Henry to usher Poe away to the hospital in order to avoid trouble for the Fourth Ward Whigs. Henry Herring, we know, still resented Poe for having attempted to court his daughter, Elizabeth Herring, with love poems when the two cousins were young at the time Poe lived in Baltimore. Here was Henry Herring's small-minded revenge for an outpouring of pure-hearted playful affection from a young poet.

The political rogues of the Fourth Ward Whigs, who kept their headquarters in the den of the Vigilant Fire Company's engine house across from Ryan's, placed the helpless poet in a cellar with other unfortunates— vagrants, strangers, *loafers* (as Americans say), foreigners. This explains why Poe, a heartily well-known author, was not seen by anyone over the course of these few days. The miscreants probably drugged Poe with various opiates.

When election day came, they took him around the city to various polling stations. They forced him to vote for their candidates at each polling venue and, to make the whole farce more convincing, the poet was made to wear different outfits each time. This explains why he was found in ragged, soiled clothes *never meant* to fit him. He was permitted by the rogues to keep his handsome Malacca cane, however, for he was in such a weakened state that even those ruffians recognized that the cane would be needed to prop him up. This cane he had intentionally switched for his own cane with an old friend in Richmond; for inside was hidden a weapon— a sword— of the most ferocious cast, and he called to mind his many literary enemies who in the past had challenged him on occasion to duels or otherwise mishandled him. But by the time he knew his danger here in Baltimore, he was too weak even to open its blade— though he would not let go of it either. In fact, he would be found with this very cane clutched to his chest.

The political club had not cooped as many victims as they would have preferred, due to the inclement weather, which kept people out of the streets. They even carried one man to the coop who was a prominent official of the state of Pennsylvania, captured on his way from the theater to Barnum's Hotel, but he was allowed to escape when it was discovered he was a big-wig. So Poe was used again and again, more than usual— and by the time his captors brought him to the Fourth Ward, located at Ryan's tavern, to vote again, he had been abused too much. After being administered an oath by one of the ward election judges, a Henry Reynolds, Poe could not make it across the room and collapsed. He called for his friend Dr. Snodgrass, who arrived in disgust. Snodgrass, a leader of local temperance groups, was certain Poe had indulged himself in drink. The political ruffians, abandoning their captive, were glad to have their foul deed hidden by this assumption. Nor would stern-minded Snodgrass be the last to make this egregious error— the wide world would soon believe noble Poe's death to be the result of moral weakness.

Yet now we have Truth come back to us.

Poe, heavily drugged and deprived of sleep, was in no condition to explain anything; and in the still rational portion of his mind, no doubt the ailing poet was devastated to see that Snodgrass, his supposed friend, looked down at him with disapproval and something like disdain. Poe was carried to a hackney carriage and driven alone to the hospital. There, under the careful ministering of Dr. J. J. Moran and his nurses, he drifted in and out of consciousness. Remembering like some distant vision his attempt to hide his own genius from its attackers through the nondescript name E. S. T. Grey, Poe deliberately told the good doctor as little as he could about himself and the purposes of his travels. But his mind was weak. At one point, no doubt remembering Snodgrass's betrayal, Poe yelled out that the best thing his best friend could do to him would be *to blow his brains out with a pistol.*

Poe, thinking of the last man who might have noticed his dilemma in time to stop the actions of his murderers— that judge, Henry Reynolds, who'd perfunctorily given the oath to all the voters— called out desperately as though he could still ask for assistance. Reynolds! Reynolds! He repeated this for hours, but it was not truly a cry for help as much as a death knell. "Oh the bells, bells, bells! What a tale their terror tells . . . Of despair!" Poe's time came to its restless end.

There. Now you alone have heard a speech that never occurred, have witnessed what the Baron Dupin would have said to electrify his audience that evening. It was a speech that, although I had eagerly reduced its pages to ashes, I'd soon be set to announce to the entire world.

30

ON THE THIRD day after my discovery of the ten-year-old *Graham's* magazine, Edwin could see my spirits were entirely demolished. I felt more poisoned than I had been when Neilson Poe had found me in front of 3 Amity Street; now it was my soul, my heart, that had been infected rather than my blood.

Edwin tried to talk to me about finding Duponte for assistance. I no longer knew Duponte, though. Who was he, *what* was he? Perhaps, I thought to myself, Poe had not even heard of my Duponte. All truth had been turned on its head. Maybe it was *Duponte* who'd deliberately and meticulously pilfered part of his character, insomuch as he was able, from Poe's tales, rather than the other way around. He was concealing himself, now, because he had known he could not fulfill the role he had imagined. Had it never occurred to me, in all the time I spent with Duponte, that his was some diseased reaction to the literature, rather than an inspiring source for it? I suppose the satisfaction of having assisted in Duponte's emergence from his isolation in Paris had led me to deny any dormant doubts. It was insignificant now, dust in the balance. I was alone.

The waters receded around the packinghouse, and with more people populating the streets nearby, Edwin advised that I must find another refuge. He secured a room in an out-of-the-way lodging house in the eastern district of the city. We arranged a time at which I would meet him to be taken to my new hiding place in a wagon covered with piles of his deliveries of newspapers. In the end, I was late, so distracted was I by the loss of Duponte.

I had requested that Edwin bring me more of Poe's tales. I read the three Dupin tales over and over whenever the packinghouse's light was sufficient. If there was no true Dupin, no person whose genius had bestowed onto Poe this character, why had I believed so fervently? I found myself first copying out sentences from the Dupin tales in a scattered fashion and then, without any particular objective, writing out the entire tales word by word, as though translating them into some usable form.

Poe had not discovered Dupin in the newspaper accounts of Paris. He had discovered Dupin in the soul of mankind. I do not know how best to share now what occurred in that upheaval of my mind. I heard again and again what Neilson Poe had said, that Edgar Poe's meaning was not in his life, not in the world outside, but in the words, in their truths. Dupin *did* exist. He existed in the tales, and perhaps the truth of Dupin was in all of our capacities. Dupin was not among us; he was in us, another part of us, a plural of ourselves, stronger than any person who might resemble Dupin slightly in name or trait. I thought of that sentence from "The Murders in the Rue Morgue" again. *We existed within ourselves alone . . .*

I found Edwin waiting for me.

"You're safe," he said, taking my hand. "I was about to search the city for you. Give me that coat and put this one on." He gave me an old pepper-and-salt coat. "Come, up hat and cut stick now. There's a wagon I've borrowed to get to the lodging house. No loafing."

"Thank you. But I cannot stay, my friend," I replied, taking his hand. "I must see someone at once."

Edwin frowned. "Where?"

"In Washington. There is a man named Montor, a minister from France, who long ago first taught me about Duponte and tutored me for my visit to Paris."

I began to walk away when Edwin touched my arm.

"He is a man you can trust, Mr. Clark?"

"No."

*   *   *

Henri Montor, the French emissary to Washington, was worried. Back home, the Red Republicans and their followers complained more loudly. *Vive la Republique!* was hollered in the public squares. Parisians grew restless if there were too many months without political struggle, thought Montor, and so now they were turning their minds against Louis-Napoleon. The results could be catastrophic.

Do not jump to conclusions. Monsieur Montor had no particular affection for Louis-Napoleon— the president-prince, a spoiled and arrogant product of fame who had made two failed and foolish grabs at power

before— but Montor enjoyed his own current position and had no desire
for it to be altered. It was not Washington, with its lukewarm food at even
the best hotels' dining rooms (even the corn cakes were only "warm" and
not hot!), that he enjoyed but the fact of being an emissary to another
country.

Montor read as many French newspapers as could be found in Washington (it was during the commission of this activity, you'll recall, that his
interest was long ago diverted by a Baltimorean reading articles about
one Auguste Duponte). Montor observed that more of the French press
was aiming at the president-prince lately. In small ways, but nonetheless.
Now Napoleon had ordered the prefect and the police to shut down un-
cooperative newspapers. What were Napoleon and his advisers anxious
about, really? What did they expect the revolutionists would do? What
grand plan could they concoct now? France was already a republic! They
could elect someone other than Louis-Napoleon. But perhaps they could
also first weaken Napoleon's position enough that an enemy from outside would come in to take advantage. . . . No, Monsieur Montor did not
guess the true plan any more than others did. Still, he worried constantly
about events around the Champs-Élysées.

He had smaller worries, too— local worries. There was a Frenchman
found shot in nearby Baltimore. It was said by some that it was that infamous rogue lawyer, the foppish "Baron" Claude Dupin, who had been living in London. What was he baron of? No matter, the fool was no doubt
involved in some mischief. Still he was a Frenchman, and Baltimore's
high constable had written with word about it to Monsieur Montor.

But this had happened a few weeks ago already, and it was not even
on Montor's mind this evening. He thought only about sleep. He had two
great pleasures in life, and to his credit neither involved superficial concerns of wealth or power. This is what separated him from men like the
prince's ministers. Montor liked most to entertain and be admired by
strangers, as we have already alluded to, and besides that he liked to
sleep, many hours at a time.

There was one of Montor's encounters with that young Baltimorean in
the reading room, studying articles on Auguste Duponte. Montor spoke
with awe about Duponte. He could not remember the last time he had
heard of Duponte performing one of his magnificent feats, but no matter.
This young man was so engrossed Montor did not wish to dissuade his
study. This was some time ago, almost six months, and Montor, who was

blessed with a short memory, only barely remembered the young gentle-man or their numerous conversations. Until this evening, when Montor walked into his house. It took him a moment to think to himself that it was strange that his hearth was already roaring with a fire, and another moment still to notice someone sitting at his table.

"Who— ? What is— ?" Montor could not think of the proper words. "Who allowed you in, sir, and what is your business?"

No answer.

"I shall call *burglary* . . ." Montor warned. "Tell me your name," he commanded.

"Don't you know me?" came the question in fine French.

Montor squinted. In his defense, the light was dim and the appearance of his visitor somewhat frightful and haggard. "Yes, yes," he said, but he could not remember the name. "That young man from Baltimore . . . but how have you come in here?"

"I spoke to your servant, in French, and told him we were to have an important government meeting that must be private. I ordered him to re-turn in two hours, and paid him for his trouble."

"You had no right to . . ." Yes! Now Montor remembered this face. "I remember. I first met you in the reading rooms, studying the French newspapers. I helped you with your French language and took you around a bit. Quentin, isn't it? You were looking for the real Dup— "

"Quentin Hobson Clark. Yes, you remember."

"Very well, Monsieur . . . *Clark*." The engine of Montor's mind was now clicking. "I shall have to ask you to leave my property at once."

Montor was alarmed to have an intruder in his lodging, even one who had previously been an acquaintance and had seemed so harmless. He was also alarmed at the name, Quentin Clark. He had retained almost no memory of the name from the reading room. But the name meant some-thing else to him as of late.

It took Montor a few moments to be able to produce any sound, and it came out as merely a breath. "Murder! Murder!"

❊   ❊   ❊

"Monsieur Montor," I said when he had finally calmed down, "I believe you know all about the Baron Dupin."

"You— " he began. "But you— " Montor was finally able to explain that Clark's name had been wired to Montor as the suspect in the attempted assassination of a Frenchman.

"Yes. Me. But I did not shoot anyone. However, I believe you know something more to assist me in determining who did."

Montor now seemed more reluctant to cry out. "Help you? After you invade my house, bribe my servant? Why are you doing this?"

"Simply for truth. I have been forced to look for it with an ungloved hand, and I will."

"They told me you were in prison!"

"Did they tell you so? Did they tell you they were plying me with poisons to manipulate me into a confession?"

Montor muttered, "I do not know what you wish me to say, Monsieur Clark! I have nothing to do with such foul play and have never even met this . . . this . . . so-called baron!"

"The men pursuing him were a pair of French rogues. I believe they were under the command of someone else— some person of great intelligence and foresight." Since Bonjour had told me they could not have been working for the Baron's creditors, and since the rogues had spoken of "orders," I knew there was more to it than the two blackguards. "You are surely aware of Frenchmen in and out of this area."

"I do not stand at the harbor peeping into the windows of ships, Monsieur Clark! Do you know the police will look for you for this . . . this outrageous trespassing." He frowned, remembering they would already be looking for me for a far worse offense. "You seem very different from when we met, monsieur."

I stood above him and looked over him coolly. "I believe you know where men like them would hide, and who would shelter them. You know all the important French citizens who reside in the region of Baltimore. Perhaps some dangerous characters like these rogues would even find you."

"Monsieur Clark, I work directly for Louis-Napoleon since he has become president. If there were French outlaws here, and they wished to hide from your authorities and ours, they would not come to *me*. You see that, don't you? Think of it." He noticed that I listened seriously to this point, and now tried to switch topics to gain my sympathies. "Didn't I help you research Auguste Duponte, the real Monsieur Dupin? Yes, what of that? Did you find him in Paris?"

"This has nothing to do with Auguste Duponte," I said. I made no threatening motion, no sudden gesture toward him. Yet he cowered; that he believed me wild and violent made me almost inclined to prove him right.

It wasn't even necessary to demand that he tell me whatever he knew. "Bonapartes!" he suddenly babbled.

"What do you mean?" I asked, annoyed.

"In Baltimore," he continued. "Monsieur Jérôme Bonaparte."

"You introduced me to some Bonapartes at that dress ball you took me to before I left for Paris. Jérôme Bonaparte and his mother. But why would someone like Jérôme Bonaparte know more about such rogues? They are relatives of Napoleon's, aren't they?"

"No. Yes. Not ones that Napoleon acknowledged, I mean. You see, when the brother of Napoleon— the true Napoleon, Emperor Napoleon, I mean— when this brother was traveling through America as a soldier at nineteen, he courted and married a wealthy American girl, Elizabeth Patterson. You met her at the ball— the 'queen.' They had a son, named Jérôme after his father, and that is who you met with her, the man dressed as the Turkish guard. When he was no more than a baby, Emperor Napoleon ordered his brother to abandon the poor bride, and after a brief struggle the brother at length obeyed. Elizabeth Patterson, now abandoned, returned with her son to Baltimore, and this family would never again be recognized by the emperor. They have been separated from their proud family line ever since."

"I understand," I said. "Continue please, Monsieur Montor."

"Outlaws would not seek to find me, an official government minister, as I say, with Louis-Napoleon as the current head of government. But such criminals might seek out those who are estranged from the name of Napoleon. Yes." His mouth loosened and he became excited, as though understanding this was now his mission too. "They might, monsieur!"

"Do you have the city directories for Baltimore?" I asked.

He pointed to a shelf in the corridor. His eyes traveled away from me shiftily, toward the window and door. He'd been caught up momentarily in my questions, but I could see he was now preparing in his mind an indignant report to the police.

It did not matter. I stopped my finger at the right page and tore it out. I could still reach the train depot before Montor's reports reached the ears of the Washington police.

. . .

And indeed, the conductor of the train did not seem at all concerned with me upon my boarding. As a precaution, I sat in the last passenger car, and to observe more I opened the window at my seat, provoking malevolent stares when pockets of cold air rushed inside. One fellow spit his tobacco pointedly close to my boots, but I only shifted my legs farther from him.

I looked for any signs of something unusual, having to will my eyes not to close for longer than a few seconds. At one point, as the train made a turn, I saw a young boy running along the front of the train boldly grab hold of the cowcatcher— this was the device in front that forced away animals like sheep, cows, and hogs that strayed onto the track— and, gripping onto this, he managed to swing into the first car. I was startled, but told myself this was just a stowaway. I soon forgot the sight of the boy dangling in front of the train through a short spell of sleep.

I was jolted awake as the train shook with a violent shudder and soon began to nudge into a slower speed as it approached a bridge over a ravine. I jumped to my feet and was about to ask what had happened when I overheard another man as he questioned the conductor and engineer. The conductor had a harum-scarum look about him, as though he were frightened even of himself.

"The train went over a chaise and horse," the engineer said coolly. "Two ladies were thrown out, and pretty well smashed, too. The chaise broken to pieces."

The conductor passed by this engineer and scurried to the next car.

"Good God, mister!" cried the other passenger, looking back to me for the same reaction. I took a few steps backward and checked the door to the freight car that was attached to the end of the train. It was locked.

My eyes were fixed on the engineer's face. I tried to think whether I had heard a crash at all, and cursed myself for having fallen asleep. The engineer seemed unnaturally calm for just having been part of a terrible accident, possibly killing two women.

"Chaise was broken to pieces," the engineer said, then looked flustered as he realized he had already said this.

I interjected casually, "I didn't hear a crash." Of course, I had been asleep, but I felt it was a test worth trying. Could they be lying? Were they slowing down for the police to come aboard?

"Funny, mister," murmured the fussy passenger in front of me. "I didn't hear any crash either, and doesn't everyone say I have the finest hearing in Washington!"

This decided it. I swung myself to the door as the train continued to cut the speed of its engine.

"You there! Stop! What do you think you are doing?" The engineer shouted this at me as he grabbed hold of my arm, but I shook him away hard and he stumbled over a piece of luggage. The passenger who had been speaking, from an overload of confusion, motioned to try to restrain me but stopped cold when he saw from my face that I would not be deterred.

Forcing the door open, I leapt onto the bank of grass alongside the tracks and rolled myself down the side of the steep arched ravine below.

31

LATER, I WOULD learn more about the Bonapartes and their quiet residence over the decades in Baltimore. Now, I wished only to find them. I could remember faintly my parents speaking of the scandal, so many years earlier– long before I was born– that ensued when the brother of Napoleon Bonaparte married Baltimore's richest young beauty, Elizabeth Patterson. That brother had long returned to luxury in Europe. It was the American descendants of Napoleon's lighthearted brother that I had to confront– the Jérôme Bonaparte I had met in costume and his family and allies– to see if they knew those rogues whose presence would prove my innocence.

But I had no particular concern for the Bonaparte family's history or ambitions at the moment. Today the question of my survival was too real.

These American Bonapartes and their offspring had multiplied and spread themselves around the city, and had maintained many homes across Baltimore through their great wealth from the Patterson family and the stipend the jilted wife received from Napoleon. The first address I visited no longer belonged to them at all– but the domestic who answered, a plump Irishwoman, received enough mistaken callers to know where to direct me. Still, it was several jaunts into different quarters, meeting various affiliated persons, before I found the most promising residence: one of the homes of Napoleon's brother's grandsons, estranged great-nephew to the legendary Napoleon himself and cousin, by my rough calculations, to the current French president.

Following the incident on the train, I felt confident I'd eluded any police agents from Washington, but I still proceeded slowly and methodically, which was maddening for such an urgent affair. It was not safe to be out in the light of day. After my escape from the train, I had waited until night in a frigid ditch and then found safe passage back to Baltimore in a covered mail-sleigh, lodging myself in the straw at the bottom of the cart with a few servants and a sleeping Hungarian peddler who, in the apparent throes of a dream, repeatedly kicked me in the stomach with a hobnailed boot. The driver rode through the night over rough stones and paths at a dashing rate as quick as any train.

Out of caution, I waited another day before going to the next Bonaparte address. The house was empty— or, rather, there were no servants and nobody responded to my knocking at the door. But I noticed the carriage house door was open and, as I stood outside, I could see shapes through the windows of the house. Propping myself on a ledge, I pressed against a window and thought I could hear men speaking in French.

When the door opened, I could see two of the figures inside more clearly. I knew one as the rogue who had almost killed me in the carriage factory, and the second to be his partner. The first wore a large bandage fastened around his arm where he had been crushed by the carriage after I had stabbed him.

A different man, the one closer to the street door, was handing over money to the two rogues, who were nodding and soon departed into the carriage house. This third man had the demeanor of being their leader. I waited until they had driven away and then rang.

The man returned to the door. He was grander than the two rogues. Not bigger, exactly, but better fashioned to provoke respect rather than mere fear, with perfectly squared shoulders. For a moment I stood paralyzed as he waited for some word from me. He looked back at me as I stared at him with a vague air of recognition.

"Mr. Bonaparte," I said finally, choking back a gasp. "You are Monsieur Bonaparte?"

He shook his head. "My name is Rollin. Young Monsieur Bonaparte is away, at West Point. You would like to leave word?" He instructed more than asked this, but I declined. There was something in his tone. . . .

I promised to return another day and hastily began backing away, terrified that one of the rogues would have occasion to return and see me at the door. But even more I feared that third one, the man calling himself Rollin. He lifted his hat, slowly, to bid me good evening, and before he returned it to its place I knew exactly where I had first seen him. It had been so brief, and long before, halfway across the world.

Remembering that first vision of him, I comprehended, gradually, as I walked through the street, how it had all happened, how it had all been connected from Paris until now. How the Bonapartes had come to be involved. How in one attempted assassination in Baltimore indeed lay the future of France. . . .

As these thoughts gathered themselves together, I walked rapidly, but somewhat carelessly, toward another boardinghouse Edwin had arranged for me upon my return from Washington. Suddenly, I felt a stinging pain travel across my back. I fell forward, then rolled onto my back. Above me, I saw flashes of a white horse, rearing upward to the sky, and a tall and powerful man on top. He unrolled his whip and this time caught my arm.

"Mr. Clark, attorney, isn't it? What a thing to see such a finely bred man wanted for murder." It was Slatter, the slave-trader, riding a perfect specimen of the largest Pennsylvania horse. I attempted to stand, but he kicked the side of my head with his boot. I writhed in pain on the ground and coughed up blood.

Slatter jumped down from the horse and, while holding me down with his dark mahogany cane, placed my wrists and ankles in shackles.

"Your sands are nearly run down, my friend! I've cleared two thousand dollars in the last month but will enjoy this even more."

"I did not shoot anyone! And I have no business with you!" I cried.

"But you had business with me the other week, didn't you? With that woolly-head young friend of yours? No, your business is not with me. It is with the city. It is always a pleasure for me to serve the police of Baltimore." The leading slave-traders often received the rolls of men and women wanted for arrest, since many of those were escaped slaves. "Perhaps you'd like to spend a night in my pen with the stock that are about to be shipped off, before you go to the police. I'm sure they will be anxious to see you again— we know you're such an avowed lover of their kind. Perhaps you even speak their nigger-tongue."

The shackles were immovable, and I had no choice but to walk along toward his slave pen as he pulled me by a long chain from his horse. Slatter seemed to relish the slow pace we took, as though he were parading me to thousands of onlookers, though, in fact, the flooded and dark streets were empty, and he bent his neck around often in order to take delight at the sight of me.

I was looking down in despair when I heard a sound of footsteps. I glanced up, and I suppose he must have seen my eyes widen with surprise. Turning around swiftly, he saw what I'd seen— a man springing from the ground with a yell to knock him over. Slatter's head hit the ground hard. He lifted his neck briefly, and then his eyes closed with a moan. Edwin Hawkins stood over him and searched Slatter's coat for the keys to my shackles.

"For goodness' sake!" I cried out. "I am desperate glad to see you, Edwin!"

Retrieving the keys, he freed me from my restraints. "Mr. Clark," he said, interrupting my exclamations of gratitude, "I must make tracks." He looked back at Slatter.

"Do not worry. He is unconscious," I said. "He won't be awake for a while yet."

"I have to leave Baltimore. Now, Mr. Clark. He knew me in my youth."

Then I realized. If Slatter had seen Edwin, and recognized the attacker as a man whom he had sold years before, or had just looked long enough to remember his face . . . Edwin would not only be convicted, he would be entered back into slavery. "Did he see you?"

"I don't know, Mr. Clark. But I can't risk finding out. I am sorry I won't be able to help you any longer. I know you will find the evidence you need."

"Edwin." I took his arm. "If only I had not shown surprise! He would not have turned at all, and you would never have been at risk of him seeing you. You have done this for Poe!"

"No. This I have done for you." He took my hand with a warm smile. "You will prove your name, and that will be reward for this. For me, you must go ahead. With heaven speed."

I nodded. "Leave here quickly, my friend," I whispered, "and be silent on your way." He disappeared into the streets.

I shackled Slatter's hands but left his feet and legs free so he could find help when he awoke. He did not look as tall as he had on the horse; in fact, he was a decrepit old man lying there, with a blank and sloppy expression. I could hardly move from this spot. With Edwin gone, I felt inconsolably alone, and I remembered longingly the comforts of Hattie's visits in prison, and Bonjour's appearance there, and the burst of strength I'd received from them.

A sudden thought forced me to my feet. "Bonjour," I gasped to myself. I heard Slatter coming to life in a series of groans, but I did not stop to look back at him. I raised myself onto the side of his horse and rode back in the direction I had come from.

"My horse!" Slatter cried. "You! Bring back my horse!"

My fears were realized when I saw that the door to the Bonaparte house I had just left was wide open. I tied the slave-trader's horse to a post outside and walked circumspectly through the front hall. It was quiet except for the sounds of audible, pained breathing. If there had been any other noises it's unlikely I would have heard them. They would have folded into the background of my mind, along with the furnishings. I was transfixed.

In the parlor, there had clearly been a struggle only minutes, maybe seconds, before I arrived. Chairs, lamps, curtains, and papers were scattered over the floor. The chandelier still shook with the violence. The victor was clear. Bonjour stood over the large figure of Rollin, who was perspiring pitifully. From the disarray at a nearby window, it was clear he had tried to jump out of it. Bonjour, though perhaps half his size, was holding him down and had a blade touching his throat.

His eyes met mine and I wondered: did he know me now too?

I had been leaving Paris with Auguste Duponte to begin our investigation of Poe's death. Climbing aboard the ship, Duponte announced there was a stowaway. You remember.

"Do request," he said to me, "Monsieur Clark, that the steward inform our ship's captain there is a stowaway on board."

"You shall want to know what I know!" cried this stowaway, Rollin, when he was revealed and accused of trying to steal the steamer's mail shipment. There was something in his tone that may have rekindled the memory in me when the same man asked, in a voice far too aggressive, "You would like to leave word?" at the door of the Bonaparte mansion. But more than that, it was the lift of his hat— revealing the square baldness that had been unwillingly shown that day at sea when he was flung from the rails. It was that sight that made me remember where I had seen him that time.

By the time I had discovered Bonjour there, the implications of this man's presence on the *Humboldt* had settled into my imagination. But to answer my previous question for myself: no, I do not think he knew me now. He had been watching for someone else that earlier day at sea.

Now he was staring right at me. Rollin's eyes burned with ghastly interest, his legs wet with water and spotted with flower petals that had spilled on the rug from a shattered vase.

Bonjour peered around. She smiled slightly, almost apologetically, at me. I could almost feel all the passion and regret of her kiss again while I looked upon her face.

"I am sorry, Monsieur Clark." She said this as though I were the one prostrate and pleading for my life.

"You," I said, standing upright with the revelation. "You poisoned me. It was not the police or the prison guards! It was you. You slipped the poison into my mouth when we kissed."

"After I found a way inside the prison, I saw that the walls of the hospital chambers were already giving way to the floods," she said. "I felt you could get out through the sewer passage, but I needed to find a way for you to be transferred there. You may say I helped you, monsieur."

"No, you did not do it to help me. You wanted to follow me to Duponte so he would find the men who shot the Baron, and whoever ordered it. You thought Duponte could still help and that I'd know where Duponte was."

"I wanted the same thing as you, Monsieur Clark. To find the truth."

"Please," begged the man on the floor. Bonjour kicked him fiercely in his stomach.

I looked on as the man twisted in pain. I took a step closer. "Bonjour, this will help nothing. The police can arrest them now."

"I have no trust in police, Monsieur Clark."

The man swallowed down some further plea and trembled pitifully.

Bonjour crouched on the floor, positioning her blade. "Leave," she said to me, pointing to the door.

"You do not owe the Baron vengeance, mademoiselle," I said. "You have fulfilled your obligations by discovering the man who ordered his killing. Murdering this villain now will only make your life wretched, will only force you to run, as you have had to before. And," I added, "I will be the sole witness to this crime. You will have to kill me, too."

I was surprised when Bonjour, after remaining dead still in the midst of contemplation, turned slowly to me with a tear at the corner of her eye. It seemed a true affection had arisen in her expression. She stepped gingerly toward me like a scared deer. She seemed to be holding her breath when she threw her arms around my shoulders with a low moan. It was less of an embrace, somehow, than when our bodies were brought together at the fortifications in Paris. It was more a need for support, and I stood straight as a pillar. "Bonjour. It will be made right. We have both helped ourselves. Let me help you." She then shoved me away as though I had been the one to pull her to me. I nearly fell against the edge of a sofa. There was something lost from her eyes that made me know that I would not see her again.

Bonjour let her dagger drop and, after a moment of looking over the scene she had created, she began kicking the man brutally across the face several times in a flurry of blows. Then she ran from the room. I breathed in relief that she had not killed him. And yet it was not my monologue that had moved her not to do so. Approaching the place where Rollin lay crumpled like a corpse, I saw what Bonjour had seen: one of the objects that had crashed to the floor during their struggle was a newspaper from that morning. On the first page was announced the death of the mysterious French baron in the hospital.

The slave-trader had not been mistaken, as I had thought, when he'd said I was wanted for murder. Bonjour, for her part, must have felt her obligation to avenge the Baron somehow burn and fade upon his death— perhaps, for the thief in her, the reward, his honor, disappeared past redemption. Perhaps, for the true criminal mind, honor did not continue beyond death; nothing continued beyond death— there was no heaven or hell for persons who sought those same territories here. Or perhaps true sorrow had made all else pale in comparison. Whatever the reason, she had abandoned her revenge.

I leaned down at the side of Rollin and found that he was insensible but only superficially injured. I wrapped his wounds with a piece of fabric I tore from a fringed curtain. Then, before leaving, I found the washbasin to try to expunge his blood from my hands.

My mind circled vigorously around what I had learned. Though I had made great strides in understanding all that had happened, I still had no evidence against the men who'd killed the Baron. I had nothing in my possession to convince the police of what I now had uncovered. Even if I waited for the two villains to return to the Bonapartes', they would not hesitate to eliminate me. Indeed, this would perhaps be Rollin's first order to them if he regained consciousness. Since the police would only want to arrest me, I would have no protection if I sent for them.

And I would remain forever *the man who killed the real Dupin.* That was what people would think. I was destroyed. I would hang for someone else's sins and, at the moment, I could not even decipher whose— these men, or Duponte's. Worst of all, I had let all this mess forever prevent the resolution of Poe's death.

· · ·

With these thoughts, I walked up and down the streets of Baltimore, stopping only at intervals to rest. I walked until the early hours of the morning, and then sunrise came and still I walked.

"Clark?"

I turned around. As I did I realized I was not far from one of the district station houses, and so you can imagine that I was not entirely unprepared to see what I did.

"Officer White," I said, and then I greeted his clerk, too.

I looked down half bemused at the blood splattered like stains of guilt across the sleeves and buttons of my ragged coat, as they grabbed me.

32

ONE WEEK LATER, as I was sitting in the most comfortable arm-chair of my library, my mind turned to Bonjour, whom I had not seen since I had first left to visit the Bonapartes' address. Although she had been driven by her desire to avenge the Baron's death, and had not had any design of assisting me in my own plight, I harbored no ill will. In fact, I had little doubt I would see her again and believed she truly cared for me. There was no earthly reason to fear for her safety, wherever she was. I suppose if I had been able to fathom something about her through all of this, it was her complete self-sufficiency in surviving, though she believed she had depended on the Baron since he had exonerated her in a Paris court. She was, in the end, purely composed of the criminal character. All means were open to her to meet threat with threat, death with death.

When Officer White discovered me after the incident at the Bonaparte house, I would have fallen at his feet if he and his clerk had not caught me. My body was debilitated. I had not realized how long it had been since I had experienced any true rest. I awoke in one of the upstairs rooms of the Middle District station house. When I stirred and lifted myself, the police clerk appeared and brought in Officer White.

"Mr. Clark, are you still unwell?" the clerk asked solicitously.

"I feel stronger." Though I am not sure this was true, really. Still, I did not want to seem ungrateful for the kindness of placing me in their comfortable apartments. "Have you arrested me again?"

"Sir!" Officer White exclaimed. "We had been searching for you for several hours to ensure your well-being."

I saw that a box of various objects that had been removed from Glen Eliza was sitting on the floor. "I escaped from prison!" I exclaimed.

"And we were quite determined to restore your place there. However, in the meantime witnesses were discovered who had seen the murderers on the night of the Frenchman's lecture. They saw two men, including one badly injured and bandaged, and thus sticking in the memory of the witness. Both had pistols drawn as they stood at the wings of the lyceum.

This was quite evidential of your innocence, but we were unable to find the men. Until yesterday." The clerk explained that a horse belonging to a prominent slave-trader had been reported stolen. It was located by a police officer at a house of an absent Baltimorean where there were, remarkably, also two men just returning from some errand who met the exact description of the witnesses to the Baron's murder! Though the men fled, and were suspected of boarding a private frigate with a third man, their behavior strongly demonstrated my innocence in the matter.

I learned, furthermore, that Hope Slatter, embarrassed to report that a black man had put him down, claimed the assault on him had been by some German foreigners. German seeming a nationality close enough to the police to French, and the horse being found in front of the house where the rogues were returning, the police felt certain that the assault on Slatter had been perpetrated by the same parties who had killed the Baron.

"So I am not to be arrested?" I asked, after some contemplation.

"Heavens, Mr. Clark!" the police clerk responded. "You are quite free! Don't you wish to be driven home?"

Others had not forgiven me for the long period of public denunciation against me. This became clear over the next months.

All that I had in possession would soon be at risk.

Glen Eliza felt empty and worthless without Hattie Blum. She and Peter were to be married and I could not in the inmost regions of my mind seek to disrupt that. They were both better people than I could be, perhaps; they had tried to steer me away from trouble, and had been deeply united by that very thing that had pushed me away from them. Hattie had risked her own reputation with her visits to my prison cell. Now that I was free, I wrote a brief letter thanking her with all my heart and wishing her happiness. I at least owed them tranquillity and peace.

For myself, I had none. My great-aunt had come to visit after I was restored to Glen Eliza, where she questioned me repeatedly about the "delusions" and "fanatical" ideas that had, in my long despair over my parents' death, ultimately led to my imprisonment.

"I did what I thought was right," I said, remembering Edwin Hawkins's words to me when I was hiding in the packinghouse.

She stood with her arms folded, her long black dress a great contrast to her snow-white hair. "Quentin, dear boy. You were arrested for murder! A jailbird! You are fortunate if anyone in Baltimore will keep your society. A woman like Hattie Blum needs a man as worthy as Peter Stuart. This house has become the very castle of indolence."

I looked at my great-aunt. She had been thrown into more of a passion over this than I had realized. "I'd have wanted nothing more than to marry Hattie Blum," I said, which was even more outrageous to her, since I was now talking about a woman shortly to be married. "Anything you can say meant to punish me further is far too little. I am happy for Peter. He is a good man."

"What would your father say! God forbid we should visit upon the dead the errors of the living. You, dear boy, are a great deal your mother's blood," she added with a dull mutter.

Before leaving that day, she flashed a glare at me intended, I later realized, as a threat. She examined Glen Eliza as though at any moment it could crumble from the moral dilapidation I had perpetrated.

Soon after, I was informed that my great-aunt had brought suit to claim possession of most of what I had inherited from my father's will, including Glen Eliza, on the basis of the mental incompetence and imbalance exhibited in my conduct since the irrational resignation of my position in Peter's practice . . . and my strong neglect of the Clark family investments and business interests, which had resulted in severely diminished value over the last two years . . . culminating in my wild, raving interruption at the fatal assembly of the Baron Dupin . . . my outrageous escape from prison, my rumored attempt to dig up a grave and encroach on a home on Amity Street . . . and all of this was proved by my complete lack of comprehension of the whole chronicle of actions.

I learned further that she had been helped in all this by Auntie Blum. It seemed that Auntie Blum had intercepted my letter of gratitude to Hattie. Inflamed to learn through my letter of Hattie's visits to my prison cell, Auntie Blum had immediately called upon Great-Auntie Clark.

Great-Auntie wrote me a letter, explaining that she was fighting for the honor of my father's name and because she loved me.

I began to ready my defense. I worked feverishly, hardly leaving the library, calling to mind the former times when Duponte would sit at the table sometimes for days without interruption.

I prepared as well as I could to defend my actions. The process was strenuous. Not only to produce responses to each accusation that my great-aunt would allege as evidence that I had squandered and misused my good fortune and name in society; but also to frame it in the language of the law that I had thought I had abandoned.

Auntie Blum had reportedly advised that the case against me emphasize the disregard of my family's wealth. She calculated that polite Baltimore would not brook the injustice of any such pecuniary offense. This was Baltimore's lynch law.

Meanwhile, I contemplated the many witnesses and friends I might call to my defense, but sadly concluded that many— like Peter, of course— could no longer speak in my favor. The newspapers, having only recently finished with the sensational news of my arrest, escape, and exoneration, now looked happily upon this lawsuit as containing an interesting sequel to my affairs, and always wrote about it with a tone of suspicion that it might prove me guilty yet of some other, larger misdoing.

At times, I felt convinced that I should peacefully leave this shattered house, Glen Eliza, which I seemed now to float inside rather than live in. As I loped through the upper stories, and climbed up one set of stairs and down another, it only seemed to confirm this feeling— word of my great-aunt's suit, indeed, left me asking myself, "Where in the land am I?" The house, with all its rambling divisions and subdivisions, with its wide spaces, still seemed to have room for only a few particles of myself.

I do not know why I stopped before one particular framed silhouette. It was one I had rarely noticed before. Even if I were to reproduce it here, it would look unremarkable to my reader's eye: an ordinary man's profile, with an old-fashioned three-point hat. It was my grandfather, who had turned furious upon hearing of my father's intention to marry Elizabeth Edes, a Jewish woman. He threatened and fumed, and stripped my father of family money rightfully owed to him. No matter, my father said, for it put him as a young man in a position not so different from my mother's family, who had built their own foundations. Through his packinghouses— "through my enterprise," he said— Father prospered enough to build one of Baltimore's unique mansions.

But while my father always spoke of his Industry and Enterprise, the traits he found opposite of Genius, I realized, looking upon this picture, that he *was* the pioneer he had always claimed not to be. For he and Mother had created this world from nothing for the sake of their happiness— and how much impatience and insistence, how much *genius,* this entailed it could not be said. My father had the very pains of genius he warned against. This is why he tried so hard to keep me away from any but the ordinary path— not because he had embraced it, but because he had deviated from it and found himself, though victorious, also wounded.

The grand old patriarch in the silhouette even unto death did not retract his objections to my mother's Jewish blood having been interjected into our orderly family line. Yet my parents had hung his silhouette in a central place in Glen Eliza, the place erected for our happiness, rather than hiding it, abandoning it, or destroying it. The meaning of this had never struck me fully until this moment. I felt an instant possession of this place and of my family and returned to my desk and to the work at hand.

I received no visitors until the evening Peter arrived.

"No servant to open the door, I see?" he commented, then frowned at himself, as though confessing he could not regulate his mouth sometimes. "Glen Eliza is still as magnificent as when we were children, playing bandits in the halls. Some of my happiest times."

"Think of it, Peter. You, a bandit!"

"Quentin, I want to help."

"How do you mean, Peter?"

He regained his usual bluster. "You never were meant to be a single attorney; you're too excitable. And *perhaps* I was not meant to have another partner other than you— I have been through two men in the last six months, by the bye. In all events, you need help."

"You mean with my great-aunt's case against me?"

"Wrong!" he exclaimed. "We will turn it into *your* case *against Great-Auntie Clark,* my friend." He smiled broadly, like a child.

I proudly welcomed Peter in that day, and he devoted as many hours as he could each evening after completing his work at the law offices. His help was of tremendous value, and I began to feel more optimistic about my chances. Moreover, it seemed I had never known anybody so intimately as my friend, and we talked as people only can before the flickering light of a fireplace.

Still, we both refrained from mentioning Hattie. Until one night, in our shirtsleeves, while making our strategies. Peter said, "At this point in the defense, we shall call Miss Hattie to testify, to show your honest bearing and— "

I looked at Peter with an alarmed expression, as though he had just screamed loudly.

"Peter, I cannot. What I mean— well, you see how it is."

He sighed anxiously, and looked down at his drink. He was taking a nightcap of warm toddy. "She loves you."

"Yes," I said, "as does my great-aunt. Either those who love me fail me, or I fail them, as with Hattie."

Peter stood up from his chair. "My engagement with Hattie is dead, Quentin."

"What? How?"

"I ended it."

"Peter, how could you?"

"I could see it every time she would look in my direction, as though she wished to be looking past me over to you. It is not that she doesn't have love for me; in a way she does. But you have something stronger, and I must not be in your way."

I could hardly stammer a response. "Peter, you mustn't . . ."

"None of your hums and hahs. It's done. And she agreed, after much discussion. I always thought she loved you because you were handsome, and so took a bit of queer joy in having won her after all. But she believed in you when there was nothing to believe in and nobody else to believe." He chuckled morbidly, then clapped his large hand around my shoulder. "That is when I realized she is a great deal like you."

I talked through in a rush what I should do, and whether I should immediately drive to Hattie's. . . . He waved me back into my seat.

"Not that simple, Quentin. There is still her family, which forbids her from communing with you, particularly now that you are under threat of losing all your possessions, even Glen Eliza itself. First, you must prove yourself, and Hattie will be yours again. Until then, it is better that they think Hattie and I are to be married. If even you see her on the street, turn the other way— do not be seen together."

I was ecstatic, and propelled into a new frenzy of industry, more determined than ever to overcome the new obstacles engendered by my great-aunt's lawsuit.

But Peter was soon oppressed with business at the office, which cut severely into his time available to give me assistance. Moreover, once the trial began, the matter became increasingly intricate and grim. Peter's clever strategy of proving Great-Auntie Clark hypocritical and malicious was stricken by the amount of support she had from the population of good society in Baltimore, especially from friends of Hattie's family. In addition, there were simply too many points of the chronology that could not be cleared up sufficiently to the public eye.

"Then there is the entire episode of spying on this baron that her lawyer has mentioned," said Peter one evening during the trial.

"But that can be explained! To find the correct conclusions about Poe's death— "

"Anything can be explained— but can it be *understood*? Even Hattie, for all that she loves you, wants to understand this, and is pained that she does not. You talk of seeking the conclusions about Poe's death, but what are they? Here lies the difference between success and insanity. To make out your case, you must adapt your argument to the understanding of the dullest man of the twelve in that box."

At length, as the case against me worsened, it became clear that Peter was correct. I could not win. However hard I labored, I could not save Glen Eliza. I could not win Hattie back. I could not accomplish any of this without a solution to Poe's death— without showing that in all of this I had found the truth that I had sought for so long.

I knew what I must do. I'd use the one persuasive story of Poe's demise that had come out of this ordeal: the Baron Dupin's. It was my last hope. It had been kept in my memory, and now I wrote it out, word for word, in the form of an address I would make to the court . . .

I present to you, Your Honor and Gentlemen of the Jury, the truth about this man's death and my life. The narrative has not been told before. . . .

I could see immediately that this would do it. Indeed, the more I read what I'd scribbled into my memorandum book, the more the Baron's story seemed possible— then plausible— likely! I knew it could not be trusted, that it had been manipulated and fashioned for the hearing and satisfaction of the public; I knew, too, that it would now be believed. *All that follows will be the plain truth.* I would speak fictions, out and out fables, probably lies. Yet I would be believed again, respected again, as my father would want. *And I must tell you this story because I am the one nearest the truth.* (Duponte, if only Duponte were here.) *Or, rather, the only one still living.*

33

DECEMBER SAW SOMETHING new and familiar in France. Louis-Napoleon, president of the Republic, decided to replace his prefect of police, Monsieur Delacourt, with Charlemagne de Maupas. He would serve as a stronger ally. "I need some men to help me cross this ditch," Louis-Napoleon reportedly told de Maupas. "Will you be one of them?"

That was a sign.

So were the new secret policemen assigned by Louis-Napoleon to monitor both the prefecture and the palace of the government.

President Louis-Napoleon assembled a team to carry out his coup. On the first of the month, he gave each member half a million francs. Early the next morning, de Maupas, the prefect, and his police arrested the eighty legislators who Louis-Napoleon feared could most effectively oppose him. They were held in the prison at Mazas. They would not have been legislators anymore, in any event, for what Louis-Napoleon did next was to dissolve the assembly, meanwhile seizing printing presses and sending his army to kill the leaders of the Red Republicans as soon as they showed themselves in the streets. Other opponents, mostly those of fine old French families, were immediately exiled from the country.

It was all rather quick.

Louis-Napoleon declared France an empire again. It was remembered that Louis-Napoleon as a boy was reported to have pleaded with his uncle, the first emperor of France, not to go off to Waterloo, at which the emperor commented: "He will be a good soul, and perhaps the hope of my race."

On my way to the courthouse each morning I read more news of the political affairs in France. It was said that Jérôme Napoleon Bonaparte of Baltimore (called "Bo"), cousin of the new emperor— the man I had met flanked by two costume swords, the man never acknowledged by his now deceased uncle Napoleon Bonaparte because of his American mother—

was to travel to Paris and meet with Emperor Napoleon III to repair the lengthy breach.

Americans were entranced with these stories from Paris, perhaps because the coup seemed so different from any upheaval that could take place here. My interest was slightly more narrow or, rather, more pertinent.

I wrote several cards to the various Bonaparte homes, hoping to find out that Jérôme Napoleon Bonaparte had not yet left for Paris and would speak with me, even though I presumed he would not remember our brief meeting at the dress ball with Monsieur Montor. I had questions. Though they might not do me any good in particular, I wanted the answers anyway.

Meanwhile, many onlookers came to court to see the continuation of my earlier humiliations. It seemed unfortunate to them, I suppose, that my previous appearances in the press had been inconclusive and had not reached an appropriate climax. Fortunately, many spectators were eventually driven away by the tedium of the technical matters that filled most of the opening days of the trial. It was around this time that I was surprised to receive a note with the Bonaparte seal, assigning me a time to come to one of their residences.

It was a larger house than the one I had seen the rogues in; it was more secluded, surrounded by wild trees and uncultivated grassy hills. I was ushered inside by a very willing servant, and on the grand stairway met at least two other servants (it was a long stairway), whose shared trait was their nervousness undertaking some task or another. The mansion was grand and in no way subdued or timid in its grandeur— showing the most marvelous chandeliers and gold-bordered tapestries, which always kept the eye looking up.

I was surprised to find seated in a massive chair burnished with silver not Jérôme Napoleon Bonaparte— the leading male of the Baltimore branch of the family— but his mother, Elizabeth Patterson Bonaparte. As a young girl she had captured the heart of Napoleon's brother and was married to him for two years before Napoleon, through various machinations, including calling in the pope to annul it, ended the relationship. Though she was not now costumed as a queen, as the first time I'd met her, the regal attitude remained.

This matron, now in her sixties, had bare arms with the most luminous bracelets, too many to count, spiraling up and down her wrists. Upon her head she wore a black velvet bonnet from which orange feathers jutted out, giving her a frightening and wild aspect. Several tables of jewels and garish garments surrounded her. On the other side of her chambers, a girl I took to be a servant rocked in a chair like an invalid.

"Madame Bonaparte." I bowed, feeling for a moment that I should lean down on one knee. "You would not remember meeting me, but I was at a ball where you were dressed as a queen and I was not in a costume."

"You are right, young man. I do not remember meeting you. But it was I who answered your card."

"And Monsieur Bonaparte, your son . . . ?"

"Bo is already on his way to meet the new emperor of France," she said, as though it were the most pedestrian reason for a tour abroad.

"I understand. I have read in the papers of the prospects for such a meeting. Perhaps monsieur could be kindly informed that I should be most obliged to arrange an interview upon his return."

She nodded but seemed to forget the request as soon as I had spoken it. "I would not quarrel with an attorney," she said, "but I wonder that you should have time to be here when you are quite occupied each day at court, Mr. Clark."

I was surprised that she knew anything of my situation, though I reminded myself of the interest taken by the press. Still, though my claim to sanity and my life's fortune was hanging in the balance, for a woman whose son was reported by the newspapers as journeying to meet an emperor, my troubles seemed rather trifling business. I sat in a particular armchair as instructed. I surveyed the rest of the room and noticed a bright red parasol, gleaming as brilliantly as her jewels, leaning against the side of a large chest. Underneath was a mostly dried puddle of water, indicating its recent use. In my mind, I saw again the scene before me at the Baron's doomed lecture hall, and the indistinct lady under a bejeweled red parasol.

Had it been she?

I realized, with a sudden chill, why this woman must have come to the lecture. As a witness not to the Baron's revelations on Poe's death, but to the revelation of a new death.

I thought I had understood most of the history of events when I'd read of the recent tales of power and death in Paris in the newspapers. Louis-Napoleon, when told of Duponte's re-emergence in Paris, a re-emergence I had stimulated, thought back to the legends of the analyst's abilities. He and the leaders of his plan for a secret coup must have believed

Duponte could jeopardize it, could *ratiocinate* and expose their goals of a coup too early. Napoleon had ordered Duponte eliminated at about the time we were leaving for Baltimore. It was meant to be an easy task for one of the men of abandoned character known to the police, with whom they sometimes made mutually advantageous arrangements.

They missed their opportunity while Duponte was still in Paris, and soon he was leaving with me. Many years later, I heard reports that they had thoroughly raided and torn apart all of Duponte's rooms while we were on the way to the harbor. Frantic, they planned his elimination at sea, only to find the expulsion of their assassin, the stowaway, one of whose aliases was Rollin. They had lost us to America.

Yet there were Bonapartes in Baltimore; indeed, there was Jérôme Napoleon Bonaparte, who had been denied his birthright. Bo had been waiting his whole life to realign himself with the branch of his family in France, to be royalty. Now came his chance to prove his worth to the heir to the power of their ancestor, to this soon-to-be emperor. The men following the Baron Dupin, the men who killed him under the guidance of the original stowaway, had not come for him at all. Rollin had hidden himself in Baltimore because he knew Duponte might recognize him from that incident on board the ship. I had seen him in my poison-induced haze in prison, where he had been incarcerated briefly for some involvement with a local criminal element. The stowaway Rollin— and his two henchmen— had been here to kill *Duponte. For the sake of the future of France.*

Except the Baron had made the mistake of disguising himself as his rival. And had been killed in his stead.

That was how I had come to understand the events since encountering the stowaway Rollin at the house of the Bonapartes. But now, meeting this woman, I had to wonder: what had she done in all this?

I turned from the parasol back to its keeper. "You knew the part of the plot your son was designing?"

"Bo?" She let out a chirp of amusement. "He is too busy with his garden and his books for such things. He is a member of the bar but never saw fit to practice. He is a true man of the world. Certainly, he wishes to assume his proper place, to regain our property and our rights as Bonapartes, but he has not the strength of spirit to be a leader."

"Then who?" I asked. "Who saw to it that you would hunt Duponte to win favor back with Napoleon?"

"I would not expect such a want of courtesy in my home from a strikingly handsome young gentleman as yourself." But her reprimand seemed light. Indeed, she leisurely passed a glance up and down my body in a way that gave me discomfort. She had been grinning, but now her face became flat and serious as she talked about her son. "Bo . . . I had endeavored to instill in my son that he was too high in birth to ever marry an American woman. Yet he disgraced himself by doing so. I wished for him in his youth to take the hand of Charlotte Bonaparte, a cousin of his, to return us to the seat of influence, but he refused."

"You refused the wishes of your parents, too, when a girl," I noted.

"I did so to be brought under the wings of an eagle!" she said passionately. "Yes, the emperor had dealt with me in a hard fashion, but I long ago forgave him. What did he say of me to Marshal Bertrand before he died? 'Those whom I have wronged have forgiven me; those whom I have loaded with kindness have forsaken me.' Ah, Napoleon, I have not let my grandsons forget that their grand-uncle was the Great Emperor!"

She lifted her hands upward and I could now observe more closely a gown that hung behind her. It was the wedding dress she had worn in 1803, in the ceremony in Baltimore that had ignited the world into consternation, that had sent emissaries from America scuttling across an ocean to try to appease the fury of the French leader. I had read about this dress recently when educating myself on the history of these episodes. It was India muslin and lace, and had caused something of a scandal as there was only one garment underneath it. "All the clothes worn by the bride might be put in my pocket," a Frenchman reported in a letter to Paris.

It hung on the wall in perfectly fossilized condition, seeming, if one were not close enough to see signs of age in the fabric, as though it was quite new, and might be rushed to a church at any moment.

Suddenly there were the sounds of a baby, a rough, brittle cry that grew increasingly loud. Startled, I looked around for its source, as though it were some supernal happening, and found that the young servant girl rocking and swaying in the corner was in fact holding a baby, no more than eight months old. This, it was explained to me, was Charles Joseph Napoleon, the youngest child of Bo and his wife, Susan. Madame Bonaparte was caring for her new grandchild while Bo and his American wife traveled to Paris to beseech the emperor for the long-awaited rights of the Baltimore members of the family.

The woman took the baby from the nurse and curled her fingers around him tightly. "Here is one of the hopes of our race. And have you ever seen my other grandson? He attended Harvard and now studies at West Point. He is everything that my husband was not. Tall, distinguished, soon to be a soldier of the most capable order." Madame Bonaparte cooed at the little creature then said, "He would make a very presentable emperor of the French."

"Only if Louis-Napoleon agrees to return your offspring to the line of succession, madame," I pointed out.

"The new emperor, Louis-Napoleon, is a rather dull man, on the order of George Washington. He shall need to secure a far stronger ingenuity for the empire to survive."

"From your family, you mean?" The baby had now begun howling, and Madame Bonaparte returned him to the nurse.

"I am too old to coquette, as was once my only stimuli. I have been tired of killing time, Mr. Clark. To doze away existence. Once I had everything but money. Here, I have nothing but money. I shall not let men of my blood be mere American colonists like my son has mistaken himself for."

"*You* did this, then. You agreed to eliminate a man, a genius, because Louis-Napoleon worried he could foresee his plot to overthrow the Republic."

She shrugged slightly. "We have given money and comfort to travelers from France, under my direction— yes— if that is what you mean. Their orders came from other parties, not from me."

"And did they accomplish what they were directed to do?"

She waved the nurse out of the room and frowned. "Dolts," she said. "They mistook one man for another. I understand they were told by the Paris police to expect your presence around this Duponte they were after, yet they saw you waiting around the hotels of this other— this false Baron, this false Duponte. No matter, for what was needed was achieved: no one interfered with Louis-Napoleon's plans, and now he has ascended." She examined me closely again and I could feel the acute judgment of her eyes growing.

"Tell me," she said. "From what we have understood, you brought along these two men of genius in some attempt to find a poet that you fancy. I have heard about this Poe. His talent has mostly been dismissed by America."

"Not for long," I said.

She laughed. "You do have faith. Perhaps you will be interested that I have heard that young poets and writers in Paris are now reading him in great numbers, your Poe. It seems he was like their own Monsieur Balzac— brilliant but luckless, doomed to be a puppet of fate. He will be brought into the European spirit, as all the better American minds are. Yet this is not enough for your Poe-worship, is it, Mr. Clark? My son is not dissimilar from how you must be; he believes books are written primarily for his personal readership."

"Madame Bonaparte, my motives are not important. This is not about me."

"But, stay! Think of it, dear Mr. Clark. You have helped by giving us an important task to perform, which has allowed us to prove our loyalty to France. We have ensured a new emperor from this, and he will create an empire in which my family can survive forever! I have spent a lifetime to see to it that my children have their proper inheritance, and would give my life for it now. What about you? You were but a chrysalis and you made the mistake of giving up what your family made you into. Tell me, what did you find?"

I rose from my chair without answering. "I have only one other question, Madame Bonaparte. If they came to know they assassinated the wrong man at the lyceum that night, did they then locate the right one? Has Duponte been killed, too?"

"I have told you," the woman said slowly, "I only provide comfort. I provide a place to start, you might say, a birthplace for noble plans. Others must decide the rest for themselves."

I had written and discarded a whole notebook of letters to Auguste Duponte. I detailed for him not only the hard reality— that Poe, apparently, had *not* modeled his character C. Auguste Dupin from any real person, but rather and remarkably only from imagination. I included not just this, but also the steps of thinking that had led me to reach this conclusion, knowing he would have an interest in the line of reasoning. However, if Duponte was still alive and escaped, I did not know where to address any letters. Not to Paris, not to his former residence, I felt certain. He would not be in this Paris, not in Louis-Napoleon's Third Empire, where his genius was seen as an enemy to the emperor's unending ambitions.

It was seeing the anxiety in Madame Bonaparte's face at the close of our interview, when I asked whether Rollin and his rogues had found Duponte, that made me decide Duponte was probably closer than I'd considered. He had been patiently waiting— not for me, exactly, but it would be me he would have to see.

Passing the bustle of porters and guests at the massive Barnum's Hotel one day, these various thoughts dissolved into an idea. Returning to Glen Eliza, I considered that my time to act might be short. I started on my way back to Barnum's. I did not leave, though, without remembering to reach into the closet for the old pistol that the police had returned along with my other possessions. This time I checked— before slipping it into my pocket— that its age and disuse had not left the hammer entirely immobile.

"Sir?"

An ashen clerk with tight whiskers glared at me suspiciously and waited for me to say something.

"Monsieur," I said abruptly and, as I'd hoped, he raised an eyebrow of interest at the French word. "There is a member of the French sovereign class currently residing in your hotel."

He nodded with all the depth of his responsibility. "Indeed, sir. He has been staying in the room once occupied by the *Baron* who visited Baltimore earlier this year. This is his brother. The *Duke.*" He leaned in to whisper this last word confidentially. "The noble lineage is most evident in both of them."

"The Duke." I smiled. "Yes. But when did our imperial Duke begin his stay?"

"Oh, as soon as his brother, I mean the noble Baron, left. His current presence is most covert— with all that is happening in France, you know."

I nodded, amused at the ease with which he'd yielded his secret. As though having the same thought, he now declaimed that he was not able to supply the location of the royal guest's room.

"You do not have to, sir," I said, and we shared a confidential nod. Of course I knew the room. I had spied on the Baron when he had stayed there.

I ascended the staircase with expectations racing through my blood.

I now remember Duponte as looking rather pale and haggard during our meeting, as though he had been all used up since we'd first met, or half used up at least. He was sitting serenely in the Baron Dupin's old hotel room when I came in. He didn't appear disappointed in having been discovered by me. I suppose I'd imagined that his remarkable composure would come unfurled by my surprise appearance, that he would speak in anger and threaten me if I seemed likely to expose him with the knowledge I now possessed of his whereabouts and his deeds. He had known the Baron would be killed in his place, and he had done nothing to prevent it.

He politely offered me a chair. The truth is, he was no less composed than ever. Then he pulled the bell for the hotel porter and told the man to take his trunk. I looked at him inquisitively.

"I had long given up on you," I said.

"It is time for me to leave," he replied.

"Now that I have come, you mean?" I asked.

He looked over at me. "You have seen the newspapers. All that has occurred in Paris."

I removed the pistol from my coat, studied it as though I had never seen it before, and placed it near him on a table.

"They might have followed me— if they are still looking for you, I mean. I have no desire to endanger you, Monsieur Duponte, despite the fact that I have been endangered by you. Keep this close to you."

"I do not know if they have still been looking for me, but if they have, they will not much longer."

I understood. The Baltimore Bonapartes had traveled to Paris in hopes of being rewarded for their loyalty to the new emperor. If they'd succeeded, they would have no motivation to continue supporting a search for Duponte, even though Madame Bonaparte and her rogues knew now they had failed to kill the real object of the assassination.

"The Baron is dead. You knew all along he would be killed in your place, and allowed it," I said. "You, monsieur, you have been the murderer."

A gong rang uproariously through the hotel. Duponte said, "Shall we dine? I have kept myself in my rooms too long. For the sake of fine food, I can afford the risk of being seen in public."

The vast dining room held approximately five hundred people sitting down to Chesapeake Bay shad. A colored "major-domo" signaled a gong to sound at each course, and all the covers on the next dishes were lifted simultaneously by waiters posted at each table.

At length I peered around to find a waiting assassin or perhaps a person who had known the Baron Dupin and would now think he's seeing his ghost. Yet, the tired countenance my companion now wore held as little resemblance to the Baron's vivid imitation of Duponte as to the old Duponte himself.

"No. I am not the murderer," Duponte now answered my earlier remark evenly. "I am not, but perhaps you are, you and the Baron, if you like. The Baron wished to disguise himself as me. Had I control over that? I tried to keep it away. I had remained in my rooms in Paris. But you needed 'Dupin,' for your own purposes, Monsieur Clark. The Baron needed 'Dupin' for his. Louis-Napoleon needed a 'Dupin' to fear. Your arrival in Paris and your persistence made me accept that however much I remained dormant, the idea of 'Dupin' would not. It was, as you said, *something sort of immortal.*"

Ah, but you are not Dupin! Never were!

It was at the end of my tongue. I was ready to seize the conversation and wrest it into my power. My thoughts were still buzzing with questions, though.

"When did you know? When did you know they were coming after *you?* That those men, supported by the Bonapartes, wanted to murder you."

Duponte shook his head as if he did not know the answer.

"But on the *Humboldt* you knew there was the stowaway aboard, that villain Rollin. It started then. Monsieur, I am witness to it all!"

"No, I did not know there was a stowaway. Rather, I knew that if there *was* a stowaway there, they were hunting me."

"I suppose you guessed!" I exclaimed.

Duponte grinned just for a flash. He nodded.

I believe that day I felt the inner pain of Duponte that had made him the way he was when I'd first discovered his stationary life in Paris— alone, unintentional in all things. Everyone had believed that he possessed extraordinary powers after he had deciphered the Lafarge poisoning case. The young Duponte was an unnaturally confident man, and he himself began to believe that his abilities were of the almost supernatural nature that others wrote about in the newspapers. The stories about him enhanced his genius, perhaps even allowed for it in the first place. Yet I still could not answer whether genius had been created through the faith of the outside world. Readers often feel that the Dupin of Poe's tales finds the truth because he is a genius. Read again. This is only part of it. He finds the truth because someone has faith in him throughout— without his friend, there would be no C. Auguste Dupin.

"Each time I saw Louis-Napoleon review his troops," said Duponte, "I could see not the future, as the superstitious fool would believe about me, but the present— he was not content with being elected president. I suppose Prefect Delacourt warned him of me after I was seen out in Paris, with you, by his spies."

"The Baron told me of what happened to Catherine Gautier. Did Prefect Delacourt warn Louis-Napoleon because you were against him in that case? Did you wish vengeance on him by escaping him?"

"The prefect's actions were motivated by him having done me wrong, not my having wronged him. Our own past perversity, not that of others, sets us against someone for life. Prefect Delacourt was removed in favor of the new prefect for many reasons, I am certain— one of those may have been the failure to successfully find me before you and I left Paris together. De Maupas is not as astute a man as Delacourt, but he is far more competent, the two traits having no bridge between them— and, as a hobby, de Maupas is quite ruthless."

"Do you believe they learned they had murdered the Baron instead of you?"

Duponte now trimmed away a piece of Maryland ham, the second course brought by our waiter. "Perhaps. You certainly proclaimed the Baron's identity to the police loud enough, Monsieur Clark! It was never clear to the public, and is likely still unclear to those concerned in Paris. Chances are, the rogues who killed the Baron here heard of the truth. For their own sakes, they probably kept the fact secret from their superiors in Paris. Instead, their leader— that stowaway sent here to have charge over the mission— has quietly hunted me. However, I knew this would be the one place in Baltimore they would not look for me: the Baron's last rooms in the city. I came here during the Baron's lecture and have shown myself in the streets only now and then at night. The hotel believes I have come to mourn for my 'brother,' the noble Baron, in peace, and has left me alone. Now that Louis-Napoleon has successfully surprised Paris into becoming an empire, and has presently held a successful vote to that effect, the stowaway surely is beginning to believe that their mistake concerning me and the Baron has passed its time of relevancy. If the American Bonaparte son succeeds in his mission, the stowaway may quietly stay in France for the rewards due to him before there are any further political changes. He and the American Bonapartes shall say nothing of their own errors, you can be sure. To Paris, I will be terribly dead."

I thought about the plain apartments of his hotel room upstairs and rehearsed in my mind what Duponte's life would have been like in the months since the Baron's murder, hiding here in plain view. He had books— in fact, the place was littered with books, as though a library had collapsed and disbursed itself at will. All of the titles seemed to relate to sediment, minerals, and general characteristics of rocks. In the darkness and gloom of these weeks, he had turned to the workings of geology. This struck me as horribly base and useless, that tomb of books and stones, and I was irritable that he was now implying a demand for my sympathies.

"Do you know the pinch my life has been in, Monsieur Duponte, since beginning our adventure?" I demanded. "I was presumed guilty of killing the Baron Dupin until the police came to their senses. Now I must fight or lose my entire estate, Glen Eliza itself, all that I possess."

I explained, through a last course of watermelon, what had happened in prison and upon my escape and my discovery of Bonjour and the rogues. After we finished our large meal, we walked upstairs to return to his rooms.

"I must relate the full story of Poe's death in court," I said to him, "in one last bid to show that in all this I acted with reason and not imbecile dreams."

Duponte looked at me with interest. "What will you say, monsieur?"

"You never intended to resolve Poe's death, did you?" I asked sadly. "You used it as a distraction, knowing it would soon enough look to the world as though you had been killed here. You were inspired when you read the Baron's newspaper announcement in Paris that he would set the trap for himself that would free you from the expectations of others. That was why you thrilled at the idea of that Von Dantker being sent to Glen Eliza by the Baron— so his imitation of you could be perfected. You only went out of the house at night to ensure the Baron's charade would succeed. You simply wanted to kill the notion, once and for all, that you were the real 'Dupin.'"

Duponte nodded at this last statement, but would not look directly at me. "When I met you, Monsieur Clark, I was angry at your insistence to see me in that light, as 'Dupin.' I then realized that only through studying Poe's tales and studying *you* would I understand what it was you and

so many others perennially looked for in such a character. There is no
real Dupin anymore, and never will be." He had a strange mix of relief
and horror in his tone. Relief that he no longer carried the burden of
being the master ratiocinator, of being the real Dupin. Horror at having
to be someone else.

I would tell him the hard truth. "You are not Dupin!" I would say.
"You never were. There was no such man ever alive; Dupin was an invention." After all, perhaps that was why I had searched so lustily to find
him again. To make him feel with me the sting of what had been lost. To
take away something and thus leave him more alone.

But I did not say it.

I thought about what Benson had said to me about the dangers to the
susceptible imagination of reading Poe. To believe you were in Poe's
writings. Perhaps, along the same lines, Duponte had once believed himself in a mental world created by Poe, had thought he was in the tales of
Dupin. Yet he *was* more present in a world like the one Poe had imagined than most of us, and who was to say that did not make him the *real*
embodiment of the character whom I had met first on a page in *Graham's* magazine? Did it matter whether he was the cause or the effect?

"Where?" I asked Duponte. "Where will you go?"

Instead of answering, he said musingly: "There is much admirable in
you, monsieur."

I do not know why, but this statement astonished me, lifting my spirits, and I asked him to elaborate.

"Some people, you understand, cannot get out of their positions. They
cannot be among the missing, even if desired. I could not, here or in
Paris, until now, and Monsieur Poe could not even until death. You could
have left all along and you did not." He paused. "What will you say in
court?"

"I will tell them the answers. I will give them the Baron Dupin's story
of Poe's death. People will believe it."

"Yes, they will. You will win the case if you do this?" Duponte asked.

"I will win. It will be as true to them as anything else. It is the only
way."

"And as for Poe?"

"Perhaps," I said quietly, "it is as good as any other ending."

"How very like an attorney you are, after all," said Duponte, with a faraway smile.

At length the porter came to secure the balance of the Duke's belongings. Duponte gave him various instructions. I retrieved my hat and bid him good evening. My steps lingered a bit as I entered the hall, but though wanting a last sight by which to remember Duponte, I only saw him struggling to arrange some unwieldy geological instruments to be transported. I wished he would turn and remind me I was not seeing any ordinary man. Call out an insult— "Dolt!" perhaps. Or "numskull!"

"I thought much of you, Duke," I muttered to myself, and bowed.

34

THE DAY SOON came for me to sit upon the witness stand and tell the full "truth" of Poe's death. To provide convincing evidence that the actions alleged as delusional and fantastical were in fact fruitful, rational, and conspicuously normal on my part. Peter had worked assiduously in my aid throughout the trial, particularly as to these points, and we had at least come to be held even with our legal adversaries in the prevailing judgment of the populace. The opposing lawyer had a lion-like voice that roared the jury into submission. Peter said that my presentation of Poe's death would be needed to obtain our victory.

Hattie, her aunt, and additional Blum family members arrived each day to court. They were perplexed by Peter's insistence on laboring over my defense ("and that after young Clark's *behavior!*"), but came dutifully to support the man they expected to marry their Hattie. I believe they also came to watch my disgrace and financial collapse. Hattie and I were able to have private words at intervals but never for long. Each time, the eye of her aunt found us, and each time she innovated new techniques to prevent any further intercourse.

This morning's testimony was widely anticipated among our society. The courtroom audience swelled from its usual numbers. I was, in particular, to prove that all of this was indeed an attempt to seek answers to a mystery about Poe's death by showing the reality of this claim: by answering the mysteries themselves. On some nights, I'd had dreams about it. In them, I thought I could see the literary figure C. Auguste Dupin—who resembled quite precisely, though not uniformly, Auguste Duponte—and could hear him dictate each particular. Yet when I woke I could describe no conclusions, could re-create no ratiocination, could find only conflicting fragments of ideas and sentences, and felt helpless and frustrated. That is when the Baron would reappear to my mind, and I would be grateful that I had his firm answers, his reliable and dramatic answers, answers that would satisfy any public demand.

Mere words that would save all I possessed.

There were stares from the onlookers, the same species of stares that had greeted the Baron on the lyceum stage. Stares of greed, the signs of a bargain between speaker and hearers to reach into the lowest part of the souls of both. Many Poe spectators who had once longed to hear the Baron were here. I would reveal how Poe died, it was said throughout the city. I could see Neilson Poe and John Benson coming into the room, men who, in very different ways, had needed those answers, any answers. I saw Hattie— for whom I would be saving a life we could have together, keeping for us a home in Glen Eliza, just by licking my lips with the Baron's honey of persuasion. Just by telling a story.

The judge called my name, and I looked down at the lines I'd written. I took a breath.

"I present to you, Your Honor and Gentlemen of the Jury, the truth about this man's death and my life. The narrative has not been told before. Whatever has been taken away from me, one last possession remains: this story."

Could I insist, as the Baron had, that what seemed true must be true? Yes, yes, why not? Wasn't I a lawyer? Wasn't it my job, my role?

"There are those of our city today who tried to stop it. There are those sitting here among you who still believe me a criminal, a liar, an outcast, a clever, vile murderer. Me, Your Honor: Quentin Hobson Clark, citizen of Baltimore, member of the Bar, a fond reader.

"This story is not about me. . . ." Here I looked down at my notes, and skipped ahead, reading almost to myself. "It was about something greater than I am, greater than all this, about a man by whom time will remember us though you had forgotten him before the earth settled. Somebody had to do it. We could not just keep still. I could not keep still. . . ."

I opened my mouth to say more, but I could not. There was another choice here, I realized. I could tell the story of what had *failed*. Of finding Duponte, of bringing him here, of the Bonapartes' men hunting him and mistakenly murdering the Baron. My words on this subject would reach the press, the Bonapartes would be in a scandal, Duponte would be stalked again wherever he had fled in the world, perhaps really extinguished from existence this time. I could completely finish what I had begun and banish it all to history.

I gripped my Malacca cane at both ends and almost felt it begin to come apart again. Then a shot rang out.

It seemed close enough to be inside the courtroom, and commotion instantly ensued. There were immediate suggestions and rumors that the courthouse was under siege by a madman. The judge directed his clerk to investigate, and then ordered all persons present to leave the courtroom until a state of calm could be returned. He said that all of us should return in forty minutes. At length there was a universal hubbub and a pair of officers began to herd everyone out of the room.

After a few moments, I was the only one remaining in the room— or I thought I was. Then I noticed my great-aunt. She wrapped her dark bonnet over her hair and straightened its peak. This was the first time since the start of the trial we were alone together.

"Great-Aunt," I pleaded, "perhaps you love me still, for you know I am the child of my father. Please, reconsider this. Do not contest the will, or my capabilities."

Her face looked cramped, withered with distaste. "You have lost your Hattie Blum— have lost Glen Eliza— lost all, Quentin, for a notion that you were a poet of some type instead of a lawyer. It is the old story, you know. You will think you have done something courageous because it was foolish. Poor Quentin. You can tell your complaint every day to the Sisters of Charity at their asylum after this, and you will not be able to afflict others anymore with excitement and worry."

I didn't reply, so she went on.

"You may think I act out of spite, but I tell you I do not. I act out of sorrow for you and for the memory of your parents. All of Baltimore will see that at my late age this is the last act of compassion I can provide, to stop you from being that most dangerous of monsters: the bustling do-nothing. May the folly of the past make you contrite for the future."

I remained at the witness stand, and was somewhat relieved and saddened when the courtroom had become absolutely silent. However, it gave me a peculiar feeling, for a courtroom was one of those places, like a banquet hall, that never felt empty even when it was. I slumped into the chair.

Even when I heard the door opening again, and heard my great-aunt murmur, "Pardon," with some offense, as she left, passing someone on their way inside, I found myself too lost in a staring spell of contemplation to turn around. If the madman who'd fired gun shots outside had come in, I suppose he could have me. Only when I heard the door closed from the inside did I start.

Auguste Duponte, dressed in one of his more elegant dark cloaks, took a few steps inside the court.

"Monsieur Duponte!" I exclaimed. "But did you not hear there is a madman in the courthouse?"

"Why, it was me, monsieur," said Duponte. He gestured outside. "I would rather the crowd not be here, in all events. I paid a vagrant to fire a few harmless shots into the air with the pistol you'd brought me so the people would have something to look at."

"You did? You used an accomplice, an assistant?" I marveled.

"Yes."

"But why did you not leave Baltimore the other day when you had planned? You can't remain here while they still may be looking for you. They may wish you harm."

"You were right, Monsieur Clark. About something you said at my hotel. I traveled to America never intending to resolve your mystery, which seemed as likely to not have a solution as to have one. I came here, as a point of fact, to end the conviction that I could do such things; the conviction that kept me for so long from living in any ordinary fashion. The conviction that frightened people, even the president of a republic, about what I might know that they wished to keep unknown. Yet people believed in the idea of it all, people wanted and feared it, even if I never appeared outside my chambers again. I suppose I could not remember if I believed in it before they did, or someone else was first."

"You wished to keep me diverted, while you plotted an escape from your pursuers and planned a sequence of occurrences that would leave behind your identity as the real Dupin. That was the nature of our inquiry to you— a distraction."

"Yes," he replied forthrightly, "I suppose at first. I believe I was tired: tired not of living but of having lived. Yet you persisted. You were certain we were here to resolve something— not only that we could, but that we were meant to. Did you tell them about the Baron's version? That mob outside the courthouse, I mean."

"I was about to tell them," I replied, with a humorless laugh, looking down at my memorandum book, where I had transcribed the Baron's entire lecture as I remembered it. Duponte asked to see it. I watched as he examined the pages.

"I will destroy this," I said when he put it back on the table. "I have decided. I will not lie about the death of a man of truth. It will never be repeated."

"But it will, Monsieur Clark," Duponte said gloomily. "Many times, probably."

"I have told no one the Baron's version!" I insisted. "I do not think he was able to tell Bonjour, or anyone else before he died. He wanted to glory in speaking it first in front of a crowd. The original document is destroyed, monsieur; I assure you, that was the only record of it."

"It is not a matter of whether he informed any associates of his conclusions. You see, the Baron is different from most only in his qualities of diligence and indelicacies and, if you wish, a certain bull-dog pertinacity not unlike your own. His ideas, however— wholly unoriginal. Thus we discover your mistake. Whether his speech burns in the prison stove or the Great Fire of Rome, his ideas shall return in the commonplace thoughts of others who inquire after Poe's death."

"But there are none— "

"There will be. Of course there will be. Other investigators, scores, hundreds of them. It may be many years, but the Baron's conclusions, and those equally appalling in their misperceptions and equally appealing in their humanity, shall rise again. They will not be stopped as long as Poe is remembered."

"Well, then, I will start with eliminating this one," I said, and tore out the first page where I had written the Baron's lines.

"Stay." He put out his hand.

"Monsieur?"

"They *should* not be stopped. Remember what I've said about the Baron?"

"We must see his mistakes," I said, a great, unexpected hope rising again in me, "to learn the truth."

"Yes. An example: I see from your memorandum book that the Baron mistakenly believed that Poe had arrived in Baltimore after being harassed on his way to New York. He concludes this merely because it was reported in the newspapers that Poe was on his way to New York to make arrangements for Muddy, the mother of Poe's deceased wife, to come live in Virginia with Poe and Poe's new fiancée, Elmira Shelton of Richmond. The Baron believes that because Poe did not board a train to New York immediately, a problem had arisen. The Baron demonstrates the common confusion of a plan that has been ruined with one that has been reconsidered. Let us follow."

"Follow?" My heart beat faster than Duponte's words.

Duponte turned stern. "Because you found me, Monsieur Clark."

"What?"

"You ask why I have risked coming today instead of fleeing safely. Because you found me. They were searching for me and you found me. Good fellow, if you will please!"

At this signal a porter wearing the Barnum's uniform now entered, pulling in one of Duponte's steamer trunks with such great effort it could have contained a human body inside. It was the very same trunk from which, in utter bewilderment, I had first picked up the Malacca cane. Duponte placed some coins in the man's hand for his labor and dismissed him, bolting the door to the courtroom after him.

"Now, as to the Baron . . . shall we follow?"

"Monsieur Duponte, do you mean . . . You confessed a moment ago that you did not in fact come here to resolve the particulars of Poe's death!"

"Dupe! Intentions are irrelevant to results. I never said we *have not* resolved it, Monsieur Clark, had I? Ready?"

"Ready."

"The Baron imagines that the ruffians at the harbor hounded Poe until the poet fled to the home of Dr. N. C. Brooks, where the same villains started a fire that all but burned down that home. The Baron's chain of natural errors begins with presuming that Poe's stop in Baltimore, because unplanned, was unintentional, that is, without intended purpose— and so only violent action could explain the extension of his stay. In fact, by the evidence of Poe's first destination, the Brooks home, we can draw an entirely different conclusion."

Duponte had discussed this with me before. "Brooks is a known editor and publisher," I added. "Poe was looking for support for his magazine, *The Stylus*, which would raise the standards for all periodical publication to follow."

"You are correct, as well as a bit dreamy as to its potential effects. In all events, if Poe were truly in danger at this point, and cognizant enough to flee as the Baron would have us believe, he may have reported it to a member of his family, however detestable they were to him— or even the police. Instead, Poe searches for an influential magazine editor! We may now erase those imagined ruffians from our picture and instead escort Poe to Dr. Brooks's house on his own will. Come."

I took my seat again at the witness table.

35

"**YOU HAVE OBSERVED** that the Baron was determined to understand the last days of Poe as a result of a sequence of increasingly violent
events. Here the Baron was gazing into a looking-glass. It is how the
Baron wished people to see his own troubles. He wished to remove from
Poe all possibility of indictment for his death by locating the cause of his
misfortune with external parties only."

"Then are you saying that the burning of Brooks's house had nothing
to do with Poe's search for sanctuary? A coincidence?"

"Not so, although we must reverse the connection in your statement.
Poe's failed search for sanctuary has everything to do with Brooks's
house burning down. Since we suspect that Poe started immediately for
Dr. Brooks's from the harbor, with his trunk, it is most certain that he anticipated finding not only literary assistance but a bed as well."

"Instead, he discovers that the house has burned, or is still burning,
depending on the exact day and hour of Poe's arrival, which we do not
know."

"Yes, and, either way, if the fire happened the very minute he came or
two days before, he is left to wander. Here is the difficulty. The doctor,
John J. Moran, who treated Poe days later at the hospital recalls that Poe
did not know *what he was doing in Baltimore* or *how he had gotten there.*
The temperance periodicals, in their search for a persuasive and incul-
cating lesson, employ this inference to suggest that Poe had begun drinking, had been absorbed entirely in a binge or spree, and this, their logic
runs, explains why he lost track of the days."

"You do not believe this?" I asked.

"It is the weakest kind of argument, not just flawed but obesely flawed.
It would be similar to you seeing me on the street one day, and then
again one week later, at which time I ask you for directions, and you
wonder how it is I had been lost for an entire week. You shall remember
we have already discussed the fact that an offer had been extended to
Poe to travel to Philadelphia and edit a book of poems by Mrs. St. Leon

Loud for a fee of one hundred dollars. An offer we know he accepted. Poe wrote to Muddy: 'Mr. Loud, the husband of Mrs. St. Leon Loud, the poetess of Philadelphia, called on me the other day and offered me one hundred dollars to edit his wife's poems. Of course, I accepted the offer. The whole labor will not occupy me three days.' These are Poe's words from earlier that summer, as we learn from the letters that have since been in print.

"If, as we have already decisively determined, Poe was in the process of collecting more capital for his magazine; and if, as we additionally surmised, Poe had added a stay in Baltimore to his itinerary at a late moment in search of enlarging this capital; and if whatever funds he did have would be diminished not by theft but by the necessity of securing a room at a hotel, then it is quite likely that, with this editing offer still standing from nearby Philadelphia, and his hoped-for conference with Dr. Brooks inhibited by the untimely fire, Poe would soon leave for Philadelphia to complete this easy work for the eager and wealthy poetess. Rather than several days 'lost,' as the temperance editors would like, no doubt Poe spent at least one night, possibly several, in a hotel here in Baltimore before securing an available train to Philadelphia. In this way, when Poe says to the hospital doctor while on his deathbed that he does not know how he came to be in Baltimore and *why* he is there, he is referring not to his arrival from Richmond, for which he would plainly know the purpose of his journey, but a *second arrival to Baltimore.* A journey back, at an indefinite time, but as early as the night before Poe's collapse at Ryan's hotel or as late as a few hours before that collapse, taken in some self-obscurity, resulting from a trip to Philadelphia."

"But you have shown, monsieur," I reminded him, "by examining her book of poetry and the poem about his death, that Poe did *not* edit Mrs. Loud's poems, and that, calling him a 'stranger,' she had not seen him in Philadelphia at any time in close proximity to his death. You remarked to me that this was only the first document of two proving this. But now you speak of Poe's trip to Philadelphia. Have you changed your mind?"

Duponte raised one finger. "Careful. I did not say Poe *arrived* in Philadelphia."

"You are correct that I have in the past alluded to a second demonstration that Poe did not arrive in Philadelphia, if any evidence is needed beyond that culled from Madame St. Leon Loud's lyrical productions. You will now remember that Poe instructed Muddy to write him in Philadelphia as 'E. S. T. Grey Esquire.' Would you re-peruse from your portfolio these apparently obscure instructions from Monsieur Poe?"

I did so: "'Write immediately in reply and direct to Philadelphia. For fear I should not get the letter, sign no name and address it to E. S. T. Grey Esqre.'" I paused and put the extract down. "Monsieur, do say you have an answer to such a strange and indecipherable cipher!"

"Cipher! Strange! The only cipher here is in the eyes of those who look and do not understand, and so decide they must be solving some puzzle."

Duponte opened the lid of the trunk that had been brought in by the porter. It was filled to the very top with newspapers. "Before coming to find you here, I stopped at Glen Eliza. Your girl, Daphne, a domestic of excellent character and dry wit, very kindly allowed me to remove a considerable portion of our newspaper collection which had sat untouched in your library these last months. Indeed, she insinuated that I should advise you to discard such papers, for they have made housekeeping in that chamber impossible. Now," he said, turning back to me, "describe for me, if you please, where precisely lies the mystery of Poe's instructions to his darling Muddy?"

I read it again silently. *For fear I should not get the letter . . .* "First, he seems to have a striking and unusual fear of not receiving the letter."

"True."

"And, in addition, he contrives a rather elaborate method by which he imagines he can prevent this. Resorting, indeed, to using this false name, E. S. T. Grey!"

"Some might say this is our best clue yet that Poe, in the end, was mad— delusional."

"You do not agree though?"

"The contention would be entirely backward! Choices, my good Monsieur Clark, are both less rational and far less *predictable* than they seem, and this is what makes them so very predictable to the thinking man. Monsieur Poe, we should remember, is no ordinary specimen; his decisions which appear so irrational seem so because they are, in truth, utterly *rational*. We may benefit from being reminded about where Poe is going, when he writes these words in the fall of 1849, and where his mother-in-law is receiving his letters."

"Easy enough. Poe, upon writing, plans to start on his way to Philadelphia prior to continuing home to Fordham, New York, to bring Muddy back to Richmond, where he will marry Elmira Shelton. Muddy receives the letter in their small country home in New York. As I say, though, *that* seems easy enough."

"Then so is your answer to his unusual instructions. You have spoken before of the many cities where Poe had lived in his adult years."

"After Baltimore, he had moved with Sissy and Muddy to Richmond, Virginia, for several years. Then to Philadelphia for around six years. And finally, in the last years of his life, he was living in New York with Muddy."

"Yes! Therefore, you see, Muddy must write 'E. S. T. Grey, Esquire.' "

I looked at my companion incredulously. "I don't see at all!"

"Why, Monsieur Clark, do you refuse outright the simplicity of the thing when it has been uncovered for us? I have been fortunate that on several occasions during my stay you have described in some precise and *exacting* detail the workings of your American post offices. In the year in question, 1849, if I have understood you, letters in your country were never delivered to particular residences but still only to the post office of a city, where one could then retrieve mail waiting for him. If a letter arrives in 1849 in New York for Edgar A. Poe, E. A. Poe comes and receives it. If a letter arrived in 1849 at the Philadelphia post office addressed to 'Edgar A. Poe,' consider then what would unavoidably follow. The postmaster in Philadelphia, consulting his list of names of those *former* residents of the city, and finding that a name matches one on that list, would forward it to the post office at the location of that person's current residence. That is to say, a letter sent from Muddy in New York to Philadelphia addressed to *Edgar A. Poe* would upon receipt at the post office in Philadelphia be treated as a mistake and instantly be returned to New York!"

"Of course!" I exclaimed.

He went on. "Muddy, being also a former resident of Philadelphia, would understand this and find nothing strange in Poe's instructions *that appear so peculiar to us.* Poe's apparently outlandish fear that he would not receive a letter sent by Muddy to Philadelphia is, in fact, completely reasonable. If Edgar Poe presented himself with his own name at the Philadelphia post office, there would surely be nothing waiting for him, for any such letter branded with his name would have been sent away; however, if he offers a fictitious name, arranged in advance with his correspondent, and a letter has been sent to that name, he would duly receive it."

"But what of his instructions to Muddy not to sign the letter?"

"Poe has been anxious. Muddy is the last remnant of his family con-
nections. *Write immediately in reply,* he says. Receiving this letter is crucial, and here he exhibits signs of some excess of care— once again, not
of illogic, but of *excessive rationality.* He knows that, in the process of
folding and sealing a letter, the signature and the address may be confused. If such a confusion were to take place, and the Philadelphia postmaster mistakenly believed the letter *addressed* to Maria Clemm, rather
than *signed by her,* the letter, once again, would take route directly back
to New York. You might notice that Monsieur Poe was generally anxious
about mail in your own occasional correspondence with him, when at
several points he expresses worry that a letter was lost or misplaced. 'Ten
to one I misdirected the letter, for I am very thoughtless about such matters,' he writes in one instance (if I rightly recall) when speaking of someone who had not replied to one of his letters. We know, too, from Poe's
history that his first infamous heartbreak was caused when his letters as
a young man never reached his young love, Elmira; and that another
early courtship, of his cousin Elizabeth Herring, was disrupted by Henry
Herring reading the letters, which contained his poetry. Indeed, the confusion over the placement of a letter, the anxiety over who possesses it,
and the perplexing variety of folding and addressing through which a letter's identity might be misapprehended form the topic of one of Monsieur Poe's better tales of ratiocination and analysis, with which I know
you are quite familiar.

"Still there is the question of the pseudonym that Poe chooses, this
E. S. T. Grey. In truth, it matters not what name he chooses as long as it
is *not* Edgar Poe, and is not so common as a George Smith or a Thomas
Jones, which would put it at risk to be taken up by another person in a
pile of other mail. Thus, Monsieur Poe desires Muddy to use a name with
not one but *two* middle initials so that it may be that much more likely
to reach him.

"Still you desire more significance to the name, I suppose? Very well.
You will see, in some of the late numbers of the failed magazine *Broadway Journal,* of which Poe was editor, that he twice inserts an advertisement
asking for capital to help secure the (doomed) future of that publication.
In these notices he asks that correspondence for such purposes be addressed to 'E. S. T. G.' at the office of the journal. Perhaps he wished to
be discreet in the collection of any money. At all events, when he writes

Muddy this letter four years later, he is once again engaged in a hopeful attempt to control his own magazine— this time *The Stylus*— and the same *nom de plume* of E. S. T. Grey perhaps automatically recurs to him from the similarity of his situation, and the corresponding position of his hopes for his delayed success. The letters of the name themselves— E. S. T. G.— need no more meaning, no more *cipher,* than the connection they hold for him between the two epochs of his life. Hieroglyphs and symmetries are for those who think too much of thinking. The mystery of Poe's instructions to his mother-in-law, then, we have entirely dismissed." Duponte, with a hint of satisfaction, returned the papers related to the topic to the trunk.

"Except . . ." I began. Seeing a flash in Duponte's eyes, I stopped myself.

"Except?"

"Did you not once say, Monsieur Duponte, that this point would form a second piece of proof most sure that Poe did not arrive at Philadelphia?"

"I did. You will remember that one of the obituaries you collected after Poe's death was from the Philadelphia *Public Ledger*? I believe you will find it also in the selection I've brought from Glen Eliza."

The obituary was in an issue of the *Ledger* from October 9, 1849, two days after Poe's death in Baltimore. I located the newspaper and passed it to Duponte.

He handed it back. "What is this?"

"Why, the very paper you asked for, Monsieur Duponte!"

"I asked for no such thing! I merely stated that it would be found in the trunk. Return it there. This obituary of Monsieur Poe in itself is as flimsy as most of the others. But you will not fail to remember that I instructed you, soon after our arrival in Baltimore, to retrieve all issues of newspapers a week before and after each article."

"I cannot fail to remember," I agreed.

"It is the set of numbers prior to that obituary to which you should direct your interest. As you find them, recall that you have already read Poe beseeching his Muddy to 'write immediately in reply' to his letter. In the very same note, he closes by pleading *again,* as though she *could* forget: 'Don't forget to write immediately to Philadelphia so that your letter will be there when I arrive.' Surely she could not ignore his urgent entreaties to hear a kind word from her along his journey."

I took up all the issues of the Philadelphia *Public Ledger* I could find in the contents of the chest. Duponte instructed me to open the paper dated October 3, 1849— the very day Poe was discovered at Ryan's inn in Baltimore. He directed me further to the post office column on the last page— the place in the paper where the postmaster cataloged names of persons with letters waiting to be retrieved. *List of Letters Remaining in the Phil. Post-Office*, it said. There, in the small print of the lengthy gentlemen's list, I found the following entry:

GREY, E. S. F.

Turning quickly to the next date that contained a post office's advertisement of remaining letters, I found the same name again.

"It must be him!" I said.

"Of course it is. Here we see E. S. *F.* Grey, rather than E. S. T. The letter *F*, we may be sure, may be readily mistaken for 'T' in the hand of those who write with flair, as Poe exhibits in his letters to you, Monsieur Clark. Muddy mistook Poe's *T* for an *F*; or the Philadelphia post office mistook her own *T* for an *F*; or the *Ledger* mistook the postmaster's *T* for an *F*. Poe's changing name has changed again— but have no doubt. This is Muddy's very letter to Poe, arriving in Philadelphia precisely, if one were to calculate the speed of mail, at the expected time after Muddy would have received Poe's letter of September 18 and, in ordinary haste, composed and deposited her letter in reply to Monsieur *Grey* with the New York post office."

"And the *Ledger* lists it on two separate days."

"Significant, Monsieur Clark, if I understand the regulations of your postal office as you have explained them."

"That's true. The first time a letter must be advertised one is charged two cents additional in postage. If it must be advertised a second and final time, one will be required to pay another two cents. Soon after, it becomes a 'dead letter'— discarded by the postmaster."

"October 3, when the letter is first listed in the Philadelphia *Ledger*, was the last day Poe was ever to see outside a hospital room again," Duponte mused absently. "On that day, we could have idly strolled through the door of the Philadelphia post office and announced ourselves as E. S. T. (or *F.*, if you please) Grey— Esquire— for you are no less Grey than Poe was— and received this letter."

"Likely this was the last letter ever written to Edgar Poe," I said sadly, looking again at the name of the addressee, and thinking it sadder still that this last, unseen, and now long-abandoned letter did not even have his name on it and, presumably, went unsigned with the name of that woman who loved him.

"Likely it was," Duponte said, nodding.

"I would like to have seen it."

"But you *need* not. I mean, not for our purposes. This listing in the newspaper demonstrates that, for the period reflected by the postmaster's advertisements, Edgar Poe was not in Philadelphia. For remember how strongly he insisted that Muddy write immediately so the letter would be there at the point of his arrival; if his arrival had occurred, we must not doubt, he would have called there with an eager heart."

"Therefore we have another reason to confidently testify that Poe did not reach Philadelphia," Duponte continued. "But we have many reasons, as we already enumerated, to believe he would have tried, and we may believe him to have come close."

"But if he tried and did not make it there, what happened?"

"You remember what we have said of Poe's drinking habits."

"Yes. That Poe was not intemperate but constitutionally intolerant to a degree unknown to most people. The fact that Poe's entire nature could be reversed by a single glass of wine, as attested by numerous people who knew him well, indicated *not* that Poe was habitually intoxicated, but rather the opposite— that Poe carried a rare sensitivity. Too many persons, in disparate places and times, have testified to this fact for one to believe it is only a polite excuse by those friendly to him. One glass, we have learned, was enough to produce a frightful attack of insensibility which could lead him to other uncertain and uncontrolled behavior. Could this have happened before he arrived to Philadelphia?" I proposed.

"Let us see in a moment. We have now surmised, using all the information available, both that Poe would have in all likelihood attempted to travel to Philadelphia and yet, despite this, that he would not have arrived. The question remains how Poe returns to Baltimore. The Baron, if his reasoning had reached this far, would then proclaim a guess, no doubt, that once Poe was aboard the train to Philadelphia, a rogue accosted him and forced him, for some inconceivable malicious motive, to return on *another train* to Baltimore, where Poe was later found. The Baron is romantic in the same way the writers of love tales and sketches are. It would make no sense at all for an assailant of any stripe to put Poe back on a train to Baltimore.

"Yet this does not mean that someone else, someone with no malicious motives, did not do so. In fact, it is an activity that a railroad conductor engages in regularly for a variety of reasons, for persons who are unruly, unconscious, sickly, stowaways, and the like. Far more likely than meeting such an aggressor on the train for someone who, like Poe, has previously lived both in the point of origin, Baltimore, and in the destination, Philadelphia— is to meet an *acquaintance* that is traveling on the same route.

"It is not much more than a *guess*, you will say, but sometimes that is all that is there, Monsieur Clark, to make sense of events. We speak of the word as inferior to trained practices of reasoning— in fact, to guess is one of the most elevated and indestructible powers of the human mind, a far more interesting art than reasoning or demonstration because it comes to us directly from imagination.

"Now, we shall imagine Poe meeting an acquaintance, rather than an enemy; and that acquaintance, by nature someone who is *acquainted* with Poe but does not know Poe intimately, inviting him for a drink on the train, or in an intervening railway station. We can imagine Poe, perhaps hoping to procure further financial support for his magazine, accepting the invitation, the insistence from this potential benefactor, of *one drink*— presented, no doubt, by one unfamiliar enough with Poe as an adult not to know his problems with the intake of spirits. Perhaps, then, a childhood friend, or let us say a classmate from West Point since, more than any other institution, former members of the army are likely to be scattered throughout the different states. Or, perhaps, a classmate from earlier, in Poe's days at college. Perhaps we have heard the name of one of such school-friends already in the facts we have collected."

"Z. Collins Lee!" I said. "He was a classmate of Poe's from college and is now the district attorney, and he was the fourth man who attended Poe's funeral."

"Monsieur Lee is an interesting possibility, a member of the funeral party we have overlooked for three others who have been more readily notable. Consider this. Besides the sexton, Mr. Spence; the undertaker; the grave digger; and the minister, there were exactly four mourners at Poe's small funeral ceremony."

"Yes— Dr. Snodgrass, Neilson Poe, Henry Herring, and Mr. Z. Collins Lee. Those were all who came."

"Think of what the first three mourners have in common, Monsieur

Clark— that they knew Edgar Poe, of course. But this would be true for many people in Baltimore, certainly more than four individuals, since Poe lived in this city for several years. Former teachers, lovers, friends, other relatives. No. More notable is the common fact that each of the three was involved in some way with Poe's *final days*. Monsieur Herring was at Ryan's hotel, where Poe was discovered and where, afterward, Snodgrass was called to assist; and Neilson Poe was present at the hospital after being notified of his cousin's condition. The funeral was not announced in advance in the newspapers or by other means and, surely, these three gentlemen could have encouraged more people to attend if they wished.

"Should we not think it highly likely, then, noticing what is true of all three other mourners, that our Z. Collins Lee would also have seen Poe sometime in his last days before his death? Lee is a wealthy man, and indeed as good a candidate as any to have been on the train and, remembering college days, which are always rather debauched, taken a single drink with Poe. Poe, on his part, would know Monsieur Lee was a person of consequence in the field of law, and would seek to be convivial in order to solicit needed support for his magazine campaign. If true, this would instantly explain two facts: not only the incident on the train, but Monsieur Lee's presence at the funeral about which so few people knew. After their meeting, if we continue, Poe begins a bout of insensibility, as you term it, from this single indulgence. This is what our other temperance group, the Richmond Sons of Temperance, to which your Monsieur Benson belonged, did not wish to accept long enough to complete their inquiry. They wished Poe not to drink a drop as much as the other traders in temperance wished him *to* drink a barrel. Thus Monsieur Benson seemed to you to be hiding something. No doubt he had discovered, after arriving to Baltimore so soon after Poe's death, this small incident."

"But stay! Back to the one drink on the train. Would not the friend," I said indignantly, "whether Mr. Collins Lee or someone unknown to us, tend to Poe when he fell ill?"

"If, as we might envision, this friend knows nothing of Poe's special circumstance in relation to drink; and if Poe, embarrassed by it, attempts as much as possible to suppress his mental and rational degradation for the sake of his personal dignity, then the friend may walk away, having little or no indication of leaving behind a person in distress. Though Poe may still feel abandoned by such an incident, that would be hardly noticeable to the innocent acquaintance. A man like Z. Collins Lee, a much-occupied attorney, might only discover something wrong days later, upon encountering his fellow attorney Neilson Poe and mentioning having seen Neilson's cousin earlier. Recall for a moment how the poet responds, if you would, when Dr. Moran at the Baltimore hospital, thinking to soothe his distressed patient, promises to find Poe's friends?"

"The best thing my best friend could do would be to blow out my brains with a pistol!"

"Yes! A friend, it seems to Poe at this late moment, can only harm him, Monsieur Clark. Can we not tell why? Can we not find the origin of these sentiments in the final footsteps of the poet? He ventures to find Dr. Brooks, and instead finds only homelessness. He meets an old friend on the train, only to feel obligated to partake in a dangerous temptation. He mentions his friend Dr. Snodgrass once he is at Ryan's, only to be confronted with Snodgrass's disapproving stares and obvious, if silent, accusations that Poe is a drunken sot. His own relative Henry Herring stands over him at Ryan's, but rather than bringing him to his own house, sends him alone to a declining hospital.

"Do you believe, we should ask the temperance press as an aside, that Poe would have summoned Dr. *Snodgrass*, of all people on earth, were he indeed in the midst of this supposed spree? We shall not deny that Monsieur Poe confessed to excessive drinking during periods in his history, and also will readily admit that he established a pattern of reforming himself alternating with a return to excess. Yet it is because of this, as an experienced drinker and reformer, that we can intelligently interpret his specific mention of Snodgrass made to Monsieur Walker at Ryan's— we can *read* this mention with proper spectacles. Were Poe in the middle of a binge, were he breaking his pledge, the last person he would name is a principal leader of the local temperance movement like Snodgrass. Moreover, Poe may have overheard in a conversation around Ryan's, while there, that Monsieur Walker was attached in the capacity of a printer to the *Sun*, so that Walker would be a direct witness to his situation. Moreover again, had Poe read any numbers of the recent papers, he would see that Snodgrass had only one day earlier been forced to renounce his organization's candidate, John Watchman, for drinking, and would be seeking to counterbalance this event as would any politician. No, Poe said *Snodgrass's* name to *Walker* as a message, as if to remark in so many words: 'I have not been in the cups; in fact, I have been so moderate, if not quite wholly abstemious, that the one name I shall single out to come to my aid will be an avid and strict temperance man, and I shall do so to a fellow who works for the press.'"

Duponte continued: "Back to our train. Poe has separated from his friend— who, let us suppose, leaves the train first, or merely returns to a different carriage. Distressed at his physical shakiness, Poe is observed by a solicitous railroad conductor, who determines that Poe has become ill— *how*, the conductor cannot know. This conductor for whatever reason presumes Poe is more likely to have some persons as caretakers back in Baltimore, or Poe perhaps mumbles something interpreted in this fashion by the conductor. The conductor, seeing this as an opportunity to be benevolent, places Poe in an opposite-moving train at the next *depot* (as I notice Americans always call your stations), perhaps at Havre de Grace.

"With this in mind, we may think of the facts at the hospital with more confidence. Poe replies to the doctor's questions that he does not know *how* he has come to Baltimore or *why*— he cannot explain these facts. It is not because of successive days of bingeing. Nor is it because he has been given opiates by political fiends, as the Baron says. It is because Poe refers to his *second* arrival to Baltimore, after he had left, and had been in a cloud of confusion about how he ended up on a train back. We have thus countered the temperance press's claims about Poe, as well as the Baron's argument that Poe had to be *kidnapped* by a political club."

I could see how we had demonstrated the temperance claims untrue, but had not related this to the Baron's argument. I proposed the question to Duponte.

"Do you recall the Baron's conclusion on this point, Monsieur Clark, as you wrote it down in your book?"

I did.

The political rogues of the Fourth Ward Whigs, who kept their head-quarters in the den of the Vigilant Fire Company's engine house across from Ryan's, placed the helpless poet in a cellar with other unfortunates— vagrants, strangers, loafers (as Americans say), foreigners. This explains why Poe, a heartily well-known author, was not seen by anyone over the course of these few days.

"Do you see, touching the issue of recognition, the Baron's misplaced logic? As a result of the Baron's own actions in relation to the press of Baltimore and elsewhere, and because of the numerous biographical volumes and articles since Poe's death, Poe's portrait has been widely circulated among the masses and his visage becomes *known* even as his death has begun to be studied. But before this, when Poe was alive, he would have been recognized, as a rule, only by literary fellows and avid readers, who at the very least would have been somewhat less likely to be out in the street and more likely to spend their daylight hours indoors, in offices, libraries, and reading rooms. Thus, that Poe was not reported to be seen over the course of these days becomes far less surprising, if even at all notable. Moreover, as he was a visitor to Baltimore, in an unannounced stay, no one would have anticipated seeing Poe around the city, even among his relations. This, if we think of the way of the human mind and eye, *greatly reduces recognition.* Have you ever had occasion to notice how, when you unexpectedly happened upon a close friend in a locale where you did not expect to see him, some greater than usual amount of time was required to register the identity of this person in your brain— indeed, more time than if you had seen someone with whom you were far less intimate? For the latter's status remains closer to the *stranger* on the street, and thus more easily identified among them.

"This is a general fault that the newspapers make, too, Monsieur Clark. Re-peruse the New York *Herald* extract and you will see."

I opened my memorandum book, where I had written the testimony I had planned to give to the court that day. The relevant portion from the week of Poe's death, written by their correspondent in Baltimore, read as follows:

> On last Wednesday, election day, he was found near the Fourth Ward polls laboring under an attack of mania a potu, and in a most shocking condition. Being recognized by some of our citizens, he was placed in a carriage and conveyed to the Washington Hospital, where every attention has been bestowed on him.

"You notice the fault, don't you, Monsieur Clark? The correspondent from Baltimore tries hard to maintain facts in their true form. For instance, it is quite accurate and specific that Poe was *placed* in a carriage by others who did not drive with him, as we shall witness shortly. And yet we know, on the other hand, that Poe was not recognized by citizens. This has been written down for us by a first-hand witness."

"Do you mean the note from Walker to Dr. Snodgrass, which we found among Snodgrass's papers?"

"I do. Walker writes, 'There is a gentleman, rather the worse for wear, at Ryan's 4th Ward polls, who goes under the cognomen of Edgar A. Poe, and who appears in great distress' and so on. To Walker, Poe is 'a gentleman'; it is only through some communication by Poe of his proper name that Walker knows who to tell Snodgrass is in distress. Indeed, Walker's language— 'who goes under the *cognomen* of Edgar A. Poe'— suggests he has some suspicions that the man is called something else entirely! As though it were an alias. Should he not write, 'The gentleman Edgar A. Poe appears in great distress' instead?"

At Duponte's request, I continued reciting to him the Baron's account of Poe's last days.

"The miscreants probably drugged Poe with various opiates. When election day came, they took him around the city to various polling stations. They forced him to vote for their candidates at each polling venue and, to make the whole farce more convincing, the poet was made to wear different outfits each time. This explains why he was found in ragged, soiled clothes never meant to fit him. He was permitted by the rogues to keep his handsome Malacca cane, however, for he was in such a weakened state that even those ruffians recognized that the cane would be needed to prop him up. . . . In fact, he would be found with this very cane. . . ."

Duponte, listening to this, pointed out with some satisfaction that the Baron's argument, though clever, seeks to find a reason for Poe's location at an election polling station and for Poe's clothing, rather than to use reason to find the truth behind that location and appearance.

"Without a home, in a place where his family once lived, where some of his family lived still, the effect on Poe's senses to be back in Baltimore, where he was once *most at home*— combined with the effects of his single indulgence in the company of Z. Collins Lee or another friend— is to make him now feel utterly alone. Without shelter he has no choice but to walk through the dreadful rain looking for it, thus soaking his clothing and exposing him to the onset of any number of additional maladies. You have already seen first-hand, I believe, the special quality of clothing most people fail to consider. When soaked, we say of our clothes, 'My shirt is useless, it is ruined.' Unlike any other 'ruined' article, its desolation, shall we say, like the great Sphinx, is temporary; you have seen that these special qualities allow Poe to trade his own outfit for dry clothes, which of course *do not fit him as does a usual tailored outfit.* This occurred likely near Ryan's. We may note that of all the detailed descriptions of Poe's clothes upon his discovery, for all the adjectives chosen to show his

dejection, none call the dress *wet*, though this should be the first word
otherwise used. The special cane with the expensively designed sword we
know Poe did not sell or trade— for even in his state of mind he remembered that it did not belong to him. He had to take care to return it to its
owner, Dr. Carter, in Richmond. It was his dignity, not his fear of violence, that kept his friend's cane clutched to his chest.

"In considering Poe at Ryan's hotel, we now reach the Baron's suspicion of the Herring family, George and Henry. It will not do, as the Baron
would have it, to confuse collateral events with the subject of our inquiry.
As you have observed in your report to me after hearing the account of
Dr. Snodgrass, when Dr. Snodgrass saw Poe's condition, he walked upstairs to secure a room for Poe before sending for Poe's relatives, whom
he knew lived in the vicinity. Yet no sooner had Snodgrass done this than
Henry Herring was standing at the foot of the stairs— *before* Snodgrass
had sent for him. Snodgrass, occupied with his private concerns and with
the state of Poe's health, did not seem to think much of this startling fact
when relating it in your presence. But we know better.

"George Herring, Henry's uncle, has been identified as the president
of the Whigs of the Fourth Ward, the group who used Ryan's hotel on
several occasions in the weeks before the election for a rally, including
once two days before the election. The Baron makes the assumption that
after such efforts, George Herring would have also certainly been at
Ryan's, this Whig fortress, on election day itself, the day Poe was found.
In this his reasoning is sound. However, the Baron then determines that
Henry and George Herring, knowing that Edgar Poe experienced bad effects from any intoxicant, conspired to choose him to 'coop' and thus become one of their voters to be brought throughout the city."

"Still, it is remarkably coincidental, I would venture to say suspicious,
Monsieur Duponte, if George and Henry Herring were both present at
Ryan's before Dr. Snodgrass even called for Poe's relatives!"

"There is one coincidental event there, Monsieur Clark, and this one
in fact is rather merely a coincidence, and renders the other occurrence
quite natural. The coincidence I mean is George Herring's presence in
the same place that Poe is discovered. George Herring is here because he
is the president of the Fourth Ward Whigs, and Ryan's is the Fourth Ward
polling station on that day. His presence is natural. Why Poe is present
here we will address in a moment. Henry Herring is Poe's uncle by marriage, to a woman who has now been deceased for some years; and whose

decease was followed, very shortly after, by another marriage, contributing, we can presume, to Poe's characterization of Monsieur Henry in a letter as a man of 'unprincipled character.' Generally speaking, then, Poe ends up in quite a threefold busy place— that is, a hotel, tavern, and polling station— with a man who is the uncle of a *former* uncle. I fear this is not in itself so much a coincidence as the Baron would like.

"At all events, the Baron proposes that George Herring selects Poe to be a member of this voting coop because Monsieur George possesses from his family knowledge of Poe's vulnerability when under the influence of even normal intoxicants. A notorious idea! Because Monsieur George is likely to know of Poe's unpredictability with intoxicants, that would be the precise reason not to choose Poe for a coop, where only men who could tolerate alcohol well would do!

"But, leaving behind the Baron's tales of the coop, we return to our so-called coincidences. Given that George Herring would have some knowledge and perhaps acquaintance with Poe through Henry Herring, upon seeing Poe in distress, Monsieur George would almost certainly send for Monsieur Henry Herring. Our mere coincidence, the presence of George Herring and Edgar Poe in the same tri-purpose building, gives rise very naturally to our second incident, the odd arrival of Henry Herring before Snodgrass has called for him.

"And what mean the subsequent events that led to Poe's being sent to the hospital? Snodgrass has offered to engage a room upstairs in the hotel portion of the building. George Herring would not want Poe to stay at Ryan's in poor condition, for as Whig president he would want to avoid *precisely* the sort of accusations of fraudulent or rough use of voters that the Baron would in fact later allege. Henry Herring was not particularly a boon companion to Poe, as the Baron is right to say— and would rather not invite Poe to his house, where Monsieur Henry still remembers with disapproval Poe's courtship of his daughter Elizabeth years before. Snodgrass could not remember whether there were one or two relatives of Poe's at Ryan's— this is almost certainly because both Henry and George Herring stood before him. Poe is therefore sent to the hospital, whose attendants then send word to Neilson Poe."

"If there was nothing insidious, if the Herrings did nothing, Monsieur Duponte, then why would Henry Herring and Neilson Poe, cousin to Henry Herring as well as Edgar Poe, be so reluctant to speak on the matter, or for the police to make inquiries?"

"You have answered your question in asking it, Monsieur Clark. Because they did nothing— that is, strikingly little— they had no wish to call attention to the matter. Think of it. George and then Henry Herring were present even before Dr. Snodgrass, and did nothing. When something was done, it was to send Poe to the hospital alone, in the prostrate position across the carriage seats. They forgot, even, to pay the driver, as you heard from Dr. Moran. They have sealed his fate, too, by assuming Poe was merely boozy, and excessively in liquor, for they no doubt passed this assumption to the doctors through the note that accompanied Poe to the hospital— so that the care given to the patient, rather than for the complex illness and perhaps multitude of illnesses that have set in from his exhaustion and exposure, would be that superficial kind given to all those who come in with too much drink. Neilson Poe came to the hospital, but could not even see the patient.

"This narrative is not one of pride for the family, particularly for an ambitious man like Monsieur Neilson, who did not want to tarnish the name Poe. This explains, too, the lack of attempt from the family to produce a larger funeral. They would not wish to draw attention to their roles in his final days, nor wish to remind anyone that Edgar Poe himself had formerly said caustic words about both Henry Herring and Neilson Poe. There is some 'shame' in it, which is the word Snodgrass writes in his poem on the subject. The methods by which it is often necessary to understand someone's motives are not by what they have done, but what they have simply omitted to do and neglected to consider."

"And yet," continued Duponte, "the Baron is not wholly misguided in looking to the fact of Poe's discovery falling on an election day as more than *chance*. The Baron wishes to find cause and effect; we, on the other hand, shall look for cause and cause. How, monsieur, would you describe the city of Baltimore on days elections are held?"

"A bit unpredictable," I admitted, "wild at times. Dangerous, in certain quarters. But does this mean Poe was *kidnapped*?"

"Of course not. The mistake of men like the Baron, who apply their giddy thoughts to creating violence, is to imagine that most violence contains sense and reason, when, by its nature, this is just what it is lacking. Yet we must not dismiss the *secondary* effects that may come from outside disruptions. Think of Monsieur Poe. Exposed to the deplorable weather, having failed to secure the ready money from Philadelphia, his

constitution weakened and confused by his single glass of spirits, Poe
would have been vulnerable to the greatest detriments to our health:
first, fear, and second, dread.

"Now, those local newspapers that you went out to collect shortly after
our arrival from Paris, will you put them on this table?"

❖   ❖   ❖

The first cutting that Duponte selected was from the Baltimore *Sun*,
October 4, the day after the election. *Very little excitement*, it read, reporting the events of the election. *We heard of no disturbance of the polls
or elsewhere.*

Another cutting from the same day read as follows:

> Yesterday afternoon a fellow with about as much liquor
> in him as he could conveniently carry, stationed himself
> at the foot of Lexington market, and for an hour assailed
> and assaulted every man that passed by, all of whom,
> very fortunately for the poor inebriate, appeared to be
> exceedingly good-natured, or they would have "tripped
> him up." He struck several of them in the face, but they
> forbore to resent it on account of his having "seen the
> elephant." He afterwards went in a tavern, and thence
> proceeded to the office of Justice Root, which was closed
> (it being dinner hour) seeking perhaps for justice.

And finally this, reported of the same afternoon:

> Assault. About dusk on Wednesday evening, as a car-
> riage containing four persons amongst whom was Mr.
> Martin Rudolph, engineer of the steamer *Columbia*, was
> proceeding past the corner of Lombard and Light Street,
> some atrocious miscreant threw a large stone, which
> struck Mr. R on the head, fortunately occasioning noth-
> ing more than a severe bruise.

"The first article," Duponte said, "insists there was *no disturbance*
anywhere in the city. Yet here, separately, we find some samples of what
we can only label disturbances. You see, in a newspaper, especially the

finest ones, one hand hardly notices the other or, rather, one column hardly notices the other, and so only by reading the entire newspaper— never just a single article— can we claim to have done any reading at all. They likely were told of the lack of disturbances by some policeman. Police in Europe want all criminals to know they are there; police in America want people to believe there are no criminals.

"Let us examine these two separate disturbances. First, we have a loud and rude fellow, alleged to have struck *in the face* several men passing by, and yet left without molestation by his fellow citizens. While the editor from the leisurely position of his desk would prefer to believe that the lack of outrage from the surrounding public was caused by the fact that the inebriate was 'good-natured,' I would ask how many good-natured fellows have been classified to be so after they punched men in their faces. Rather, we can safely surmise that the nature of the disturbance, remarkably, was common enough that day as to not sufficiently arrest the attention either of the authorities or the common people. That is, there were so many like this one that he could not claim much public response. This may give us more idea of the goings-on during election day in the rest of the city than the editors imagine.

"Taking now the third extract, describing a scene not far in distance, I believe, from the location of the polling station where Poe was discovered on Lombard and High; read again this cutting, which describes an engineer and his fellow carriage passengers being struck by a large stone thrown by some miscreant. We may imagine Poe, too, having to dodge a tempest of wild stones on those streets or, perhaps, now ill from the drink, the terrible exposure of many hours to the weather, and complete lack of sleep, Poe may have himself been disoriented enough to be throwing stones at perceived or real villains, thugs, and rascals that filled the streets that day. It hardly makes a difference if we think of Poe as target or as targeting, or involved in this incident not at all. What we know is that Poe would likely possess a manic fear at this point in reaction to whatever wild and disorderly actions he might witness along the streets that day. The polling station, rather than being a dark dungeon of cruelty— as your Baron finds it necessary to envision it— may well have been seen by Poe as a sanctuary, a place where there would likely be the semblance of some order. Poe went in for help that, alas, was too late to be found. In this way, we have thoroughly followed Poe from his disembarking to his futile rescue by Snodgrass."

"But Poe's words from the hospital," I said. "His shouts of 'Reynolds'—could this not be an indication of some responsibility or knowledge on the part of Henry Reynolds, that carpenter who served as ward judge for the election in the location where Poe was found?"

Duponte's face broke out in genuine amusement.

"Do you not believe it?" I asked.

"I haven't a reason to disbelieve it as a factual possibility, if that is your meaning, Monsieur Clark. Others will think they can guess what is unusual in Poe's mind— an impossibility to do for anyone, much less for a genius. To do that, read his tales, read his poems; you shall get all that is extraordinary and singular— that is, not repeated in mental currents outside of Poe. But to understand the steps in his death, you must accept what is ordinary in him, in anyone, and in all around him that crash into his genius— these will be answers.

"That Poe called this word, 'Reynolds,' for many hours the night of his death in the hospital is exactly what we should *not* pay attention to— if our purpose is to understand how he died. Poe was not in his clear mind, arising from the joining of disparate circumstances that we have already enumerated. That the Baron, that other observers might fixate on it demonstrates the common lack of understanding about how and why people think and act as they do. Even without profound consideration of the matter, we may remember that Poe is in a state of feeling completely alone. In truth, he could have been calling for anybody. It might have been the last name he had heard, perhaps belonging to that same carpenter who visited us in your parlor, or it might have been the name of a man whose part in a deadly affair of several years past renders it far too dangerous for either of us to speak about.* Most likely, though, it has something to do with a matter far distant from his death that we must never know about, for that is what Poe would be thinking about, just as a man trapped in a pit would be thinking of escape, not of the pit. Not about the death that is all too close upon him, but about life left behind.

"You understand now. All this, all that he did in the days since stepping off the boat from Richmond, was an escape from Baltimore— from his lack of home. This city had *once* been his home, the land of his father and

---

*I implored Duponte to expand on this ill-omened statement in full; he relented only under the condition that I never write of it publicly. If I am at a future date able to relate Duponte's revelations touching this point, it must be at a site far more private.

grandfather, the birthplace of his wife and adored mother-in-law, whom he called Muddy, Mother, yet he had no home there any longer—

> *"I reach'd my home— my home no more—*
> *For all had flown who made it so."*

Here Duponte seemed ready, quite unconscious of me, to recite more of Poe's verses, but stopped himself. "No, he had no home here. Not this Baltimore, where he did not trust his remaining relatives of the name Poe even to inform them of his presence, and indeed they were afterward ashamed enough of their response to his demise to say so little about it as to appear suspicious. Nor was home New York, where his wife, Virginia, was dead and buried and he was preparing to flee forever; not the city of Richmond either, where the marriage with a childhood love was still only a plan, however attractive, and his memories of losing that place as a home once before and losing his mother and adoptive parents were still strong. Not Philadelphia, where he once resided and wrote, where he was obliged to use another name or risk losing the last loving letter of the one relation still devoted to him, where somehow he found now that he could not even reach it on a train.

"You see clearly now the map of Poe's attempted movements in his last epoch of life— from Richmond to try to go to New York, from Baltimore trying to go to Philadelphia— it is no small fact that these four cities were all ones where he had once lived and was rolling incessantly between. If there were twenty men named Reynolds standing around in his hospital room, Poe's Reynolds, man or idea, would still be far away from there— not of sickness, not of death— somewhere he would *long to be.* That name, monsieur, reveals to us nothing of the circumstances of Poe's death, and will ever remain the possession only of Poe himself. In that way, it is the most crucial and most secret of all the particulars."

❋   ❋   ❋

Forty minutes after the court had been abandoned, when it was found that the doors to the courtroom were fastened from the inside, there was another commotion. It was later declared that I was mad as a March hare for risking such behavior toward the judge, who was indeed irate. But I had not yet finished with Duponte when the doors began violently rattling. After the analyst concluded in full his demonstration, which presented but a few more details than transcribed faithfully above, Duponte looked at the door, and then turned back to me.

"You may tell this to the court," he said. "I mean, all we have said. You will not lose your fortune; you will not surrender Glen Eliza. All the precise points shall not be comprehended by some of the simpletons among your peers, of course, but it will do."

"I am not dramatist enough to claim these ideas were mine, not huckster enough to say they were the Baron's. I must speak of you, monsieur, must reveal your genius, if I tell them this. And if I did I might by chance reveal something that leads those men back to you. If they hunt you out— "

"You may tell them all," interrupted Duponte. He nodded slowly to show he understood the risk to himself and was genuine in granting his permission.

"Monsieur Duponte," I began with gratitude.

I looked at the fragments of faces and hollering mouths through the windows in the doors to the courtroom. The crowd was demanding them opened. I suppose the sight mesmerized me. When the doors were finally unbolted, I lost sight of Duponte in the stream of people. Peter rushed to me and pulled me aside.

"Was that . . . who was that man with you?" he asked.

I did not reply.

"It was him. Auguste Duponte. Wasn't it?" he asked.

I denied it, but was not very convincing.

"Quentin, it was!" Peter said with unchecked exuberance. "Then he has told you! He has given you all you need to know to uncover the mystery of Poe's death? And to extricate yourself from all troubles! A miracle!"

I nodded. Peter did not stop smiling as I was led back to the witness stand. The judge, apologizing for the interruption, reprimanding me for bolting the doors, and assuring us that the vagrant outside the building had been disarmed, now asked me to resume my testimony.

"No," I whispered.

"What, Mr. Clark?" the judge said. "We must hear the balance of your testimony. Speak up, please!"

I stood up. The skin around the judge's eyes wrinkled in irritation. The onlookers whispered across to one another. Peter's smile dropped from his face. He closed his eyes at what he realized was about to happen and rolled his head into his hand.

I looked across the crowd to my great-aunt. Peter began waving demoniacally for me to sit. I pointed my cane right at her. "The memory of my parents belongs to me, and Glen Eliza and all that is in it belongs to the name I bear. I shall fight for all this, Great-Aunt, even though I will probably not win. I will live happily if I can, and die poor if I must. I shall not, not by you or Auntie Blum or the whole arsenal of Fort McHenry, be compelled to give up. A man named Edgar Poe died in Baltimore once, and perhaps it was because he was a man with dreams better than our own and we used him for it— used him all up until there was nothing left. He shall watch no one use him again. And," I thought I might as well add, swinging the aim of my cane elsewhere in the audience, "I shall marry Miss Hattie Blum come tomorrow morning in the valley below Glen Eliza, at sunset, with all of Baltimore invited, and all will be right!"

I thought I heard one of Hattie's sisters fall to the floor in a faint. Hattie, who was beaming despite being wrapped by her aunt's vise-like arms, shook herself free and rushed toward me. Peter was required to hold back the Blum family with explanations and assurances.

"What have you done?" Hattie said to me in a nervous whisper. The throng had become louder, and the judge was now straining to silence them.

"Proved my great-aunt correct, perhaps," I said. "Your family will give us nothing, and I have already entered debt. I may have thrown away all we have, Hattie!"

"No. You've proved me right. Your father would be proud today— you are a chip off the old block, Quentin." Hattie kissed me quickly on the cheek and, pulling herself from my grasp, hurried to try to soothe her family.

Peter grabbed my arm. "What is this?"

"Where is he?" I asked. "Have you seen where Duponte went?"

"Quentin! Why did you not simply repeat whatever it was that Frenchman told you? Why did you not tell the court the truth of what you and he found?"

"And to what purpose, Peter?" I asked. "To save myself. No, this is what they hope for me to do so they might feel they know me, and that I am inferior because different. No, I do not think I will. Send public opinion to the devil today— this history will remain unspoken for now. There is one person I will tell today, Peter. I wish her always to understand me, as she has before, and she must hear for herself."

"Quentin, Quentin! Think of what you're doing!"

36

I DID NOT share the narrative of Poe's death with that courtroom, not that day or any other. Instead, I worked alongside Peter and became, as he later liked to say, an unrecoverable lawyer, finding each item of inconsistency and weak supposition in the case against me. In the end, we won. I received official recognition of my sanity and did so quite handily, by the judgment of most who observed the entire proceedings. Though there were few who *believed* I was, in fact, completely sane, they admitted that the trial pointed to that fact.

My reputation for an original bent of legal acumen spread. I rejoined Peter as an equal partner and we became one of the more successful law practices in Baltimore in mortgages, debts, and the contesting of wills.

The practice also added a third attorney, a young man from Virginia of habitual industry, and Peter soon married the equally industrious sister of that gentleman.

Though the police did not look for Edwin Hawkins in relation to the infamous assault on Hope Slatter, the slave-trader was said to have privately declared that he would know the man when he met him. But only a few months after the incident, Slatter decided that Baltimore had begun to be unreliable for his line of business, and he moved his slave-trading firm to Alabama, permitting the safe return to Baltimore of Edwin Hawkins. Edwin, meanwhile, deprived of his situation at the newspaper offices, had begun reading more books on the law and became a first-rate clerk in our expanding practice and later, at age sixty, an attorney.

Nearly nine years after my last visit, I returned to Paris with Hattie, and brought along Peter Stuart's young daughter, Annie. There was none of the general surveillance and spying that I had once experienced. Indeed, in some ways Paris was a more *comfortable* place to be as an empire under Louis-Napoleon than as a republic under the same man. As an American from a nation that was a republic, I had been an unwanted influence by a man planning an overthrow of that very form of government.

As an emperor, Louis-Napoleon had the power he wished for, and so no longer thought to exercise its full range from day to day.

The Baltimore line of the Bonaparte family, after Jérôme Napoleon Bonaparte's conference with the new emperor, received by decree the right to the Bonaparte name for all of the descendants of Madame Elizabeth Bonaparte. But the emperor would yield no rights to succession or imperial property as Madame Bonaparte had instructed her son to demand. When Louis-Napoleon died years later, neither of Madame Bonaparte's two grandchildren, both as handsome and as tall as could be hoped for, became emperor of the French. She lived for many years in Baltimore, and could be seen often in her black bonnet and red parasol in the streets, outliving even her son Bo.

Bonjour, meanwhile, had become a popular member of the small French circle in Washington, and was much admired and sought after for her independence and wit. She found she had perfect freedom as a widow here in America. One who also called herself a widow (though her husband, the elder Jérôme Bonaparte, was still alive in Europe), Madame Bonaparte, for many years, found joy in instructing and encouraging Mademoiselle Bonjour regarding various schemes and romances, though Bonjour did not usually heed her advice. Bonjour refused to marry again even when she experienced serious financial trouble. Through certain friends she had made through Monsieur Montor, Bonjour was soon entered into the theater and became something of a minor sensation as an actress performing in several cities here and in England, before settling on the writing of popular novels.

That day in the courtroom was the last time I saw Auguste Duponte. There were only a few more words passed between us than I have mentioned already. I believe I had some second sight in the courtroom, some foreboding that this was to be our final meeting. Once the crowd had settled down, I escaped outside and located Duponte exiting the court building. I tried to think what I might say.

"Poe," I said, "it is Poe . . ."

In my mind, there was some coherent and important statement to convey before parting, but I could not now, facing him, imagine what it was. I thought about the letter I had anticipated for so long from Poe from his time in Richmond, which might have revealed that he had tried to arrange to meet me in Baltimore— the letter had not come and never would, yet on this morning I felt an almost exactly equivalent sensation as though it *had*, if such can be rightly judged.

Duponte was looking out from high on the courthouse steps, gazing over Monument Square at a man and woman laughing together and an old slave leading a young horse, knowing there could be those who had seen him on the streets and recognized him. Peter and a few other attorneys were calling for me to come back inside. I remember what I saw with the unfading vividness of today. Duponte's jaw seemed to loosen, his lips slide together, and that queer grin he had given the portrait artist, that very face of mischief and accomplishment and genius, passed over him for one extravagant moment before it disappeared with him across the street.

I would always search for mentions of him— under some assumed name, of course— in newspaper columns about far-off places.

Sometimes I was certain I found reference to my old friend, though he never revealed himself directly and, as far as was known to me, never returned to the United States. There were times I had a vague presentiment that he would appear unexpectedly when he was most missed— for example, during a period when Hattie fell bafflingly unwell, or in those months when no sign of Peter could be located during his much-talked-about time as a general in the war.

I felt myself for many years, in some ways, waiting. I waited to tell my story, Edgar Poe's story, waited for a time when Poe's mind had been uncovered; waited for a day when others would need what I had found from Edgar Poe. I wrote this story in careful hand in memorandum books— it took up more than one of these books, for I was forever adding to the impressions; and I then would wait and write more.

Sometimes I'd remove the Malacca cane from its place to feel its weight in my hands, and when alone unsheathe the shimmering blade, and I'd laugh with a start and think of Poe, dressed handsomely on his arrival to Baltimore, the Malacca confidently securing his steps.

Hattie wished to know more about Duponte. She even expressed envy of her aunt for having had a few encounters, though that subject was forbidden from being discussed with Auntie Blum even in the old woman's advanced years. Hattie often asked for my final assessment of him and his character. I could not say. I could formulate nothing close enough. I kept the portrait that had been painted so many years earlier, but what had seemed an exact replica before looked nothing like Duponte to me now or, for that matter, like the Baron. Or, rather, it resembled nowhere near as well Duponte as the images preserved in my mind.

Still, it remained in the library of Glen Eliza, where he had sat. When told of him, supper guests might marvel that there was such a rare man. Here Hattie's interest in the subject of Duponte would diminish. "It was you there also, dear Quentin, who did it," Hattie would say; and then to see my stern look at the proposition, she would lightly admonish me: "Yes, it was, it was you."

HISTORICAL NOTE

Edgar Allan Poe died at the age of forty in a Baltimore hospital on October 7, 1849, four days after being found in distress at Ryan's inn and tavern. On September 26 or 27 Poe had left Richmond, Virginia, by steamer on his way to his cottage in New York, with an itinerary that included a stop at Philadelphia to edit a book of poems by a writer named Marguerite St. Leon Loud. Poe asked his mother-in-law, Maria Clemm, to send him a letter in Philadelphia addressed to the pseudonym E. S. T. Grey. But Poe, from what we know, never reached Philadelphia or made it home to New York; instead he came on an unannounced and final visit to Baltimore. The details of his whereabouts for the next five days— from his arrival by ship to his appearance at Ryan's on an election day— have been almost entirely lost. This remains one of literary history's most persistent gaps.

A small funeral for Poe was conducted by Reverend William T. D. Clemm at the Westminster Presbyterian burial yard on October 8. There were four mourners in attendance: Poe's relatives Neilson Poe and Henry Herring, his colleague Dr. Joseph Snodgrass, and his former classmate Z. Collins Lee. Reports about the circumstances and causes of his death were hazy and conflicting and were further confused by the publication of a memoir by Rufus Griswold, in which facts and even quotes were fabricated. As the decades passed, theories and rumors about Poe's demise multiplied, told by those who had known Poe and those who had not.

The Poe Shadow features the details about Poe's death determined to be the most authentic, combined with original discoveries that have never before been published. All of the theories and analysis related to Poe's death in this text use the historical facts and leading evidence. Original research through numerous resources, including archives and depositories in six different states, has aimed to endow the novel with a definitive examination of the subject. Some of the new additions to the knowledge of Poe's death appearing here for the first time include: the fire at N. C. Brooks's house around the time of Poe's Baltimore arrival and attempted visit;* the role of George Herring as president of the Whigs of the Fourth Ward and his presence at Ryan's at the period of the election, and the probable connection between this and Henry Herring's previously unexplained arrival at Ryan's on October 3; Joseph Snodgrass's prominence in the temperance committees for the Sunday-law issue and his prime role in repairing the damage of candidate John Watchman's disgrace immediately before the October 3 election; the existence of Philadelphia writer Marguerite St. Leon Loud's 1851 poem "The Stranger's Doom"— possibly the first poem published on the death of Poe, which this novel for the first time identifies as related to Poe, analyzes, and reprints; and the never-before-discovered existence of a letter to "Grey, E. S. F." waiting at the Philadelphia post office in the last weeks of Poe's life (in all likelihood the last letter written to Poe), as well as the original analysis introduced here of the reasons for Poe's strange use of the "Grey" pseudonym.

Other rare details referred to are: the specifics of Poe's interaction with and initiation into the Shockoe Hill Sons of Temperance, the gesture of Baltimore *Patriot* employees to raise money for Poe's grave site, the preparation of a longer oration by Reverend Clemm for Poe's funeral than was used, the physical description of the Walker note, and the little-known poem about Poe's death by Dr. Snodgrass partially reprinted here.

Even as it incorporates as much original research as possible to clarify the events, the novel attempts whenever possible to remain historically faithful to what the characters would have known about Poe around the year 1850, which sometimes differs from what we know now. (Good examples include the year and place of Poe's birth and the status of his adoption by the Allan family, which remained under dispute for decades after Poe's death, in part because Poe himself shaded the details of his biography.) All quotes from newspapers about Poe's death and its surrounding features are from actual nineteenth-century articles, and all quotes attributed to Poe were written or spoken by him. Edgar Allan Poe at age twenty did indeed act as an agent for his future mother-in-law, Maria Clemm, in selling a twenty-year-old slave named Edwin for forty

---

* The notion that Poe tried to visit Dr. Brooks's house has been under dispute. Poe's unsuccessful attempt to visit Brooks was first reported by nineteenth-century biographer George Woodberry. Later scholars objected on the grounds that Woodberry did not name a source. In addition to the fire, I have been able to uncover Woodberry's unmentioned source as Brooks's son.

dollars to a black family in Baltimore, one way of removing a slave from the slave trade.

Baltimore and Paris as they would have been around 1850 have been reconstructed from many memoirs, guidebooks, maps, and literary texts of the time. The Baltimore and Paris police departments, Louis-Napoleon in Paris, and Hope H. Slatter and Elizabeth Patterson Bonaparte in Baltimore are situated within the fictional events of the novel, using the interests and motives history shows them possessing.

Quentin Clark is a fictional character, but in him live some of the viewpoints and words of a few readers who were devotees at a time when Poe's literary output was undervalued and his morals and character frequently vilified. The main sources for Quentin and his relationship with Poe are George Eveleth and Phillip Pendleton Cooke, both of whom exchanged letters with Poe. Many of the characters connected here with Poe and his death, including the sexton George Spence, Neilson Poe, Henry Herring, Henry Reynolds, Dr. John Moran, Benson of the Shockoe Hill Sons of Temperance, and Dr. Snodgrass, are real, and their depictions based on the historical figures. They reflect the different moral and literary agendas that frame the events of Poe's death even to this day.

For more than a century, there have indeed been attempts to identify the "real" Dupin who inspired Poe's mystery tales. Auguste Duponte and the Baron Dupin are fictional but take their forms from the wide range of "Dupin" candidates who have been uncovered. This long list includes a French tutor named C. Auguste Dubouchet and a preeminent lawyer, André-Marie-Jean-Jacques Dupin.

Though many people have obsessively combed through the death of Poe in attempts to solve its mysteries, Quentin's quest is fictional. Still, his actions and some specific discoveries channel the earliest amateur investigators, who preceded by decades the scholars and theorists who later took up the subject. Maria Clemm, Neilson Poe, and Mr. Benson were quietly endeavoring to collect information immediately after Poe's death, when traces of his final days might still turn up anywhere.

ACKNOWLEDGMENTS

This book owes so much to four people: first, to my literary agent and friend, Suzanne Gluck, brilliant and inspirational at every step; and to Gina Centrello of Random House and my editors, Jon Karp and Jennifer Hershey, for their vision, their passion, and their faith.

Superb publishing professionals at my literary agency and publishing houses contributed to all facets of the process. At William Morris Agency, Jon Baker, Georgia Cool, Raffaella De Angelis, Alice Ellerby, Michelle Feehan, Tracy Fisher, Candace Finn, Eugenie Furniss, Alicia Gordon, Yael Katz, Shana Kelly, Rowan Lawton, Erin Malone, Andy McNicol, Emily Nurkin, and Bari Zibrack. At Random House, Avideh Bashirrad, Kate Blum, Sanyu Dillon, Benjamin Dreyer, Richard Elman, Megan Fishmann, Laura Ford, Jonathan Jao, Jennifer Jones, Vincent La Scala, Libby McGuire, Gene Mydlowski, Grant Neumann, Jack Perry, Tom Perry, Jillian Quint, Carol Schneider, Judy Sternlight (at Modern Library), Beck Stvan, Simon Sullivan, Bonnie Thompson, and Jane von Mehren. I have also received support and insight from Chris Lynch at Simon & Schuster Audio, Stuart Williams and Jason Arthur at Harvill Secker UK, Elena Ramirez at Seix Barral, and Francesca Cristoffanini at Rizzoli.

Thanks to those who have helped this book progress through reading and reinforcing. This includes, as always, my family; my parents, Susan and Warren Pearl, and my brother, Ian Pearl; as well as Benjamin Cavell, Joseph Gangemi, Julia Green, Anna Guillemin, Gene Koo, Julie Park, Cynthia Posillico, Gustavo Turner, and Scott Weinger; and Tobey Wiggins, who lent amazing encouragement and supportiveness.

Additional thanks: the archivists and librarians at Boston Public Library, Harvard University, Iowa University, Duke University, Maryland Historical Society, Enoch Pratt Public Library of Baltimore, Johns Hopkins University, New York Public Library, the Library of Virginia and the University of Virginia. Also, for generous input related to Poe and specific areas of nineteenth-century life and culture: Ralph Clayton, Dr. John

Emsley, Allan Holtzman, Jeffrey Meyers, Scott Peeples, Edward Papenfuse, Jeff Savoye, Kenneth Silverman, and Dr. Katherine Watson.

Further appreciation to the generations of scholars who have assembled our current knowledge about Poe's life, including the exceptional Burton Pollin (who first noticed the appearance, mentioned in this novel, of the initials "E. S. T. G." in the *Broadway Journal*). A note of praise for the Edgar Allan Poe Society of Baltimore website (eapoe.org), created by Jeff Savoye, which should set the standard for all online literary resources. Finally, thanks to the staffs and supporters of the Poe homes and museums in Baltimore, Fordham, Philadelphia, and Richmond, as well as the Westminster burial yard in Baltimore, for sustaining the story of Poe as a living experience and allowing all of us a chance to visit.